FORBIDDEN SENSATIONS

"You and I have nothing to say to one another." Sky Dancer jerked her arm free of his grasp.

Morgan's eyes narrowed. "I have a great deal to say to you. I came here today to ask you to be my wife!"

Sky Dancer felt as if a sharp knife had just sliced through her heart. How ironic it was—moments ago he had voiced his hatred for the Indian race, and now he was asking one of that race to be his wife.

"I don't want you, Morgan. Go away and leave me alone. You and I are not suited to one another!"

"Aren't we?" he hissed, pulling her roughly into his arms. "I can damn well prove to you that you are wrong."

His arms tightened about her like iron bands and his lips sought hers brutally. The kiss was not one of love, but of anger and passion. Sky Dancer tried to pull away, but the blood in her body seemed to run hot. She found her lips opening to receive his kiss. She felt her head spinning and her heart pounding. Her struggling ceased as she gave in to the wondrous feelings he awoke in her body.

She knew it was wrong to be in his arms—he and men like him were enemies to her people. But she couldn't stop the tide of passion that flowed through her . . .

Savage Summer

CONSTANCE O'BANYON

ZEBRA BOOKS
KENSINGTON PUBLISHING CORP.

ZEBRA BOOKS

are published by

Kensington Publishing Corp.
475 Park Avenue South
New York, NY 10016

Second printing: June, 1988

Printed in the United States of America

Friendship is golden, and you are 24 karat, Julie Persik, Emma Frances Merritt (Bennett) and Catherine Creel

SAVAGE SUMMER

Alike yet unalike came two maidens fair.
To walk among mortal man with courage and
   with dare.
Each would leave her family to wander far from
   home.
Both would find her future in the great unknown.
Oh fair maidens weep no more, merely reach out
   your hand.
You will find your own true love in the far
   forbidden lands.

Like the storm on a summer's evening; like the fall
   of the summer's rain.
Gone are the worlds they once knew, leaving only
   the echoes from whence they came.

CONSTANCE O'BANYON

Prologue

Valley Forge, Pennsylvania, 1849

Taggart James bent over his sleeping daughter's bed and studied her face. How angelic Danielle looked with her dark hair spilled over the white bed covering. She was a lovely child, and had such a happy disposition.

As if the child sensed her father's presence, her eyes opened, and she favored him with a sleepy smile. He knelt down beside her and gathered her close to him.

"Baby?" she questioned in her childlike language.

"Your baby brother's sleeping, just as you should be."

Danielle put her chubby arms about her father's neck and laid her face against his. "Mama?" she asked sleepily.

"Your mama is sleeping," Tag told her, referring to his second wife, the only mother Danielle had ever known. "You can see her tomorrow. Close your eyes and go to sleep," he said, kissing her smooth cheek.

He touched his daughter's silken hair and felt a lump

in his throat. Her skin took on a soft golden glow in the dimly lit room. Tag knew that even though she was beautiful, she would always look different from other children because her mother, Morning Song, had been an Indian.

As Tag held his sleeping daughter in his arms, he was overcome with many emotions. His thoughts drifted to his first wife, Morning Song. She had been killed the day Danielle had been born. His daughter would never know the soft gentle ways of her mother. Of course Danielle had Alexandria, who was kind to her and treated her as if she had been born of her body.

Tag wanted his daughter's life to be filled with happiness, but he feared if anyone discovered she was half Indian she would become an outcast in Philadelphia society.

He realized the time would come when Danielle would have to face who she was, but not for a long while. He knew how cruel the white world could be to those who had the least bit of Indian blood in their veins. It wouldn't matter to the white world that Danielle's mother, Morning Song, had been a Blackfoot princess, and adored by her people. They would only see that she was different from them.

Tag's eyes hardened when he remembered the callous way two white men had killed Morning Song. It made him angry at how the white race he belonged to thought they were better than the Indians.

In that moment, Tag vowed that Danielle would be educated in only the finest schools where she would be taught to be a lady. He would lavish money on her clothing and lift her so high no one would dare look down on her. He would arm her against whatever came, hoping to give her confidence and pride in her white and Indian heritage. He felt at peace, knowing that Morning Song would have understood and approved.

Until the day when Danielle had to deal with who she was, he and Alexandria would protect her from as much hurt as they could. Even though Alexandria was Danielle's stepmother, Tag took comfort in the fact that she loved his daughter as if she were her very own.

Tag blew out the lamp and silently moved across the room to the door, closing it softly behind him.

Danielle sighed in her sleep, not knowing of the concern her father had for her future. She was well past her first birthday and had never known anything but love in her life. She was too young to know that one day her strength and courage would be tested, and she would stand with her feet in the white and the Indian world! He feared the day would come when her world would be shattered and she would have to search for her true identity!

Blackfoot Territory

Many miles away from Valley Forge, Pennsylvania, in the Blackfoot village, there dwelled another half-Indian, half white, baby girl. She was the daughter of Tag's sister, Joanna. Not only were Tag and Joanna brother and sister, but Joanna's husband, Windhawk, had been the brother of Morning Song.

It had been eleven years ago when Tag and Joanna had been traveling on an ill-fated wagon train that had been attacked by the Piegan Blackfoot Indians. She

11

and Tag had both been saved by Windhawk, chief of the Blood Blackfoot. Joanna had fallen in love with Windhawk, choosing to become his wife and remain in the Blackfoot village.

It was early evening as Joanna held her sleeping daughter in her arms, wondering what the future held for the child, Sky Dancer. The child was fair of skin and looked enough like Joanna's niece, Danielle, to be her twin sister instead of her cousin.

Joanna couldn't help being concerned about her daughter's future since she looked more white than Indian. When Sky Dancer had been born her eyes had been a nondescript color, but now that she was older, they were a bright violet-blue, like Joanna's.

Sometimes it frightened Joanna to know her daughter would walk in the ways of the Indians. She was determined that Sky Dancer would learn about both the Indian and white world.

Joanna didn't worry about her son, Little Hawk—he was a small replica of his father and looked every bit like an Indian. He would be groomed to one day take his father's place as chief of the Blood Blackfoot tribe.

Sky Dancer smiled in her sleep, and Joanna remembered her mother once told her that when babies smiled in their sleep, they were seeing angels. She pushed the ebony hair away from Sky Dancer's face and hugged her tightly.

After much discussion, Windhawk had agreed that when she was older Sky Dancer could go to Philadelphia. She would stay with Tag and Alexandria to be educated on how to become a proper young lady. Joanna wanted her daughter to have all the advantages she had been brought up with—for the James family

12

possessed great wealth and social standing.

Joanna hadn't noticed that Windhawk had come up behind her. She didn't see the softness in his dark eyes as they rested on her. She watched as Sky Dancer slowly opened her eyes and smiled.

Windhawk reached across Joanna, lifting his daughter into his arms and she giggled with delight. When he looked into Sky Dancer's eyes he couldn't help but be warmed. His heart seemed to contract when she threw her arms about his neck and kissed him on the cheek.

Little Hawk ran up to his father and grabbed him around the legs. Windhawk bent down and lifted his son in his arms as well.

The whole family left the lodge for a walk down by the river. The sun was going down and it painted the countryside with a soft rosy hue—there was peace and contentment here in Blackfoot land.

Joanna glanced across the Milk River and sighed happily. She had never known it would be possible to obtain such complete satisfaction. Windhawk had not only filled her life with the joys of the heart, but joy of the flesh as well. She often missed Tag and Danielle, but they would be coming to visit before long. She felt Windhawk's eyes on her and glanced up at him. His eyes spoke of the deep love he had for her and she leaned her head against his shoulder contentedly.

With Windhawk beside her, they would teach their children the important things in life.

Joanna's son held his hands out to her and she lifted the child into her arms. As the first stars twinkled in the ebony sky, Windhawk and Joanna walked back toward their lodge. Their love was so strong, it had reached across the gap that had separated their two worlds. Joanna had no desire to ever leave this land. She would be content to remain beside her tall, dark husband until the end of time.

Both Joanna and her brother Tag had found their destiny; but what about their half-white, half-Indian daughters? Would the time come when they would be tested to the limit? Would the day come when they would have to face who they were, and search for their own destinies . . . ?

Chapter One

May, 1865

The old trapper, Farley, saw several Indian tipis in the distance. He urged his tired horse forward, glad that he'd found Windhawk's camp at last. When he entered the camp, Farley was greeted by several Blackfoot braves who seemed genuinely glad to see him. Throwing his leg over his horse, he jumped to the ground.

Farley was an imposing figure with his long flowing white hair and his equally white beard. Dressed in buckskins, he moved with the agility of a young buck. No one knew his age for sure, but the one thing they did know—wherever Joanna was, the old trapper wouldn't be far behind.

He ambled past several of the tipis until he came to a big white one with a huge black hawk painted on the front. This was Windhawk's lodge and the old man knew he'd find Joanna inside.

"Joanna, you here," he called out.

The flap was thrown aside and a beautiful woman

15

with flaming red hair smiled at him. She was dressed in soft buckskins, a beaded headband circled her head.

"Farley, I am glad to see you, my friend. When did you get here?" She spoke in the Blackfoot tongue, and he answered her in kind.

"As you know I have been trapping in the Canadas. When I got back to the village, I was told that you and Windhawk had left for St. Louis. I came to find you."

"Is anything wrong?" she asked, with a worried frown on her face.

He grinned widely, lapsing into English. "Nope, I just wanted to be here when you traded Sky Dancer for Danielle. I musta misfigured, 'cause I didn't realize this was the year the girls was to be swapped."

"Sky Dancer isn't too happy about this exchange in the least. I came very close to backing out." Joanna also lapsed into English.

"Did I tell you 'bout the last time I was in Philadelphia, Joanna?"

Farley made a trip to Philadelphia every summer where he would spend several weeks with Joanna's brother Tag. The old man was very dear to Joanna and Tag, and both of them always made him feel welcome. However, he preferred to spend most of his time in the Blackfoot village so he could be near Joanna. Everyone knew he adored her.

She suppressed a smile. "At least a dozen times, Farley."

"Well, you will recall I told you that Danielle was the spitting image of Sky Dancer?"

"Yes, I remember you saying this to me. Tag has said much the same thing."

"Now you are gonna see that I wasn't stretching the truth one bit."

Her laughter bubbled out, and she placed a kiss on his rough cheek. "You never stretch the truth, Farley; you only bend it a bit."

"How'd you ever get Windhawk to come clear to St. Louis?" Farley wanted to know.

"It's very simple. He wouldn't allow me to come without him."

Farley nodded, knowing how possessive and protective Windhawk was of his wife Joanna. "Where is Windhawk?"

"He has gone hunting. I expect him back any time now."

"Will he be going into St. Louis with you?"

"No, he will stay here and wait my return." She quickly changed the subject. "You've had a long journey. Are you hungry, my friend?"

He grinned widely and the creases in his face formed several deep laugh lines. "I thought you'd never ask. I'm very near starved. You got any of that stew I like?"

"Yes, I do—come in and I'll feed you," she said, disappearing inside the tipi.

As Farley sat shoveling the warm stew into his mouth, his eyes followed Joanna around the tipi. He read the pain of uncertainty in her eyes. As always, he knew her so well, he could guess what was troubling her.

"Don't fret none, Joanna. The summer will pass soon enough. Afore you know it, Sky Dancer will be back home."

She smiled at the old man. "I know . . . but . . . Yes, you are right, Farley."

The lazy years of happiness and growing up had

flown by for Sky Dancer. Now the time had come when she would meet her cousin Danielle again. The two girls hadn't seen each other since they were five summers old. They were both in their nineteenth year, and it was said they looked very much alike. The plans that had been made by their parents, long ago, were about to come to pass.

Sky Dancer had ridden with her father, mother, and a group of Blackfoot warriors to St. Louis, where she would be exchanged for her cousin, Danielle. There was no happiness in her heart at leaving all that was dear to her. She didn't want to spend the summer with her uncle and an aunt she hardly knew.

Sky Dancer thought of her older brother, Little Hawk, who had gone with his cousin and their grandfather James for a tour of Europe. She thought what a strange year this was—Little Hawk had gone away, and she was to be handed over to her Uncle Tag and Aunt Alexandria.

Looking down at her soft buckskins, she knew that tomorrow she would have to change them for the clothes of a white woman. Blinking her eyes, she held back the tears that threatened to fall. A Blackfoot princess was not supposed to cry, she reminded herself.

Why was she being forced to go to a place that she didn't want to see? She knew her mother and uncle had long ago made the plans for tomorrow. Sky Dancer had heard about her cousin Danielle all her life, but she didn't remember her at all. Uncle Tag, she knew very well since he had often visited the Blackfoot village. What about her Aunt Alexandria? She would be a stranger.

Feeling a dull ache deep inside, she turned her head,

looking toward the dense woods where her father had set up camp. Sky Dancer was soon to enter a world she knew very little about. That frightened her beyond belief.

Pushing a wisp of ebony hair out of her face, Sky Dancer raised her face to the sun. She prayed Napi, the great one, would make time pass quickly so she could return to her home.

Danielle glanced at the dusty streets of St. Louis with a look of horror on her face. There were hordes of humanity pressed together from all walks of life. Many wore filthy buckskins, while others were dressed in an out-dated fashion. The streets were noisy and the stench was almost more than she could bear. To her St. Louis seemed like the very foundation of hell. Being a frontier town, it in no way resembled Philadelphia, with its gentle life-style.

Danielle's eyes were red from crying. She had grown weary of begging her father to take her back home. She tried to convince him that she didn't want to spend the summer with a bunch of filthy Indians. In truth she was frightened at the grim prospect. Her blue eyes sparkled with anger, knowing that she would make everyone suffer for forcing her to do something that was repugnant to her. She thought about her cousin, Sky Dancer, and wondered if she had similar thoughts about this exchange.

Joanna stood on the hill, looking down on the Missouri River, knowing that St. Louis was around the bend just out of sight. It was twilight, and the mud-colored river reflected an eerie yellow glow. How strange it felt to be in the white world again. Her violet-blue eyes watched the water churn and break against the shore. Her thoughts were troubled—she had no desire to return to "civilization." In fact, she no longer thought of herself as being white.

Joanna was married to Windhawk, chief of the Blood Blackfoot. He had long ago won her heart and given her happiness beyond her wildest dream. She had borne him a son and a daughter. That alone should give her the right to feel she was as much a Blackfoot as one who had been born into the tribe.

She didn't hear the soft footsteps that came up behind her. When a hand went about her waist, she leaned back against a hard muscled body. Looking up into the face she loved so well she was struck by his handsomeness. His long ebony hair hung loosely about his shoulders, encircled with a plain leather headband. He was tall with broad shoulders and narrow hips. A man born to command others.

Joanna laid her head against Windhawk's shoulder. They were both silent for a long time. A wisp of red-gold hair blew across Windhawk's face and he glanced down at the woman in his arms. How Napi had smiled on him by giving this woman into his keeping. She had been his wife for many summers, but still he never grew tired of looking upon her lovely face. She had brought about a change in the chief. He no longer walked in the ways of war—she had gentled him, if not changed him completely.

"What were you thinking, my husband?" Joanna

asked, turning around and putting her arms about his neck.

He smiled slightly. "I was thinking that with you I have found peace and contentment. You keep my lodge, tend my children . . . you fill my heart. What man could ask for more."

She placed a kiss on his bronzed cheek. Looking up into his dark eyes, she saw a softness that she knew he reserved for her alone. "We do have a good life together, my husband. My one and only regret is that I have been unable to give you more children."

His hand tightened about her waist and he looked into her deep blue eyes—eyes that he had often seen flash with fire, or soften with desire. "We do not need other children, Joanna. With you beside me, I fall asleep each night with joy in my heart. I cannot wait for each new day to come, knowing you will walk beside me."

"You have made me very happy, my husband. If the whole world had what we share, there would be no more war. I feel blessed among all women that I was chosen as the wife of the mighty Windhawk."

He watched her eyes cloud over with sadness. He knew she was worried about their daughter, and he wanted to comfort her. Cupping her face in his hands, he gave her a look that melted her heart. "You are still worried about sending Sky Dancer to Philadelphia?"

"Yes. I know it has been planned for years that we would take Tag's daughter, Danielle, and my brother would take Sky Dancer for a summer. With our son in Europe with my father and Sky Dancer going away, it will seem very strange. I wish there weren't this Civil

21

War going on."

"I have heard that the war may be over. It will be good for our daughter to see the world her mother comes from. You must know your brother will take care of Sky Dancer. As for Little Hawk, we both agreed this journey over the big water will be good for him."

"I know. I am just being selfish, I suppose."

"Not you, my wife. Your heart is filled with love for the whole world. It is only right that a mother would want to keep her young near her."

Joanna knew Windhawk was every bit as troubled as she was about sending their daughter so far away, yet he was trying to comfort her. "Was it a mistake, this bargain we made with Tag when the girls were but babies, Windhawk?"

"This I cannot tell you, Joanna. My heart is also heavy that our daughter must travel so far away from home, but I am also gladdened that we can come to know my dead sister's child."

Joanna shook her head, causing her red-gold hair to swirl away from her face. "You can hardly call them children, my husband. Both Sky Dancer and Danielle are in their nineteenth summer."

Windhawk smiled slightly and she could see the love dancing in his eyes. "The years have passed quickly, since I took you as my wife. When I look at you, I know you are even more beautiful now than you were as a young girl. How well I remember the day I first saw you. Your beauty warmed my heart and I knew you must have been meant for me. I will never forget that you gave up your world to live in mine."

She rested her cheek against his broad chest,

22

knowing how gladly she had taken his way of life. She couldn't imagine ever loving anyone but Windhawk. "I made my choice long ago, my husband. But is it right to force Sky Dancer to leave her home and go to a world she has only read about in books?"

"We will give our daughter and Danielle a chance to know both worlds. The path they choose to walk will then be up to them."

"You are very wise, my husband. I will put my worry aside. I know that we are doing what is best for both girls." Her eyes drifted down to the river once more. "I do wish you could come to St. Louis with me, Windhawk. I don't like to leave you here."

Windhawk's eyes followed hers. He knew what she was feeling, but deep inside she knew he must wait for her to return. "You know this is the best way, Joanna. I cannot go with you to this white man's town. I will be here for you when you come back—then we will journey back to our village with Danielle."

Joanna pushed a lock of ebony hair out of his face. "Sky Dancer and I will leave for St. Louis tomorrow morning. I know Tag will want us all to get together before we go our separate ways, so I will see you in a few days." She paused and looked at him with troubled eyes. "I suppose the summer will pass soon enough."

"Yes, it will pass, Joanna."

"Did you know that Farley rode into camp today?"

Windhawk raised a dark eyebrow. "That old man would follow you wherever you went. He has been the only burden I have been forced to bear because of you."

"You like Farley and you know it."

"How can I not like someone who looks after you like a watchdog? I know you are safe when he is on guard."

"He is like part of the family."

Windhawk's mouth quirked briefly. "The hour grows late. Let us not spend our last hours together talking about Farley. I want to hold you in my arms tonight," Windhawk told her, leading her away from the river.

Joanna could feel Windhawk's unrest. She knew he was wondering if she would want to stay in the white world. Would she never be able to convince him that her life was with him? As they reached the tipi, he pulled her into his arms and buried his face in her red-gold hair.

"I will always return to you, my husband," she whispered. "As long as I live, I will never want to be anywhere that I cannot reach out and touch you."

He crushed her in his arms and breathed her name over and over. "Time is the enemy, Joanna. Let it pass quickly until you return to me."

Taggart James smiled at his wife Alexandria, who was turning down the covers of the bed. "Not exactly what you would call luxury, is it?"

She tossed her mink-colored hair and looked up at him with her unusual golden eyes. "I don't mind the discomfort of this hotel. You can hold me in your arms and I would be comfortable anywhere."

"Is Danielle sleeping?" Tag asked with a worried frown on his face.

"I think so, at least she didn't answer when I went into her room a moment ago. She isn't happy in the least, Tag. I hate to see her upset."

24

"She will get over it," he stated stubbornly. "This summer will be good for her. I think perhaps we have spoiled her by always allowing her to have her way. She may learn humility by being with the Blackfoot people. The Blackfoot respect a person for his worth and not for his social position."

Tag sat down in a stiff horsehair chair and pulled Alexandria into his lap. "What is the troubled frown I see on your face?" he asked.

"It's nothing," she said, turning her head away. "I was just wondering if you ever miss living with the Blackfoot. I know you grew up in the Indian village. Do you ever regret returning to Philadelphia?"

"Of course not." He forced her to look at him. "There's more on your mind than you are saying. Tell me what's really troubling you."

"I . . . it's just that I was wondering if you ever think about Danielle's mother, Morning Song. We never talk about her anymore."

"You are wondering if I still love her?"

"Yes, I suppose."

Taking Alexandria's chin firmly in his hand, he forced her to meet his eyes. "The man who loved Morning Song no longer exists. When she was killed and I was driven by hatred to avenge her death, you helped me find my way. It was the boy in me that loved Morning Song—she was the love of my youth. You are the true love of my life, and the one I will grow old beside."

"But you did love her."

"Yes, but she is no more than a fleeting dream. I do regret, however, that Danielle never knew her mother."

Alexandria felt the sting of his words in the depth of

25

her heart. She had come to think of Danielle as her own daughter, and it was hard sometimes to realize Danielle hadn't been born of her own body. She was saddened by the fact that Tag was sending her away for the summer. Danielle had never liked to hear about her mother's people; it was almost cruel to make her spend the summer with them.

"Danielle is going to be very unhappy, Tag. She's cried almost daily for weeks."

"Be that as it may, the plans are made and I will not back out now. You will like getting to know Sky Dancer. She is a lovely young girl. You will be astounded when you see how much she resembles Danielle."

Alexandria sighed unhappily, and laid her head against Tag's shoulder. "I pray this will not end in disaster. Danielle can be very strong-minded when she wants to be."

He tilted her chin up again and smiled down at her. "Yes, in that she is not unlike you. The two women in my life keep me up to scratch."

Alexandria tugged playfully at his hair. "We have to look sharp to keep up with you, Taggart James."

His deep laughter was silenced as she pulled his head down to receive her kiss. He sighed contentedly as she melted against him. He had not erased her concern, but he had caused her to put it out of her mind for the moment.

The forest was sweltering after the morning rain that had moved across the valley. It was now early afternoon and the steamy heat was almost unbearable.

26

A noisy bluebird chattered from its perch high in the branches of a tall oak tree, scolding the young girl who had invaded its sanctuary.

Sky Dancer was oblivious to her surroundings. She pushed a strand of ebony hair away from her face and plucked at the scarlet-colored ribbon which was laced across the bodice of her gown. Her heart felt heavy as she raised her head to gaze across the meadow at the five tipis that had been erected beneath the canopy of bright blue sky.

This land was alien to the Indian girl. She yearned for the green valley and the high mountains of her home. She was frightened of what tomorrow would bring. She would be leaving her mother and father to travel to the hub of the white world.

The young girl spotted an unknown variety of crimson-colored wildflowers and absentmindedly bent down to pluck one of the delicate blossoms. Raising the flower to her nose, she found it to have a pleasant aroma. Sitting down amid the tall thick blades of grass, her eyes moved over the unfamiliar countryside.

Sky Dancer knew she was unlike the other maidens of the tribe, because she didn't look like an Indian. Her hair was as dark as midnight, but her eyes were startlingly blue in color. Her skin was not bronzed like the other Blood Blackfoot, but instead was a soft ivory color. She was as much a child of her white mother as she was of her Indian father.

Plucking the petals from the flower, she allowed her mind to wander. She had missed her brother and wished he was going with her to Philadelphia. Maybe if he were with her, she wouldn't be so frightened. Shaking her head she knew Little Hawk wouldn't be

27

returning until after winter covered the land. It seemed this year would be filled with change for her as well as her brother. She missed Little Hawk because they had always been so close. She knew that if he were here he would understand how lost she was feeling.

Sky Dancer caught a glimpse of movement in front of one of the tipis. There were a dozen Blackfoot warriors who had traveled with her family for protection. She saw her good friend Wolfrunner, and waved to him. Sky Dancer's father and Wolfrunner's father had grown up together, and their families were very close. Sky Dancer loved Wolfrunner as she would a brother—she was glad he had been chosen to come with them. Her attention was drawn to the main tipi and she watched as her mother walked toward her.

Sky Dancer felt a lump in her throat, thinking about being separated from her family. As her mother drew near, Sky Dancer could see her red-gold hair gleaming in the midday sunlight. Flaming Hair, she was called affectionately by the Blackfoot tribe. She was so lovely that Sky Dancer could easily see how her father had chosen her as his one and only wife. Many of the Blackfoot warriors had several wives, but her father wanted no one but his Flaming Hair.

The young Indian maiden always liked to hear her mother tell about how she had met and fallen in love with Sky Dancer's father. Flaming Hair's white name had been Joanna James. Sometimes, when the family was alone, Sky Dancer's father would still call her mother Joanna.

"What a pretty picture you make nestled among the lovely wildflowers, Sky Dancer," Joanna said, sitting down beside her daughter. She looked into the young girl's blue eyes, catching a glimpse of sadness and uncertainty. Taking Sky Dancer's hand in hers, Joanna squeezed it, and gave her daughter a reassuring smile.

"There is no need to be disturbed by your visit to your Uncle Tag's home. I promise that you will have a most enjoyable summer. Before you know it the time will pass and you will be back home."

Sky Dancer looked away from her mother and fixed her eyes on the distant horizon. "I am frightened of that which I do not understand. I do not think I will like the white world, my mother."

"Speak in English, Sky Dancer," her mother urged gently. "Your English is very good, so you must not forget and speak in Blackfoot when you reach Philadelphia."

"Tell me again about Philadelphia. I have read many books and seen pictures of the town, but I cannot imagine what it will be like."

Joanna slipped her arm about her daughter's shoulder, knowing what she was feeling. She would miss her, but she must think what was best for her daughter, and take comfort in the fact that it would broaden her education.

"I haven't been back since I was seventeen, two years younger than you are now. I am sure it has changed a great deal since that time. We have talked on this before, and you will remember all that I have told you. You will be able to carry yourself well, because you have been taught the ways of the white man since you were small."

"Yes, but could I not go next year? I do not want to leave you and Father at this time. You have said there is unrest in the white world. Would it not be better to go when the war is ended?"

"Your father has said the rumor is that the war is growing to a close."

"Do you think I will make friends in Philadelphia, my mother?"

Joanna knew many of the young warriors of the tribe had begun to show an interest in marrying Sky Dancer. So far her daughter had shown no preference for any of the warriors who had paid her marked attention. Joanna had decided long ago that her daughter would know both the white and Indian world before she made a decision to settle down to being a wife and mother.

"I believe everyone you meet will love you, Sky Dancer. How could they not. You are a sweet, lovely young girl. You speak English as well, if not better, than most white people." Joanna smiled. "You have a charming accent, I might add."

Suddenly Sky Dancer reached for her mother's hand and held it to her cheek. "I have never understood why you were so insistent that I learn to speak the white man's tongue. Nor do I know why I had to learn how to act like a proper white lady. Although I am half white, I feel like a full-blood Blackfoot."

Joanna looked into the blue eyes of her young daughter. There were many things she couldn't tell her daughter. Sky Dancer was not like her friends. In many ways she was more white than Indian, though she didn't know it yet. Joanna wanted her to be able to compare the two cultures, so she could decide where her future lay. Joanna hoped her daughter would choose the Indian world and return to her and Windhawk, but Sky Dancer had to be allowed to make that choice for herself.

"Time has a way of passing, my daughter. If it is God's will that you come back to your father and me, I will feel joy. If you are fated to stay in the white world, then I will understand and accept this also."

Sky Dancer knew that her mother's heart was breaking at the thought of her going away. She knew how difficult it was for her mother to send her to Philadelphia. In that moment Sky Dancer decided not to cause her mother further anguish. She would go, if not with a happy heart, at least without complaining. After all, she would be back home before winter set in.

"I will go to this place that was once your home, my mother. I will learn all that I can so you will be proud of me. But I will be home before the first snowflakes fall," she said with conviction.

Joanna merely nodded. "How much do you remember about the trip we took to St. Louis when you were five, Sky Dancer?"

"I remember only that it was a big noisy place that frightened me. There were many white men there with hair on their faces like Farley."

"Do you remember meeting your cousin Danielle?"

"No, but everyone said we looked very much alike, although I cannot remember her at all."

"That's understandable since you were both very young the last time you met. As you know, I will be taking Danielle home with me. Like you, she is half Indian, and her father wishes her to know about her Indian heritage. I am sure she is feeling every bit as apprehensive as you at this moment."

"Tell me again how you and my Uncle Tag were rescued by my father," Sky Dancer urged.

Joanna got a far away look in her eyes as if she were

remembering. She knew Sky Dancer had heard the story many times before, but she never seemed to tire of hearing it. "As you know, Sky Dancer, your Uncle Tag and I were traveling on a wagon train which was heading for Oregon Country. Our mother had died and we were on our way to join our father." Joanna paused and smiled at her daughter. "The first time I saw your father, the wagon train was camped beside the Platt River in what is known to you as Sioux country. He and many of his warriors were meeting at the trading post to hold games and contests with the Piegan Blackfoot."

"The chief of the Piegan saw you and wanted to take you away, didn't he?" Sky Dancer asked eagerly.

"Yes. He raided the train and killed almost everyone. He left me for dead, but took Tag as his prisoner. Later, your father heard about the raid and found me among the wreckage of our wagon. I was injured so he nursed me back to health and took me to his village."

"At that time you thought he was responsible for the raid and you thought my uncle was dead."

Joanna smiled as her daughter helped her tell the story she'd heard many times. "Yes, that's true. Tag was only twelve years old at that time and he suffered greatly at the hands of the Piegan chief, Running Elk. Later, your father discovered that Tag was alive and rescued him from Running Elk."

"Father said he loved you from the first moment he saw you. He told me he knew you would one day be his wife."

Joanna laughed. "Oh, yes, your father can be very persuasive when he wants something."

"You married my father and later, when Uncle Tag

was older, he married my father's sister, Morning Song."

"This is true. Tag and Morning Song had been married less than two years when she was killed by two white men. Before she died, Morning Song gave birth to Danielle."

"My uncle was enraged and went to Philadelphia to find the ones who were responsible for Morning Song's death," Sky Dancer supplied. "He avenged her death. That's when he met and married Aunt Alexandria."

"That's right. He decided to stay in Philadelphia, but not before he came back to the Blackfoot village for his daughter. That's why Danielle was raised as a white girl. Can't you see how important it is that you spend time with your Uncle Tag and Aunt Alexandria? It is also important that Danielle come to know her mother's people."

"Why did Danielle have to be raised as white, my mother?"

Joanna took a deep breath, knowing that would be a hard question to answer. Sky Dancer had never before faced prejudice. It would be hard for her to understand how the white race scorned its red brothers. "There are many things I have taught you about the white world, Sky Dancer. I have neglected to tell you that the white man does not love the Indian. That is why you will change your name while you are in Philadelphia. While you are staying with your Uncle Tag, you will go by the name of Skyler Dancing—you must not forget."

"Yes, I will remember. Sky Dancer wrinkled her brow in thoughtfulness. "My grandmother says that the world is large enough for all men to live in peace. Is this not true of the white man?"

"Sun Woman dreams of a world where the white man and the Indian will walk in harmony. But that is not the way it is, and probably never will be, Sky Dancer. The white man despises and distrusts anyone who is different from himself. That's one of the reasons that you must not mention that you are half Indian while you are in Philadelphia."

Sky Dancer stood up and gazed down at her mother. "I will not like denying who I am. I have no shame in me for the Blackfoot blood that flows through my body. I will not like to live with a people who want me to hang my head in shame."

Joanna saw the defiance in her daughter's blue eyes and felt pride in her. Standing up, she took Sky Dancer's hand in hers. "I would never want you to be ashamed of who you are. Always remember that you are an Indian princess. You are the daughter of Windhawk, a brave and noble chief. There may be times when you will feel hurt. At those times feel pride in who you are, and know that you are very special to the Blackfoot tribe. Also remember that your Uncle Tag and Aunt Alexandria love you. They will be there for you should you need them."

Sky Dancer couldn't understand why her mother was sending her away if she thought she might be hurt. She only knew that it was important to her mother that she go to Philadelphia. For some reason, her father had agreed.

"I will be glad when the time has passed and I can return to you and my father. I will go to this place and I will remember all the things you have taught me about the white man. I will do my best not to shame you or my father."

Joanna hugged Sky Dancer tightly to her. "I could

never be ashamed of you. You are the kind of daughter every mother wishes for." The most difficult thing she would ever have to do in her life would be to let her daughter go, but deep inside she knew she was doing it for Sky Dancer's own good.

A shadow fell across Joanna's face and she looked up to see Windhawk watching her closely. He knew what she was feeling and gave her an encouraging smile. Taking his daughter's hand, he pulled her into his arms. "The time has come for you to leave, Sky Dancer. Your horse has already been saddled and is waiting for you."

Sky Dancer looked up at her father. His dark hair held no trace of gray, and his face was handsome enough to make any maiden's heart beat faster. He was the leader of the fierce Blackfoot warriors, and yet she knew him as a kind and gentle father.

"Can you not come into St. Louis with us, Father?" she asked hopefully. There was always the chance that her father might change his mind and take her back home, she thought.

He enfolded her in his arms and laid his face against her dark head. "No, I will stay here and wait for your mother to return." His dark eyes became soft as they drifted across Sky Dancer's face. "The sun will not shine so brightly until you return, my daughter. When you leave, you will take with you that part of my heart that belongs to you."

Sky Dancer could feel tears building up behind her eyes and she prayed she would not cry in front of her father. "I will be home soon, my father," she said, turning away quickly and rushing toward the waiting horses.

Windhawk watched his daughter, feeling an ache of

loss at their parting. Sky Dancer was his only daughter and it tore at his heart to think of her going so far from home. He turned to Joanna and saw the tears sparkling in her eyes, and knew that she was feeling much the same as he.

"I did not know it would hurt so much to let her go, my husband. I wonder if it wouldn't be better if I were to go to Philadelphia with her?"

Windhawk's eyes caressed the face he loved so well. "It is difficult to let Sky Dancer leave—it would be impossible to allow you to leave."

Joanna looked into the dark eyes of her husband. "I will return soon, Windhawk."

"You could always change your mind and bring Sky Dancer back with you, Joanna. You know there is the possibility that our daughter will want to stay in the white world."

"We both know that is a possiblity. We will deal with that, when and if it occurs."

Windhawk touched Joanna's face softly. "Hurry back to me, my love. I will be waiting for you," he told her, lowering his dark head and kissing her deeply.

As Sky Dancer and Joanna rode away from the camp, Farley was with them. Sky Dancer couldn't help turning back to look at her father. Windhawk raised his hand to her and then disappeared into the tipi. Sky Dancer had the urge to dismount and run to him so he could hold her in his comforting arms. She nudged her horse forward, knowing she must not weaken. It would be a strange world she was going to, but she would put on a brave front for her mother's sake.

Chapter Two

Danielle James sat on the edge of the stiff horsehair settee looking about the hotel room with a distasteful frown on her face. The rug on the floor was torn in several places and frayed about the edges. The loosely woven curtains at the window fluttered in the afternoon breeze and the open window had allowed several pesky flies to enter the room and they buzzed about her face. What was she doing in this hovel? she asked herself for at least the tenth time. St. Louis had a long way to go before it would ever come up to Philadelphia's standards, if it ever would. The town itself was no more than a few makeshift buildings and a street that was as smelly and muddy as a pigsty.

Moving across the room, Danielle stood at the window to stare down on the street below. Had it been only last summer that her father had taken her on a holiday to France? Why had he insisted that she spend this summer with her mother's people, the Blackfoot Indians? Indians were savages, weren't they? Her friends would be horrified if they ever learned she was half Indian. The fact that her mother had been an Indian was the closest-guarded secret in Philadelphia. Her father and stepmother had taken pains to hide that fact from their friends and neighbors, knowing they would never have accepted her as a half-breed. She only wished they had hidden the knowledge from her as well.

Closing her eyes, she tried to block out the shame she felt because of the Indian blood that flowed through her veins. She felt humiliated and degraded every time she thought about that part of her that was Indian.

Danielle could vaguely remember the one other time she had traveled to St. Louis to meet her Aunt Joanna and Uncle Windhawk. They had gone to a place in the woods where many tipis had been set up. Danielle could recall being terrified by the Indian warriors and even the man who was her uncle. Every time her father would mention taking her to visit the Blackfoot village, Danielle would cry and carry on so much that he had relented. This time, however, her tears and pleading had fallen on deaf ears. Her father, who was usually so indulgent with her, stubbornly insisted that she was going to spend the summer in the Blackfoot village. It had something to do with a promise he had made long ago to her Indian grandmother, Sun Woman.

The door opened and Danielle turned to watch her mother enter the room. Danielle had never thought of Alexandria as her stepmother. Since her own mother had died the day of her birth, Alexandria was the only mother she had ever known. She loved Alexandria with all her heart and wished that she was indeed her real mother.

"It's hot here in St. Louis. I want to go home,"

Danielle exclaimed as she wiped the perspiration from her forehead with a lawn handkerchief.

"Yes, it's much warmer here than it is in Philadelphia, Danielle, but you will find the weather much milder when you reach the Blackfoot village."

When Danielle hurried across the room, the wide bell hoop beneath her gown caused her skirt to sway gracefully. She threw herself into Alexandria's arms as tears spilled down her face.

"It's not too late for you to make Father change his mind. I beg you, Mother, help me!"

Alexandria took Danielle's handkerchief and dried the girl's tears. She loved Tag's daughter as if she were her very own, but she knew Tag had long ago made this decision and no one would be able to change his mind.

"Danielle, I cannot help you in this. You would make things much easier on yourself and your father if you would accept this as an adventure. Think of the fun you will have learning about the Blackfoot people. I know your Aunt Joanna and Uncle Windhawk are looking forward to you spending the summer with them. Think of the joy you will bring to your grandmother. I understand she has been ill."

"I don't want to go! I don't like my grandmother; she is nothing more than a . . . savage!"

Danielle hadn't heard her father enter the room, and when he spun her around to face him, she saw the anger etched on his face, and there was a dangerous glint in his eyes. "Don't you ever, ever let me hear you speak of your grandmother in that way again, young lady. Sun Woman is a wonderful woman, and you could learn many things from her, not the least of which is not to be so selfish."

"But, Papa, she is an Indian," Danielle cried. "How can you care so little about me that you would abandon me to people that I don't even know?"

"You know your grandmother very well. At least you have heard us speak of her. You must remember the times she came to Meadowlake Farm to visit you. The last time she came you treated her so badly she was deeply hurt. She knew you were ashamed of her. You hurt one of the finest women I have ever known, and you had better not allow such a thing to happen again. Do I make myself clear?"

Danielle lowered her head, no longer able to meet her father's eyes. How well she remembered the visit her grandmother had paid to Meadowlake Farm. Danielle had been six years old at the time. Sun Woman had tried to tell her about her mother, but she had cut her off, refusing to listen. The final blow had fallen, however, when her grandmother had reminded her father of a promise he had made to her when Danielle had been but a baby. Evidently he had promised the woman that Danielle would one day spend time with the Blackfoot people. The time she had always dreaded had arrived, and it seemed that she was to be exchanged for her cousin Sky Dancer.

"I'm sorry, Papa, but I am so unhappy about this arrangement. Please take me back home with you."

She saw the muscles tighten in her father's jaw and knew he would never relent. In the past she had often managed to get her way with tears, but that was not to be the case this time. Danielle felt as if he was throwing her to the wolves. "You don't love me or you wouldn't cast me aside," she insisted, trying one last time to reach his heart.

"You are wrong, Danielle. It's because I love you that I am doing this. I know in the past that Alexandria and I have spoiled you too much. Perhaps spending time with your mother's people will open your eyes in many ways. At least I hope it will."

Danielle realized that no amount of pleading on her part would change her father's mind. Turning away, she crossed the room and threw herself down on the bed. If she were going to have to go to the Blackfoot village, then she was determined to make everyone else as miserable as she felt. She would show them all that they couldn't treat her this way. She would make them all pay!

Sky Dancer stepped out of the scented bath and dried herself with the thick towel. She looked at the gown her mother had laid out on the bed for her to wear. How could anyone feel comfortable with so many undergarments, she wondered, picking up the wire hoop with its stiff webbing and bindings. She shook her head, studying it curiously. She had seen many pictures of ladies garbed in their finery, but she had never had the desire to wear the ridiculous clothing herself. Running her hand down the creamy white petticoat, Sky Dancer thought she had never felt anything so soft. Her mother had told her that her Uncle Tag would be bringing her new clothing from Philadelphia and she would be abandoning her buckskin gowns for the duration of her visit.

Joanna entered the room through the connecting doors and smiled at her daughter. Sky Dancer could only stare in awe at her mother, who was wearing a pale green gown that seemed to shimmer when she walked. "Mother, you are so beautiful. I wish Father could see you now."

Joanna laughed. "Your father is a very determined man. He would prefer to see us both wearing buckskin, I'm afraid. We haven't much time—my brother will be waiting for us to join him shortly. Let me help you dress."

Sky Dancer followed her mother's direction and stepped into the pantaloons. She drew in her breath as her mother laced the stiff corset about her waist and cinched it in tightly. When Joanna lifted the gown over her head, Sky Dancer was sure she would neither be able to move nor breathe. Before Sky Dancer could complain about her discomfort, her mother turned her around and fastened the gown up the back.

Joanna stood back and admired her daughter, thinking how lovely she looked. Giving Sky Dancer an encouraging smile, she led her over to a mirror so she could see her reflection. "This is the way I always wanted to see you dressed, Sky Dancer. You are breathtaking."

The young girl stared in disbelief at the image which was projected in the aged and cracked mirror. The gown was white muslin, with tiny puffed sleeves. The waistline was pointed in the front and back. The skirt was embroidered with tiny flowers, white on white. As Sky Dancer's eyes traveled up to her own face, she stared in wonder at the image that was reflected in the mirror. Her skin was not white, but a soft ivory color. Her blue eyes seemed to sparkle with youth and good health. Black hair draped over one shoulder and fell to her waist. Could that stranger in the mirror be her?

Suddenly Sky Dancer felt fear of the unknown life that awaited her just beyond the bedroom door. Sky Dancer sought her mother's eyes, and could tell by the expression on her face that Joanna knew what she was thinking and feeling.

Joanna pulled Sky Dancer's hair back to the nape of her neck and tied a white ribbon about it. "You are so beautiful, my daughter," she whispered through trembling lips.

"Is that really me?"

"Indeed it is," her mother said with pride. "I know you are feeling a bit frightened at the moment, but that will pass. Come, let us go to your Uncle Tag's suite, he will be wondering what's keeping us."

Taggart James crossed the room and opened the door. His eyes softened when they rested on his sister's lovely face. Taking her hand, he pulled Joanna into his arms. There had always been a special bond between the brother and sister which time and distance had not weakened.

Joanna lifted her face and smiled into her brother's blue eyes. "You have hardly changed at all since last I saw you," she said, kissing his cheek and hugging him tightly.

"No woman in the world can rival your beauty," he said with a humorous light in his eyes.

Alexandria stepped forward and took Joanna's hand. She had realized a long time ago that Tag and his sister shared a special kind of love. She had never been jealous of their love, but at times perhaps she was a bit envious. As the two sisters-in-law embraced, Sky

Dancer stood nervously in the hallway. For many months she had been dreading this meeting. She knew her Uncle Tag very well since he visited the Blackfoot almost every summer, but she was unsure about how to greet her Aunt Alexandria and her cousin Danielle.

Tag grabbed his niece and tightly hugged her to him, and she smiled up at him. He was indeed a handsome man with no gray to lace his blonde hair and no wrinkles to mar his face.

"Sky Dancer, you are all grown up, and nature did a beautiful job on you, too." Suddenly his eyes rounded in astonishment. "I . . . swear you are the very image of your cousin Danielle. If I didn't know better, I would say my eyes were playing tricks on me." Tag was indeed shocked as he realized that the two young girls could pass for twins.

Taking his young niece's hand, he led her into the room and over to the girl that Sky Dancer had dreaded meeting. The beautiful young girl was dressed in a pink and white candy striped gown and her hair was arranged on the top of her head. To Sky Dancer the lovely girl looked like she could have just stepped out of the pages of a fashion book.

When the two girls stood face to face, their eyes met and widened in surprise. In that instant they both realized that they did look like twins! They each had the same deep blue eyes and midnight black hair. Their features were finely chiseled and they had the same high cheekbones. There wasn't a hair's breadth difference in their height.

Danielle was overcome by the irony of the situation and she smiled brightly. "I had heard that we were alike, but until this moment I had no notion just how true that was. It is as if I were looking into a mirror at my own image, Sky Dancer," she beamed, warming to her look-alike immediately.

Farley ambled into the room, and looked from one girl to the other. "Well, I can't hardly tell which one's which. Didn't I tell you that they was like two peas in a pod?"

Tag vigorously shook Farley's hand, and Alexandria kissed his rough cheek." We're glad to see you, Farley." Alexandria said with affection. "I hope you're going home with us."

"Nope, I 'spect I'll be going back to the village." Farley was made to feel he was welcome in Philadelphia and in the Indian village. "Which one of you gals is Danielle?" he asked, lumbering over to the look-alikes. "I want to give Danielle a hug since I ain't seen her in so long."

Danielle smiled impishly. "Can't you tell I'm me, Farley?"

"Yep, I knowed it was you, I just wanted to see if you knowed who you was." He gave her a tight hug and then stood back. "I declare, you are both the same."

Sky Dancer shook her head in confusion. "I . . . did not know we were so alike." She had dreaded this meeting with her worldly and sophisticated cousin, but she saw only joy and acceptance in the young girl's eyes.

"Papa, how can you be so cruel as to separate me and my cousin now that we have only become acquainted? I declare I will cause a scene if you don't allow us to spend this summer together." Danielle's eyes sparkled mischievously as she winked at Sky Dancer. "What fun we could have fooling all my friends in Philadelphia."

45

Before Sky Dancer could voice her opinion, she was enfolded in the arms of her Aunt Alexandria. The tiny woman stood inches shorter than Sky Dancer, and had the strangest golden-colored eyes. Alexandria's mink-colored hair was pulled back in a bun at the nape of her neck, and Sky Dancer thought that her aunt had a soft, subtle kind of beauty. She was immediately warmed by the older woman's smile.

"We are going to have such fun, my dear. There are so many things that we want to show you."

Suddenly some of Sky Dancer's apprehension left her. She could feel this newfound love reach out to her.

Joanna approached her niece and took her hand in hers. "Although I haven't seen you since you were very young, please know that I love you. I am going to love having you for the whole summer. I will always remember when your mother died and I nursed you along with my own daughter. That gives us a special bond, don't you think?"

Her aunt's words came as such a surprise that Danielle had no ready reply. She had often wondered what her Aunt Joanna would be like. She couldn't understand what would cause a white woman who had been brought up in polite society to abandon her way of life to live with an Indian. "Your portrait which was painted when you were a young girl hangs on the wall in my father's study. You were lovely then; you are beautiful now" was all Danielle could think to reply.

Joanna smiled. "I thank you for the compliment. You cannot know how long I have looked forward to this summer. There are so many people who are anxious to meet you, not the least of whom is your Uncle Windhawk."

Danielle looked down at the toe of her satin slipper which was peeking out of the hem of her gown. She couldn't meet the blue eyes that held so much love and understanding. She didn't want to like this woman. Hadn't she sworn that she would make everyone miserable for forcing her to spend four months with a tribe of savages?

"If you have any influence with my father, I beg you to intercede on my behalf. I do not want to spend the summer with the Blackfoot. All I want to do is go home."

Joanna turned quickly and looked at her brother. She had expected Danielle to be apprehensive, but she hadn't expected her to be defiant.

"Danielle, I am warning you," her father said, giving her a look that clearly told her he was angry with her. "Apologize at once to your Aunt Joanna!"

Danielle raised her chin stubbornly. "I will apologize because you ordered me to, Papa, but I will not say I'm sorry, because I'm not. I want to go home."

Tag's eyes sought his sister's and she read the hopelessness there. "Danielle, you cannot possibly know how much you are loved by many of us in the Blackfoot tribe. Your grandmother, Sun Woman, marks the passing days off on a piece of buffalo robe. There are many who impatiently await your visit. We have planned many exciting adventures with which to entertain you," Joanna said, watching the young girl's eyes fill with anger, or perhaps it was apprehension.

Danielle crossed her arms and tapped her foot. "I'm not in the least interested in what a bunch of Indians have planned for me. I was brought up to be white; I will not act like a savage!"

47

Tag's face showed the rage he was feeling. When he would have vented that anger on his daughter, Joanna silenced him with a glance. Taking Danielle by the shoulders, she turned her niece to face her. "You only say these things because you are frightened, Danielle. I understand what you are feeling because at one time I felt the same as you. Give yourself this chance to experience a whole new way of life."

Again it was hard for Danielle to look into her aunt's eyes. She wanted to cry out her anguish because no one seemed to understand what she was feeling except her aunt. "I won't go, and no one can make me!" she cried, throwing herself into Joanna's arms.

Joanna raised her niece's face and stared into her eyes. "Danielle, you are forgetting one very important thing. You are the daughter of Morning Song, and as her daughter, you, in your own rights, are an Indian princess of a proud and noble family. It is your duty to act accordingly.'

"I . . . am a real princess?" Danielle asked in shocked surprise. "No one has ever told me this before."

"I can assure you it is the truth," her father concurred. We have never mentioned it to you because, as you know, we had to keep your identity a secret. We wanted you to lead a normal life, which wouldn't have been allowed had the neighbors known that you were half Indian."

Danielle was thoughtful for a moment as she looked at Sky Dancer. They were both half white and half Indian, yet her cousin didn't look or act like a savage. Perhaps she had been wrong in not wanting to visit her mother's people. If she were a princess, would she be treated like royalty? "I will go with you, Aunt Joanna," she said reflectively. "But only because I am forced to. I am unimpressed with the title of Indian princess."

Joanna saw the anguish on her brother's face as he sent her a grateful glance. She realized that Danielle had a long way to go before she would be able to come to terms with who she was. The way would be a difficult one, but she was determined to help guide this girl in finding true happiness. She owed it to her brother and to Danielle's dead mother, Morning Song.

Tag held his arm out to Sky Dancer and gave her a bright smile. "Let us proceed to the dining room. I will have the distinction of escorting the four loveliest ladies who ever stepped foot in this town. St. Louis will never see the likes of you again."

Alexandria took Joanna's arm and gave her a woebegone look. They both knew that they were tampering with nature to transplant two young girls into a world they didn't belong.

"Danielle will come around, Alex. She just needs time to grow up."

"I will take the greatest care of Sky Dancer, Joanna. She is so sweet and lovely. I wish Danielle could be more like . . ." She shrugged her shoulders. "I just hope we haven't made a mistake."

"Me too," Joanna agreed. "Me too."

That night the two girls went into Danielle's room while their parents visited in Tag's and Alexandria's room. They were sitting in the middle of the bed getting better acquainted. Danielle reached out and touched her look-alike's face. "We really could pass for twins, you know. I bet if we put our minds to it, we could fool

49

almost anyone."

Sky Dancer removed the ribbon from her hair and tied it about Danielle's head so it resembled an Indian headband. "Yes, I believe you are right. It is truly a wonder, is it not?"

Danielle's face became thoughtful and secretive. "I have an idea, Sky Dancer," she said, smiling mischievously. "Tomorrow we are supposed to spend the day with your father. My father said it had all been arranged this morning. What if . . ." She giggled and stood up, dancing around the room, causing her gown to swirl out about her. "What if you pretended to be me, and I pretended to be you?"

Sky Dancer scooted off the bed and caught her cousin's hand. "It might be fun—do you think we could get by with it?"

"Let me see now . . ." Danielle began thoughtfully. "Your voice doesn't sound like mine. You speak English with an accent. Do you think you can talk like me?"

"Do you think you can talk like me?" Sky Dancer mimicked her cousin perfectly.

"That's it, you did it!"

"Now, listen to this. Tomorrow I will dress in one of your gowns, and you will wear mine. I will wear my hair straight like yours, and we'll put yours up on your head."

"Wouldn't it be something if we could fool them well enough so I wouldn't have to go to Philadelphia, and you wouldn't have to go to my village," Sky Dancer said, giggling delightedly.

Danielle's eyes narrowed. "Who knows, if we are very clever we might just pull it off. Would you be willing to do that?"

"No, I would never try to trick my mother and father in that way, Danielle. It would be fun for a while, but not for what you are suggesting."

"I thought Indians were supposed to be devious and sly," Danielle said in a haughty voice.

"I had heard that white men often say things that are not true," Sky Dancer replied in an angry voice.

Both girls glared at each other until at last Danielle's face eased into a grin. "You know what—I think I like you. All right, we will just try to fool them for tomorrow."

Sky Dancer was slower to get over her anger than Danielle. She didn't like the things her cousin had said about the Indians. "I am not so sure I like you at all," she admitted.

Danielle, who was always a tease, made a face at Sky Dancer. "How can you not like your twin. Come on, let's plan what we are going to do tomorrow."

Slowly Sky Dancer's temper cooled. No one could stay mad at Danielle for very long.

From across the hall Tag heard Sky Dancer and Danielle's laughter. "I knew the girls would get along once they got to know one another. It's a shame that they haven't known each other over the years."

"Well they won't get to know each other this year," Alexandria stated. "How can they, when they will each go their separate ways?"

"I believe they will always remember this summer," Joanna predicted. "Let us hope they will look back on this year with fond memories."

*   *   *

Sky Dancer was aware that she was dreaming and yet it seemed so real. She stood alone overlooking a strange and wondrous garden. There was a sweet aroma in the air, and she knew it came from the many flowers in bloom. Turning her face up to the moon, she felt a loneliness in the very depths of her being.

If it were only a dream why did she feel so alive? She knew something extraordinary was about to happen. Glancing down, she found herself dressed in a lovely shimmering gown of the white woman . . .

A voice she didn't recognize spoke from out of the shadows. "I wonder what you were wishing for just now? A new gown, perhaps, or maybe a new bonnet?"

Sky Dancer slowly turned to face the stranger. He was a head taller than she was and wore the blue uniform of a Cavalry officer—he was a white man! She couldn't see his features very well since they were cast in shadows, but his eyes seemed to sparkle with mirth.

"I do not know you, sir," she heard herself saying.

He reached out and captured her hand, stilling her movement. She looked into laughing silver-gray eyes. Those eyes gleamed as he gathered her in his arms. She felt his nearness like a pain in her heart. Who was this man who controlled her dreams.

Sky Dancer wanted to leave—wanted to wake up— but she seemed hypnotized by the deep chord in his voice and the way he was looking at her. Since she had never been kissed by a man—no Blackfoot brave would ever have dared touch her—she didn't suspect his intention until it was too late.

When their lips met, her mouth trembled beneath his. She was bewildered by the touch of this man's lips on hers. A warmth seemed to surround her heart, and it frightened her so much that she pulled away from him.

Placing her hand to her lips, she looked at him quizzically. What should she do? Surely it was wrong to allow a strange man to kiss her. "My father will kill you for this," she said, voicing the first thought that came to mind.

He laughed. "Surely not for just one stolen kiss." The mocking laughter danced in his eyes.

Sky Dancer knew she should leave but he seemed to hold her prisoner with his strange silver eyes. She also realized she was still dreaming and didn't want to wake up. She wanted to stay in this dreamworld with her silver-eyed lover.

Her face was flushed, and she placed her hand to her lips. She hadn't known it could be so pleasant to be kissed by a man. The blue uniform fit his broad shoulders and six-foot frame to perfection. His features were bold and handsome. His hair and sideburns were golden in color. His most disturbing feature was his silver-colored eyes. They reminded Sky Dancer of the color of a frozen pond, except there was warmth and humor in his glance.

What was his name? she wondered. Why was she dreaming about him? No, surely it was more than a dream—it was a vision—perhaps a prediction of things to come!

She found herself reaching out to him, but a swirling shadow world had already enveloped him in its darkness. She cried out to him to take her hand and hold her in this shadow land, but already she could feel herself waking.

Her eyes opened and she focused them on the ceiling of the hotel room. She felt strangely empty and bewildered. Had the dream been a glimpse into the future, or merely a nightmare? She didn't know. She was fully awake—the dream was gone. Shaking her head she tried to clear it. Still sleep-drugged she tried to remember what she had dreamed but couldn't—it was lost, gone.

The dream had left her drained. Trying to fall asleep, she wanted to recapture the fleeting vision, but couldn't. It was almost daylight when she again closed her eyes in sleep. Even then the dream did not return. . . .

Chapter Three

Sky Dancer waited until her mother had gone across the hall to her uncle's room, then she dashed down the hallway into Danielle's room. Her arms were laden with a gown, slippers, and undergarments.

"Hurry, Sky Dancer, we don't have much time," Danielle breathed. "Someone might come in and catch us in the act of trading clothing."

Both girls quickly changed into each other's gowns and shoes. Danielle sat Sky Dancer down on the bed and arranged her hair on top of her head, with one long trailing curl hanging over her shoulder. They then stood back and surveyed each other.

"Yes, it will work if you can remember to talk like me," Danielle said with mischief dancing in her eyes. "You talk so proper, Sky Dancer. Try to drop your accent and remember to say *can't* instead of *cannot*, and *don't* instead of *do not.*"

"I'll try to remember. What do we do next?"

"Here's where the true test comes in. You go to my father's room, and I'll go to your room and wait for your mother."

"I am very nervous, Danielle."

"No, say, 'I'm very nervous,'" Danielle corrected.

"I'll try to remember," Sky Dancer said, feeling the excitement building up inside her.

"Hurry, before someone comes! Let's see how long we can fool everyone," Danielle urged.

"No, say, 'Let us see how long we can fool everyone,'" Sky Dancer said, giggling.

Danielle shoved Sky Dancer toward the door. "Go on, you little imp—but be careful."

Sky Dancer moved quickly down the hall. When she neared her uncle's room, the door opened and her mother stepped out into the hall.

"Hello, Aunt Joanna." She held her breath wondering if her mother would discover the deception, and hoping she had correctly imitated Danielle's voice.

"Good morning, Danielle. Are you excited about the picnic?"

"Yes," Sky Dancer said, brushing past her mother and entering the room before she doubled over in a fit of laughter. This was going to be fun, she thought.

"Good morning, dear," Alexandria said, planting a quick kiss on her forehead. "I was going to come to your room and help you with your hair, but I see you have done it yourself."

Tag was reading a newspaper, and he laid it aside. "There is a special bloom to your cheeks this morning, Danielle. Did you sleep well?"

"Yes, Papa. When do we leave for the picnic?"

"When Joanna and Sky Dancer are ready," he answered. Pulling her down into his lap, he held her close for a moment. "I'm going to miss you, honey. Tell

56

me, how did you get along with Sky Dancer?"

"I liked her very well," Sky Dancer answered, hiding a smile behind her hand.

"Didn't I tell you Sky Dancer was wonderful? If you were of a mind to, you could learn some manners from your cousin. She's special."

"Well, I can tell you I was charmed by Sky Dancer." Alexandria added her views to the conversation.

"Don't you think she's a little savage?" Sky Dancer said offhandedly.

Tag turned her to face him. "Don't you ever let me hear you say th—" His eyes widened in shocked surprise as he recognized Sky Dancer. A smile eased his lips into a smile. "Well, perhaps she has a few rough edges," he said, winking.

Sky Dancer knew her uncle had recognized her, but he seemed willing to play along with the little game.

"Tag, how can you say such a thing?" Alexandria cried. "I think she's lovely."

"Yep, I can't argue with that, can you, Danielle?"

Sky Dancer's eyes danced merrily. "I think she is breathtaking."

Danielle watched her aunt go about the room gathering up scattered clothing and placing them in the trunk. Lifting a sparkling pink ball gown, she held it against Danielle. "This is lovely. I wish I could be in Philadelphia when you wear it."

"I would rather wear my buckskins, Mother. Will you not take me back home with you?"

"We have already discussed this, Sky Dancer. Besides, I'm looking forward to getting to know Danielle better."

"Do you like her?"

57

"I love her."

"But do you like her?"

"I'm sure when I get to know her better, I will like her very much. I suspect she can be a very charming young lady." Joanna folded the pink gown, and carefully placed it in the trunk.

"Come, it's time to go. Your uncle will be wondering what's keeping us."

The picnic was being held in the woods so Windhawk could be with them. Joanna and Alexandria had hoped a picnic would break the tension and allow the two young girls a chance to become better acquainted. It would also allow Tag time to visit with Windhawk. Tag had always looked up to his brother-in-law. He would never forget that Windhawk had saved his life many times. Windhawk had taken him in and raised him, instilling a sense of values in him that Tag still lived by today.

The girls continued to play their roles. Sky Dancer had told Danielle that her Uncle Tag knew about the switch, but no one else seemed to catch on.

Danielle stood beside Joanna as Windhawk arrived. This was the most frightening moment of all for her. When he walked up to her, she cringed inside. His dark eyes moved over her face, and he smiled. Glancing at Sky Dancer he shook his head. "Which one of you is my daughter, and which is my niece?" To Danielle's surprise, his English was perfect.

"Father, do you not know me?" Danielle said, feeling that no one could fool this man with the probing black eyes.

"I am glad to see you, my daughter." He made no attempt to draw her into his arms, but went over to Tag. The two men clasped arms in Blackfoot fashion. Anyone could see they were happy to see one another. "Do our daughters try to play a trick?" he said under his breath so only Tag could hear.

"Play along with them for a while. It seems they have fooled everyone but you and I."

Windhawk moved over to Alexandria. "It has been many years since I have seen you, my sister. It is good to look upon your face."

Alexandria had always been a bit intimidated by the Blackfoot chief. She could never completely forget that he was Tag's first wife's brother. "It's always good to see you, Windhawk."

He smiled, putting her at ease. "Today we are blessed, because we are all together."

"All but our two sons," she reminded him.

"This is true." He turned to Sky Dancer and knew he must pretend she was his niece Danielle. "I have long looked forward to seeing you, Danielle. You are as pretty as my own Sky Dancer."

She smiled. "I am glad to see you, Uncle. I have heard many things about you."

He took her hand and pulled her into his arms. "Have you also heard it is not nice to try and fool your father?" he whispered against her ear.

"How could you tell?" she whispered back.

He chuckled. "It's a wise father who knows his own flesh."

He moved away, and held his hand out to Joanna. "Let us give thanks for this day. We are with the people that we love," Windhawk announced.

Farley chose that moment to amble into the family circle. Without a word to anyone, he walked right up to Sky Dancer. "Why are you wearing your hair up like that, Sky Dancer? I like it better hanging down."

Joanna and Alexandria looked at the two girls in surprise, then they burst out laughing. "It took you to point out our own daughters, Farley." Joanna was laughing so hard, she had to stop to catch her breath.

"Farley, you spoiled everything," Danielle cried. "Why did you have to do that?"

Farley looked at the smiles on everyone's face. He couldn't understand what was so funny.

"We did fool you for a time," Sky Dancer said. "Of course our fathers knew from the start who was who."

The broad, muddy Mississippi River flowed lazily toward the sea, oblivious to the green slopes and dense forest that grew along its banks.

Sky Dancer stood on a hill overlooking the place where the Missouri and Mississippi rivers joined in the endless flow to the sea. These rivers with the strange-sounding names might be larger and wider than the Milk River of her homeland, but they couldn't compare with its life-giving water.

The young girl wore a gray and white pin-striped gown, with its cumbersome steel hoop swaying with the warm breeze. How she longed for her soft buckskins and moccasins.

"What are you thinking," her look-alike asked, coming up beside her and following Sky Dancer's eyes down to the river.

"I suppose I am homesick. Like you, I wish I didn't

60

have to venture so far from home."

Danielle sat down on the green grass and motioned for Sky Dancer to join her. "Perhaps, if we were to band together and present a united front, our parents would listen to us and relent."

Sky Dancer shook her head. "I have given my word and cannot break it. Would it not be better to go forward with a happy heart and make the best of a bad situation, suffering only in silence?"

Danielle sighed heavily. "I suppose," she declared ruefully. "Tell me about your life in the Indian village. Somehow I cannot fathom you living with savages and enjoying it. You seem so civilized."

Sky Dancer didn't take offense at her cousin's words. At the moment she felt years older than Danielle, even though they were only a few weeks apart in age. "I have known no life other than the one I was born into. I love the people of the Blackfoot tribe. Both you and I are what others less kind might call half-breeds. Yet if I were to resent anything in life, it would be the white blood that flows in my veins. It seems you resent the Indian that is a part of you."

"I suppose you are right," Danielle admitted. "I didn't intend to like you or my Aunt Joanna, but I find that I do. Wouldn't it be fun if we could spend the summer together? La, I can just see the ladies of Philadelphia turning green with envy when the two of us walk into a room. We are both beautiful, you know."

Sky Dancer couldn't help but laugh at her cousin's observation. "Are we? I suppose I never thought much about how I looked until I met you. You *are* very lovely."

61

Danielle chewed on a long stem of grass. "If I am beautiful, then you are too. Have you never had a young man tell you that you are pleasant to look upon?"

"No, they wouldn't dare say such a thing to me. I am daughter to the chief."

"How very dull. I love all the attention I am showered with when I go to balls and parties. Is there no one special whom you like in the Blackfoot village?"

"No, not really, although . . . I do think Wolfrunner is very handsome. He has not looked at me as a woman though. We are no more than good friends. You will meet him since he is traveling with my father and mother."

"Tell me about him," Danielle said with interest.

"Wolfrunner is the son of a powerful war chief, Gray Fox. He is five summers older than I, and very handsome. He is a very brave warrior. Many of the maidens of my tribe wish he would look at them, but he does not."

"I know someone like him. His name is Morgan Prescott. Actually, he's a doctor and is serving in the Cavalry. His family lives on the estate down the road from ours. He is very handsome and dashing. All the girls make fools of themselves over him, but he hardly notices them."

"Is he interested in you, Danielle?" Sky Dancer wanted to know.

Danielle tossed aside the blade of grass she had been chewing. "Not in the way you think. He has always treated me like a child. I declare he can be the most irritating man sometimes. He is a colonel in the Cavalry and doesn't come home very often. I haven't seen him in over a year. How dashing he looked in his uniform the last time I saw him. He did kiss me once, but it was all in fun."

"The war is very bad, isn't it?"

"Didn't you know the war is over—we won. General Lee surrendered to General Ulysses S. Grant at Appomattox Courthouse. But to answer your question, yes, the war was awful and for more reasons than one. There are never enough handsome dancing partners at a ball. I am ofttimes forced to dance with bearded old men. It will be wonderful when our men come home again. Of course, if they come home while I am away, all the most eligible ones will be snapped up before I return."

"Do you love this Morgan Prescott?"

"Goodness, no."

"You said he kissed you."

"That was nothing. Morgan kisses all the young ladies. He is the most sought-after bachelor in Philadelphia, but he isn't marriage minded. I was very angry with him the last time we met. I believe I damned him to the enemy."

"I have never kissed a man other than my father and brother, with the exception of Farley."

Danielle giggled. "Isn't it strange. That crusty old trapper is a big part of both our lives. I just adore him, don't you?"

"Yes, he lives in my village. Farley is like one of the family."

Danielle frowned. "Just think, your brother and mine are traveling in Europe this summer with our Grandfather James. Men have all the advantages, don't you agree?"

"I have never thought about it. I know Little Hawk was very excited about going abroad with Grandfather."

"I would settle for a party or a ball at the moment. I like excitement in my life," Danielle admitted.

Sky Dancer laughed. "My mother has taught me how to dance, but I wouldn't want to dance with one of your young gentlemen. I would be too frightened."

"Father told me that your mother taught you to speak English as soon as you could talk. I suppose she was preparing you for this summer."

"Yes, she taught me what she calls all the niceties of society. I hope I can put them into practice when we reach Philadelphia. I would not wish to shame your father and mother."

"I don't think you have anything to worry about. You realize, of course, they aren't going to tell anyone that you have an Indian father. They will guard the truth as they have for me all these years."

"Yes, I have been told this. I wonder why I cannot be honest about myself. I feel only pride for the Indian blood that came to me through my father."

Danielle's eyes turned cold, and she frowned at Sky Dancer. "The one thing you must not do is let anyone find out that you are half Indian. You may not care, but I would be humiliated if they were to find out about me. I will hate you forever if you betray me!"

Sky Dancer blinked her eyes. "I will not betray you, but neither will I feel shame for who I am. You are a fool if you shun the noble race that your mother belonged to."

"I don't want to talk about my real mother. As far as I'm concerned, Alexandria is my mother. All of

Philadelphia believe this to be true."

Sky Dancer stood up and brushed away the grass that clung to her skirt. She was deeply disturbed by her cousin's views. Today was the first time in her life that she had come up against prejudice and it left a bitter taste in her mouth. She realized more than ever that she would not like this white world she was going into.

As her cousin walked away, Danielle watched her with a troubled expression on her face. She had come to realize that even though the two of them looked alike, they were nothing alike on the inside. She felt again bitter resentment burning deep inside because she was being forced to leave her home and live among the Indians.

Joanna and Alexandria spread the colorful cotton cloth on the grass, then set out the food that had been provided for them by the hotel. Farley was stationed nearby with his hat pulled over his eyes, pretending to be asleep, but knowing everything that was going on around him.

Alexandria bit her lip and gazed at her sister-in-law. "Joanna, sometimes I fear this exchange was a mistake. Danielle is very unhappy about the arrangement. Tag and I should have eased her into this. If we had brought her to the village when she was younger, perhaps she wouldn't be feeling this hostility. We tried so hard to keep people from finding out about her Indian blood, not realizing we were causing her to resent that she is only half white."

"You did what you thought was right at the time. Sky Dancer isn't all that happy about the thought of leaving home, either. Perhaps in the end, this will all turn out for the best."

"Let us hope so. I suppose Tag and I have spoiled Danielle terribly, but deep down she is a loving girl. Have patience with her, and give her a chance. She will soon show you her better side, Joanna."

"Have no fear, Alexandria. You forget that when Danielle's mother was killed, it was I who nursed her at my breast. I love her very much."

Alexandria closed the lid of the picnic basket and looked directly into Joanna's blue eyes. "Please put your fear aside for Sky Dancer. Your brother and I will take the best care of her."

"I know you will. In truth I will be happy when the summer has passed and each girl is back where she belongs."

"Joanna, you are concerned that Danielle will hurt Sun Woman again, aren't you?"

"Yes, I confess I am. Sun Woman is getting old, and her one wish is to spend some time with her dead daughter's daughter."

Tag came out of the woods and joined the two ladies. Sitting down, he picked up an apple and bit into it. "I just left Windhawk, and he is most anxious for you and Danielle to meet him at his camp early tomorrow morning. He says he wants to get an early start, Joanna. I think what he really meant was that he misses you," he teased.

Farley stood up and stretched his arms over his head. "I 'spect I'll be getting back to camp now." He ambled off without another word to anyone.

Joanna and Alexandria turned their attention to the two girls who were making their way across the glen.

Joanna looked at Tag and sent him a quizzical glance. He smiled at her reassuringly.

"Don't worry about either of them," he said lazily. "They both come from good stock."

The afternoon passed slowly as the two girls found out about each other's lives. They talked of their homes and many of the customs.

Danielle faced the coming day with a heavy heart. She was trapped into a situation over which she had no control. Her father had no sympathy for her plight, and if Alexandria felt pity for her, she didn't show it.

Sky Dancer watched her mother laughing with her uncle. She tried to picture her mother living in the white man's world. How easily she wore the silk gowns and strange-looking shoes, but then she had been born into that world.

"Will I be facing any kind of danger in your village?" Danielle asked, breaking into Sky Dancer's thoughts.

"No, none that I can think of. You will be well protected by the warriors." Sky Dancer paused and looked into eyes not unlike her own. "I would ask you to be particularly kind to our grandmother. She is a frail old woman and she loves you a great deal."

"I don't think of her as my grandmother. But . . . I will not be unkind to her."

"You will like my father, Danielle. He is very wonderful."

"My father is not at all wonderful at the moment. If he were, he would take me back home," Danielle said with a pout on her pretty lips.

"Let us not think about tomorrow or the day after." Sky Dancer smiled, and lay back on the grass. "Let us both pretend that tomorrow is years away."

Danielle lay back on the grass, and stared at her cousin. "You may be able to fool yourself, but I can't. Tomorrow will come, and we will both be taken far from our homes."

Sky Dancer had the strongest urge to run to her mother and throw herself into her arms. Instead, she closed her eyes and willed herself to be strong. There would be many tomorrows before she was back home in the Blackfoot village.

Danielle reached for Sky Dancer's hand. "I truly believe I willl miss you. It was fun today, wasn't it?"

Sky Dancer nodded. "Yes, it was fun trying to fool everyone." She felt a sense of loss. She hardly had time to get to know her cousin, and now they would be parted.

As the two girls gazed into each other's eyes, they knew they shared a common bond. They had more in common than just their looks. They would each have to come to terms with the white and Indian blood that flowed in their veins.

Chapter Four

Sky Dancer's head swayed back and forth with the restless motion of the coach. She had the feeling they would never reach their destination, but would ride on forever into oblivion.

They had spent a week at Meadowlake Farm, her aunt and uncle's country home, which was located in Valley Forge. Sky Dancer hadn't been unhappy at the farm. There had been just the three of them staying at Meadowlake. Alexandria had told Sky Dancer her uncle had sent the servants away so she could be eased into the white world. Sky Dancer had discovered many wondrous things at the farm. Most of all she enjoyed the library with books reaching clear to the ceiling. She spent a great deal of her time riding the blooded horses that her uncle kept there. She was almost sorry when her uncle announced that they would be leaving for Philadelphia.

Early this morning, they had climbed into the coach, heading for Philadelphia. The young girl wished they could have remained in the country. From what she had been told, Philadelphia would be entirely different from Meadowlake Farm.

She had lost count of the days that she had been traveling with her aunt and uncle. The mode of transportation had varied to suit the situation. When they left St. Louis they had gone by boat. On some of the smaller nameless rivers they had been transported by barge. Now, lastly, but far less comfortably, they were traveling by coach. It had rained every day since they had been in the coach, and as a result they had made slow progress. Several times the heavy coach would become bogged down in the mud and mire, forcing them to get out and stand in the rain while the wheels were freed.

Her Uncle Tag had assured her that barring any more trouble, they would reach Philadelphia before nightfall. Sky Dancer gazed out the window and watched the scenery. She felt no kinship with this strange land. Each mile that passed took her farther and farther from her homeland. She was a long way from all that was dear and familiar to her.

Sky Dancer felt totally miserable. It wasn't that her aunt and uncle hadn't been kind to her. In fact, they had gone out of their way to try and make her as comfortable as possible. It was more that she felt like she had been abandoned by her own mother and father.

Gazing at the dense treeline outside the coach window, she watched the steady rain drench the countryside. If only the sun would come out, she thought miserably. How she would like to be standing on the Sweet Grass Hills right this moment, with the warm sun beating down on her face. How wonderful it would be to abandon the tight uncomfortable clothing, with all the laces and wires, for the soft buckskin gown she was accustomed to wearing.

Suddenly the coach hit a huge rock in the road, and Sky Dancer was almost unseated, saved only by the steadying hand that her Uncle Tag placed on her shoulder.

She smiled at her uncle who moved over to sit beside her. Aunt Alexandria was sleeping soundly and hadn't been awakened by the mishap.

"In about another hour we shall reach the outskirts of Philadelphia. After that, depending on the traffic, we should be home within no time at all," her uncle assured her.

"My mother told me that your home is very big and grand. I fear I shall lose my way with so many rooms to wander through."

"Sky Dancer, the one thing that you must remember is that this is your home, the same as it's Danielle's. I don't know if your mother has informed you of the fact that you are an heiress of some means."

"She told me that the James family is very wealthy," Sky Dancer admitted, little impressed with white man's wealth. To her way of thinking, money could never be compared with one's peace of mind.

"Yes, we are, honey. Do you know what that means where you are concerned?"

Sky Dancer shook her head. "Soon I will be returning to my own home. I do not think money will affect my life one way or another."

Tag's laughter rang out. "How like your mother you are. I can't tell you what a joy it will be for me to get to know you better. I wish Danielle was more like you,"

71

Tag added ruefully. "I'm afraid her stubbornness will get her into trouble one day."

Sky Dancer smiled, and in that moment Tag saw a fleeting shadow of his sister's loveliness. Taking the young girl's hand, he placed it against his cheek. "I have loved you since you were a baby. If, while you are staying with us, you are troubled about anything, I hope you will come to me. Will you promise me that?"

Sky Dancer nodded her head. Uncle Tag was the only familiar thing in her life at the moment. Since he had visited the village almost every summer, she had come to know and love him. "I promise," she said softly.

Tag looked into his young niece's eyes, dreading what he must say to her now. He knew about her proud spirit, and he feared she wouldn't understand his reasoning. "Sky Dancer, from this moment on, you will go only by the name Skyler Dancing. Did your mother explain the reason for this?"

"Yes, but I can't say that I like it. I don't feel ashamed of who I am. I don't like the notion of having to change my name."

Tag slid his arm about her shoulder. "I pray the day will come when no one will judge another for no reason other than the kind of person he or she is. That day has not yet come, Skyler," he said, deliberately using her new name. "You must believe me when I tell you, no one must ever know your true identity."

"Are you ashamed of me, Uncle Tag?"

He could read the sadness in her eyes, and shook his head. "The reverse is true, my dear sweet niece. I am proud of you. I know of no other young lady who has your qualifications. Let me tell you a little about myself and perhaps you will better understand my feelings. You know about my being raised in the Blackfoot village?"

"Yes, of course."

"What you may not know is that I admire your father more than any man, living or dead. He took a young, lost white boy and taught him the important things in life. I give him full credit for the man I am today."

"You are a fine man."

Tag gave her a crooked smile. "That's debatable, but I do think I know what's important in life. Like you, I know it isn't money or possessions that are important. However, I feel I didn't pass that knowledge on to my daughter."

"Perhaps my father can teach her as he did you and me," Sky Dancer said earnestly.

Tag looked out the window and vaguely noticed that the rain had stopped. "Perhaps he will, Skyler. I certainly hope that he will."

When the coach made its way up the tree-lined avenue, Sky Dancer could see the big house that seemed to rise out of the mist, and she pushed down the fear that threatened to cut off her breathing.

Alexandria patted her hand and gave her a bright smile. "It will be all right, my dear. You'll see."

As the coach came to a stop, Sky Dancer watched a procession of servants line up on the steps to welcome the travelers home. Tag touched Sky Dancer's shoulder to draw her attention. "Remember that once you step outside this coach you will be known only as

Skyler Dancing, my niece. Sky Dancer no longer exists as long as you reside in Philadelphia." His voice was kind but firm at the same time. She nodded her head in acceptance, feeling as if she had just lost her identity.

Alexandria accompanied Skyler up the stairs and led her down a long, wide hallway. "You will be staying in the room which your mother occupied as a girl. Little has been changed in this room, except we had it newly painted and new coverings made for the bed and windows."

When Alexandria paused before a door and opened it wide, Skyler stepped inside hesitantly. She blinked her eyes at the lovely sight that confronted her. The walls were white, and the bed covering and curtains were lemon yellow, giving the room a bright, airy appearance. There was a vanity table with a stiff yellow skirt and a lounge and chair covered in yellow and white stripes.

"This is lovely," Skyler exclaimed. "Was this truly my mother's room?" she asked, turning around in a wide circle.

"Yes, indeed it was. Your uncle didn't want to change it very much. You will find that many of Joanna's possessions still remain."

Skyler walked over to the vanity and ran her hand over the surface of an ivory-handled mirror. Suddenly she could feel her mother's presence, and she felt less lonely.

Turning to Alexandria, she smiled. "I will love staying in this room, even though it is difficult for me to

74

envision my mother as a young girl living in this house."

Alexandria reached out and slid a comforting arm about Joanna's daughter. "You are so welcome here, my dear. I want you and I to become better acquainted. It's not hard to know what you are feeling at the moment. Once you have become accustomed to this house, you will begin to enjoy yourself. Your uncle and I have a glorious summer planned for you."

Skyler suddenly felt an uneasiness at what lay ahead for her. "Will I be meeting many people?"

"Yes, but not right away. First you will be allowed to settle in."

"I want my mother to be proud of me, Aunt Alexandria. I will try very hard to fit in."

Alexandria laughed. "I have a strong feeling you will be at home in no time." She crossed the room and opened the door. You have had a long and arduous journey. Why don't you rest for a while before you come downstairs. Should you require anything, you have only to ask one of the servants."

With a feeling not unlike panic, Skyler watched her aunt's departure. She wanted desperately to return home. The summer months seemed to loom ahead of her like a painful ordeal to be endured.

She would endure whatever she must, because by the autumn she would be on her way back home to the Blackfoot village.

As she stood before the wide window that gave her a view of the garden below, she tried to imagine her mother as a girl, standing just where she was.

How strange it was to have stepped back into her

mother's past. The last time Joanna James had been in this room, she had been only a girl of seventeen.

Sky Dancer was in a deep sleep. She felt a coldness move over her and tried to awaken. She realized she was going to dream about the strange white man again. She felt her senses become alert and a swirling cloud engulfed her body. Once more she was in a shadow world but she wasn't frightened. She felt that something wonderful was about to happen—wonderful but sad.

The dense clouds lifted and she found herself in her aunt's garden. In the distance she saw a summerhouse amid a flower garden—the smell of them was sweet to her nostrils.

Sky Dancer tried to throw off the sense of sadness. Something was about to happen that made her heart heavy. She didn't know what it was . . .

"Do you wish upon a star?" a deep masculine voice asked.

Spinning around she saw the same man she had dreamed about at the hotel in St. Louis. It seemed the most natural thing in the world that he had come to her again. "No, I was thinking about you," she freely admitted. He gazed up at the night sky while she watched him, trying to fill her heart and mind with his nearness.

"This is the last time I will ever see you. I am going home tomorrow. This is good-bye for us," she heard herself say . . .

Sky Dancer tossed and turned on her bed. Why was she sending this man away when deep inside she wanted him to stay?

His hands gripped her shoulders and he pulled her back against him. "No, this isn't good-bye. Don't you know you are tearing my heart out? Don't you give a damn that I love you?"

Her eyes were tear-bright. "I would rather tear out my own heart than to cause you pain. I do love you, but you will have to understand I must go away."

"I can't believe that you are going away—leaving me with nothing to hold on to." He raised her face and rested his against it. "I want you for my wife."

Sky Dancer shook her head. "That can never be." She tried to close her eyes against the tears, but was unsuccessful. "I can never be your wife, but I will give you what should only be for my husband on my wedding night."

He searched her face. "Are you saying what I think you are?"

"Yes. I will be with you tonight. This is all I can ever give you."

Anger moved over his face. "You are leaving me, so you think to pacify me with a few crumbs. I don't want what you offer . . . now or ever."

She knew it was his hurt that was talking. "You do want me. Your words may deny it, but your eyes never could. It will cost you nothing to take what I give you tonight."

"How many other men have you offered yourself to? Am I the next in a long line of men to whom you have offered crumbs?"

She reached up and unfastened the neck of the robe she was wearing. "I have never given myself to another. I want to give myself to you so you will know how

77

deeply I feel about you. I don't want you to remember me with anything but kindness and love."

"No! I will not take what you are so willing to give. If I can't have all of you, then I don't want anything at all. I can find plenty of women who are willing to give me what you offer so freely."

Even as he denied his need for her, his eyes were drawn to her. He watched as she let her robe drop onto the floor of the summerhouse. He took a step toward her, but stopped when she raised her arms to him.

The bright moonlight seemed to turn her body a golden color. The man could no longer resist the lovely vision that stood before him with her arms outstretched.

Suddenly she was in his arms, and his hands were running up and down her back. He sought and found her lips as his hunger for her deepened into a maddening whirlwind.

Sky Dancer felt his hands sliding blissfully up and down her back and across her hips. She would give him all she had to give, for she couldn't bear to go away and leave him with nothing. There was no doubt in her mind that he loved her, and she doubted she would ever love another man as deeply as she loved this white man . . .

Sky Dancer felt herself waking up and tried to hold on to her dream world. Moaning in her sleep, she reached out her hand and touched her dream lover.

Sky Dancer's hair was streaming across her golden-colored breasts like a black velvet curtain. Her lover was in a half-dazed state, wanting her with every fiber of his being. His body trembled and he felt a need to touch her, to hold her against him forever.

"Damn you," he growled. "You know I want you, but not this way. Why are you doing this to me . . . to us?"

She could feel the strength of his arms as he pushed her aside. She could sense there was pain as well as anger in him. He took the cushions from the window seat and angrily tossed them to the floor of the summerhouse.

"If you want me to lay you down, I'll do it. I hope you know what you are letting yourself in for. But I don't think you do," he said in an angry voice.

Her body trembled visibly as she watched him strip his shirt off and toss it aside. This wasn't what she wanted, she thought in a panic. She had wanted to give herself to him with love, not with anger.

When he had cast the last of his clothing aside, he walked toward her slowly. His eyes were burning into her, and she could see that his jaw was set in anger. Her eyes went to the magnificence of his body. She started shaking all over as he drew nearer. Her eyes fastened on the golden mat of hair on his chest that ran further down his body than her eyes were willing to go.

He reached out for her and slammed her against his naked body. His form was lean and hard and the feel of his hardness pressing against her caused her to gasp.

"Damn you for making me love you, and damn you for making me want you," he growled in her ear.

"Please, I don't want it this way," she pleaded . . .

Sky Dancer reminded herself that this was just a dream and tried to wake up. She couldn't bear the contempt she saw in those silver eyes.

"How do you want it?" he demanded to know. "I wish to hell I knew."

"I . . . wanted to give you this night to remember," she whispered through trembling lips.

He forced her head up so she would have to meet his gaze. "I don't need this to keep you in my mind and heart. Wherever I go and whatever I do, the thought of you will always be with me. How many ways do you want me to say I love you? How many times must I prove that I want you for my wife?"

Tears blinded her, and she quickly brushed them away with the back of her hand. "I love you more than my own life. Am I not proving that to you tonight?"

His head dipped, and she met his kiss eagerly. His hot body was pressed against her soft curves, and she felt a new awakening from deep within. His tongue parted her lips savagely and his mouth plundered hers. She was vaguely aware that he was lowering her back against the cushions.

"This isn't what I envisioned for you and me. I had thought to take you on our wedding bed," he whispered hotly in her ear.

"Tonight I will be as your wife," she answered. "Take what I would have given you as my husband."

His lips moved down her throat and across her silken breasts. Sky Dancer gasped for breath as his tongue circled the rosy peaks. A white-hot sensation rushed through her veins, and she felt as if an earthquake shook her body. She experienced the after-shock all the way to her toes.

"Sweet, sweet," he murmured, and his hot breath sent shivers down her spine.

Sky Dancer could sense a reluctance in him, so she drew his face up to her lips. "Take the gift I offer. It is all I have to give you," she whispered.

He moaned as her lips sought his. He could no longer reason past the wild desire that kept pounding in his brain. Kissing her all the while, he spread her legs and positioned himself between them. One hand pulled her head closer to receive his burning kiss, while the other wandered slowly and sensuously down to the valley of her womanhood. His hand shook as it moved carefully into the velvety softness of her.

Sky Dancer groaned as her body reacted to his soft touch. She felt something akin to pain, yet beyond pain as his hand gently massaged her inner core.

She felt him move forward. When he slowly entered her body, she clamped her lips together tightly to keep from crying out at the beautiful feelings that encased her whole being.

"You belong to me. Surely you can feel that," he murmured.

His damp hair clung to the side of his head, and she ran her fingers through it. With an instinct that is born of woman, she moved her hips up, inviting him to drive deeper into her softness.

He groaned as his body reached dazzling heights. "You are me, and I am you," he whispered in a raspy voice. "I love you more than life, my dearest love. Say that you love me," he demanded, needing to hear the words spoken.

"Yes," she groaned as the tempo inside her body was heightened by his softly spoken words. She gasped with pleasure when he thrust forward, searing the insides of her with his stamp of ownership. "I love you," she whispered against his ear. "I love you with all my heart . . ."

Sky Dancer knew she was crying even in her sleep. In

her vision she was witnessing a love so beautiful it tore at her heart. What she didn't understand was why she was leaving the man she loved. Thick fog swirled about her head. She felt her lover gently stroking her skin as he spoke soothing words in her ear.

"Do not cry, little love. I shall move mountains if that will make you happy. I will sweep aside anything that stands between us, and I shall walk over anyone who tries to take you away from me."

Sky Dancer closed her eyes, knowing the pain she was causing him. She raised her head and looked into his eyes. "Kiss me good-bye," she cried softly. "My dearest, dearest love, kiss me one last time . . ."

The dense fog was closing in on her and she felt him slipping away. "Who are you?" she cried. "Why do you torture me? Why do I love you?"

Knowing it was only a dream, she moaned. Why was she tortured by dreams of this white man? She loved a ghost—an image—someone who didn't really exist.

Suddenly she was fully awake. Her body was trembling from emotions and her cheeks were wet with tears. As before, she couldn't remember what she had dreamed—she only knew it had made her sad. There was a great emptiness deep inside. The dream was forgotten when she awoke, but the agony it had invoked within her heart and body still remained . . .

"I am going to try to do what will please you, Mother."

Leaning her face against the soft lace curtains, she hoped never to shame the people who loved and believed in her. She was so homesick, that she ached all over. This world wasn't for her. She longed for the home of her heart.

Chapter Five

Danielle was dressed in her gray riding habit with a pert little hat set at an angle on her raven tresses. Never having ridden any way except sidesaddle herself, she was appalled that her aunt rode astride like a man. Farley rode along beside them, his eyes always alert. Danielle was sure the old trapper could see things nobody else could.

As they drew near the place where they would be meeting her uncle, the young girl felt as though her stomach was tied in knots. Her cousin had mentioned that there were several warriors who would be traveling with them. Her heart leapt in fear at the thought of facing the wild savages.

They had ridden all day and were a long way from St. Louis by now. It was almost nightfall when she saw a campfire just ahead. Her hands tightened on the reins and she felt as if she were going to be sick.

She was about to be forced to meet that part of herself that she despised. She had always tried to deny that part of her that was Indian. Soon now she would come face to face with that reality.

As they rode into the camp, the first thing Danielle saw was the tipis. Her heart was pounding so loudly that she could actually hear it throbbing in her ears. Her eyes fell on several Indians who stood watching her—their dark eyes seemed to burn into her.

Danielle was startled when one of the warriors broke away and rushed over to her. Before she had time to react, he had grabbed her about the waist and swung her to the ground. All the while the Indian was saying something in his guttural language that she couldn't understand.

She cried out and beat against his chest. Surely this savage didn't intend to ravish her, right here before her aunt!

Joanna came quickly to Danielle's rescue. She drew her away from the Indian and spoke to him in the Blackfoot tongue. The Indian looked startled for a moment. His dark eyes raked across Danielle's face and he stepped back as if the touch of her skin had burned him.

Joanna put her arm about Danielle's waist and patted her soothingly. "This is Wolfrunner. He has mistaken you for Sky Dancer. Since you know how much you resemble Sky Dancer, I'm sure you will forgive his mistake. Wolfrunner is much more confused than you are at the moment."

Farley dismounted, and led the horses away, laughing aloud. He was clearly amused by the incident.

Danielle turned back and looked at the Indian who was watching her now with guarded indifference. He was the warrior that Sky Dancer had told her about the day of the picnic. In her mind she quickly assessed the man. He wore buckskin leggings but his body was bare from the waist up. His skin was dark—too dark for her taste. His hair was so black it was almost blue, and his eyes were almost the color of the raven's wing. Indeed there was a strong handsomeness about him, but not the kind she admired. He was a savage and she vowed she would never allow him to come near her again.

Before she could utter a word, riders approached the camp, the air suddenly seemed sharp with tension. The Indians that were seated by the campfire stood up as the newcomers drew reins.

Danielle turned to watch her uncle ride into camp with several of his warriors. He was different than he had been at the picnic. She supposed it was because of his surroundings. She was immediately aware of the fact that he was the kind of man who commanded and received respect. His dark eyes went first to his wife and visibly softened. When he looked at Danielle she saw them sparkle with warmth.

Dismounting slowly, he walked leisurely toward her. There was nothing about him that incited fear in Danielle. As she looked into his eyes, she read the strangest emotion. Love . . . Her uncle loved her! How could it be she hadn't seen that in his eyes at the picnic.

He didn't attempt to touch her, but merely smiled slightly. "Danielle, how long I have wanted the chance to get to know you. I feel the part of you that is my dead sister."

She swallowed a lump in her throat, knowing he was pulling at that part of her that was Indian—awaking her other self, the part that she had denied existence.

"I am pleased to see you again, Uncle," she said, surprising herself. Indeed there was a part of her that was thrilled at the chance to get to know, and understand, the man who had been a legend to her. She had heard so much about his daring deeds, she could hardly believe he stood before her in the flesh.

Windhawk could sense in his niece a great unrest. Knowing it would not be wise to hug her to him as he wanted to do, he turned his attention to Joanna.

His eyes were so alive and spoke of how he had missed her. "Did it go well for our daughter?" he asked his wife in English for his niece's benefit.

"Sky Dancer was apprehensive, but I believe all will be well with her." Joanna reached out her hand and Windhawk clasped it in his.

Danielle could feel someone's eyes burning into her, and she turned to see the Indian Wolfrunner staring at her. When she met his eyes, he turned away and she shivered. Her heart was pounding and she could feel these people pulling at her. She would never allow them to make a savage of her. Her Indian blood had long been denied, but now some part of her felt akin to these people.

"Come," her uncle said, holding the tent flap aside for Danielle to enter. Without a backward glance she walked into the tipi, glad to get away from Wolfrunner's probing eyes.

There were some kind of skins spread inside the tipi, and Danielle gathered this was where they would sleep. She was weary, and she sank down on one of the soft skins too tired to think or reason. The very worst had already happened to her. She would be forced to live like an animal until she could return to Philadelphia.

"Why don't you rest, Danielle," Joanna said kindly. She could see her niece was totally exhausted. "I will bring you food and then you can go to sleep."

Danielle sank back against the soft robe. Feeling emotionally drained, she closed her eyes. She was asleep when Joanna returned with her food.

Danielle awoke feeling bruised and stiff. It was not yet daylight, so she turned to face the campfire. Stretching her arms above her head, she looked up at the overhead branches and frowned. If this was what it was like sleeping under the stars, she could well do without it. She was accustomed to sleeping in a downy feather bed with soft bed sheets next to her skin.

Sitting up, she frowned in distaste at the animal skin she lay upon. It had done little to cushion her against the hard ground. How much more of this would she have to endure? This was the worst torture she could think of. Would her father feel pity for her, if he could see her now?

"I see that you are awake," her Aunt Joanna said, dropping down beside her. "I have always liked sleeping beneath the sky, don't you? Of course sleeping in a tipi isn't quite the same, is it?"

Danielle was quiet for a moment. She could hardly credit that her lovely aunt liked the hardships she was forced to endure as the wife of a Blackfoot chief.

"I much prefer to sleep in my own bed. I fail to see what you could possibly like about sleeping on the ground."

Joanna smiled in understanding. "I can see where you might feel that way now, but wait until you have become accustomed to our ways. Everything is new to you and I can imagine you might feel frightened too."

"I want to go home. Why is my father punishing me?"

Joanna drew the young girl into her arms, knowing very well what she was feeling. "Your father isn't trying to punish you, Danielle. He made a promise to your grandmother that he would allow you to get to know your mother's people. He has merely honored that promise."

"Alexandria is my mother. I don't want to think about the woman who gave me birth. She isn't my true mother. I do not want to think about being half Indian!"

Joanna stood up and motioned for Danielle to do the same. "Walk with me. I want to tell you about your mother. She was not only very fair of face, but she was beautiful on the inside as well."

Danielle rose reluctantly. She didn't want to hear about the woman who had given birth to her. She had always been ashamed of the Indian blood that ran in her veins. Her father had often wanted to talk about her true mother, but Danielle wouldn't listen.

As they walked through the woods the sun painted the sky with a soft rosy hue. The birds in the branches of the cottonwood trees were singing sweetly to welcome the new day.

"Danielle, are you aware that your mother died the day you were born?"

"Yes, I knew that," she said with a pout on her lips. Apparently her Aunt Joanna was going to talk about her mother whether Danielle wanted to hear about her or not.

"How she would have loved you, had she lived. Her last thoughts before she died were of you. Did your father tell you that?"

"Yes, but I never really listened when he spoke of such things. I didn't know Morning Song, so therefore I do not love her."

Joanna felt tears sting her eyes. "It seems you have closed your heart to anything connected with your mother. What a pity. Do you realize Morning Song was your same age when she died?"

"I . . . no, I never thought about that. Was she really beautiful?"

"Indeed she was, Danielle. Her hair was midnight black, and she had the most beautiful brown eyes. Her voice was soft, and I rarely heard it raised in anger. Morning Song was a kind person. Everyone loved her, including your father. You were a child born of that love. If you deny your mother, you deny the love your father had for Morning Song."

"She was an Indian princess?"

"Yes, that's true, and so are you."

Joanna studied her niece's face for a moment. Danielle looked so like her own daughter that it was like a knife in her heart. The biggest difference between the two girls was their disposition. Sky Dancer was sweet and kind, while Danielle was stubborn and willful. Joanna feared her niece would suffer greatly before she came to terms with who she was.

"Your grandmother is marking off the days until you come. She has talked of nothing else but your visit for months. She loves you a great deal, Danielle."

The young girl stopped and leaned against the trunk of a tall tree. "I wish I didn't have to see her. How am I supposed to act with her? What will we find to talk about?"

Joanna took a deep breath. "Shall I tell you a secret? This last year, Sun Woman has been learning to speak English just so she could converse with you. Let your heart guide you, Danielle. Sun Woman has so much love to give you. If you will only allow it, she has many worthwhile things to teach you."

Tears welled up in the young girl's blue eyes. "I . . . am afraid of her," she admitted. "I have always been afraid of Indians."

Joanna pulled Danielle into her arms and stroked her dark hair. "Oh, my dear, dear child, there is nothing for you to fear in the Blackfoot village. You are going to be received with so much love it will astound you."

Danielle pulled away and turned her back. "I am not afraid of my Uncle Windhawk."

Joanna smiled. "Why do you suppose that is?"

"I . . . don't know."

Joanna sat down on a fallen log and motioned for Danielle to join her. "Shall I tell you something?"

Danielle sat down and folded her hands in her lap. "Yes, if you aren't going to tell me more about my . . . mother."

"I was going to tell you about Windhawk, but your mother may come up in the conversation."

Danielle turned troubled eyes to her aunt. "Why did you abandon your life in Philadelphia to remain with the Blackfoot? You are so beautiful, and my father says that you could have had your pick of young gentlemen to marry."

Joanna smiled, wondering how she could tell this young girl how Windhawk had swept through her life one autumn and stolen her heart. "When I first met Windhawk, I was frightened of him. I had been injured,

90

and he nursed me back to health and then took me back to his village. I can still remember that first day in the Blackfoot village so clearly. The only friendly face I saw that day was your mother's. She was so kind to me, and later we became the best of friends. Since she died, I have never found a friend to replace her in my heart."

"Why did you decide to stay with the Indians, Aunt Joanna? My father said you could have returned to Philadelphia had you wanted to."

Joanna's eyes took on a faraway look, her mouth curved into a smile. It would be hard to explain all-consuming love to someone who hasn't experienced that emotion for herself. She turned her blue gaze on her young niece. "Have you yet met a man whom you love?"

"No." Danielle shook her head. "I have had many beaux who have liked me, but I never felt I could marry any of them. I always feared that if a man found out about me being a half-breed, he wouldn't want to love me."

Joanna tilted the young girl's face up, feeling her heart break. She thought perhaps it was a good thing that Danielle was spending the summer with the Blackfoot. She needed to learn many lessons, but most of all she needed to learn to be proud of who she was.

"Danielle, when you find the right man, and if he truly loves you, it will not matter who your mother and father are."

"I could never love an Indian," Danielle said as her blue eyes sparked with something akin to fear. "I don't want a dirty Indian to even touch me."

Joanna closed her eyes, remembering the awful day when Morning Song had died. How well she could recall taking this girl to her own breasts and nursing her. She realized that Danielle needed help and understanding before she could come to terms with her heritage. Her young niece was obviously being torn apart by having denied that side of her that came from her Indian mother. Joanna hoped, with all her heart that she could find a way to help her niece end the torment she was living through.

"Danielle, if you are expecting to live like a princess when you get to the village, then you will be sadly disappointed. The Blackfoot people work very hard and have no respect for anyone who doesn't do the same."

"Are you saying I will have to labor like a . . . servant?"

"No, I am simply saying that if you want to gain the respect of your mother's people, you will have to prove you are worthy. They are anxious to reach out to you in friendship because of your mother, but they will judge you on your own merits."

"I never had to do anything around our home in Philadelphia, and I have no intentions of laboring in some dirty Indian village," Danielle cried defiantly.

Joanna could feel her temper rising, but she tried to keep it in check. Perhaps Danielle couldn't help it if she was spoiled. "You will not find the people of the Blackfoot dirty, Danielle, but neither will you find the comforts you are accustomed to. Why don't you open your heart and give us all a chance. Perhaps you will even enjoy yourself this summer."

Danielle's eyes clouded over. "All I want to do is go home. I will be counting the days until I can leave all this behind forever."

Joanna sighed deeply, knowing she had a heavy task ahead of her. Danielle would be miserable if she didn't change her attitude toward the Blackfoot.

"Come, the warriors will be breaking camp by now. We must eat before we start out. Your uncle Windhawk travels at a very fast pace, and you will need all your strength to keep up with him."

The scantily clad Indian was hidden by a thick bramble bush as he peered at the Blackfoot village across the Milk River. His eyes narrowed as they moved to the center of the village where Windhawk's lodge stood. His heart burned with bitter hatred, when he thought of the chief of the Bloods. His hatred had festered and grown over the years. He had been but a young boy when Windhawk had ridden into the Piegan Blackfoot village and slain his father, Running Elk.

Scar Face remembered standing over Running Elk's dead body and vowing revenge against the man who had taken his father's life.

He looked for signs of life in Windhawk's lodge, but saw no smoke coming from the top of the lodge. This could only mean that Windhawk and his family were away from the village.

Hearing footsteps behind him, he turned to see his friend, Tall Bear, bend down beside him.

"Scar Face, will you not give up this foolish plan to kill Windhawk? It is said that he is not of this world, and cannot be slain. It is said that his enemies all die a horrible death."

Scar Face stood up, and his hand automatically went to the scar that ran the length of the left side of his face, thus giving him his name. The scar was another reason to hate. It had been given to him in a fight with Wolfrunner, one of Windhawk's Blood warriors. His eyes narrowed as he gazed at the setting sun.

"If you are afraid, then you can leave, Tall Bear. My fight is not your fight. It is I who will avenge my father by taking the life of the mighty chief of the Bloods," he spat out.

"I have heard it said that Windhawk is protected by the Great Spirit, Napi, and no man can harm him."

"I do not believe this to be true," Scar Face ground out between clenched teeth. "Windhawk is no different from you or me, Tall Bear. When you stick him, he will bleed red, the same as any man."

"I have heard of his power and strength—it must be true. You must leave with me now!"

"No, I have asked myself what could I do to this man that would be worse than taking his life? I think I know the answer."

Tall Bear studied his friend closely. Scar Face had acquired his name when he was but twelve summers. He had challenged Wolfrunner for a horse and had lost not only the horse, but nearly his life as well. It was said that he cheated in the fight and tried to strike Wolfrunner down from behind, but Tall Bear didn't believe his friend would do such a cowardly deed. Scar Face had been a good friend to him. However, he knew the driving force in his friend's life seemed to be to avenge his father's death.

"If you are thinking to kill Windhawk's white wife, I can tell you that would be very unwise. He would avenge her by burning our village and slaying our people. I heard it said that not too many years ago, two

Assiniboin warriors abducted Windhawk's white wife. The great chief's vengeance is still talked about around the Assiniboin campfires. It is said he killed many brave warriors that day. Is this what you want for our people?"

Scar Face thought back to last year's hunting council, when the Piegan and Blood tribes had come together in friendship. At that time he had seen Windhawk's white wife and his half-white daughter. It was then that he had begun to plan his revenge.

"It is said that Windhawk guards his wife jealously and no man could get near her, but what about the daughter, Tall Bear?" Scar Face's eyes burned with hatred as he looked back toward the Blood village.

"I have seen his daughter, Sky Dancer. She has great beauty. I was once near enough to her to see her sky-colored eyes. At the time the young maiden's brother never left her side, and I dared not speak to her. No, my friend, you had better forget about killing Sky Dancer."

I have also seen the Blood princess many times, but she never spoke a word to me. I will see the day she will beg me for mercy and curse the day she was born from Windhawk's seed," Scar Face said, realizing the hatred he felt for Windhawk had now been transferred to the daughter. She would be the target of his revenge!

"What do you plan to do?" his friend asked, feeling great fear at the thought of harming anyone that belonged to the mighty Windhawk.

"I shall wait and watch until I find the young maiden alone. Windhawk will know what it feels like to lose someone he loves. He will cry out in pain many times before he learns of his daughter's fate."

"What will be her fate, my friend?" Tall Bear wanted to know.

Scar Face's eyes narrowed. "I will take her to the Canadas and sell her to one of the French trappers. Windhawk will never know if she is alive or dead, nor will he know until I tell him that she will be paying the price for my father's death."

Scar Face mounted his horse and rode toward the Blood Blackfoot village, knowing he would be welcome there because he belonged to the Piegan Blackfoot tribe.

Tall Bear urged his horse forward, following Scar Face. He feared that his friend would meet an early and agonizing death, but he was his friend and Tall Bear would help him if he could. When Scar Face neared the chief's lodge, his eyes burned with hatred. He would bide his time, and when the moment was right, he would take from Windhawk the daughter of his heart. He didn't yet know how that would be accomplished, but she would suffer greatly at his hands before he was through with her!

Reaching up, Scar Face stroked the scar on his face, and hoped that he might also meet Wolfrunner again. He had an old debt to settle with him as well.

Danielle was bone weary and thought they would never reach their destination. They had been traveling for three weeks at breakneck speed. Each morning she was forced to rise early and climb onto her horse. The terrain they were riding through was primitive, and there were no roads. At Joanna's suggestion, Danielle had finally agreed to abandon her sidesaddle, but she refused to wear the buckskin gown her grandmother had sent her—even though she was told Sun Woman had made the gown with loving care despite her failing eyesight.

She was resigned to the fact that she would have to live with savages, but she would never become one of them!

Danielle walked beside the river, feeling misplaced and lonely. This was not her world, and she resented the fact that she was forced to endure these hardships. She thought of her half-brother, who was spending the summer in England with her grandfather. Why did *her* blood have to be tainted with Indian blood? Why couldn't she have been born to Alexandria? In that moment she almost hated the Indian woman who had given her birth. In Danielle's estimation, her mother had placed a lifelong curse on her.

A dark shadow fell across Danielle's face and she looked up to see a young Indian warrior standing beside her. She remembered his name was Wolfrunner. Since the night he had mistaken her for Sky Dancer he had not again approached her. Now she assessed him as a woman would and found him to be very handsome. His dark hair was worn free but for the leather headband that circled it. His chest was bare but for the porcupine necklace he wore. His dark eyes sought hers and Danielle turned away.

"Who are you?" she asked in English.

"I am called Wolfrunner, son of the war chief, Gray Fox."

She sat down on the riverbank and gazed into the

distance. "You speak English well for an Indian," she couldn't help observing.

His handsome face eased into a smile. "You speak English well for a half-white woman."

Danielle glanced up to see if the man was mocking her but there was genuine interest in his smile. "How did you learn to speak my language?" she wanted to know.

He sat down nearby and studied her with his dark eyes. "I, like many of the Bloods, was taught by your Aunt Joanna. Windhawk wanted his people to learn the language."

"A fat lot of good English will do you in an Indian village," she couldn't help but say.

"It has enabled me to talk to you. Your uncle tells me that you do not know the language of your mother's people . . . why is this?"

Her eyes grew stormy at the mention of her mother. Why must she always be reminded that her mother was an Indian? "I do not wish to know your heathen tongue, and I don't want to talk to you either," she said, turning away and staring at the distant sunset.

Wolfrunner was quiet for so long that Danielle glanced up to see if he had left. Her eyes collided with brilliant black eyes, and she shivered at the anger reflected there. If there could be such a thing as a look of hatred, it was on Wolfrunner's face now.

"I am a good friend of your cousin, Sky Dancer. We grew up together. I came to you in her behalf, thinking you might be lonely and need someone to talk to. Sky Dancer told me to look after you. I see you do not need looking after."

He rose to his feet with an agility that surprised

Danielle. She knew she had made him angry, but why should she care. What did it matter what Wolfrunner, or any of these Indians thought of her?

"Don't think because you are a friend of Sky Dancer, that you would be counted among my friends. I am nothing like my cousin."

She saw his jaw tighten. "That is true, you are nothing like Sky Dancer. She would never look down at another human being as inferior to her. Pity you are not like her in more than looks."

Danielle felt her cheeks flame as he walked away. Even though she was angry, she couldn't help noticing the proud tilt of his head and how straight he carried himself. For the first time in her life, she regretted speaking without first weighing the consequences.

In the days that ensued, Danielle would often find herself watching Wolfrunner. He was always in the group of warriors who rode beside her, but as far as she could tell, he paid not the slightest attention to her.

The days seemed to stretch ahead of Danielle, and she watched as civilization as she knew it disappeared into the wild untamed wilderness.

To her surprise she was beginning to warm to her Uncle Windhawk. He was so patient with her, never losing his temper when she asked to stop and rest.

Danielle rode along beside Windhawk, and she became aware that he was watching her closely. "How much longer will it be until we reach your village, Uncle Windhawk? I am so very weary of traveling."

Windhawk smiled kindly at the young girl, thinking how much Danielle reminded him of his own Sky

Dancer. He realized she was having a hard time adjusting to the Indian ways. He remembered when Joanna had first come to his village, and how difficult it had been for her to adjust to the Indian way of life. Given time, he was sure Danielle would come to accept her mother's people.

"Just beyond that mountain lies my village," he said, indicating the barrier of rock and stone which seemed to bar their path. "You will sleep in my lodge tonight, Danielle."

Chapter Six

Sky Dancer or Skyler Dancing, as she now tried to think of herself, was amazed by the many strange things she'd discovered in the white world. She was most impressed by the kitchen where the food was prepared. There were wondrous things to behold, such as the beautiful dishes and shining silver on which the food was served.

Each day at the noon meal Alexandria would take Skyler to a little table in the corner of the kitchen, where she would instruct her in how to eat with the fork and spoon. Skyler was intelligent and it didn't take her any time at all to master the art of eating manners. She could deftly unfold her napkin and place it on her lap. She learned which fork went with what course.

Three afternoons a week a dancing instructor would come to the house to teach her the latest dance steps. At those times Alexandria would play the spinet and the dance instructor would lead Skyler through the steps.

Alexandria had taken Skyler shopping and she now had gowns, petticoats, undergarments, shoes, bonnets, and silk stockings to match every occasion. She neither enjoyed wearing the tight corset, which was laced tightly about her waist, nor the cumbersome crinolines with their steel rings.

At first, Skyler didn't think she would ever learn to walk in the stiff, pointed-toe shoes that laced about her ankles. But she practiced walking in them every day, until at last she could at least move about reasonably well.

Skyler was sweet-natured and did everything she was told. She danced with the aged dance master, and she learned to curtsy and bow. She was taught to offer a young gentleman her hand only when she was wearing gloves, and only then if it was her wish. There were so many rules of do's and don't's that it made her head spin. She doubted she would ever remember everything she'd been taught.

It was late in the afternoon when Skyler walked out into the garden. It was lovely and quiet, and she loved to move among the beautiful flowers, smelling the sweet aroma that seemed to fill the air. Everything in this world was so orderly. The flowers had been planted in neat rows, and even the trees formed a line along the drive. It was hard for her to comprehend that one would plant flowers, when they grew so profusely on their own in Blackfoot land.

It was truly lovely here, and her aunt and uncle had been so kind to her. Still she felt a loneliness, and wished she could soon return to the land of her birth.

She often thought of her brother who was traveling in Europe with her grandfather and cousin. Was he, too, lonely for the land of the Blackfoot?

"It's not so bad once you become accustomed to it, my dear." Her Uncle Tag's voice interrupted her thoughts.

She smiled at him sweetly. "You are reading my mind."

"That's not too difficult. I sometimes miss the life I led with the Blackfoot. It is only natural that you should be thinking of your home."

"Do you ever wish to return to live with my people, Uncle Tag?"

"Yes, but I never will. I have great responsibilities here. When I feel everything closing in on me, I go to Meadowlake Farm for a while, and that helps." Tag noted the sadness in her eyes. "Are you terribly unhappy here, Skyler?"

"No, you and Aunt Alexandria have been wonderful to me, and I love you a great deal . . ."

"But?"

She smiled at her uncle. "But I do get homesick sometimes."

He placed his arm about her shoulder and they walked along the garden path together. "This summer will not last forever. Before you know it you will be leaving us. It is my hope that when you leave, you will look back at this summer with fondness."

She leaned her head against his shoulder. "I will always remember your love and thoughtfulness. My mother loves you a great deal, and I can now see why."

He stopped and gazed down into her face. "To look at you one would think you were a well brought up young lady. You have a kindness of heart that seems to draw people to you. You look so like Danielle, and yet I wish she had more of your gentle nature."

They stopped beside a pond, and Skyler looked at her own reflection. She hardly recognized the image that stared back at her. Suddenly it felt as if she was losing her own identity. Glancing at her uncle, she didn't realize that much of what she was feeling was written in her eyes. At the moment she reminded him of Morning Song, more than Danielle ever had, and he felt a pain surround his heart.

"Never fear, my dear, you will never lose the person you are. Those things that make you the person you are will stay with you forever. Even when you are gone from this world you will be remembered for the person you are today." He was thinking about his dead wife, Morning Song, something he rarely did anymore.

Skyler stood on her tiptoes and planted a kiss on his cheek. "You are very gallant, Uncle Tag. I would wager that Aunt Alexandria counts herself fortunate that you are her husband."

Tag smiled. "I have been very fortunate for having known two exceptional women. Morning Song and Alexandria. They were as different as two women could be, but each special in her own way."

"Do you still think of Morning Song?"

"I hadn't until lately. Morning Song was a part of my past, but she gave me a daughter. Since being with you she is never very far from my thoughts. What I felt for her isn't the same feelings that I have for Alexandria. Morning Song was the love of my youth—Alexandria is the love of my heart." Morning Song's image danced fleetingly through Tag's mind. He saw a vision of soft brown eyes and a gentle smile. "Yes, I remember her very clearly at times."

"I don't think my mother and father could ever love anyone else, do you?"

"No. Windhawk and Joanna were meant to be together. You will one day meet a man who is right for you, then you will understand love better."

"I suppose, but it is not easy being a Blackfoot princess. My father has told me I cannot marry just anyone."

Tag chuckled. "I doubt that Windhawk would think anyone is good enough for you. Fathers are like that. Is there no young warrior whom you favor?"

"No, not yet. I began to think I will never meet a man who will love me."

Again he chuckled. "My dear young niece, I don't think that will be a problem. You are very lovely and the Blackfoot warriors would have to be blind not to see that. No . . . I am sure all the young men are put off because of who your father is. I would not like to be the one to have to ask Windhawk for your hand, would you?"

Her laughter joined his. "No, my father can be very formidable to those who do not know him."

Tag reached over her head and plucked a large white blossom and handed it to her and watched her face carefully. "Did your aunt tell you that you will be going to a ball at the end of the week?"

Skyler lowered her eyes, feeling fear at the thought of meeting so many strangers. "Yes, but I wish I didn't have to go. I might make a mistake that would shame you and Aunt Alexandria."

"You will do no such thing. I think it is very important for you to meet young people your own age. Your mother wanted you to learn about the difference

105

between your two worlds. The best way to accomplish that is by being with those of your age. Don't you agree?"

Skyler sighed heavily. "I will go, but I won't have fun."

He patted her hand affectionately. "We will see, my dear, we will see."

As they walked to the house, the sun was setting, and Skyler was overcome with melancholy. There was a restlessness within her that she couldn't explain. It went deeper than just being homesick. Perhaps it was the fact that she was a young lady and there was no young man in her life. She had never thought much about the love between a man and a woman. Until now she had been content with life the way it was.

As they approached the house, Skyler tried to imagine her mother walking this same path as a young girl. Her mother had been surrounded with wealth and beautiful things and yet she had given it all up when she had met Skyler's father. Would she ever love a man that much?

Tag drew her into the house and smiled at her tenderly. "Don't be in such a hurry to grow up, my dear little niece. That time will come all too soon. You must enjoy life while you have the chance." Tag had the strangest feeling that Skyler didn't belong to the Indian world. Her grace and beauty seemed to shine forth like a beacon. Perhaps Joanna had taught her daughter the white man's ways too well. Skyler was more white than Indian.

Skyler lay in the big soft bed watching the shadows

flicker across the ceiling. She felt strangely close to her mother. Here in this room that had been her mother's, Skyler could almost hear her laughter. Her thoughts were heavy as she examined her mother's love for her father. She had never thought about it before, but it must have been very difficult for her mother to turn her back on this world to live in the Blackfoot village.

The bedroom door opened and Alexandria entered. "I saw the light on under the door and knew you weren't sleeping. Would you like me to sit and talk to you for a while?"

Skyler sat up and patted the bed. "Yes, I would welcome your company."

Alexandria sat down and reached for Skyler's hand. "I realize everything has been strange to you, but you have come along beautifully. I have little doubt that you will be the belle of the ball Friday night."

"I wish I didn't have to go," Skyler said, looking into her aunt's strange, golden-colored eyes.

"Nonsense, you are going to have a wonderful time. I wish I was young again."

"You are not old, and you are so lovely."

Her aunt smiled at the compliment. "Thank you for that, but I feel very old tonight."

For the first Skyler noticed that her aunt seemed pale. "Are you not feeling well?" she inquired with concern.

Alexandria smiled. "It is nothing to worry about. In fact, I am deliriously happy. I just learned today that I am expecting a baby. Your uncle is beside himself with joy."

"That is wonderful! I am so happy for you and Uncle Tag."

"Children are such blessings. You are a shining example of that. I have been blessed with a son, and Danielle is like my own daughter. Your mother feels very much the same about children as I do. It's a pity she and Windhawk didn't have more babies."

"I know my mother would like nothing better than to have another baby, but she has been told by Matoka, the medicine woman, that it would be impossible. Matoka is very wise. She always delivers all the babies of the women in our village."

"Yes, it's a pity. Joanna is such a good mother," Alexandria said sadly.

"You must allow me to help you. I would be only too delighted to do anything to make your load lighter. You have only to say what you want me to do."

Alexandria stood up and kissed Skyler's cheek. "I may very well take you up on that. The doctor has told me I must take it easy, and your uncle is most insistent that I do just that."

"We shall see that you do not overdo, Aunt Alexandria. When will the baby be born?"

"Not until around Christmas. I fear you will be back home before your new cousin comes into the world."

Skyler scrambled out of bed. "Would you like me to see you to your bedroom?"

Alexandria laughed at the concern on the young girl's face. "No, I am not yet an invalid. I have given birth once before without difficulty; I expect I shall again."

Skyler watched her aunt leave and then climbed back into bed. She wondered what it would be like to have a baby. Would it not be truly a miracle to give birth to a child of the man you loved?

She blew out the lamp and then lay back against the soft feather pillow. One day she would marry, but would it be to the man of her choice, or to someone her father had chosen for her? Closing her eyes, she felt herself drifting off. There were many unanswered questions about her future, but she was too sleepy to ponder them now.

Feeling as if she was lost and adrift between two worlds, Skyler didn't know where she really belonged. When she returned home, would she be able to pick up the threads of her life and go on as if this summer had never happened?

Her body settled into the soft downy mattress and her thoughts were of home. In her mind she was riding her horse across the vast prairies, with the cool breeze kissing her face.

Skyler turned over on her stomach and faced the window. How often had her mother lay in this very bed and pondered her future?

Sighing wearily, she drifted off to sleep.

Chapter Seven

The inside of Windhawk's lodge was dark, and Danielle could hear the far-off howl of some wild animal that sounded almost like a woman screaming.

Joanna had prepared her bed in a curtained-off area to allow her more privacy. Danielle lay on a soft mink-skin, unable to sleep.

Her mind was filled with horror and disgust for the Indian way of life. As always her thoughts drifted to her home, to her soft bed, with its cool, white, lavender-scented sheets that had caressed her skin. If she were in Philadelphia right now, the chances were she would be at a ball. Her dance card would be filled with the names of many dashing young soldiers.

She turned to her back and watched the shadows play across the top of the lodge through a mist of tears. She didn't belong here. She felt no kinship with these people.

Her mind wandered back to yesterday when she had first entered the village, riding beside her Aunt Joanna. Many dark eyes had watched her silently, causing her heart to race with fear.

When they had reached the center of the village, her Uncle Windhawk had helped her down from her horse. She'd hardly had time to gather her wits about her when a tall gray-haired warrior had come rushing out of one of the tipis. He had picked her up, tossing her into the air. She had screamed out in fear, fighting for her release as he hugged her tightly to him. It wasn't until her Aunt Joanna had come to her rescue that the Indian had placed her on her feet, looking puzzled. Danielle had been told that she had again been mistaken for Sky Dancer. The Indian who had greeted her so aggressively turned out to be Gray Fox, the war chief, father of Wolfrunner.

After the people had been told that Danielle was the daughter of their dead princess, Morning Song, many of them came up to her in friendly greeting. Since she couldn't speak the Blackfoot language, and they didn't seem to speak English, she didn't know what they were saying to her.

It had been a relief when Joanna had taken her hand and led Danielle to the tipi of her grandmother, Sun Woman.

Danielle would never forget the shock of seeing her grandmother. The last time she'd seen Sun Woman, she had been energetic and spry. But now, she had wasted away to skin and bones—a mere shell of a woman. Sun Woman now looked so frail and old, with little resemblance to the woman Danielle had once known.

The old woman's eyes had lit up and she had weakly reached out a trembling gnarled hand to her grand-daughter. Danielle had been amazed at the strength in her grandmother's hands as they clasped hers tightly. She felt pity for her, knowing she was obviously very ill, but she didn't like to think that the sickly Indian woman was her grandmother. The high cheekbones were sunken, and the once proud tilt of her head was no longer in evidence. It had been five years since Sun Woman had visited Meadowlake Farm. Five years that robbed her of her health.

The tipi had been hot and stifling, smelling of medicine and sickness. Danielle had been glad when Joanna intervened and announced that Sun Woman needed to rest from the excitement and they should leave.

Danielle clamped her eyes tightly together, trying to imagine what it would be like to grow up as an Indian. Running her hand down her smooth cheek, Danielle knew she wouldn't ever want to toil in the sun until her skin became hard and wrinkled as aged parchment. She had been raised to have fun and attend parties, not to be buried in some obscure Indian village.

Tears rolled down her cheeks as she thought of the agonizing days that stretched ahead of her. It was a long time until she would be able to return to Philadelphia. What she couldn't change would have to be endured. She remembered Alexandria once telling her, what could not be cured must be endured. The truth of those words came home to her now. She would never allow the Indians to pull her down to their level. She would rise above them and remain herself, no matter what happened.

The bright morning sun hung in the sky like a huge

ball of fire. Danielle glanced at Wolfrunner who was mounted on his horse, glaring down at her. Aunt Joanna had been busy this morning, so she'd asked Wolfrunner to take her niece for a ride. The Indian's face was grim and he seemed to look right through Danielle.

"I am not any happier about the prospect of riding with you than you are," she declared, trying to hoist herself onto the sidesaddle. She had refused to give up her saddle and ride astride like a man. She had also refused to wear the Indian gowns her aunt had given her.

Wolfrunner, seeing the trouble she was having, dismounted and walked over to her. Picking her up about the waist, he plopped her on the saddle without ceremony. He then turned away to mount his own horse.

When they crossed the river and rode toward the mountains, Danielle nudged her horse into a swift gallop. She had always loved horseback riding, finding it exhilarating. She looked forward to these daily rides, just so she could get away from the village. Usually her aunt and Farley went with her, but today neither of them was available.

Wolfrunner stayed even with Danielle, but he avoided looking in her direction. As the wind whipped at her hair, she felt the pins come undone, and the dark tresses fell about her shoulders. Deciding she couldn't very well pin it back up, she allowed it to blow free.

After they had ridden for about an hour, Wolfrunner pulled up his mount. "This is as far as you are allowed to go," he said, dismounting. "We will rest the horses here, and then start back."

"I'm going to ride farther," she stated flatly. "I want to see what's on the other side of that valley."

"No. Joanna said you were to go no farther than the Sweet Grass Hills," he insisted.

Danielle's eyes ran over him in anger. He was dressed in only a breechcloth, and powerful muscles rippled across his back. His long, lean legs seemed to grip the side of his horse, easily controlling the animal. He was handsome, and some primitive feelings stirred in Danielle's body. She was shocked at her daring thoughts, and kicked her mount into a run. In her confusion, she wanted to get away from the man who seemed to trouble her thoughts.

She could hear Wolfrunner riding after her, so she nudged her horse forward at a swifter pace. Looking back she saw he was gaining on her. Danielle's horse was in a full run, and still the Indian had almost drawn even with her. Applying her riding crop to the horse's hindquarter, she suddenly felt afraid. What would he do when he caught her?

With a startled cry she felt herself being lifted into the air and placed on the horse in front of Wolfrunner. Glancing quickly at his face, she saw the naked anger etched there. She didn't notice that her own horse had stopped. All she could think about was what was going to happen to her.

Danielle slammed back against Wolfrunner's bare chest as he pulled his horse to a halt. "Let me down!" she cried, hitting out at him. Her hands were flying and she felt them come in contact with his face. She saw the red mark on his face, and shivered in fear. She must have hit him harder than she thought, because blood was trickling down his cheek. With a look of horror she realized she still held her riding crop in her hand. She must have hit him with it!

For just a moment she looked into flashing eyes that were dark storm centers. She was miles from nowhere, alone with a savage, and she didn't know what he was going to do to her!

Danielle could feel his bitter rage. "I . . . didn't mean to hurt you. Don't hurt me," she said in a shaky voice, shrinking away from him.

Suddenly he dropped her to the ground. Before she had time to think, Wolfrunner kicked his horse into action. She thought he was going to ride off and leave her until she saw him gather up the reins of her horse, and guide him back to her.

Without a word, and without looking at her, he dismounted. Lifting her onto her horse, he held onto the reins. Danielle felt indignation as he swung onto his horse and led her tired mount forward in a slow walk, back in the direction of the village.

Neither of them spoke, nor did they look at the other. Danielle bit back angry words, knowing she dared not push him farther. There was no telling what he might do.

When they were in sight of the village, he handed her the reins, and rode across the river. Filled with anger, and knowing she was safely within reach of the village, she yelled out at him. "You are a savage, and I hate you!"

Either Wolfrunner didn't hear, or he didn't choose to answer. She watched as he left the river and rode out of sight within the village.

Her temper hadn't cooled by the time she reached

her uncle's lodge. She stormed inside glad there was no one there. Dropping down on her knees, she took a deep drink from the water jug. It did little to quench her bitterness. She hoped she would never have to see Wolfrunner again.

Danielle had been in the Blackfoot village three weeks, and it seemed to her that the days crawled by. Danielle hadn't seen Wolfrunner since that day they had gone riding. Bored and restless, she tried to find ways to fill the lonely hours. Many of the Indian maidens had tried to befriend her, but Danielle refused to join in their games. The only times she enjoyed herself were when she went riding with her Aunt Joanna and Farley.

The thing Danielle resented most of all were the times when she was forced to sit with her grandmother. Each day Joanna insisted that the Danielle visit the ailing Sun Woman. At those times, the old woman would ramble on and on about her dead daughter. Sometimes Sun Woman would talk in the Blackfoot language, other times she lapsed into English.

Apparently Sun Woman was too ill to notice that her granddaughter rarely contributed anything to their conversation. Joanna had managed to cover up for Danielle's lack of interest in what her grandmother was saying.

It was hot inside Sun Woman's tipi and Danielle could feel rivulets of perspiration running down between her shoulder blades. She almost wished she had taken the white doeskin gown Joanna had offered her this morning. Anything would be cooler than her heavy cotton gown with its numerous petticoats.

As she looked on the sleeping face of her grand-mother, Danielle almost wished she had agreed to go berry picking with Joanna and the rest of the women. She had declined, claiming that the heat made her head ache. Joanna had asked her to stay with her grand-mother until they all returned that afternoon, and she now felt bored and restless.

Sun Woman moaned, and Danielle reluctantly placed her hand on the old woman's forehead and found it hot to the touch. Sun Woman opened her eyes, which were fever-bright, and stared at her grand-daughter.

"Morning Song, you have come back!" she cried, sitting up and taking Danielle's hand. "Have you come to take me to walk among the dead with you?"

"Grandmother, it is I, Danielle. You are very ill and mustn't overexcite yourself," she said, trying to push the old woman back on the buffalo robe.

Sun Woman gasped for breath as she lay back. Her eyes seemed to clear as she looked at Danielle. "I thank Napi, the Great One , for allowing me to look upon your face before I die, Danielle," she said in a weak voice.

"You shouldn't talk nonsense, Grandmother. You will outlive us all." Danielle couldn't understand the feeling of sadness that took over her reasoning. This woman was nothing to her, and yet she wanted to comfort her. For the first time, she realized that the blood of this woman flowed in her own veins. This was the woman who had given life to her mother. It was as if

118

Danielle was watching a part of herself die.

"I am thirsty, child," Sun Woman wheezed. "Give me a cool drink of water."

Danielle picked up the water jug and found it to be empty. "I will just run to the river to fill this, Grandmother, I won't be gone long."

As Danielle made her way through the village on her way to the river, she noticed it was almost deserted, since most of the men had gone hunting and the women were out picking berries.

There was an urgency about her as she ran past the tipis. She couldn't bear to think that her grandmother might die. As she bent down to fill the water jug, her foot became tangled in her green cotton gown, and she almost fell headfirst into the rushing water.

Feeling a steadying hand on her shoulder, Danielle spun around to face the Indian brave who was holding on to her arm. Her eyes widened in fear when she saw the long deep scar that ran from his left eye and across his lower jaw, giving him a sinister appearance.

"I am fine now, you can let me go," she said, trying to move out of his grip.

Scar Face stared with hatred at the half-white girl. He had been watching her for many days, waiting for the opportunity to get her alone. Since the village was almost deserted and there was no one in sight, now was the time for which he had planned. He had thought out everything down to the last detail, and it was working better than he had hoped.

"I said 'let me go'," Danielle cried, beginning to feel uneasy at the strange way the Indian was acting. He seemed to be watching her with something akin to hatred in his dark eyes, and it frightened her. She couldn't remember ever seeing this Indian in the village. If she had, she would have recognized him. His wasn't the kind of face one forgot.

"Why do you speak in the filthy white man's tongue?" he asked angrily.

Danielle shook her head, not understanding his words. "I don't understand what you are saying, but if you value your life, you will let me go."

Scar Face quickly scanned the village. Seeing no one about, he clamped his hand over Danielle's mouth so she couldn't call out for help.

She began to struggle and kick out at him, but he merely picked her up in his arms and waded through the river so they wouldn't leave any footprints.

Danielle gasped for breath as his hand cut off her breathing. When she saw the two horses which were tied behind a clump of bushes, she realized he was taking her away from the village. With all the strength she possessed, she struggled and kicked out at him, but his grip only tightened painfully on her.

He spoke a harsh command in her ear, and pulled her up against him, cutting off her breathing.

Scar Face urged the horse forward while keeping to the river so the hoofmarks would be hidden. He knew while he was near the village there was danger of being discovered, but his hatred for Windhawk made him risk the danger. He would hide his tracks so no one could follow them.

Wild unbridled fear took over Danielle's reasoning when she realized the Indian was taking her away from the village. She bit the hand that was clamped over her mouth, and the Indian muttered harshly in her ear. His grip tightened about her waist mercilessly.

Danielle didn't feel the hand that came down hard against her temple until her head exploded in pain. Blackness engulfed her and she slumped back against the man in unconsciousness.

Chapter Eight

As the buggy pulled up in the circular driveway, Skyler could hear the beautiful music coming from inside the huge brownstone house. She felt nervous and unsure of herself as a footman rushed forward and helped her out of the buggy. Skyler gave her hand to her Uncle Tag and he helped her up the steps with an encouraging smile.

"You aren't to feel frightened, my dear. You are going to have more fun tonight than you can imagine."

Skyler smiled slightly, wishing she didn't have to go to the ball tonight. Suppose she were to shame her aunt and uncle, by committing a faux pas. She was so unaccustomed to the white man's ways. She had listened intently to the dance master as well as her Aunt Alexandria when they had instructed her on etiquette and manners. But could she remember everything they had taught her? She had decided the best way to proceed was to talk as little as possible, and speak only when spoken to.

The ballroom was crowded when Skyler entered on

the arm of her Uncle Tag. She noticed that every man under forty wore a blue army uniform, while the ladies wore gowns made up of every color in the rainbow.

Feeling her hand tremble, her Uncle Tag leaned close to her ear. "Don't be frightened, honey. Just remember you are a princess. The way you carry yourself and the proud tilt of your chin will prove to the people here that you are someone special."

Skyler was encouraged by his words. Yes, she had nothing to fear; no one here would know who she really was. If she could just get through this evening without shaming her uncle, she would have accomplished something.

"I wish Aunt Alexandria could have come with us tonight," she said wistfully.

"She wanted to be with you, but you know the doctor ordered her to stay off her feet for a while. I will be the perfect escort and introduce you to all the most eligible young gentlemen."

Uncle Tag was proud to introduce Skyler to his friends and business associates. They were all startled at the close resemblance between Skyler and Danielle, commenting on how the two girls could pass for twins.

Skyler danced with several gentlemen and found that she could easily keep step with them.

Midway through the evening, Skyler found it stuffy in the ballroom. Her feet were hurting and she wanted a breath of fresh air. Seeing the door that led out to the balcony, she made her way across the room, hoping no one would stop her and ask for a dance.

Skyler stood on the balcony, overlooking the garden with a feeling of déjà vu. She had been here before—stood on this very spot! Looking around expectantly she held her breath and waited for something to happen.

There was a strange sweet aroma in the air, and she knew it came from the many flowers in bloom. Turning her face up to the moon, she felt a loneliness in the very depths of her being. Somewhere, far away, this very same moon shone over the Blackfoot village. What were her mother and father doing at this moment, she wondered. Was Danielle standing under this moon, wishing they could change places again, as Skyler wished?

Colonel Morgan Prescott stood in the shadows of the balcony and watched who he thought to be Danielle James. He hadn't seen her in over a year. He had no way of knowing that the girl he was watching wasn't Danielle at all, but her cousin Skyler.

Morgan watched almost breathlessly as the bright moon shone down on her lovely face. He saw what could only be a wistful look in her eyes. He had never thought of Danielle as other than a spoiled, overindulged little girl. But as he watched her now, something stirred to life within him.

Stepping into the light, he moved to her side. "I wonder what you were wishing for just now? A new gown, perhaps, or maybe a new bonnet?"

Skyler slowly turned to face the stranger—but he wasn't a stranger. She had heard his voice before, but when? He was a head taller than she was and wore the blue uniform of a Cavalry officer. She didn't know the bars on his collar signified he was also a doctor. She couldn't see his features very well since they were cast in shadows, but his eyes seemed to sparkle with mirth. She had been taught enough of the white man's ways to know it wasn't acceptable for a young unescorted lady to converse with a man she didn't know.

Suddenly her heart started pounding and she waited for him to step into the light. She was frightened because she remembered her dream when she had stood on this balcony with this man.

"I do not know you, sir," she said, stepping around him with the intention of returning to the ballroom. She was frightened and wanted to get away from him.

He reached out and captured her hand, stilling her movement. "What new game is this you are playing, Danielle? Surely you couldn't have forgotten your old friend in only one short year."

"You are mistaken, sir. I am not—"

"I know, don't tell me." He laughed down at her. "You are not glad to see me. If my memory serves me right, you said you wished a Rebel bullet would find my heart, and you consigned me to the devil."

Skyler looked into laughing silver-gray eyes. The man, whoever he was, had mistaken her for Danielle. "You do not understand, sir, I am not—"

Again he interrupted her. "I know, Danielle, you aren't interested in talking to the likes of me. You told me repeatedly that you weren't interested in a man who wasn't marriage-minded. Well, I haven't changed; I still don't contemplate marriage. But we have said all this before. If my memory serves me right, you called me a rake and a rogue."

All of a sudden Skyler began to lose patience. How dare the man in her dreams—the man she had loved—how dare he mistake her for her cousin. Shouldn't he have known who she was? "You have an irritating habit, sir, of not allowing one to finish a sentence. Had you allowed it, I would have explained to you that I am not Danielle, but her cousin."

Morgan frowned while he studied her face carefully. "Now I know you are playing a game with me. No one else in the world could look like you. I'm not put off by the fact that you are even trying to disguise your voice. You can drop the phony accent, Danielle."

"I told you I am not Danielle! If you will just move aside and allow me to pass, I would be most appreciative." Skyler was beginning to be irritated with the man, and wanted nothing more than to join her uncle. If he were the man in her dreams, he wasn't supposed to mistake her for Danielle.

His silver eyes gleamed as he gathered her in his arms. Skyler stiffened, too taken aback to react at first. He was going to kiss her just as he had in her dream!

"There is one sure way to end this discussion, Danielle. I have once tasted your lips, and I believe I shall just do so again. I never forget the way a woman's lips taste. Every woman is unique."

Skyler wanted to leave, but she seemed hypnotized by the deep chord in his voice and the way he was looking at her. Since she had never been kissed by a man—no Blackfoot brave would ever have dared touch her—she wanted to run but couldn't.

As Morgan looked into her luminous blue eyes, he remembered the other time he had kissed Danielle. She had flirted with him outrageously, as if she had been begging for him to kiss her. When their lips had met, he had felt nothing past a pleasant sensation. In the year since he had seen her, she'd hardly crossed his mind. Now he felt intrigued and touched by her soft beauty.

When their lips met, he felt her mouth tremble beneath his. Somewhere deep inside he felt a sweetness and longing to do more than kiss her. He wanted to deepen the kiss and tap her sweetness to the fullest. Startled by his strange reaction, he lifted his head and stared at her in amazement.

Skyler was bewildered by the touch of this man's lips on hers. A warmth seemed to surround her heart, and it frightened her so much that she pulled away from him. Yes, her heart sang, this was the man she was to love. She didn't know why, but the Great One had picked him out for her. As an Indian she put a great deal of importance on visions.

Placing her hand to her lips, she looked at him quizzically. What should she do? Surely he must know she wasn't Danielle by now. Did he also know the two of them were destined to meet?

"My father will kill you for this," she said, voicing the first thought that came to mind.

Morgan laughed. "Tag might be a bit miffed with me, Danielle, but I shouldn't think he would go so far as to kill me." He looked down on the garden below. "Even if he did call me out, Danielle, it was worth it for the stolen kiss."

He turned his strange silver eyes on her. "It is odd, though, Danielle. You have changed somehow. I would swear you had never been kissed before, and you and I both know that isn't true. Perhaps what you need is to be kissed more often. Haven't the young gentlemen been taking care of you while I've been away?" The mocking laughter danced in his eyes.

Her heart ached at his mistaken assumption. "Sir, I have told you repeatedly who I am. I do not intend to stand here and take any more of your insults. If my cousin Danielle called you a cad and a rake, she had well-founded reason!"

His laughter followed her when she brushed past him and reentered the ballroom. Edging herself along the wall, she made her way to her uncle, who was talking with a group of men. Not wanting to interrupt him, she stood at his side, allowing herself to relive the incident on the balcony. Her face was flushed, and she placed her hand to her lips.

The music was playing, and Skyler watched the people dance by in a haze. Everything about this white world was a mystery to her. The man on the balcony had indicated he'd kissed her cousin before. Was it considered all right for a young woman to give her kisses so freely to a man in this white society?

As Skyler reached her Uncle Tag's side, he turned to her and smiled. "You certainly haven't sat down from lack of dancing partners. Are you enjoying yourself, honey?"

She hesitated, not wanting to seem ungrateful since he had planned on her having a good time. "I love the music, Uncle Tag, and the ladies' gowns are so very lovely."

Out of the corner of her eye, Skyler caught the flash of a blue uniform. Turning a defiant glance on the man who approached, she found herself blushing at his rakish smile. His smile was slow and his eyes gleamed with merriment. When they had been on the balcony, she hadn't been able to see him all that well—in her dream his face had always been in shadows. Now, under the brilliantly lit ballroom, he seemed to stand apart from all the gentlemen in the room. The blue uniform fit his broad shoulders and six-foot frame to perfection. His features were bold and handsome. His hair and sideburns were golden in color. His most disturbing feature was his silver-colored eyes. They reminded Skyler of the color of a frozen pond, except there was warmth and humor in his glance. How well she remembered those mocking eyes.

Tag turned to the young officer, delight written on his face. As they shook hands vigorously Skyler could tell they were glad to see each other.

"It's good to see you, Morgan—or should I say Colonel Prescott. I'm delighted to see some trigger-happy southern youth hasn't parted your hair."

Morgan smiled and caught Skyler's eye. "Danielle doesn't share your wish for my good health." There was again the twinkle of mirth in his eyes.

Tag winked at Skyler, sending her a silent message of humor. Realizing at once that Morgan had mistaken his niece for his daughter, he decided to play the game to its fullest. "Morgan, you are said to be an authority on beautiful women. Tell me, do you think my daughter has changed much?"

Morgan's eyes now seemed to caress Skyler's face. "I find her more beautiful, if possible, but . . . I'm not at all certain I care much for her newly acquired accent."

Tag grinned down at Skyler, who was unaccustomed to being the butt of a jest so therefore had said nothing. She was mulling the man's name over in her mind, knowing she had heard it somewhere before—but where?

"I'll tell Danielle you said so the next time I see her, Morgan. She is away just now visiting my sister. I don't believe you have had the pleasure of meeting my niece,

130

Skyler Dancing."

Tag could hardly control his facial muscles as he watched the color drain from Morgan's face. Morgan's eyes seemed to sparkle like quicksilver when he looked at Skyler through half-closed lashes.

"No, I have not had the pleasure," he said, bowing slightly. "I am at your service, Miss Dancing," he added gallantly. He seemed truly humble and embarrassed at the moment.

Suddenly Skyler caught the irony of the situation and decided to make Morgan Prescott squirm even more. "But you are mistaken, Mr. Prescott. Have you forgotten we met moments ago on the balcony. I believe you said something about not being marriage-minded."

The twinkle was back in his eyes. "Perhaps I should clarify that statement, Miss Dancing. I should have told you that I had not yet met the woman for whom I would wish to give up my freedom."

"What a pity, sir. The young ladies must be pining away for you to take notice of them," she stated flippantly.

Tag flashed Morgan a smile. "You can see that Skyler is like Danielle in more ways than one. I believe she can give tit for tat, should the occasion call for it." Tag turned to his niece. "Skyler, Morgan is a neighbor of ours. He is a doctor in the Cavalry. Danielle has pestered him since she was small, and has looked up to him much like an older brother. If you can fool him into thinking you are Danielle, then you could fool anyone."

"That's true, Miss Dancing. Danielle always delighted in causing me grief. When she was small, she put frogs in my saddlebags and a burr under my saddle."

Skyler gave Morgan a cold stare and it seemed her eyes had turned to blue ice. "Do not expect me to look on you as an older brother, Mr. Prescott. I have a brother of my own." She still hadn't forgiven him for taking liberties with her, even if he had thought that she was Danielle at the time. Most of all she couldn't forgive him for not knowing her. If she had dreamed so often of him, shouldn't he have known her?

"No, Miss Dancing," he said, smiling. "I wouldn't want to be your *brother*."

Skyler caught the hidden meaning in his words. She was more than a little disturbed by this man. She was having a difficult time standing here having polite conversation with the man when she had visioned the two of them making love. Her face burned red when she remembered the intimate parts of her dream.

"You have a very unusual accent, Miss Dancing. I cannot place its origin."

Tag saw his niece's discomfort and spoke up. "Skyler is from a small place that is hardly on any map. She is spending the summer with us, while Danielle is staying with Skyler's mother and father. It's kind of a swap so we could each get to know the girls better."

Morgan smiled slowly. "Then I will be seeing you, Miss Dancing. Perhaps sooner than you think."

Oh, yes, she thought to herself, I shall certainly see you again, Morgan Prescott. Aloud she said, "Uncle Tag, I am weary, and I want to see how Aunt Alexandria is feeling. Do you think we could go home now?"

"Miss Dancing, surely you don't intend to leave until

I've had a dance with you." Morgan spoke up, his slow grin easing the lines of his sensuous mouth.

"Go ahead and dance with him, honey, while I have the buggy brought around," her uncle urged.

Skyler had little choice but to comply. As Morgan took her hand and led her onto the ballroom floor, she was still confused. She tried to avoid his eyes as he swung her into a lively dance step.

"You really put one over on me this evening, and I'm not easy to fool, Miss Dancing."

"So my uncle indicated. I believe he said that you were an authority on women."

"If that's so, I am not where you are concerned. I find myself very intrigued with you, Miss Dancing. Everything about you I find different from other women. Your accent, the proud way you hold your head, the golden tinge to your cheeks. Even your name is intriguing. I find myself wanting to know all about you."

Skyler felt panic. This man could see and sense too much. She couldn't allow him to find out who she was or where she came from. It wouldn't matter as far as she was concerned, because she would be gone in a few months. But he might put two and two together and discover that Danielle was also half-Indian. Perhaps there was nothing she could do to stop the two of them from fulfilling their destiny. It could be that they were meant to walk together.

Skyler feared Morgan Prescott. "I don't wish to know you better, Mr. Prescott. I found out more than I wanted to about you in this one evening." As she spoke the words she knew they were untrue. She wanted very much to see him again.

His laughter was deep. "You have hardly scratched the surface, my dear, and I will get to know you better, mark my words."

She glanced up into stormy eyes and couldn't seem to look away. This man seemed to be pulling at her. Why couldn't he just leave her alone?

Skyler was relieved when the music stopped. Without pausing to think she moved quickly away from Morgan Prescott. She was glad to find her uncle waiting at the front door to take her home.

Just before Tag led her out of the room, she couldn't resist a backward glance at Morgan Prescott. He was standing alone, staring at her with the oddest expression on his face. Some inner instinct told her she hadn't seen the last of him. She would see him again—this she knew. Their paths would cross many times in the future. A shiver ran the length of Skyler's body and she didn't know if it was from delight or fear.

Chapter Nine

Danielle regained consciousness slowly. Her head was pounding painfully, and when she opened her eyes the sun was so bright, she quickly closed them again. As her memory slowly returned, she sat up looking about her fearfully. A hand tightened about her waist to still her struggling.

She didn't know how long she had been unconscious, but it must have been several hours, because the sun was sinking in the west, and there was no sign of the river that ran beside the Blackfoot village.

The motion of the horse was making her feel sick at her stomach. Danielle clamped her mouth tightly together, hoping the sickness would pass. Fearfully glancing up at the man with the scarred face, she shivered uncontrollably.

Out of the corner of her eye, she saw that a second Indian had joined them. A choking sob escaped her lips as she felt terror encase her whole being. The Indian who held her tightly against him clamped his hand over her mouth, hissing what could only be a command to

135

be silent.

"Why are you doing this?" she cried out after prying the man's hands away from her mouth. "I don't even know you. Let me go!"

As before, the man spoke harshly in her ear, and she felt renewed fear. Evidently he couldn't speak English, and she knew very few words in Blackfoot.

Danielle felt tears of hopelessness sting her eyes. What did this Indian want with her? She tried not to think about what his intentions might be. Closing her eyes, she thought instead of her home back in Philadelphia, her father, Alexandria, and her brother. Would she ever see them again? Surely the Indian intended to kill her. Why else would he have taken her away by force?

Would her Uncle Windhawk come after her? Yes, he would come, but suppose he didn't find out about her disappearance until it was too late.

The Indian shifted her weight, causing Danielle's body to come back more firmly against his bare chest. She shuddered, not wanting to be in such intimate contact with the filthy savage. His chest was wet with sweat and again she felt her stomach churn.

A sob broke from her lips, and she felt her body begin to tremble. Uncle Windhawk, she prayed silently, come and get me! Please save me!

For some unknown reason Danielle wondered what Wolfrunner's reaction would be when he found out she had been abducted. She remembered all the unkind words she had hurled at him and wished she could take them back.

Danielle's fear seemed to make her mind clearer. Never had the sky looked so beautiful. Never had she

136

wanted to live so desperately. As the sun sunk slowly in the west, she wondered if it was the last sunset she would ever see.

Sun Woman was worse, and Joanna feared Windhawk's beloved mother wouldn't last through the night. As she bathed the old woman's forehead with cool water, she wondered where Danielle had disappeared. She had been irritated when she returned from berry picking and found Sun Woman alone. How could the girl be so thoughtless? Didn't she care in the least that her own grandmother was dying?

Joanna was too angry to search for Danielle at the moment. Fearing she would say things to her niece in anger that she might regret later, she tried to put the incident out of her mind.

Sun Woman opened her eyes and looked at her daughter-in-law. "Joanna," she said weakly. "I am so weary, my spirit longs for its release."

"Do not say that, my mother. I am going to help you get better. I have made you some of the nice herb tea that you always liked."

The old woman shook her head. "I have lived a full life, my daughter. You have brought joy into my life, but I want to walk with Morning Song. I will leave you before the sun makes its appearance for a new day."

Joanna felt the tears gathering in her eyes. She dearly loved Windhawk's mother and couldn't bear to think of her dying. She remembered the woman her mother-in-law had once been. Sun Woman had been strong in word as well as deed. Joanna now realized how much she had come to depend on Sun Woman.

Gazing at the wrinkled face that was etched in pain, she felt as if her heart would break.

"Hush, my mother. You are but weak from the illness. When you are stronger you will forget that you said these words to me. Come, take a sip of the tea—it will make you feel much better."

"No. I don't want the tea. Where is my son?" Sun Woman asked, trying to rise. "I want to see him."

"Windhawk rode out with the hunting party early this morning. I will send someone for him if it would make you feel better."

"Yes, send for my son, Joanna. I also want to see all my grandchildren. Why is Sky Dancer not here?"

Joanna knew Sun Woman was not thinking clearly, or she would remember that Sky Dancer had gone to Philadelphia. "Don't you remember, my mother, Sky Dancer is visiting with Tag and Alexandria."

The old woman nodded. "Yes, that is so. Sky Dancer will weep when she learns of my passing. Tell her . . . tell her, that she was the joy of this old woman's heart."

It was becoming increasingly difficult for Joanna to hide her tears from Sun Woman. "You can tell Sky Dancer yourself when she comes home, my mother."

Sun Woman sighed wearily. "Where is Danielle? I want to tell her something."

Joanna felt her anger burn deep. Sun Woman loved Danielle so much and the girl hadn't even given her a thought when she had left her alone. "I will send someone to find her, my mother. You try to rest now."

Sun Woman closed her eyes. Time was slipping away as quickly as was her strength. She would meet Napi, the Great One, before the night was over. She would walk in the mountains with her beloved husband and daughter, and together the three of them would wait for the time when the rest of their family would join them. Her gnarled hands gripped the beaded necklace her husband had given her on their wedding day. A smile curved her lips as she drifted off to sleep.

Matoka, the medicine woman, touched Sun Woman's forehead and shook her head sadly. "She grows weaker, Flaming Hair."

Joanna leaned her head against the lodge pole. Her body shook from the deep sobs that she was trying to hold back. Suddenly strong arms went about her and she was turned against a hard chest.

Windhawk held his wife tightly, silently sharing her grief.

The sun had set and it was a bright moonlit night. Danielle wondered if they were ever going to stop riding. Even though she hated to be in such close contact with the Indian, she was weary, so she rested her head against his shoulder. She wished they would stop, and yet she feared that they might. As long as they were on horseback she was safe enough, she reasoned.

Danielle became aware that the second Indian was hanging back to cover up any tracks they might have left behind. Why were they taking such pains to cover their tracks, and what were their plans for her?

She could hear the steady heartbeat of the Indian who held her, and wondered if she dared try to question him again. Remembering his reaction when she tried to speak to him earlier, she decided to remain silent.

Her mind wandered back to the Blackfoot village,

and to her ailing grandmother. Sun Woman should not have been left alone in her condition. What had her Aunt Joanna thought when she returned and found her missing? Did she think she was off somewhere pouting? She hoped her aunt would know her well enough to realize she would never leave someone in her grandmother's condition alone.

Taking a deep breath, Danielle closed her eyes. For the first time in her life, she was in a situation that she could do nothing about. If she were to die, would her father not regret forcing her to leave her home to spend the summer with the Blackfoot?

It seemed every bone in her body ached, and her eyes burned with unshed tears. Danielle was so frightened she didn't know if she would be alive to see the sunrise the next morning. If she were going to die at the hands of these savages, she hoped that God in his infinite mercy would make it a quick and painless death.

The moon was high in the sky when the Indian halted his mount. Danielle had fallen asleep and hardly stirred as he handed her down to his companion before dismounting himself. She opened her eyes when the Indian set her on her feet, and in her sleep-drugged state, she clung to his arm.

Danielle came fully awake when the Indian who had abducted her began tying rawhide strips about her wrists and bound her to a tree. She was past feeling fear as she sank down to her knees and rested her head against the rough tree bark.

She couldn't see the two men very clearly since a cloud had passed over the moon. Straining her eyes in the darkness she watched the Indian who had abducted her spread his blanket nearby and sit down upon it, while the other one led the horses away.

Danielle could feel the Indian's eyes burning into her, and wondered why she sensed such hatred there.

The ground was hard and cold and she was hungry, thirsty, and tired, but she dared not complain. Silently she cried tears of self-pity, wondering how this nightmare was going to end. She expected the two Indians to pounce on her at any moment.

When the second Indian returned from tending the horses, he dropped down beside his friend. They didn't light a fire, and were no more than dark shadows as they talked together quietly. Danielle wished she could understand what they were saying so she might learn her fate.

Tense moments passed and she tried to work her hands free of the rawhide ropes which were cutting into her skin painfully.

Danielle's eyes were fastened on the two men and she felt relief when one of them took his blanket and lay down, while the other rested his back against a tree. Apparently they feared pursuit, so one of them would sleep while the other stayed on guard.

Leaning her face against the tree trunk, she felt weary and drained—there wasn't a place on her body which didn't ache. With her hands tied about the trunk of the tree, she couldn't lie down, but was forced to sit up in a most uncomfortable position. At last, too weary to think or reason, her eyes closed and she drifted into a troubled sleep.

*   *   *

Windhawk had sent runners out in every direction to try and find some sigh of Danielle. By now, they had all reported back to him and none had found the slightest clue to her disappearance.

He turned troubled eyes on Joanna. "I do not understand this. Danielle would never have gone off on her own, she would be too afraid. How can a young girl just disappear without a trace?"

Joanna moved into her husband's strong arms. "I don't know, Windhawk, but I am concerned. It is dark and she must be very frightened."

"Did you have the women search the village?" he asked, feeling uneasiness in his heart.

"Yes, I did, but she wasn't found. What is so strange is that no one has seen her since she came with me to your mother's tipi early this morning."

Windhawk glanced over to the buffalo robe where his mother lay sleeping. "I must go and search for Danielle, and yet how can I leave my mother when she needs me?"

Joanna raised her face and her eyes were tear-bright. "I know this is tearing at you. I will go with you to search for Danielle. I am so frightened that something has happened to her. Tag trusted us to keep his daughter safe."

Windhawk's expression was grim as he crossed the tipi and knelt beside his mother. "You cannot leave my mother, Joanna. One of us must stay with her in her last hours. I fear she will not see the morning sun." Joanna could hear the grief in Windhawk's voice. She knew what it was costing him to leave Sun Woman at such a time.

Kneeling down beside him, she laid her head on his

142

shoulder. "I will stay with Sun Woman and give her what comfort I can. Take heart in the fact that I will not leave her alone for a moment."

Windhawk stood up and lifted Joanna to her feet. Leading her away from where his mother lay, he whispered in a pain-laced voice. "My heart is heavy, Joanna. I grieve for my mother's passing and for the daughter of my dead sister. I can do nothing about my mother, but you have my word that if Danielle is alive I shall bring her back to you."

Without another word, Windhawk swept out of the tipi. Joanna gripped her hands together tightly. Looking upward, she sent a silent message of prayer that this night would not end in two tragedies.

Kneeling down beside Sun Woman once more, she took the old woman's hand in hers. She had loved this woman as a mother and a friend. She couldn't bear to think that this woman who had been so vibrant and had wielded so much power and strength was nothing more than a wasted body—an empty shell. Her heart ached for Windhawk, knowing what he was feeling.

At that moment, the wrinkled old hand that Joanna held tightened and Sun Woman opened her eyes. "My . . . son . . ." she said in a weak voice. "I . . . must see Windhawk."

Joanna jumped to her feet and ran out of the tipi, hoping she could catch Windhawk before he left the village. Seeing a group of mounted warriors in front of her lodge, she hurried toward them.

The men moved their horses aside to allow their chief's wife to approach him. One look at his wife's face, and Windhawk moved to her side. "What has happened? Has my mother—"

"No, not yet, my husband, but she is asking for you. I think you had better come at once."

Hand in hand Windhawk and Joanna hurried to his mother's tipi. Once inside Windhawk sat down by his mother and took her frail hand in his.

"I am here, my mother," he said softly.

The tired old woman smiled. "I . . . feared I would walk in the spirit world without . . . saying what is on my mind . . . my son."

"Don't talk, my mother, save your strength," Windhawk gently urged.

The dark eyes seemed to clear as Sun Woman stared at her son. "No, just listen . . . I have so much to say and such a short time to say it in."

Windhawk nodded grimly, knowing he could not deny his mother her chance to speak her mind.

"I wanted to tell you, my son, not to grieve for me." Her voice seemed to grow stronger as her eyes caressed Windhawk's face lovingly. "No mother had a finer son than you. I have been well proud of you. You have led our people through many hard times, but I have seen a vision and I must tell you about it."

Windhawk touched her face softly, knowing that when one saw a vision on his deathbed it came from the Great Father, Napi. "I am listening, my mother."

"In the vision I have seen our people herded like cattle by the white men. I have seen women and children slaughtered as the white men take over our lands."

Windhawk took a deep breath. This was nothing new to him. He knew the time would come when the Blackfoot would have to fight for their land to stop the encroaching white man.

"The Great Father has sent me a message from your father, Windhawk!" Sun Woman said excitedly. "Your father wants you to move our people into the Canadas so they will be safe. I know you, my son. You are a proud man and would never run from the white man, but you must promise me that you will consider what I have told you tonight."

"I will think on what you have told me, my mother."

Sun Woman's eyes wandered past her son, to the white woman whom she loved as her own daughter. "I will not mind leaving you . . . my son. You . . . have this woman to take care of you. I . . . have loved you both so well."

Joanna dropped down beside Sun Woman. "I have loved you, my mother. You have been my friend and have taught me many valuable lessons."

Sun Woman smiled sadly. "You have also taught me many things . . . my daughter." In that moment Sun Woman's eyes seemed to cloud over and her slight body trembled.

"Do . . . not grieve for . . . me," she whispered.

Joanna watched as the old woman's eyes seemed to go blank, and she knew Sun Woman's spirit had just flown to the sun. Tears spilled down Joanna's face as Windhawk turned to clasp her in his arms. Their tears mingled as they both looked on the face of the woman who had given them so much.

After a long moment of silence, Windhawk stood. Joanna knew inside he was grieving, but he must show a strong face to his people. She knew he would cry no more tears, and no one but her would ever see his weakness.

"I must go and search for Danielle," he said in a deep

voice as if he were dazed by what had just happened. "Look after my mother," he said, turning away.

Joanna did not watch Windhawk leave the tipi. Her grief was so deep she had been trying to hold it in until he left. Deep broken sobs issued from her throat as she took Sun Woman's still warm hand and raised it to her lips.

By now others had heard of Sun Woman's death and had gathered outside the tipi. Joanna heard Windhawk and his warriors ride away, and she stood up, knowing there was much to do. She had the heartbreaking task of directing the building of a scaffold which would be Sun Woman's final resting place, and her gateway to the sky. Sun Woman had been much loved and the moans of the death chant reached Joanna's ears.

Several women entered the tipi weeping loudly. Matoka, the medicine woman, came to help Joanna dress Sun Woman in her best doeskin gown.

Touching the old woman's face, Joanna closed Sun Woman's eyes. She whispered, "Rest easy, my mother—I have loved you well."

Chapter Ten

Skyler slowly slipped into her life in Philadelphia. Since the ball she had attended several teas and luncheons. She found the people she met to be warm and friendly. They were curious about her background, but she managed to tell them very little about herself.

She did make one good friend. Priscilla Wendham was Skyler's age and lived in the house next door. The two of them seemed to talk easily, and Skyler found that Priscilla had a sweet and generous nature.

Alexandria was often ill. Her pregnancy didn't seem to be going well, and as a result it gave Skyler an excuse to turn down many dinner invitations to stay home and look after her aunt.

The James family owned a big shipping firm and her uncle was often away tending to business, so Skyler and Alexandria spent a lot of time together. Skyler was growing close to her lovely aunt and she could see how Danielle would love her as a mother. Many times Skyler would be overcome with homesickness, but she tried to hide it from her aunt and uncle.

It was early afternoon. The house seemed unbearably hot, so Alexandria had suggested that she and Skyler spend the afternoon in the summerhouse.

The summerhouse was one of Skyler's favorite places. It had been built in a circle with a dome-shaped roof, the top half of the walls open but for the white trellises that supported many climbing rose bushes. Inside, cushioned seats were built around the lower wall. In the middle was a lounge, with a table and chairs.

A cool breeze was blowing and the birds were singing sweetly in the nearby trees. Skyler and her aunt were sewing baby clothes and enjoying a quiet kind of companionship.

"You do lovely work, dear," Alexandria said, examining the embroidery on the blanket her young niece was stitching.

"My grandmother taught me to sew, but usually I use colored beads instead of silk threads. See, I have made the pattern of the blue wildflowers that grow on the Sweet Grass Hills near my village."

Alexandria smiled brightly. "My dear, it is simply lovely. I shall always treasure this blanket because you made it for me."

Standing up Skyler poured a glass of lemonade and handed it to her aunt. "I am going to miss you and Uncle Tag when I return home, Aunt Alexandria. I didn't expect to enjoy myself this summer, but I have had wonderful times with you and my uncle."

Alexandria raised her glass and took a sip of the cool liquid. "I don't want to think about your leaving. I have grown so accustomed to having you here. I am just sorry that I am not in a condition to show you a better time." Her aunt's face lit up as she gazed up the walkway. "I do believe that is Morgan Prescott coming to call. He is such a nice young man and I always enjoy his company."

Skyler nervously ran her hand across the chair she was sitting in. She had thought often of Colonel Prescott; in fact she had looked for him at all the functions she had been invited to, but he hadn't attended any of them.

For some strange reason her heart began to beat faster as he approached. The brass buttons on his blue uniform shone brightly as the sunlight hit them. He carried himself straight and tall. His knee-length boots made a crunching sound as they struck the pebble walkway, while his spurs made a slight jingling sound.

Skyler seemed to notice everything about him. She wondered why he had been on her mind so much lately. She had met many handsome young gentlemen since she had arrived in Philadelphia. Why did Morgan Prescott stand out so vividly in her mind?

Morgan slowly climbed the steps of the summer-house. His eyes were dancing merrily as they rested on Skyler. She gave him what she hoped was an indifferent glance, hoping he wouldn't guess that her heart was thundering against the wall of her breasts.

"Morgan, what a delightful surprise," Alexandria exclaimed, happily extending her hand to him.

"It is always a pleasure to see you, Alex. My mother sends her greetings, and says to tell you she will be calling on you the moment she returns from Paris."

"How is your mother and your sisters?"

"Mother is well, and Margo is enjoying her season in Paris. As for myself, I am looking forward to your barbecue at the end of summer." His eyes traveled to Skyler. "Are you also looking forward to the barbecue, Miss Dancing?"

"I do not know, since I have never been to a barbecue, sir."

He eased himself down on a cushioned seat that ran the length of the wall of the summerhouse. "How can that be? Everyone has been to a barbecue. It is a custom we have adopted from our southern neighbors."

Alexandria laid her sewing aside and picked up the pitcher of lemonade, and poured a glass for Morgan. "Everything in Philadelphia is new to Skyler, Morgan. It has been a real delight showing her around."

"Have you ever been on a boat ride down the Delaware River, Miss Dancing?"

Glancing up, she shook her head. "No, I have not, but my uncle has promised to take me one day. I think it will be a very delightful and new experience."

He took the glass of lemonade Alexandria handed him, and thanked her with the nod of his head. "You must come from a very strange place indeed if you have never been on a river ride or attended a barbecue. As it happens, I have come here today with the express purpose of asking you to attend a riverboat party some friends of mine are giving tonight. Will you accept my invitation? I realize it's kind of short notice." His silver eyes twinkled and he gave her a devastating half-smile.

Skyler pricked her finger with the needle and laid the sewing aside, raising the injured member to her lips. "No. My aunt needs me to stay with her." She had never known a man like Morgan Prescott. He was polished and sophisticated with a glib tongue. The fact that he was handsome added to the overall picture she had drawn of him in her mind.

Alexandria smiled at her young niece. "Nonsense. You will certainly not stay home on my account." She turned her eyes on Morgan, realizing for the first time his interest in Skyler. "My niece will be only to happy to go with you tonight. What time will you pick her up?"

"Around five?"

Skyler opened her mouth to protest, but the look in her aunt's eyes stopped her. Feeling trapped into a situation she could do nothing about, she clamped her mouth together tightly.

"I wonder if the two of you would excuse me?" Alexandria said, gathering up her sewing and standing up. "I want to talk to the cook about dinner tonight."

Skyler came to her feet. She was shocked that her aunt would leave her alone with a man. In the Blackfoot village such a thing was never done. "I will go with you." She wasn't at all pleased that she would be going on a riverboat ride with Morgan Prescott. The last thing she wanted was to be left alone in his company now.

"No, dear," Alexandria told her firmly. "You stay and entertain our guest. "I think I'll just lay down a bit before dinner."

Morgan's eyebrows came together in a frown. He could tell that Miss Dancing didn't want to be alone with him. Then he remembered their first meeting and smiled. He couldn't really blame her. It was highly unconventional for a man to kiss young lady on their first meeting. After the ball he had found himself unable to put her out of his mind. There was something so refreshing and totally different about her.

"Have a good rest, Alex," he said, raising his glass to her.

"Thank you for stopping by, Morgan. We never get to see enough of you anymore."

He chuckled. "We will have to correct that situation. Now that the war is ended, I'll be home for a while."

Skyler reached for her glass of lemonade and took a sip. She was trapped into entertaining Colonel Prescott, and she was nervously hoping she wouldn't make any mistakes he would pick up on. She knew she wasn't as polished as the women he was accustomed to. She must carefully guard her true identity from this man. She could only imagine what his reaction would be if he found out she was a half-breed.

Morgan watched Alexandria make her way up the path to the house. When she was out of sight, he turned his silver eyes on Skyler. She had again picked up her sewing and seemed bent on ignoring him. Standing up, he moved to a chair next to her.

"The real reason I came this afternoon was to apologize for the other night. In my defense I can only plead ignorance to your identity. Now that I look at you I can see there are many differences between you and Danielle. Your eyes are a deeper blue, almost violet in color. Your features are softer and you don't seem to smile very much. Danielle is a little imp, always playing tricks on people; whereas you are much too serious about life."

She raised her head and met his dancing silver eyes. "I tried to tell you who I was, but you wouldn't listen to me. I am not inclined to forgive you for your ungentlemanly conduct."

His lips curled into a smile. "I am almost positive

that you had never been kissed by a man before. I can see where my actions might have come as a shock to you."

"I do not understand many things about your land, Colonel Prescott, but I am told that in your country men do not usually force their unwanted attentions on young ladies."

His eyes narrowed in confusion. "What do you mean when you say my land? Are you not from the United States?"

Skyler realized her mistake. "I . . . no, I am not."

"But surely you are not from the South?"

"South of what?" she asked.

He laughed softly. "I was thinking about south of the Mason-Dixon line, but I can see you are not. Where do you come from?"

Skyler could feel him drawing her deeper and deeper into a web. He was confusing her. "If you were from my land, you would never have dared touch me. Men have died for far less than what you did."

"What kind of bloodthirsty society do you come from? This is the nineteenth century."

Suddenly Skyler knew she must put an end to the converstaion. Morgan Prescott was becoming entirely too inquisitive and familiar. Standing up, she brushed past him. "You must leave now. I really need to be with my aunt," she said without looking at him.

"No, I won't leave until you tell me what you are talking about. Where is this land that you come from? I thought I knew everything about your family. I have known Tag and Alexandria for many years. I knew Tag had a sister, but he rarely talked about her. I gathered she lived in Europe somewhere."

153

Turning around slowly she faced him. "I come from a place far away from here. There is an invisible line between our lands that should never be crossed by the people of the United States; even so, my father says your people will one day cross that line."

He leaned against the railing and folded his arms across his chest. "Now I know you are from the South. You must put the thoughts of war behind you. One day the wounds of war will heal and we will be reunited in spirit once more."

Skyler gazed across the garden. She watched a brightly colored bluebird take flight and suddenly wished she could be free. It was becoming a heavy burden to try and hide who she was. She was proud of her Indian heritage. To be ashamed of it would be to deny her own father. Suddenly she was weary of all the pretending.

"Your country has not yet fought against my land. If you ever do, you will find my father is far more powerful than you can imagine."

"You speak as if your father were a king or something," Morgan said with amusement. "One would think he is an absolute ruler."

"No, he does not rule absolute, but his word is law. He has a wise council that advises him sometimes. "

Morgan's eyes narrowed. "I can hardly credit what you are saying. You have had me in a spin ever since I met you." He looked at her as if he doubted the truth of what she was telling him. "Should I address you as 'your majesty'?" he asked, tongue in cheek—almost mockingly.

His manner had suddenly turned arrogant. Skyler had never had her word doubted by anyone. She was barely able to curb her anger. She wanted nothing more than to put this man in his place, so she forgot to be cautious.

"I am a princess in my land, but my uncle and my parents think it should be kept a secret while I am in your country. If you were in my land you would not be allowed to approach me, let alone take rash liberties." Fearing she had said too much, Skyler lowered her lashes. "Now I have said too much. No one was supposed to know about my identity—it was to be a closely guarded secret."

The arrogant look left Morgan's face, and he released a long breath. Now he knew what was different about her. Yes, she did carry herself like royalty. There was a certain aura about her that other women didn't have.

"If this is your secret, it is safe with me, Miss Dancing. I will not press farther. I can only tender my apologies once more."

Before Skyler knew what was happening he reached out and took her hand, raising it to his lips. She felt a shiver race down her spine and jerked her hand free.

Deep laughter filled the air as Morgan bowed slightly. "Until tonight, Miss Dancing," he said, turning away and walking out of the summerhouse.

Skyler placed her hands to her flaming cheeks. Had she said too much to Colonel Prescott? Would her uncle be displeased with her? She didn't want to go with that man tonight, but she didn't seem to have a choice. Her aunt and uncle didn't seem to understand how difficult it was to try to hide who she really was. Surely they couldn't know what a burden they had placed on her small shoulders.

*   *   *

As Skyler came in from the garden she found her uncle was waiting for her in the sitting room. She smiled and kissed him on the cheek before putting her sewing away in a basket.

"Your aunt tells me that you are going with Morgan tonight. He is a fine young man. I had always hoped he and Danielle would become closer, but that wasn't meant to be. She was never his type."

Skyler looked deeply into her uncle's eyes. "I am not his kind either, Uncle. I wish I didn't have to attend the party this evening."

Tag studied her face carefully. "Do this for me, Skyler. I want you to have all the fun you can before you leave us. Your mother wants this for you also. You need not be afraid, Morgan is a gentleman and he will take care of you."

"He is far too curious about me. He asks too many questions."

Tag laughed humorously. "What young man wouldn't be curious about a young lady as lovely as you. That is the most natural thing in the world."

"You do not understand. Just a few moments ago, he had me admitting I was a princess. Surely there can be harm in that."

Tag pulled her into his arms. "I see no harm done, my dear; after all, you *are* a princess."

"You are not angry with me for telling Colonel Prescott?"

"Of course not, but I would caution you about saying too much. Just go out and enjoy yourself tonight. You are far too serious about life—be young and carefree."

"I know nothing about Morgan Prescott, Uncle Tag.

He is a stranger to me."

"I can tell you he's a fine man. His father died when he was young, but Morgan took on a man's responsibilities. He's also a very fine doctor. I understand he is very sought after by the ladies, but you will be safe with him. If I didn't believe this, I wouldn't allow you to go with him. Just have fun tonight."

Skyler sighed deeply and pushed a tumbled curl out of her face. She felt her heart sink. How could she have fun when she was with Colonel Prescott? He had a disturbing way of reaching inside her and stirring up emotions and feelings she wasn't even aware of. Her heart told her this man could be dangerous to her peace of mind.

Chapter Eleven

Danielle felt someone grasp her shoulders and roughly shake her awake. She was tired, so she pushed the hand away, wanting to sleep just awhile longer. Whoever it was became more insistent and jerked her forward, demanding that she awaken. Her eyes slowly opened and she was back in her nightmare world. She'd hoped it had been a bad dream—that she hadn't really been abducted by the hideous, scar-faced Indian, but this was stark reality.

Fear seemed to cover her like a blanket of needles, prickling her skin, cutting off her breathing. She gulped in a breath of air, trying desperately to hide her fear.

The Indian untied the rawhide ropes about her wrists, and dragged her to her feet. Danielle avoided looking at his hideous face, because she knew there would be hatred burning in those dark eyes.

Jerking her head up, the man tied the rawhide rope about her neck. Leading her forward as if she were an animal, he yanked her down to a sitting position.

Danielle made a frightened muffled sound as the Indian knelt down beside her. He held out his hand to her, and she saw he was offering her food, if one could call a few kernels of corn, food. As hungry as she was, she wasn't about to eat from this savage's hand like some animal. Shaking her head no, she clamped her mouth together tightly. Her eyes burned defiantly, as if challenging him to force his corn past her lips.

This seemed to anger the Indian, and he grabbed her by the hair and jerked her head up. Forcing her mouth open, he crammed the corn inside.

Danielle coughed and sputtered as the dry kernels stuck in her throat. Spitting out the corn, she felt her anger reach its zenith. For the moment, anger overruled her good judgment. Turning her head away she spat the corn out upon the ground, and then cast the man an angry glance.

"I will not eat from your hand," she cried. "You are nothing but a dirty Indian!"

His dark eyes narrowed to slits. Danielle watched helplessly as he raised his hand. The blow he delivered caught her across the temple, and thousands of stars exploded inside her head. Then she was in a world of swirling darkness. She felt herself slipping into a state of unconsciousness.

As the two Indians rode away from their night camp, Scar Face carried the unconscious Danielle in front of him. She was unaware that the two men again took pains to cover their tracks, nor did she know of the fear that beat in each of their hearts. They looked over their shoulders many times, and backtracked often, fearing the legendary chief of the Bloods would overtake them. Both knew if Windhawk were to find them they would die a slow and agonizing death.

Windhawk stood motionless as his eyes surveyed the deep valley below. How was it possible for one to disappear without leaving a trace? His warriors were good trackers, and yet they hadn't even found a blade of grass crushed or a stone out of place. Whoever had taken his niece knew what they were doing. They must have planned it well in advance.

He turned his eyes homeward, realizing he would have to return to the village to inform Joanna that he had found no sign of Danielle. His heart was heavy, knowing he would also have to send someone to Philadelphia to inform Tag that his daughter was missing, perhaps dead.

Hearing movement, Windhawk turned to see Wolf-runner behind him, staring down at the valley. "I have this feeling that whoever took your sister's daughter did not come this way, my chief," the young warrior observed.

"Why do you say this?"

"I have been thinking which way I would take if I wanted to throw someone off the trail and make it difficult to be tracked. I believe I would go to the north toward the Canadas. There are many mountains and rivers to cover one's tracks in that direction."

"As you know, I have sent your father and seven warriors toward the Canadas. They reported back that they found nothing."

The young warrior looked at his chief. Like the rest of the tribe, he loved and admired this man. His heart was heavy for his chief's grief. "I will go to the north and look for signs. No one can disappear without leaving some sign. If it is possible, I will bring your niece back to you."

Windhawk looked at Wolfrunner. The young man was the eldest son of his good friend, Gray Fox. He remembered a time when Wolfrunner had been a baby, and Joanna had saved his life by slaying a wild boar. Since that time, Wolfrunner had been a favorite of Joanna's, and she loved him almost like a son. He was a brave and fearless warrior. Several winters past, Windhawk had given him the name "Wolfrunner" because of his daring and bravery.

"If that is your wish, I will not say no. Perhaps you can find something which has been overlooked."

"If she is out there, my chief, I will find her and bring her back," he vowed once more.

Windhawk smiled at the young warrior. "I will trust you to do that. I cannot think who would dare lay hand to someone who belongs to me. I have many enemies, but this one is bold if he will come into my village and take from me. If you find who has done this thing, bring them back to me if you can. Take someone with you if it is your wish."

"I would rather go by myself, my chief, because I can travel faster alone," Wolfrunner said, turning his dark eyes northward. His mind wandered to the slight girl who was not accustomed to the harsh ways of the wilderness. He didn't like her very well, but for his chief's and Joanna's sake he would not give up until he found her, dead . . . or alive.

Danielle looked down at her soiled and torn skirt.

162

Her hair was a mass of tangles. She knew her face was dirty and streaked from the tears she had shed. Her hands were tied behind her. A second rope was tied about her neck then looped over the arm of the scar-faced Indian.

They were camped in a deep canyon, with high rock walls on three sides. It appeared to Danielle that the Indians no longer feared pursuit, because they had built a campfire. She had lost count of the days they had been traveling, but she knew they always moved in a northerly direction.

Danielle was almost weak with hunger, having eaten nothing since her abduction. She wished she'd eaten the corn the Indian had tried to force on her that morning. She could smell the delicious aroma of the rabbit that was cooking on a spit, and felt her stomach growl. Would the Indians share their bounty with her tonight, she wondered, or would they try to force her to eat the dry corn?

For the most part, the two men ignored her, and that suited Danielle just fine. She listened to their guttural talk wishing she could understand what they were saying. She knew they were discussing her by the way they kept nodding in her direction. Perhaps they were at that very moment deciding her fate . . . good or bad.

Danielle still had no notion as to what these Indians wanted with her. She studied them both now. The one with the scar down his face was much older than the other. He always seemed sullen and quiet. The younger of the two she judged to be about her own age. He seemed to look at her strangely as if he feared her, or perhaps he feared what would happen to him because of her. A new thought came to her—he was frightened

163

of Windhawk!

The scar-faced man removed the rabbit from the spit. Carving off a small slice, he threw it in Danielle's direction and it landed on the ground. She couldn't reach for the meat since her hands were tied behind her, so she strained forward to pick the meat up with her mouth. She had almost reached the delicious-smelling meat when the Indian yanked on the rope that was tied about her neck and dragged her back.

Tears of pain and humiliation stung Danielle's eyes. The harder she struggled, the more the man pulled on the rope, causing it to cut off her breathing. Just when she thought she couldn't stand the pain any longer, Scar Face kicked her in the stomach and sent her sprawling backward. She gasped for breath—the pain in her throat was like an open wound. Doubling up in agony, she felt a burning in her stomach. Just when everything started going black, he released the rope. Apparently the man grew weary of his cruel game—or perhaps he didn't want her dead.

Danielle lay with her face in the dirt, feeling as low as a human could sink. The man had made her grovel, but he wouldn't do it again, she vowed. Raising her head, she gave him a cold glare. As hungry as she was, she wouldn't touch the meat. Let him kill her if he wished; there were far worse things than death. The loss of one's pride was much worse than dying. Danielle didn't realize she was changing. She didn't know that the part of her that came from her Indian mother cried out in protest against being humbled by this man.

Scar Face seemed to sense the change in Danielle. He motioned for her to pick up the meat, but she merely stared at him defiantly.

Standing up, he walked toward her slowly. Jerking on the rope, he pulled her to her feet. Again Danielle felt her breathing closed off, and she threw her head back, gasping for precious air.

"You will eat the meat. Eat or I will slice your heart from your body," Scar Face ordered in a harsh tone.

Danielle couldn't understand his words, but she knew what he said. She shook her head. "I will not eat. I would rather you kill me now."

In spite of his hatred for this Blood Blackfoot maiden, Scar Face had to admire her spirit. Surely this daughter of Windhawk was also touched by the spirits. Her courage bothered him, as bravery will always make a coward feel uneasy. "Why do you speak to me in white man's tongue, Sky Dancer?" he asked in halting English.

Danielle stared at him in disbelief. This man had abducted her, thinking she was Sky Dancer! Perhaps if she could make him realize he had made a mistake, he would release her. "I am called Danielle James—I come from Philadelphia. Sky Dancer is my cousin. I speak to you in English because I cannot speak the Blackfoot language." She spoke slow and distinctly, hoping to make him understand.

His eyes half closed, and he smiled, causing the hideous scar to pull the corner of his mouth up, distorting his whole face. "Do you think me a fool? Do I not know who you are? Have I not seen you with your brother one summer back at the Piegan village? Do you not know me, Scar Face?"

"That wasn't me you saw. I only recently came to the Blackfoot village to stay with my aunt and uncle. My father is not Windhawk; my father is Flaming Hair's brother, Taggart James."

Sinister laughter issued from his lips. "You speak not the truth. I know about the Flaming Hair's brother. When he was but a boy, he was once a captive of my father, Running Elk. It was because of him that my father is dead. Windhawk came to my village to get him, and slew my father. I took you to avenge my father's death."

Danielle was thoughtful for a moment. She had heard the story of how Windhawk had rescued her father from the Piegan Blackfoot chief. What this Indian didn't know was that it was not Windhawk who had killed his father that day, but her own father, Taggart James. Scar Face unknowingly had the right person in Danielle, but he didn't know it. She decided it would do no good to try and prove who she was, he wouldn't believe her anyway.

"What are you going to do with me?" she asked, raising her eyes to him and trying to mask her fear.

"It is not for you to know. When the time comes you will cry and beg me for mercy. I will hear you cry out many times before I am through with you. You are dirt beneath my feet, half-white woman."

His eyes dropped down to Danielle's blouse that had been ripped open in their struggle. She cringed inside, knowing a new fear. Her breasts were clearly visible and there was no way she could cover herself since her hands were tied. She could do no more than suffer his leering glance in silence.

His hand went up to stroke the scar on his face, while his eyes traveled over her scantily clad body. "Yes, Sky Dancer, you will cry out many times before I have had my fill of you. You will not look like a Blood princess

166

when I have finished with you. You will be dead like my father."

Scar Face jerked forward on the rope and brought her tumbling against him. A shudder racked her body as his filthy hands came up to the back of her neck and he forced her to look at him.

"I say you have never been with a man before. No man would have dared touch Windhawk's daughter . . . but I would dare."

Danielle turned her head away from his foul breath. Her heart was beating with fear. She had to think of a way to save herself.

She remembered her father once telling her that when Windhawk had been a young warrior, he had a vision of a white buffalo. At that time the Blackfoot were starving and her uncle had led his warriors to a place where the vision had told him to go. There they spotted a large herd of buffalo and among that number was the albino buffalo. Windhawk had walked among the animals until he came to the white beast. He slew the animal and ate its heart as the vision had told him to. Her father had told her that because of this, the Indians believed Windhawk to be the chosen of the Great Father. His enemies feared to harm him, lest they incur the wrath of the Napi. She decided it was best to pretend to be Sky Dancer and try to use the Indian's superstition against him.

"Do you know why no man would touch me?" she asked, looking into the Indian's eyes—showing no fear.

"I do not fear Windhawk as others do, Sky Dancer," he said, smiling slightly. "If I wanted you, the thought of your father would not stop me."

"That is a pity, because if you touch me you will die a

long and agonizing death. Have you not heard of the white buffalo my father killed?"

For the first time she saw uneasiness creep into the Indian's eyes. His friend appeared at his side and tugged at his arm. "What she says is true, Scar Face. Windhawk has the power of the white buffalo. Do not touch this Blood princess or you will die!"

Scar Face shifted his weight. He knew about Windhawk's awesome power, and he decided it would not be worth testing it. Shoving Danielle down to her knees, he gave her an angry growl.

"You will eat the meat. I do not want you dead yet. I am taking you to a French trading post where you will be sold. Let the man who buys you suffer from Windhawk's wrath. I do not want to touch you."

Danielle felt herself go weak all over. A sob rose up in her throat and she bit her lip. Apparently Scar Face had believed the story about her uncle and didn't want to chance the consequences.

Feeling herself fortunate to have gotten off so easy, she picked up the meat and ate it hungrily. She didn't want to test Scar Face's patience any further. It would be best to avoid provoking his anger if possible.

That night as she lay on a bed of soft green grass, Danielle looked at the star-bright sky. She felt different somehow. It was as if all semblance of civilization had been stripped from her. The only thought in her mind at the moment was how to survive. She closed her eyes, calling on all her strength to face what lay ahead.

She didn't know which would be worse—to be sold to some French trapper, or to have the Indians kill her.

For the first time in her life, Danielle knew what it felt like to be cold and hungry. She felt so alone—was there no one to come to her rescue? Tears spilled from her eyes and her thoughts were of her father who was far away.

Since the Indians no longer feared they might be followed, they must think that her Uncle Windhawk would be able to track them. Her thoughts turned to her Indian mother. "Mother, I have denied you for so long. Please send your people to save me," Danielle whispered in a painful voice.

Wolfrunner bathed his face in the small stream, and gazed up at the sky. It seemed as if someone, or something, was beckoning to him—pushing him almost beyond endurance. He had ridden for days and nights, only stopping to rest his horse. As he lay back on the cool grass, he could see Danielle as she had been the day they had gone riding. She had been haughty and insulting, but she had spirit. How long could she survive in this country?

Again it seemed he could hear a voice whispering to him, or was it only the wind?

Chapter Twelve

Skyler stood very still as her aunt laced up the back of her satin gown. Drawing in a deep breath, she hoped she could get through the evening without bursting out of her lacings.

Glancing in the mirror, she saw that the deep, wine-colored gown made her skin appear delicate and golden in color. A satin ribbon of the same color was wound through her hair, and Skyler wondered if Morgan Prescott would think her beautiful.

"My dear, you are simply lovely. It makes me yearn for my younger days just to look at you," Alexandria observed, smiling brightly.

Skyler glanced at the deep vee that slashed down the bodice of her gown. The swell of her breasts was just visible above the neckline—her eyes went to her aunt. "Is it proper for a girl to show so much of her bosom, Aunt Alexandria? It feels almost indecent."

Her aunt smiled and turned her around. "It is very proper, my dear. Just take satisfaction in knowing you will be the prettiest girl at the party tonight."

171

"I wish you and Uncle Tag were coming with me," the young girl said wistfully.

"Don't fret, you are going to have a wonderful time tonight. Morgan Prescott is very respectable and he will see to it that you are not left alone."

Skyler knew it would do no good to tell Alexandria that she didn't want to be alone with Mr. Prescott. She would just have to endure the evening, but she was very sure she would never again accept an invitation if she knew Morgan Prescott was also going to attend.

Skyler ran her hand down the skirt of the wine-colored creation, loving the feel of the soft satin. Alexandria gave her niece a look of approval as she handed her a pair of white lace gloves to complete her toilette.

"You look lovely, my dear. One would think you were born to wear satin and lace."

"It all seems so senseless to me to dress in such a fashion to ride on a boat. One would expect to dress more practically for such an occasion."

Alexandria laughed. "You would cause quite a stir were you to show up in buckskin and moccasins. Before too long you will become accustomed to wearing all the folderol that goes into the dressing of a young lady."

"That would be foolish since I will never again have an opportunity to dress in such a fashion once I return to my home, Aunt Alexandria."

"I have something for you that I think you will like very much, Skyler." Her aunt's eyes sparkled.

"What is it?" Skyler asked, watching her remove some kind of necklace from a black velvet chest.

Alexandria held up a golden locket that shimmered

172

in the lamplight. "This locket was your mother's when she was a young girl. I'm told it was given to Joanna by her mother on her sixteenth birthday."

Skyler reached for the golden locket feeling tears moisten her eyes. "It is lovely."

"Let me show you something," Alexandria said, opening the locket and handing it back to Skyler.

"Oh, it is a picture of my mother and . . . Uncle Tag when they were young."

"Indeed it is."

"May I wear it?"

"Yes. It belongs to you." Alexandria turned Skyler around and fastened the necklace about her neck. "There are many jewels that belonged to your mother and grandmother James that Tag has been saving for you. Many of them are valuable."

"Shouldn't the family jewels go to you and Danielle?" Skyler asked, touching the locket that fell between her breasts.

"Some of them have, but Tag and your grandfather James decided that you are to have most of them. I'll show them to you one day next week."

"Thank you" was all Skyler could manage to say past the lump in her throat.

Alexandria ushered her toward the bedroom door. "Come. You are not to dwell on homesickness tonight. I want you to have a good time. In fact I insist upon it."

Skyler took a deep breath as they neared the staircase. She felt like she was being forced to do something against her will, and there seemed no way out. She feared spending the whole evening with Morgan Prescott. Suppose he drew all her secrets out of her? Suppose he made her tell him things that were better left unsaid?

Morgan was standing in the entryway talking to Tag. Hearing someone coming down the stairs, he glanced quickly up and saw a vision of loveliness floating down the stairs in a frothy, wine-colored satin gown. His eyes drank in Skyler's beauty. His heart seemed to stop and he felt as if he were seeing her for the first time. Her back was straight and her head erect. There was a proud, almost stubborn tilt to her chin.

Even from the distance that separated them, he could see her eyes sparkling—he drew in his breath. Never had there been a woman to rival Skyler Dancing. Her beauty was of such that poems and sonnets were written. In that moment he felt compelled to look away. She was so lovely it was almost physically painful to look upon her.

Tag moved forward to take his niece's hand and help her down the last few steps. "You are a vision, my dear. I wish your mother could see you now," he said softly in her ear.

Skyler's eyes traveled to Colonel Morgan Prescott. His blue dress uniform fit his tall frame to perfection. The brass buttons and gold epaulets lent elegance to the uniform. She felt a tightening in her throat as she watched the soft light fall on his golden head. To her he appeared like some young golden god out of a Greek myth.

Stepping forward, he bowed and his eyes laughingly caressed her face. "Good evening, Miss Dancing. I will be the envy of every man tonight when I enter with you on my arm."

Skyler was unaccustomed to receiving compliments, and felt embarrassed. Lowering her eyes, she allowed her lashes to cover her shyness.

Tag kissed her on the cheek and walked her to the front door. "Have a nice time."

She gave him a half-smile and allowed Morgan to escort her outside. He helped her into the buggy and arranged her gown so it wouldn't get wrinkled. His eyes sparkled when he climbed in beside her and picked up the reins, urging the horses forward at an easy gait.

A brilliant sunset lit the western sky as they rode along the cobblestone streets of Philadelphia. There were warm glows coming from the windows of the homes they passed. Skyler tried to think what was taking place in those houses. Perhaps the people were just sitting down to dinner and the children had already been tucked into their snug little beds. She cast a sidelong glance at Morgan, who smiled at her warmly.

"What were you thinking just now?" he inquired. "You had the most thoughtful look on your face."

She smiled stiffly and glanced down at her folded hands. "I was just wondering what the people in those houses were doing."

He chuckled. "I will tell you. Let's see . . . take that white house on the corner there."

"The one with the yellow trim?"

"Um huh. Let us pretend that the Pinwinkles live there. Mr. Pinwinkle works at the bank all day counting someone else's money. Mrs. Pinwinkle tends the house, and tries to keep up with her sixteen children, ranging in ages from one to sixteen."

Skyler smiled at his wild fabrication. "Surely not sixteen children. The house seems very small to me."

"Yes, poor souls. They hardly have room to draw breath. Today Mr. Pinwinkle received a shock."

Skyler was so caught up in his game that unknown to her she had begun to relax and lose some of her apprehension. "What caused his shock?"

"Mrs. Pinwinkle informed him just before dinner that they would soon have another addition to the family."

Skyler covered her mouth in mock horror. "Surely not another baby?"

"I'm afraid so. Six, in fact."

"How can that be?" she said laughingly.

"Easy. Sport, the dog, just delivered six rollicking puppies on the kitchen floor."

Skyler laughed delightedly. "You have just relieved my mind. I feared the Pinwinkles would have to move to a larger house."

Morgan felt his heart tighten at the sound of her laughter. She was weaving an invisible web about him. She was lovely and exciting and he wanted to know everything about her.

For a time neither spoke. Skyler was watching the sunset, and when she glanced up, she found Morgan's eyes on her. He smiled and she felt her heart turn over.

"I feel very frustrated, Miss Dancing. You have me totally confused."

"Not by intention," she said softly, wishing he wouldn't look at her so closely. "What have I done?"

"I cannot seem to find words to describe your beauty," he answered, half-serious, half-teasing.

She looked quickly away, feeling her shyness cut deeply. "I do not like a man to say pretty things to me.

176

It makes me feel uncomfortable."

He maneuvered the buggy toward the riverfront and chuckled. "I have never met a woman who didn't enjoy compliments. Your cousin Danielle thrives on them."

"I am not my cousin."

"No, you are not. If you were, you wouldn't be sitting beside me at this moment."

She turned back to him in wonder. "Why? I thought you liked Danielle."

"Oh, I liked her right enough. But . . . I have never felt anything more than brotherly toward her. With you it's a different story."

Skyler would like to have asked him what he meant, but they had reached their destination and Morgan stopped the buggy. The waterfront was thriving with activity. Many buggies lined the riverbank. Many gentlemen and their ladies were making their way up the gangplank of the riverboat where the party was being held.

Morgan jumped from the buggy and helped Skyler down. A young lad rushed forward, offering to watch the horses for a price. Morgan tossed a coin at the boy before taking Skyler's arm and leading her up the gangplank.

Music was filtering through the air, and Skyler felt a stirring of excitement. Suddenly she was very aware of the man who was beside her. Something rare and beautiful was happening to her, and she didn't yet know what it was. She was excited and confused at the same time. She had a feeling that something very unusual had taken hold of her.

As Morgan led her into the big salon, her heart

177

seemed to he keeping time with the music. Without a word, he took her in his arms and led her into a waltz. It seemed that she was floating. It was as if there was no one in the room but the two of them. Morgan's eyes locked with Skyler's and she held her breath.

"I like the way you fit in my arms," he told her in a deep voice. "It's almost as if we were created for one another, don't you think?"

Skyler was startled by his words, but not half so startled as Morgan himself was. He hadn't been aware that he was going to make such a statement. He watched the blush tint her cheeks and drew in his breath. Just before she lowered her eyes, he saw confusion reflected there.

Nothing was said as they both tried to cope with the new emotions they were feeling. Whatever the feelings were, they were as old as time and as new as bright spring flowers. It was a fragile thing—too fragile to examine very closely at the moment.

The evening passed in a daze of music and gaiety for Skyler. Morgan was fun to be with; he made her laugh and feel happy. He didn't say anything personal again, but was light and teasing. Skyler was dancing around the fringes of a whole new world. She felt lighthearted and frivolous. It was as if she stepped outside herself and was a completely different person. There was no sign of the Blackfoot princess; only a lovely young lady, enjoying the company of a charming gentleman.

There was excitement in the air. She felt herself being caught up in the warm glow of Morgan's silver-gray eyes. There was electricity flowing between the two of them, and she was at a loss as to how to handle herself.

"Are you glad you came?" he asked, as he waltzed her across the room."

"Yes, very," she answered him breathlessly.

When they stopped dancing to take a breather, Morgan introduced Skyler to many of his friends. Most of the young gentlemen were in uniform. Skyler learned that Morgan had met most of the gentlemen while the war had been going on.

When the soldiers began talking about their war experiences, Morgan took Skyler back on the dance floor.

As the evening progressed everyone else seemed to fade into the background. Nothing existed but the feelings that ran feverishly between Skyler and Morgan.

Later Morgan led her out onto the deck, and they both stood silently gazing across the river. Hundreds of stars were twinkling in the ebony heavens. She slowly turned to face him and found him staring at her.

"What would you say if I told you I wanted to spend the rest of my life with you, Miss Dancing?" he asked softly, again startling not only her but himself as well. Morgan had no warning that his feelings were so deep for this lovely, mysterious girl. He drew back a moment as if to gather his thoughts.

Skyler could feel her whole world crumbling around her. This man was trying to pull her into his world. If he knew who she really was, would he turn away in disgust?

"I do not think you should be saying such things to me, Colonel Prescott," she said softly, trying to hide the sadness in her heart. She knew she was not the woman for this dashing, young gentleman.

His good humor returned almost immediately. "You are right, of course. I believe I just jumped off the deep end, so to speak. I should have waited until you got to know me better. If you are confused by what I just said, what do you think I am feeling? I have never said those words to a woman before. Are you some kind of goddess that has the power to bewitch a man, Miss Dancing?"

"I have no power to bewitch anyone, Colonel. I am no more than a woman."

When his eyes searched Skyler's face, she felt a weakness wash over her body. Suddenly she became afraid. Again this man was pulling at her heart and making her feel things she couldn't understand.

"The hour is late—I would like to go home now," she said, turning away.

"Are you sure?" he asked in a deep voice. "Actually the evening is still young." Morgan somehow dreaded to let her go, fearing she would disappear in a puff of smoke.

"Please take me home."

"If that is your wish." Taking her arm, he led her across the deck of the ship and down the gangplank.

On the ride home, the stars didn't seem to shine as brightly for Skyler. She could feel Morgan's eyes on her, but she refused to look at him.

When they reached the driveway that led to the Jameses' estate, Morgan halted the team and turned to look at Skyler. His hand was resting on the back of her seat, and he moved forward, picking up her locket. When his fingers brushed her skin, Skyler gasped.

"I think you know we need to talk, Skyler."

She said nothing about his use of her first name. As he walked around the buggy and lifted her to the ground, she wished he would pull her into his arms and tell her that the two of them could breach the gap that separated them.

His hand slowly drifted up her arm and with gentle pressure he pulled her into his arms, as if reading her thoughts. "I remember the taste of your lips, and have wondered if they would be as sweet a second time." His voice was deep and shook with emotion.

Skyler knew she should pull away, but it was as if she belonged in the circle of his arms. This man whom she hadn't even known until a few short weeks ago had crept into her heart, destroying her peace of mind and turning her whole world upsidedown.

Morgan's head descended, and she knew he was going to kiss her. His mouth was warm as it covered her lips and she felt herself being drawn tightly against him. Her whole body seemed to be filled with new and exciting feelings. It was as if she were being reborn—he was filling her heart with a warmth and tenderness that she couldn't fully understand.

Skyler's arms moved about his neck, and she could feel her head spinning dizzily. She clung to him as if he were her lifeline—indeed, her very life. So many different emotions tripped through her mind. Emotions that were new and unexplored. Soft feelings that warmed her heart—deep emotions that awakened her body as well as her mind.

When Morgan raised his head, he stared down at her in amazement. The moonlight fell softly on Skyler's face, and he thought he had never seen anyone so lovely. Her eyes were shining and he could see the confusion in the violet depths.

There were so many things he wanted to say to her, so many feelings he wanted to share, but the intensity of his feelings overwhelmed him.

He pulled her head to rest against his shoulder and ran his hand down her back. "What have you done to me, Skyler Dancing?" he whispered. "You have shaken my world to its foundations."

She felt his warmth reach out to her. She had no thought of how improper it was to be in the arms of a man she hardly knew. It felt so right to have him hold her.

Raising her face to him, she shook her head. "I do not know what has happened. I need time to think."

He stared at her for a long time and then nodded. "You are right. This has happened so quickly we both need time to think it through. I have to go to Washington for two weeks. When I return we will talk then."

Morgan led her back to the buggy and lifted her up and placed her inside. When he pulled up to the house, Skyler had a heavy feeling around her heart. It would be terrible not to see him for two whole weeks.

When he walked her to the door he didn't attempt to touch her. "I will see you in two weeks," he said, before turning away.

She watched the buggy pull away in complete confusion. Her whole world had come crashing down on her. Skyler wished with all her heart that she had her wise mother or grandmother to talk to.

A feeling of loneliness surrounded her heart, but this

time it wasn't for her home in Blackfoot country that she yearned. She missed Morgan and knew the two weeks he would be away would crawl by.

As she ascended the stairs to her room, tears flooded her eyes. What was she going to do? She couldn't tell Morgan about her background. What did the future hold for her and the man she now knew she loved?

Chapter Thirteen

Wolfrunner raised his head into the wind and caught the scent of meat cooking in the distance. Scanning the horizon, he saw the smoke from a campfire rising into the sky in the valley just below. He dismounted and examined the ground with an expert eye. There was evidence that two unshod ponies had passed this way. With his tracking ability, Wolfrunner could easily tell that one of the horses was carrying double. He had picked up a faint trail three days back, and each day the trail had become easier to follow. As of yet, he didn't know if he was following a false lead, or even who he was after. He only knew he must find Danielle.

Wolfrunner had begun to feel pity in his heart for the young maiden who must be frightened at this moment. Many times he almost turned back to the village. But the thoughts of Danielle kept pushing him onward at a punishing pace. Each night he would fall on his blanket in an exhausted sleep. He remembered Danielle's gentle beauty. She was neither as strong as Sky Dancer nor would she be able to endure the cruel ways of the wilderness country for very long.

Mounting his horse, Wolfrunner decided to watch the camp from a distance until nightfall. Then he would venture closer to find out who he was following. Perhaps it would prove not to be Danielle. If it wasn't her then he had wasted valuable time chasing a false trail.

Danielle tested her mouth with her finger and found it to be swollen and bleeding. She had incurred Scar Face's anger again tonight when she had refused to eat the raw fish he offered her. In the end she had been compelled to eat the fish because she had no choice. She could still smell the fish on her breath, and it made her stomach heave. Danielle swallowed the bitter taste of bile that rose in her throat. She had to concentrate on something else or she would be sick.

Danielle was so tired but couldn't seem to fall asleep. The horses were hobbled nearby and she heard them acting up. Apparently Tall Bear had heard it also, because he got up, and moved off into the shadows to check on the animals. Scar Face became alert and unsheathed his knife, waiting and watching for his friend to return.

Hope fanned to life within Danielle only to be dashed into bitter disappointment moments later. She had hoped that it might have been her uncle coming to rescue her who had disturbed the horses, but Tall Bear soon returned and lay down beside his companion.

As her hopes died, she closed her eyes, wishing for the sleep of forgetfulness—but in that she wasn't successful, for sleep eluded her.

Moments later the horses began stomping the ground and pulling at their ropes nervously. This time Tall Bear mumbled to himself as he got up and left his bed for a second time. Scar Face paid little heed to his friend now, but merely grunted and rolled up in his blanket, drifting back to sleep.

Danielle waited for what seemed hours, and when Tall Bear didn't come back, she became puzzled. The shadow of a man fell across the dying embers of the campfire, and at first Danielle thought it was Tall Bear returning. Her eyes moved over the man, and she wondered why he was acting so strangely. He didn't lie down beside Scar Face, but kept in the shadows, edging his way toward Danielle.

Soon he moved out of view and moments later she felt a knife slice through the ropes that bound her hands. Turning around quickly, she saw nothing more than a fleeting shadow. If it was Tall Bear, why had he cut her loose, she wondered, scrambling to her feet.

Danielle could feel her pulse drumming in her head. Moving back against the trunk of a tree, she forgot that the rope that was about her neck was also tied to Scar Face's arm. The rope pulled her up short, and Scar Face roused up and stared into the darkness. Suddenly he became alert and jumped to his feet. Mumbling something Danielle couldn't understand he jerked her forward and she landed at his feet.

Danielle watched as Scar Face unsheathed his knife, while his eyes scanned the darkness. He knew he was an open target since he was standing in the light of the campfire, so he pulled Danielle to her feet, and half dragged her toward the woods. She fell several times, and he jerked he up, muttering something unintelligible.

Danielle knew that Scar Face mustn't reach the horses, because the man who had sliced through her bonds must have come to rescue her. Throwing her weight against Scar Face, she caught him by surprise. He fell to the ground, dragging her down with him.

Out of nowhere, the shadow of a man appeared. Before Scar Face knew what was happening, he was hauled to his feet with a knife at his throat.

"I am not surprised to find you, Scar Face," Wolfrunner hissed in his ear. "I will take pleasure in ending your life and ridding the world of a plague."

Scar Face felt great fear as he recognized the voice of his old enemy. He knew he must act fast or Wolfrunner would do just as he threatened. He was maddened with fear. He could see his life being ended here in the wilderness. All he could think of was preserving himself. With a strength which came from that fear, he jabbed an elbow into Wolfrunner's stomach. Acting quickly while Wolfrunner was doubled over in pain, he cut the rope that bound him and Danielle together. Moving rapidly into the shadows, he fled into the night.

Danielle lay in a daze of pain. She couldn't yet see who her rescuer was, nor did she know if she had been rescued, or if she had simply become another Indian's prisoner. Rolling to her knees, she tried to clear her mind. She didn't know whether to run or just stay where she was. Suppose this Indian was one of her uncle's warriors? But he was alone—surely if this man was a Blood Blackfoot, her uncle would be with him.

She'd heard his voice when he'd spoken to Scar Face, but since he hadn't spoken in English, she hadn't recognized him as anyone she knew.

Hearing the sound of horses' hooves, Danielle knew that Scar Face had ridden away. Realizing that she had no time to waste if she was going to gain her freedom, Danielle jumped to her feet and ran into the woods. This was her bid for freedom. She had to get away from the Indian who had frightened Scar Face away.

Bushes reached out and tore at her clothing and her skin. It was so dark she stumbled over something and fell. A scream issued from her lips as she groped in the darkness and discovered a dead body and knew it must be Tall Bear. Her desperation came as much from her fear as from the need to be free and she staggered to her feet, pushing onward. She feared that if the unknown assailant were to catch her, she would meet with the same fate as Tall Bear.

She had hardly gone any distance when the man reached out and captured her from behind, swinging her up into his arms. Wild unleashed fear tugged at her heart. She struggled and kicked out at the man, but he twisted her around and held her firmly against his body so she couldn't move.

"You have nothing to fear from me. I am not your captor. I have come to take you back to your aunt and uncle, Danielle."

Danielle's struggling suddenly ceased, and for the first time in days she felt safe. She trembled as a feeling well-being washed over her. She recognized Wolfrunner's voice and knew she had been saved! Resting her head against his shoulder, she allowed tears to wash freely down her face. For a long moment

Wolfrunner held her, gently stroking her tangled hair, comforting her without saying a word.

When she stopped crying, he set her on her feet, and she sank to her knees. "How can I thank you for saving me?"

"You are not safe yet, Danielle. We must not stay here. Scar Face could return at any time. Are you well enough to travel?"

"Yes, let's leave this place at once!" she cried, looking back over her shoulder. "Where is my uncle?"

"He is looking for you."

"Are there others with you?"

"No. I am alone."

Danielle allowed him to lead her forward. She was so overcome with relief, she couldn't think past being free. She was like a child who had no will of her own and was allowing Wolfrunner to lead her where he would. She knew she was dependent on him for her very life: in fact she owed this man her life.

When they reached the clearing where Wolfrunner had tied his horse, he muttered under his breath. "It seems I underestimated Scar Face—he has taken my horse. The fight is not yet ended."

Danielle's senses were too dulled to hear what Wolfrunner was saying. She was so tired and emotionally drained that all she wanted to do was lie down and rest.

Wolfrunner knew that they were vulnerable, and he must find shelter to hide Danielle for the night. When she stumbled and fell to her knees, he picked her up and carried her. Closing her eyes, she rested her head against his shoulder. In no time at all she had fallen asleep, wrapped in a warm blanket of safety.

190

As Wolfrunner came out of the woods and into the moonlight, he looked down at the girl he carried in his arms. There was no evidence of her former beauty. Her lips were swollen and her face bruised and dirty. He didn't imagine that Scar Face and his companion had left her untouched. He felt pity in his heart for the poor pathetic girl who was more white than Indian. He doubted she would ever again be the same proud beauty she had once been.

After walking for a long while, he found a safe place against the face of the cliff. It had two boulders on either side and would be easy to protect. Here they would rest for the remainder of the night.

Placing Danielle down on the soft grass, he sat down beside her, with his senses alert to any danger. He knew that Scar Face would be following them. Now the hunter had become the hunted. Wolfrunner knew if he had been alone he could easily outsmart Scar Face, but the girl would slow him down, making his task of saving her much harder.

Danielle moaned in her sleep and Wolfrunner placed his hand on her face. That seemed to relax her and she curled up close to him.

He glanced down at her slight body and wondered how she had lasted as long as she had. Surely Scar Face had been overly cruel to her. He thought of Joanna and how happy she would be to have her niece back. Wolfrunner would do anything to make his chief's wife smile. She was and always had been a ray of sunshine in his life. He didn't love her as a man loves a woman, but rather as one would worship the brightness of sun without wanting to possess it.

His eyes watched the dark shadows, for he knew he

191

must not fall asleep. This girl was his to take care of and he must protect her with his life, if need be.

He couldn't help but think of the strange quirk of fate that had placed her in his hands. She thought she was so high above him, but now she would have to depend on him to survive.

He watched the rise and fall of her chest and couldn't help noticing that her creamy white breasts were poking through her torn blouse. Feeling a stirring in his loins, he turned quickly away. He didn't want to desire this girl. He didn't even like her.

Chapter Fourteen

On the train ride back to Philadelphia, Morgan was deep in thought as he pondered his future plans. He was oblivious to the crowded condition of the train, and was hardly aware when the train made a stop to take on more coal.

In searching his heart he found that he wanted to ask Skyler to be his wife. His head was filled with plans for their future together. He had received his orders to go to Fort Laramie in Idaho Territory to help put down an Indian uprising. If he could convince Skyler to marry him, she could go with him. Did he really want to stay in the Cavalry? He was a doctor, and a damned good one, but he'd seen so many wounded and dying in the war, that he had been sickened by it.

As a field doctor he had been forced to operate under the most appalling conditions. Ofttimes he had removed an arm or leg simply because he hadn't had time to save them.

He thought back to the battle at Fredericksburg, Virginia, in December of sixty-two. The Union forces had sustained heavy losses. In the four days of that battle, a continuous stream of boats brought the dead and dying down the Rappahannock River to the field hospital. The Union casualties had numbered twelve thousand after that battle. Morgan had gone for days without sleep. He thought of how he would have to stop every so often so the bloody table he had used to operate on could be washed down. He hadn't felt like a doctor that day, but more like a butcher.

Looking back, he knew he could have done no differently. Time had been against him and the other three doctors who had fought the life-and-death battle. They had been forced to work with speed instead of compassion. Perhaps that was why he wanted to go to Fort Laramie, so he could redeem himself in his own mind.

Pushing the morbid memories out of his thoughts, he allowed himself to think back to the first night he had met Skyler Dancing. Little had he known that their meeting would change his whole life.

He smiled to himself. One would have thought that bells should have gone off and the sky should have become awash with bright colors when he first met her. He hadn't had any warning that the mysterious niece of Taggart James would touch his life so deeply.

He wondered what it was about her life that she wouldn't share with him. There was definitely something she was keeping locked inside. He leaned back and closed his eyes thoughtfully. What if she didn't feel as deeply about him as he did about her? He was sure she felt something, but it might not be love. He thought of her soft smile and the haunting sound of her voice. It seemed to him that she could easily be the role model for what the perfect woman should be. Many lovely young women had moved through Morgan's life, but at the moment none of them seemed to stand out. His whole heart was filled with violet eyes, ebony hair, and a voice so hauntingly sweet it sounded like music to his ears.

Never having been a man to wait until things came to him, Morgan was armed with self-assurance. He was confident that Skyler would one day belong to him.

Skyler stood in her Uncle Tag's business office which overlooked the giant James shipping yard. There were huge wooden skeletons of ships, with dozens of men laboring to turn out the finished product. It was hard for her to imagine that one could get on a ship and sail to far-off places.

"How do you feel about all this, my dear?" Tag asked, gesturing toward the shipyard.

"It is all a little overwhelming. Is it true that James ships sail all over the world?"

"Yes, and right here is where we build the ships that are bought by countries all over the world. What do you think about that?"

"I am impressed."

"I brought you here today so you would be aware that you own a part of this business. Yours and Little Hawk's share comes to you through Joanna."

"I cannot see that I would ever have any need for money, Uncle Tag. I was perfectly content with my life as it once was."

Skyler stared out the window, watching the men climbing on giant scaffolds in the belly of the ships, without really seeing them. "I am confused about many things," she admitted. "There is so much I do not know about. You and Aunt Alexandria brought me to your home and taught me many things about your way of life. But you forgot to tell me how this might leave a lasting effect on my life."

Tag moved over to stand behind her. "Alexandria and I have sensed that you are troubled, but we passed it off as homesickness. Were we wrong?"

She turned around and looked at him with sad eyes. "I do not miss my home as much as I did in the beginning." She looked past him and stared at the rolls of charts and papers that were piled on his desk. "I am so confused, Uncle Tag. I don't know what I am feeling."

He saw the troubled expression in her eyes and his heart went out to her. At the moment she reminded him of Joanna, and he wanted to comfort her if he could. "Do you want to tell me what is bothering you?"

"I have to tell someone. Help me understand what is happening to me, Uncle Tag."

He took her arm and seated her in a chair, then bent down so he would be on eye-level with her. "If you should want to talk, I am a very good listener, my dear."

Skyler lowered her lashes, at a loss as how to tell her uncle about her feelings for Morgan Prescott. "I don't know how to begin," she said with feeling.

He placed his hand on hers. "This concerns Morgan, doesn't it, Skyler," he said with a perception that surprised her.

"Yes, but how did you know?"

Tag smiled at her. "It wasn't so hard to deduce. I

could see that he was interested in you. Your aunt and I have noticed you moping around since Morgan has been away."

"Uncle Tag, I don't know what to do," she said, tightening her grip on his hand. "I think I love him."

"How does he feel about you?"

"I don't know. He said we would talk about our feelings when he returns."

"Honey, I have known Morgan for a long time. If he says he has strong feelings for you, then you can believe him."

"I cannot allow him to love me, Uncle Tag. He doesn't know that I must leave at the end of summer."

Tag took her hand and pulled her to her feet. Leading her out of his office, he pointed her toward the town of Philadelphia. "This may be where your future lies, my dear. Your mother knew when she allowed you to leave your home that you might choose to stay here. Only you can decide where your life will go from here on out. You will have to ask yourself if you love Morgan enough to leave your mother and father. If you do, you must know what you will be giving up. Weigh the consequences before you decide."

"Uncle Tag, if I tell Morgan about myself he may not understand. What would he think of me if he knew I was half Indian?"

"I don't know, Skyler. I have to be honest with you. Morgan may turn away from you when he finds out. Many people don't understand the Indian way; Morgan may be one of them."

Tag turned Skyler around to face him. "I'd like to tell you Morgan would understand about you, Skyler, but I just don't know. I can't advise you on this; you'll have to decide for yourself whether you want to tell him. I can tell you that people who aren't willing to take a chance oftentimes miss out on happiness."

Skyler looked over her uncle's shoulder toward the west, the direction of her home. She could feel something tugging at her heart. If she returned home without telling Morgan who she was, she wouldn't have to face his rejection. He would be coming back to Philadelphia any day now, and she would have to make a decision one way or the other.

Tag patted her affectionately. "I don't think the situation is as grim as you believe it to be. Nature and time have a way of solving many of our dilemmas. Would you like me to speak to Morgan about your background?"

"No. I will have to do it myself. I just hope I have the courage when the time comes."

"If he truly loves you, it will not matter to him who your mother and father are."

"Perhaps," she answered with a faraway look in her eyes. "Then again I may have misread Morgan. It could be that he has no strong feelings for me at all."

It was a lazy Sunday afternoon without a cloud in the sky. The warm breeze picked up the scent of wild honeysuckle, and a hummingbird flew through the air, moving from flower to flower. Skyler was in the summerhouse with her aunt and uncle as they enjoyed a quiet companionship. Tag was reading a newspaper and Skyler was helping Alexandria wind a ball of wool yarn. The usual pitcher of lemonade was sitting on the glass table along with a plate of honeycakes.

Hearing someone coming down the graveled pathway, they all looked up to see who it was. When Skyler saw the blue uniform, her heart skipped a beat. She had wanted to see Morgan, but now that he had come, she felt shy and nervous.

Tag caught her eye and gave her a wink. "Well, it seems Morgan has become partial to our company. Why do you think he pays us so much attention lately, Alex?" he asked, chuckling aloud.

"I believe he likes my lemonade," she answered, smiling at her young niece.

Morgan slowly climbed the steps to the summerhouse. His eyes were on Skyler and he was thinking how lovely she looked in her rose-colored gown. "Hello, ladies," he said, smiling. "I came to rescue you in case Tag's conversation is beginning to bore you." His eyes rested on Skyler, and he smiled at her slight blush.

"How did you find Washington?" Tag asked, laying the paper aside and indicating the young doctor should join him on the window seat.

"Hot and noisy," Morgan answered, sitting down and stretching his long legs out in front of him. "There is quite a stir over the Military Commission's trial to convict the accomplices in the assassination of President Lincoln. The people are in a fever pitch and crying for blood."

"I was just reading about the trials. What was the outcome?" Tag asked with interest.

"All eight were found guilty. Four were sentenced to hang; Doctor Samuel Mudd and two others have been sentenced to life in prison, while Edward Spangler received a six-year sentence."

"I hope the hue and cry will die down now," Tag said thoughtfully. "It's time now to get on with pulling the country back together."

"I agree, Tag, but it will be a long and painful process. If President Lincoln had lived, I believe he could have better accomplished reuniting our country. I'm not sure Johnson is up to the task."

"Did you happen to see President Johnson while you were there, Morgan?" Alexandria wanted to know.

"Yes, I attended a White House luncheon, where I was introduced to him."

"What was your opinion of him?" Tag asked.

"He is rather forceful and speaks more to the common people. I believe he is out of his depth with trying to run this country."

"Let us pray that he finds his way," Alexandria observed as she took the ball of yarn from Skyler and placed it in her sewing basket.

Skyler watched Morgan as he talked. He was highly intelligent and knowledgeable. He talked of things that she knew nothing about. How could she have thought for one moment that he was interested in her? she wondered sadly.

"I received my orders while in Washington," Morgan said, looking at Skyler. "I fear I have been sent to the end of the earth."

"Where?" Tag asked, watching Skyler's face.

"General Conners has been sent to Fort Laramie in Idaho Territory, and he has asked that I accompany him."

"Why should you be sent so far away?" Alexandria asked.

"There is trouble with the Arapaho. They have been

attacking the Overland Mail stations and stages. They have even started cutting the telegraph lines. Washington wants the raids stopped."

Tag watched Skyler closely as he asked the next question. "How do you feel about the Indians, Morgan?"

He shrugged his shoulders. "They are savages. I suppose I share many soldiers' views, that the only good Indian is a dead Indian!"

Skyler gasped aloud and felt the pain of his words in the depth of her soul. He could have said nothing that would have wounded her more deeply. Out of his mouth had come the words that had condemned her love to a slow death. He hated and despised all she stood for. Her mother had been right, the white race could never understand the Indian.

"Would you then want to kill all the Indian women and children, Colonel Prescott?" She rose to her feet and faced him with an angry sparkle in her eyes.

"I am told an Indian, be it man, woman, or child, would cut your throat as easily as you would take an afternoon stroll, Miss Dancing. But you shouldn't concern yourself with such matters. You shouldn't ever have to worry about anything past what lovely gown to wear."

"You are wrong, sir. I am not some milksop that has no mind of her own. I have been taught to think for myself, and I will leave the choosing of what gown to wear to some weak-kneed ninny!"

Morgan frowned. What had he said that set Skyler off? How lovely she was with her eyes blazing and her black hair flowing in the warm breeze. No, she wasn't the kind of woman who would think only of frivolities.

One of the things he loved most about her was her strong will. "I can see that the Indians have a champion in you. I hate to disillusion you, but they are unworthy of your concern. We have tried to educate them, with little success. We have tried to teach them how to live, but they prefer to live like animals."

"Do you think it so strange that a people would want to live as their ancestors did? What makes you think the way you live is so wonderful, that you should have the right to cram it down the Indians' throats?"

Morgan looked at Skyler in amazement. Oh, yes, she was different from all other women. She had a brain and wasn't afraid to use it.

Tag and Alexandria exchanged glances. They knew what this was doing to Skyler, but they didn't know how to stop what was happening.

"Why do you condemn a whole people just because of a few renegades?" Tag asked hurriedly, fearing Skyler would say too much.

"You are far too generous, Tag. If I were a soldier instead of a doctor, I would have no qualms about doing my duty. I would much rather be shooting at the Indians than fire on my brothers to the south. But I am not a soldier—I am a doctor. My job is to save lives, not take them."

Skyler felt her whole body tremble with rage. How could she have thought she had any feelings for this man. He was not worthy of her love or her tears. Morgan was the kind of man her mother had warned her about. A torrent of feelings rushed through her body, and she didn't know how to deal with them at the moment. She needed to be alone to think.

"If you will excuse me, I feel a headache coming on,"

she said, running down the summerhouse steps and racing toward the house.

"Wait!" Morgan called after her, but Skyler didn't acknowledge him. She ran for the safety of the house as if her life depended on it.

Tag and Alexandria watched with troubled eyes as Morgan rushed after their niece. They both knew the young doctor had wounded Skyler—perhaps beyond repair. Tag started to go after her when Alexandria placed a restraining hand on his arm.

"Let them work it out among themselves, Tag. You can do nothing at this point."

"He hurt her badly, Alexandria."

"I know, but I fear if we interfered, we would only make matters worse."

"Damn it, I never knew Morgan to be so merciless. How can he condemn a whole race of people, for the sins of a few?"

"Like many people we know, Morgan speaks out of ignorance. He has never had the chance to know the Indians as you and I have. Give him time."

"I don't think even time can help him now. If Skyler is anything like Joanna, she will never forgive Morgan for what he said today."

Morgan caught up with Skyler and spun her around to face him. He saw the tears in her eyes and was at a loss as to what had caused them. "I need to talk to you, Skyler," he said softly, aching at the sight of her tears, and knowing he was somehow responsible.

"I have nothing to say to you. Release me this moment!" She was hurt and angry. The last thing she wanted to do was talk to him.

"I don't understand what has come over you, Skyler.

I kept thinking the whole time I was in Washington about how I would approach you. I have something very important that I want to ask you."

"Whatever it is, I do not want to hear it, Colonel. You and I have nothing to say to one another," she replied, jerking her arm free of his grasp.

His eyes narrowed. "I have a great deal to say to you. I came here today to ask you to be my wife!"

Skyler felt as if a sharp knife had just sliced through her heart. How ironic it was—moments ago he had voiced his hatred for the Indian race, and now he was asking one of that race to be his wife.

"I don't want you, Morgan. Go away and leave me alone. You and I are not suited to one another!"

"Are we not?" he hissed, pulling her into his arms. "I can damned well prove to you that you are wrong."

His arms tightened about her like iron bands and his lips sought hers brutally. The kiss was not one of love, but of anger and passion. Skyler tried to pull away, but the blood in her body seemed to run hot. She found her lips opening to receive his kiss. As when he had kissed her before, she felt her head spinning and her heart pounding. Her struggling ceased as she gave in to the wondrous feelings he awoke in her body. Her mind knew it was wrong to be in his arms—he and men like him were enemies to her people. Still, she couldn't stop the tide of love that filled her heart.

When he raised his head, his eyes were fever-bright. "Tell me we aren't meant for each other, Skyler. I know damned well I love you. If you say you don't feel the same about me, I'll know you are lying."

"Leave me alone, Morgan. I don't want to be pulled into your world, and you could never fit into mine," she cried, turning away from him.

He grabbed her by the shoulders and spun her around to face him. "I don't understand this talk about your world and my world. My God, don't you know what has happened between us? Are you not aware that I—"

She clamped her hands over her ears and shook her head. "Do not say it. You and I can never be together. If you knew the truth about me, you would only hate me."

"What is this secret that you try so hard to cover up? No matter what you have done in the past, I will love you. Nothing can change that."

"I do not want you, Morgan. Men like you are the enemy." Tears were streaming down her face as she looked into his eyes. "Just leave it alone. It would be far better for us both if you were to just leave and never look back."

"What could you have done that you are so ashamed of? I find it hard to believe that you could have anything in your past to hide."

Her eyes seemed to gleam, and she raised her head proudly. "I am not ashamed of who I am, Morgan. I am proud of both my mother and father."

He shook his head in exasperation. "I am not understanding anything about this conversation. What have your mother and father got to do with the way I feel about you? If you are trying to tell me that you are illegitimate, I can assure you it won't make one damned bit of difference to me."

Skyler turned her back to him and closed her eyes. What she really wanted to do was be in his arms and pour out her heart to him, but her secret must never be told. Would it not be far better for him to think she didn't love him than to tell him the truth. She realized more than ever that she must not allow her secret be known. If she did, Danielle would have to live with the consequences.

"I can tell you no more, Morgan. This is the last time I will ever see you. I am going home before too long, and I will never come back to Philadelphia. This is good-bye for us."

Without giving him a chance to digest what she had just told him, she turned and ran into the house. Morgan stood as if turned to stone, and his mind was in a turmoil. If that was the way Skyler wanted it, then so be it. He didn't need her in his life.

After a time, he walked to the front of the house, mounted his horse, and rode away without a backward glance.

Skyler stood before her bedroom window, looking out on the lawn. Her heart felt so heavy that it actually ached. Her family had been right in this pretense to protect her from men like Morgan Prescott. Had she come to Philadelphia as Sky Dancer, she would probably have been shunned in the streets.

What kind of race was it that preached Christian charity, and then condemned a whole race, just because its people had different beliefs.

Oh, Morgan, Morgan. I don't want to love you. You will destroy me, and yet . . . I cannot help myself.

Chapter Fifteen

Danielle woke when someone lifted her to a sitting position. It was still dark, and she couldn't see very well. Her first thought was that it was Scar Face whose insistent hands shook her from her sleep. She flung out her hand and caught her tormenter with a stunning blow across the face. As Danielle came fully awake, she saw the red handprint on Wolfrunner's face and felt ashamed. Fearing he would retaliate in kind, she scrambled to her knees and moved back away from him; after all, this wasn't the first time she'd struck him. She remembered his anger on the other occasion when she'd lashed out at him.

"I'm sorry, I thought you were—"

His face was grim and his dark eyes flashed. "I know what you thought," he cut in, touching his cheek. "You look to be but a weak woman, but you deliver a powerful blow."

"I said I was sorry." He seemed almost amused, but she couldn't be sure. She still watched him carefully for any sign of anger.

He stood up and moved away. "I am glad to see your spirit has not been broken by Scar Face and his friend." She saw the smile now playing on his lips. "You are much stronger than you appear." He reached up and touched his cheek once more.

She staggered to her feet, finding she wasn't as strong as he thought her to be. Her legs felt shaky—she was weak from hunger, and she wasn't sure she could stand for very long. "I'm glad you killed Tall Bear, and I wish you had killed Scar Face as well. I detest them both—they were revolting."

"You may have much cause to wish for Scar Face's death. We have not seen the last of him."

Danielle looked at her rescuer. "Do you mean he will come after us?"

"I am sure of it. He has a powerful hate in his heart. He will think he has the advantage, since I have you to slow me down."

Danielle felt his insult hit home. "If you feel I am a burden, why did you come after me?"

"Do not think I came after you for your sake. For my part, Scar Face and Tall Bear would have been welcome to you. What I have done was for Flaming Hair, since she was suffering over your disappearance."

Danielle turned away, not wanting him to see how his words wounded her. She couldn't blame Wolfrunner for feeling as he did. She had said some horrible things to him that she now wished she could retract. There had to be a way for her to show him she had changed. She was no longer the spoiled little girl who had always insisted on having her own way in everything. Suddenly a thought came to her. In all her troubles she had almost forgotten that her grandmother was dying.

"How is my grandmother?" she asked.

"Not that you would care, but Sun Woman now walks in the spirit world."

Hot tears burned her eyes. She *did* care about her grandmother's death. When she had first come to the village, she'd been angry because she had been forced to come against her will. She'd struck out at everyone wanting to punish them because she was miserable. Danielle would always have to live with the fact that her grandmother had died thinking she didn't care about her.

"Come, it is almost daylight and we must be on our way. I would not like to be caught in this valley when the sun comes up."

"Are we not going to eat?" she asked.

"I fear all the food I had was on my horse, and Scar Face has it now."

Danielle sighed heavily. There was no need to complain about her plight. Was she not better off now than she had been this time yesterday? She walked along behind Wolfrunner, thinking she could sleep for a week without ever waking. Visions of roast turkey and buttered bread danced in her head. She remembered the times Alexandria had tried to coax her to eat, and she had refused. She doubted that she would ever take food for granted again.

Wolfrunner set a steady pace for Danielle to follow, and she was determined to keep up. Many times she was so weary she thought she might drop, but she dared not complain. For some strange reason she found herself wanting to win Wolfrunner's respect. She also feared that if she didn't keep up with him he'd leave her behind.

It was long after the noon hour when they finally did stop to rest. Danielle collapsed on the ground and closed her eyes, too exhausted to move.

It was quiet and peaceful among the tall pine trees. A steady breeze cooled her overheated body, and she felt herself getting drowsy. Moments passed, and suddenly Danielle felt a sensation like someone was staring at her. Opening her eyes slowly, she found Wolfrunner sitting nearby with his eyes resting on her face.

Moving to a sitting position, she realized her torn gown did little to cover the upper half of her body.

"I'm hungry," she said, pulling the bodice together. She must not forget that she was alone with a savage, and if she wasn't careful, there was no telling what he might do, Danielle cautioned herself.

"I have nothing to give you," he said, turning away. "You will have to wait until I can kill some game. There are not even any berries for you to eat in this valley."

She noticed he was whittling on a tree branch, and looked at him questioningly. "What are you doing, Wolfrunner? Are you making a weapon?"

"I am making a spear. The only weapon I have is this knife. We will need a spear for protection before we reach my village."

"Do you really think Scar Face will come after us? Perhaps you frightened him into never coming back."

"He will come. I am the one who gave him the scar that earned him his name. He has never forgiven me for that. What I do not know is why he risked Windhawk's wrath to capture you. He is a very foolish man."

Danielle looked into troubled dark eyes and felt something like fear race down her spine. "Scar Face thinks I am Sky Dancer. He hates my uncle because he thinks Windhawk killed his father, Chief Running Elk."

Wolfrunner shook his head. "Windhawk did slay Scar Face's father many summers ago."

"No, you are wrong. It was my father who killed Running Elk."

"That is not what I have been told by the Piegan," Wolfrunner said, looking at her doubtfully.

"My father was but a boy when he killed Running Elk, so it was decided to let the people think Windhawk killed the man. My father said Windhawk took the blame to protect him in case anyone wanted to seek revenge. Apparently that is just what happened. It's strange, though, that Scar Face would wait all these years to act."

Wolfrunner stood up and tested the point of his newly carved spear. "It does not matter who killed the Piegan chief. Scar Face thinks you are Windhawk's daughter. Even if he knew you were only Windhawk's niece, he would still come for you. His honor is at stake now. He fears I will tell the Blackfoot that he is a coward. He also knows he is a dead man if Windhawk finds out he was the one who took you. There will be nowhere he can hide to escape Windhawk's wrath. That gives him two reasons to try and stop us from reaching the village." Wolfrunner knew there was also a third reason that Scar Face would come after them: Scar Face hated him almost as much as he hated Windhawk.

Danielle's eyes fearfully searched the countryside. "I am frightened, Wolfrunner. How will we ever make it back to the village?"

Wolfrunner balanced the spear in his hand and then took aim and launched it through the air. The missile sailed through the sky and landed with its point sticking into a dead tree stump. "You need not worry. Scar Face will not harm you as long as I am alive," he said, walking away to retrieve his spear.

Danielle's eyes followed the man who had saved her from Scar Face. For the first time, she took a long look at him. He wore only a leather breechcloth, which did much to call attention to his hard lean body. A breastplate of porcupine quills rested against his wide chest. His ebony hair hung loosely about his shoulders and was ornamented with two black raven feathers.

Retrieving his spear, Wolfrunner turned to her and she studied his face. His dark eyes seemed to move past her with bored indifference. His cheekbones were high, his chin was stubbornly set. He would be considered handsome, she supposed, but not to her. She had never found dark skin appealing, and his eyes were too fierce to suit her.

Danielle owed this man her life. He had rescued her even though he barely tolerated her as a person. She was sure he was waiting for her to collapse into a heap, but she would show him that she could keep up with him if it killed her. She would prove to him, and herself, that she could last as long as he could.

"We must go," he said, giving her a look she couldn't define.

It took all Danielle's strength just to stand. She wondered if she would really be able to keep pace with this man who was trained to withstand many hardships.

When Wolfrunner bent down in front of her with his

knife drawn, she stepped back fearfully.

"I must cut the bottom of your gown. You will trip over it and slow me down."

Danielle bit her lip and nodded, knowing he was right. Looking away, she couldn't watch as he cut the material up to her knees, showing off her pantaloons. He stood back and gave her a dark look, then nodded.

"You must take off the undergarment. It, too, will only slow you down."

"No! I will never remove my— No, it is unthinkable. What would people say?"

"You will do as I say, or I will do it for you," he threatened. The dark look he gave her was enough to send shivers down her spine.

"I will do it," she said quickly as he moved toward her. "You must turn your back though."

He gave her a look that showed he didn't care to look at anything she had to show. When he turned his back, she quickly stepped out of her pantaloons, and then tossed them behind a bush. Looking down at her appearance, she felt almost naked. Her blouse was ripped down the front, and her legs were showing all the way to her knees. If her friends in Philadelphia could see her now they would be horrified.

Wolfrunner turned back to her and looked her over. "Good, now you can move more freely. I warn you that I will not stop for you if you fail. You are nothing like Sky Dancer. She would know how to follow a warrior's orders without question."

He moved away, and Danielle knew he would indeed leave her if she didn't keep up with him. She followed along behind him, mentally forcing one foot in front of the other. She had the feeling that Wolfrunner was right about her cousin, Sky Dancer. She would have very little trouble keeping up with Wolfrunner. But she imagined that if she were her cousin, Wolfrunner wouldn't say such cruel and cutting things to her either.

Danielle was beginning to see how shallow and useless her life had been until now. Left alone, she would never survive in this wild untamed wilderness. She had begun to examine her life, and she wasn't at all pleased with the picture she had of herself. Danielle knew if she were to come out of this ordeal alive, she would be a different person—hopefully even a better person.

Danielle and Wolfrunner had been traveling southward all day. Danielle was unaware that by late afternoon Wolfrunner had slowed his pace so he wouldn't push her beyond her endurance. Not that he cared for her, she thought bitterly; he just didn't want a sick woman on his hands.

As the sun began to set, he stopped and motioned for her to rest. Danielle leaned her head against a trunk of a tree and took a deep breath. She was exhausted, but proud of the fact that she hadn't complained. Of course, she reminded herself, this was just the first day of traveling on foot. She had little doubt her strength and courage would be tested to the limit before they reached the safety of the Blackfoot village.

"Do you know how to use a knife, white woman?" Wolfrunner asked, breaking into her thoughts.

Danielle turned to face him and saw him watching her closely. "I . . . no. I have never had any need to use a knife," she admitted, wondering why he should call her white woman. She had as much Indian blood in her veins as Sky Dancer. Now wasn't the time to belabor the point, however.

His eyes narrowed. "I will leave the knife for you. Let us hope if the need is such, you will learn quickly to use it."

She reached out her hand toward him. "You aren't leaving me alone, are you?"

"I will not be gone long. You should be in no danger. You have but to call out and I will hear you."

Danielle wanted to beg him not to leave her, but pride sealed her lips. Taking the knife he held out to her, she turned away. His movements were so quiet she didn't hear him as he melted into the evening shadows. When she turned back, he had disappeared from sight.

Sinking down to her knees, Danielle felt alone for the first time in her life. It was so quiet, even the birds seemed to be silent. She felt as if she had been abandoned and was the only person left on earth.

She sat huddled in her misery, watching the night shadows move across the land. Strange sounds now came from the woods. Danielle laid her face against the rough tree trunk, trembling with fear.

"You are a coward," she said aloud, hoping the sound of her own voice would bring her courage. "Sky Dancer wouldn't be frightened if she were left alone."

Clutching the knife in her hand, she stood up and leaned her back against the tree. What would she do if Scar Face came upon her? Suppose some wild animal were to attack her?

With the darkness came a cold wind blowing out of the north. Danielle kept her back to the tree while her eyes searched the darkness. Her hunger was all but forgotten, because it had been replaced by the stronger emotion—fear. Fear seemed to seep through every pore of her skin and dance down the back of her spine. The eerie sounds coming from deep in the woods seemed magnified, and she expected a bear or some other fierce animal to come charging out at her any moment. She shuddered, and her hand tightened on the hilt of the knife. She prayed that Wolfrunner would soon return.

Wolfrunner backtracked to find out if they were being followed. Finding no sign of Scar Face, he set out at a steady run to find food for the white girl.

So far the girl had surprised him. He had expected her to cry and complain. His jaw clamped into a grim line. She would cry out in anger and fear many times before they reached the village. She was soft, and he did not admire her. He would feed her and keep her alive, but should she fall behind or become too much of a burden, he would leave her.

When Wolfrunner returned to where he had left Danielle, he found her huddled by a tree, fast asleep. She still clutched the knife in her hand and didn't even wake as he sat down beside her.

He placed his small bounty of berries and roots in his pouch, thinking the girl needed sleep more than food.

Hearing Danielle's deep breathing, he turned his face away and closed his eyes. Even though he appeared to be asleep, his ears were attuned to hear any danger that might come. He had been trained since birth to fight and survive in the wilderness. He had little doubt that he could outsmart Scar Face if it weren't for the girl. He realized that he must not take the trail that Scar Face would expect him to take. He would have to go the long way around, through the grassy prairies. It would take many days longer to reach the village that way, but it would be safer for the girl. He couldn't allow Scar Face to get his hands on her again.

Opening his eyes, he allowed them to roam over the girl. How could she look so like Sky Dancer and yet be so different. He had always looked on Sky Dancer with awe and reverence. She was a Blackfoot princess, but then so was this girl. Danielle provoked deeper and more disturbing emotions within him. He found himself wanting to reach out and cradle her in his arms so she would feel warm and protected. His body seemed to stir to life and this troubled him more than anything. He frowned, knowing what her reaction would be should he take her in his arms. She would scream and struggle, thinking he was trying to ravish her.

Turning his dark eyes away, he knew he was in danger of losing his heart to this unworthy white girl. The sooner he returned her to Windhawk and Joanna, the sooner he would be rid of her. She was beginning to creep into his mind more and more. There were many Indian maidens for him to choose from. Why had he never wanted one of them? Why should this girl he didn't even like make his blood run hot?

He wrestled with himself, trying to cleanse his mind of this girl, but was not successful. Yes, she did make his blood run hot, and he had to admit that he wanted her.

Turning over on his back, he watched the stars twinkle in the ebony sky. Was he not a warrior in command of his own destiny and feelings? He would never allow a woman to enter into his heart unbidden. This girl was unworthy of a Blackfoot warrior.

He watched as a shooting star streaked across the sky, leaving a fiery trail in its wake. He knew he was going to have to be strong and deny his desire for Danielle. Was he not Wolfrunner, one of Windhawk's most trusted warriors?

His dark eyes moved across the heavens, and he sought inner peace within himself. That peace did not come, not even when the first hint of the morning sun lit the eastern sky.

Chapter Sixteen

Morgan had called at the James house on several occasions, but Skyler always refused to see him. He also received a cool reception from Alexandria and that puzzled him. What had he done?

Skyler had come to the agonizing realization that to see Morgan, and talk to him, would only prolong her pain and make forgetting him even more difficult. She rotated between loving and hating him. She couldn't understand how he could be so small-minded as to hate a whole race of people just because they were different from him.

When she was in the privacy of her room at night, she often cried herself to sleep. She had begun to count the days until it would be time for her to return to her village. Perhaps when she was back home with her family again she would forget all about Morgan Prescott.

Skyler tied the pink bonnet beneath her chin and

rushed out the front door to join her Aunt Alexandria, who was already waiting for her in the buggy. They were going to have tea with Mrs. Wendham and her daughter Priscilla. Skyler wished she didn't have to go. It was very apparent that her aunt was trying to keep her busy so she wouldn't dwell on her unhappiness.

Her aunt and uncle had said very little to her about the incident in the summerhouse. She knew they were sorry she had been hurt, but there wasn't anything anyone could do about it now.

Entering the carriage, she arranged her pink and white gown so it wouldn't wrinkle. As she gazed out the window, she saw it was an overcast day, and it looked as if it might rain before the day was over.

Since the Wendham's home adjoined the Prescott estate, it took no time at all to arrive at the neighbor's front door. As they climbed the stairs to the stone house, Mrs. Wendham and her daughter came out to greet them. Priscilla linked her arm through Skyler's and led her into the house, declaring her gown was the loveliest creation she had ever seen.

There was polite conversation over tea, and afterward Priscilla took Skyler up to her bedroom. They were seated at the window seat, and Priscilla smiled brightly.

"I have a secret to tell you if you promise you won't tell another living soul, Skyler." Priscilla had light brown eyes and red hair. She was so light-complected, she tended to freckle across her nose. Pretty, was the only way Skyler could describe her friend.

"I promise," Skyler said, puzzled.

"I am madly in love. If my mother ever found out, she would confine me to the house and never let me out again."

"Why would she do such a thing? Does she not want you to love a man?"

"Of course she does, but only if she thinks the man comes up to scratch. She expects me to marry in my own class."

"I do not think I understand. What is your class?"

"Skyler, you are such a silly goose sometimes. You know what I mean—a man with the same interests and who comes from the same background as I do."

"Oh, yes, I see. It is the same with me. My father would never allow me to marry . . . one who . . ." Skyler's voice trailed off. She had been about to say her father would never allow her to marry a warrior who was not from one of the wealthier families. "Who is this man, and where did you meet him?" she asked instead.

"His name is Billy Kirby, and he works at Donaldson's Printing Shop. He hopes to own the shop one day. I met him in the park one Sunday and we were both drawn to each other immediately. We try to meet in the park every Sunday when I can get away."

"Priscilla, I do not think it is a good thing to go behind your parents' back. Could you not tell them about your feelings for this man?"

"Heaven forbid! They would never understand."

"Tell me about this Billy. What is he like?"

Priscilla's eyes took on a dreamy look. "He is very handsome, with blond curly hair and bright blue eyes. I wish you could meet him." Priscilla giggled. "No, perhaps I don't want you to meet him. You are much too pretty."

Skyler ignored the compliment. "I do not have a good feeling about this, Priscilla. It is not right to go against what your father and mother would want for you."

"If you loved someone and you knew your parents wouldn't approve, would you just give him up?"

Skyler closed her eyes for a moment. "If someone is wrong for me, even if I loved him, I would turn away from him. The man I marry will have to understand me."

"You are stronger than me, or else you have never loved someone as I love Billy. His language is coarse and his manners are appalling, but still I love him."

Skyler thought of Morgan and felt renewed pain in her heart. She loved him so deeply that it hurt to even think about him, but he was not for her. "To love is to feel pain sometimes. I do not think I want to love."

"Sometimes you talk in riddles, Skyler, and I don't understand you. Even though we are the same age, I sometimes feel you are years older than I. There is something very mysterious about you."

"My mother would say I am too serious about life. I take after my father."

"It has not escaped my notice that you never really talk about yourself other than in general terms. I like you very much, but I don't really know that much about you."

Skyler smiled at her friend. "There is nothing to know. My life has been very dull up until the time I came to Philadelphia."

"I know a secret that you don't know," Priscilla said, clasping .her hands together and looking at Skyler smugly. "I know someone who is very intrigued with you."

"Who?" Skyler couldn't help but ask.

222

"None other than Dr. Morgan Prescott himself. I would simply die if he was interested in me. He is so handsome, and when he looks at me with those silver eyes, I could just swoon. All the young ladies in Philadelphia would be ready to scratch your eyes out if they knew how Morgan feels about you."

"No, you are mistaken," Skyler said, moving to the vanity table and picking up a china figurine. She didn't want to hear about Morgan today.

"It's the truth. I had it straight from his best friend's mouth. Jeb Taylor told me that Morgan is extremely interested in you. Aren't you excited?"

Skyler turned the figurine over in her hand and pretended to be examining it to hide her distress. She felt tears gathering behind her eyes and prayed she wouldn't cry. Crying had always been foreign to her nature, but lately she had succumbed to that weakness a great deal.

"Jeb Taylor is wrong, Priscilla. Mr. Prescott does not care for me—not really," she managed to say.

Priscilla stood up and studied Skyler's face. "You are the one who is mistaken. Morgan has never paid marked attention to any young lady, although many have tried to catch his eye. I have seen the way he looks at you, and so has my mother. Mama declares Morgan has lost his heart at last. She says it's strange that Morgan should care for you, when he never gave a second look at Danielle. The two of you do look a great deal alike, you know."

"Your mother is wrong." Skyler wanted to end this conversation before she burst out crying.

"I have heard that Morgan took you to the riverboat party. He would never have done that if he hadn't been interested in you," Priscilla insisted.

Skyler knew if she didn't escape she wouldn't be able to hold the tears back. "I have a dreadful headache, Priscilla. I believe I will ask my aunt to take me home now."

Without giving her friend time to answer, she rushed down the stairs. When Skyler announced that she wasn't feeling well, her aunt immediately took her leave of Mrs. Wendham.

On the ride home, the tears Skyler had been trying to conceal fell down her face. Alexandria held her while she cried, knowing that something must have been said about Morgan. Her heart felt as if it had a weight on it, knowing the pain her niece was going through so needlessly. How well she could remember what it felt like to be young and hopelessly in love. She was reminded of a time when she first knew she loved Tag, and how hopeless she had thought that love had been. Alexandria had no words of comfort to offer Skyler. All she could do was hold her and share her pain. She could see no solution for the problem that faced Skyler and Morgan.

"Cry it out, Skyler. Get it all out of your system, and then perhaps you will feel better," she said, dabbing at the young girl's face with a handkerchief. "What in the world happened that brought this all on?"

Skyler bit her trembling lip, trying to gain control of her emotions. "It was nothing really. Priscilla just said that Morgan was . . . interested in me. I don't know why I am acting so foolish."

Alexandria drew Skyler into her arms, and held her tightly. She knew it was a hopeless situation. Perhaps it would be best if Skyler returned to the Blackfoot

224

village. She hated the thought of Skyler leaving, but she could see no other solution. If Skyler stayed in Philadelphia she was bound to run into Morgan, and that would only keep her wound open.

"There, there, don't dwell on this," Alexandria soothed. "Tag and I wanted so for this summer to be a wonderful experience for you. I can't tell you how I grieve for your heartache."

Skyler smiled through her tears. "Even with what happened to me with Morgan, I wouldn't have missed getting to know you and my uncle better. I love you."

Alexandria felt tears in her own eyes. "We love you too, dear—very much."

The house was quiet and everyone had gone to bed. Alexandria curled up in Tag's arms, and he rested his hand on her stomach.

"How was your tea with Mrs. Wendham this afternoon?" he asked, brushing his lips against hers.

"It was a mistake to go, Tag. Priscilla brought up Morgan's name and Skyler fell to pieces. I barely got her to the buggy before she started crying. It breaks my heart to see her so unhappy. I believe it would be better for her if you would take her back to her home."

"Damn Morgan for what he said to her. The humorous thing in all this, if there is any humor, is he doesn't even know what he's done wrong. I believe he cares deeply for Skyler. It's all so tragic."

"I don't think he will ever be able to bridge the gap between the two of them. Some people are just not meant to fall in love."

Tag tilted her chin up and looked into the golden

225

eyes that still moved him deeply after all the years they had been married. "We are fortunate, Alex. Do you know I believe you are more beautiful than you were when I fell in love with you. Your beauty seems to deepen as the years go by."

She looked into his eyes and felt his love for her like a soft blanket of security. "If I am beautiful, it is because I'm carrying your baby."

He gathered her close to him. "We will think about a solution to Skyler's problem. I don't want to take her back just yet. I have loved having her here with us. Let's just wait a few more days and see what happens."

Alexandria pulled Tag's head toward her. "I pray that there is an easy end to all this, Tag. Skyler is lost and confused. I am frightened that Danielle might be feeling lost herself. We may have made a mistake by forcing the two girls to leave all that was dear to them. Perhaps neither of them can function in a world they are not accustomed to."

Tag rested his lips against her smooth cheek. "Perhaps you are right, but it's too late to look back. Let's just take one day at a time and see what happens."

As Tag's hand moved over Alexandria's back, she closed her eyes. Her heart was so filled with fear for the two girls who now walked in worlds they didn't understand.

Skyler had been unable to sleep so she got out of bed and went for a walk in the garden. The big yellow moon seemed to hang suspended against the ebony sky, while kissing the landscape with its silvery light. She was a child of nature and she felt akin to earth and sky. She

226

drew her strength from the land, but not this land. This land was foreign to her.

Suddenly she wanted to stand on the banks of the Milk River and walk among the Sweet Grass Hills. She wanted to go home and find herself again.

"You look like a moon maiden who was sent to earth to walk among mortal man." A deep voice spoke up from behind her.

Skyler whirled around to face Morgan. Her heart was racing so fast she could hardly breathe. "What are you doing here?" she asked through stiff lips.

"Damned if I know. I started walking after dinner and ended up here in your aunt's garden. I suspect my subconscious brought me here. I never dared hope I would see you."

"I have to go in now," she said, trying to sidestep him.

Morgan reached out and caught her arm, restraining her. "Why have you been avoiding me? If you would just tell me what I have done to offend you. I have searched my mind, and haven't come up with the answer. You were all right when I went to Washington. When I came back you had changed. Why?"

"I have not changed, and I . . . am not avoiding you."

"Are you not? What would you call it?"

"I simply . . . don't like you."

He pulled her to him so tightly that she was forced to look into his face. The silvery light of the moon seemed to be reflected in his eyes, which sparkled luminously. "What have I done that would turn you against me? Was it wrong to declare my feelings for you?"

"I cannot love you, Morgan. We come from different

227

worlds. You could never fit into mine, and I no longer want to stay in yours."

He stared down into her eyes, unable to comprehend what she was saying. Refusing to be diverted, he tried another approach. "If you detest me, I could understand why you are withdrawing from me, but I know that isn't the reason. I know what you were feeling when I kissed you, Skyler. Help me understand what has happened to turn you away from me—help me retain my sanity!"

"I . . . do not want to talk to you, Morgan. Why can you not just go away?" she said, looking past him, since she couldn't bear to look into his eyes any longer.

"Look at me!" he said in a commanding voice. "Look me in the eye and tell me that you want me to leave you alone—then I will believe you."

Skyler met his glance and she saw many emotions in the silvery depths. Pain, uncertainty, hope . . . love.

"I'm waiting, Skyler. Tell me you don't love me. Let me hear from your own lips that you despise me."

She felt her heart skip a beat. Her lips began to tremble from the lie she tried to speak. "I . . . cannot!" she cried. "I cannot speak it."

He pulled her to him and she buried her head against his shoulder. Morgan could feel her slight body tremble as he held her to him. He was overwhelmed with a magnitude of feelings. This girl had come into his life and swept him into a sea of uncertainty. She was nothing like the woman he had imagined he would one day love. She was mysterious and secretive. He knew nothing about her past, and less about her future. He knew she had some deep feelings for him, but still he could feel he was losing her.

228

He tightened his arms about her as if he could hold on to her by sheer force. "Say you love me, Skyler. Admit the truth . . . I have."

Raising her face once more, he saw she was crying. "Do not cry, little love. You will find that loving me will be the easiest thing you have ever had to do. I will make your life beautiful if you will only give me the chance."

Skyler could feel her heart melting. She knew without any doubt that Morgan loved her and she loved him. But love was not enough to overcome their differences. "I do not want to love you," she cried. "Why can you not leave me in peace?"

His hands slid down to her throat and he could feel the pulse beat throbbing madly. He raised her chin and gazed into her face longingly. "You're killing my soul, Skyler. Can't you see that?" he whispered.

She was caught by the pain in his eyes. She wanted so badly to comfort him and find some comfort for herself. In that moment she forgot about the invisible line that divided the two of them. Cupping his face between her hands, she stood on tip-toes and pressed her lips against his.

The moment their lips met, all their hidden feelings came rushing to the surface. Morgan crushed her in his arms and took command of her heart and body.

Skyler felt as if she were flying on silver wings, soaring across the heavens to a place known only to lovers. How could it be wrong to love this man when she needed him desperately? Home and family were forgotten, and she wanted to follow him wherever he led.

"You love me," he murmured against her lips. "You know you do. Love me tonight, tomorrow, next year, and all the rest of our lives. I've never asked this of a woman before, but then I have never loved a woman before you. I need you as a man dying of thirst needs a drink of water."

Yes, her heart agreed—yes, I need you too. But she couldn't bring herself to say the words. "There is no tomorrow for us, Morgan. There isn't even tonight. I do not want you in my life." Skyler spoke the cruel words that tore at his heart, and in so doing, felt her own heart cry out for his pain.

His grip tightened on her arm, and he glared down at her with angry eyes. "Damn you, why? You have to tell me why you are throwing happiness away with both hands. Is it because of who you are, or because of who I am?"

"It is a little of both," she whispered through trembling lips.

"Tell me what I can do to reach you?"

"Why do you insist on the impossible. You would not walk in my world, and I would not be welcome in yours. Just go away and leave me alone."

Skyler sadly watched the love that had been shining in his eyes become replaced with confusion and arrogant pride. "I get the feeling I'm wasting my breath. Tell me!" he demanded. "Am I not good enough for you?"

"My father would not think so, Morgan. It would be far better if you never tried to see me again."

He stepped back a pace as if she had struck him. "If that is your wish, then I will grant it. I fear the day will come when you will realize what you have thrown away tonight. My love for you is so strong I cannot wish you the pain I am feeling. I only wish you happiness." His eyes swept her face in a long, lingering glance. It was as if he wanted to remember every detail after she had gone.

Without another word, he turned and walked away, soon to be swallowed up by the dark shadows of night. Skyler wanted to call out to him, but she knew it would do no good.

As Skyler walked down the path toward the house, she noticed that a dark cloud had moved over the moon, casting the garden in darkness. Her heart was heavy, and tears ran down her face. She could feel the hopelessness of her situation. She loved Morgan and he loved her, but she could never stay in his world. Skyler realized he was also frustrated because she couldn't even tell him what was wrong between them. Her young body craved the love that would give her fulfillment, and she knew Morgan felt the same.

Morgan's anger and confusion had been like a knife in her heart. Deep inside, she wished him only happiness. She didn't like to think of him being sad. It seemed such a tragedy that the two of them loved so deeply, and yet they could never be together.

As the first drops of rain began to fall, she lifted her face to the heavens and the raindrops mixed with her tears. It was as if the whole universe was weeping with her.

"Morgan, Morgan, it would have been better had I never met you," she cried. "If I had never known love, I would not now feel such pain."

Morgan felt the first drops of rain hit his face. Flexing his tired muscles, he directed his footsteps homeward. For so long he had searched for the ideal woman for him; now he'd found her in Skyler Dancing. What had gone wrong, for God's sake? Nothing he'd said to her tonight had penetrated that wall she'd built between them.

Seeing the light of his house in the distance, he slowed his steps. As the rain peppered down on Morgan, he knew it wasn't the only wetness on his cheeks.

Chapter Seventeen

Danielle stood atop a smooth rock that jetted out over the Missouri River, gazing at the sea of grassland that seemed to stretch on and on forever. The only break in the land was the occasional cliff or butte which had been carved by the river over the past century. Shading her eyes against the bright sunlight, Danielle saw the cottonwood trees that grew along the river and thought they would make a good cover for one to hide.

She was puzzled, knowing Scar Face hadn't taken this route when he had abducted her. Her mind wandered to the silent, brooding Wolfrunner. They had been traveling together for over a week, and he seldom spoke to her. She found herself wanting to know more about him. What was he really like? Did he ever laugh? Did he have a sense of humor? Surely she couldn't judge him by the way he treated her. He didn't seem to like her and considered her to be a burden.

A shadow fell across her face, and she turned to face Wolfrunner himself. His eyes brushed past her as they always did, giving her the impression that he didn't like to look at her.

"This is unfamiliar to me," she said with a wide sweep of her hand. "Why are you taking me this way? Surely there is an easier way."

Still he didn't look at her but fixed his eyes on a nearby cottonwood tree. "Scar Face will not expect me to take this way home. It will throw him off for a time."

"Do you mean we will no longer have to worry about him following us?" she asked hopefully.

"He will not be fooled for long, but for a while we will not have to worry about him following us. Soon he will discover that I have tricked him, and he will backtrack to search the prairies for us."

"Does that mean we can stop long enough for me to bathe in the river? I am not accustomed to going so long without a bath. I have never been this filthy in my life."

His dark eyes moved over her with seemingly bored indifference. Danielle didn't know that Wolfrunner was thinking that even in her dirty and tattered condition, he still found her desirable.

"Come. You can wash yourself while I hunt game so we will have meat. You can go into the river if you stay out of the deep part. I will not be here to pull you out should you get in trouble."

"My father taught me to swim, so I will not drown, if that's what you are worried about."

"I was not worried, but your aunt would be. I owe it to her to see you safely back."

Danielle watched as he turned and walked away from her. His dislike for her seemed to grow with each passing day. Had she not obeyed him in everything?

Why did he continue to treat her with such disdain? Apparently he would be satisfied if she would drown in the river. Then he wouldn't have to worry about her anymore.

Sighing inwardly, she made her way down the side of the hill to the river edge. Wolfrunner was a mystery in more ways than one. He seemed to despise her and yet he was going out of his way to keep her safe. Of course he never missed an opportunity to tell her he was taking her back only for Joanna's sake.

Coming upon a spot where the river had washed upon a kind of sandstone pit, she noticed it was somewhat like a small pond. It would be an ideal spot for bathing since it was surrounded by cottonwood trees and would offer her some degree of privacy.

Gazing into the clear water, Danielle got her first look at her own reflection, and was horrified by what she saw. Her hair was a mass of tangles and her face was streaked and dirty. She hardly recognized herself.

Without further consideration, she stripped off her skirt and blouse and tossed them aside. Easing herself down into the pond, she dunked her head down, allowing the cool water to wash over her. How wonderful it would be to feel clean again. After she scrubbed herself as best she could without soap, she rinsed out her tattered skirt and blouse.

As she climbed out of the water, she stretched her arms up to the heavens, allowing the sun to kiss her golden-colored body. She smiled, thinking how Alexandria would scold her if she could see her now—naked as the day she was born.

Wolfrunner stood on the cliff, staring down at the

girl. His eyes roamed hungrily over her golden body, and he felt a tightening in his loins. Her beauty bordered on perfection and he couldn't seem to tear his eyes away.

Forcing himself to turn away, he made his way down the side of the cliff. Taking his knife, he proceeded to clean and gut the two rabbits he had killed.

He knew it was too late to run away from the feelings that had come upon him so unaware. The girl had somehow gotten inside him and touched a part of him that no other woman had found. He knew he had been drawn to her from the first day he had seen her. It didn't matter that she was more white than Indian. It didn't even matter that she was spoiled and willful. He knew he would always carry an image of her in his heart. He had begun to admire her spirit and courage, and he hated himself for wanting her. Wolfrunner was honest enough with himself to now admit he hadn't searched for Danielle for Joanna's sake alone. He had searched for her because he had been compelled to find her.

As Wolfrunner slit the first rabbit open and cleaned it, he tried to push the girl out of his mind. Perhaps it had been a mistake for him to take the longer way back to the village. Could he continue to hide his heart from the girl whose name he couldn't even pronounce? It was all so strange and confusing. How could he want a girl who looked down her nose at him merely because he was an Indian? Deep down he had always admired the white race since all he had to judge them by were Joanna, Tag, and Farley. He had been ripped apart the day Danielle had belittled him, and it wasn't likely he would ever get over it, he thought.

Picking up the rabbits, he looked toward the river.

The girl seemed to be pulling at him even now, and he didn't know how to battle these newfound feelings.

Danielle sat in the sun, allowing its warm rays to dry her hair. Running her fingers through the thick mass, she tried to remove the worst of the tangles. She knew her gown was torn and wrinkled, but at least it was clean.

She felt, rather than heard, Wolfrunner when he came up behind her. Turning slowly, she favored him with a smile, but as always he merely seemed to look right through her.

"I see you have not squandered your time. Can we build a fire to cook the rabbits?"

Without answering, he handed her his kill and proceeded to gather up dried branches to build a fire. In no time at all, the two rabbits were roasting on a spit, and the aroma was enough to make Danielle's mouth water.

Sitting by the fire, she continued trying to remove the tangles from her hair. Some of the tangles would be impossible to remove, she thought in horror, fearing her hair would have to be cut.

Suddenly Wolfrunner appeared at her side. She was shocked into silence as he turned her around and began to comb her hair with a branch from a bramble brush. His stroking movements were very gentle, and he took great care not to stick her with a thorn.

Danielle closed her eyes, loving the feel of his gentleness. When he ran a hand softly down her hair, she shivered and caught her breath.

"You must turn the spit," he said, as he proceeded to

plait her hair into one long braid.

Danielle noticed her hand was trembling as she reached for the spit. What was happening to her? she wondered. She was somehow disturbed by his touch, and yet she wished he could go on touching her this way. She had gone so many days without a kind word from anyone that she now basked in his tender attention. She hadn't realized that one with such strength could be so gentle.

Her breathing seemed to be affected by his nearness, and suddenly she turned to face him. When their eyes met and locked, she felt a weakness in the very depths of her being. His dark eyes suddenly moved away from her, and he tossed the makeshift comb aside.

"You will find your hair will not tangle now that it is braided. It would be wise if you would wear it this way until we reach the village."

Once again he was the cold stranger. Not knowing what to say, she reached back and touched the single braid, finding he had tied one of his black raven feathers in her hair. "Thank you," she said, lowering her eyes.

By now the meat was roasted to a golden brown, and Wolfrunner removed it from the spit. Since the meat was hot, he placed one of the rabbits on a flat stone and motioned for Danielle to help herself. He watched as she daintily tore a piece of meat and held it to her lips.

"This smells delicious. I had never eaten rabbit before . . . before I was kidnapped. I believe I am becoming quite fond of it, or perhaps it's just that I'm hungry."

"To a starving man, there is nothing better," he told her, sitting crossed-legged and taking a bite of the meat.

238

Danielle soon cast off her pretty manners and savored every bite of the succulent meat. She thought she had never tasted anything better.

Every so often, her eyes would roam to Wolfrunner. He seemed not to be aware of her, so she studied him carefully. What was there about this man, this Indian, that had evoked some unknown emotion in her? she wondered. He was nothing like the men she was accustomed to. He was a savage, and she had the feeling that no amount of education would civilize him. Perhaps her feelings were no more than gratitude because he had saved her from Scar Face. There were many things she wanted to know about him—dare she ask him about himself?

"How did you get the name Wolfrunner?" she asked, thinking he couldn't possibly object to such a question.

Tossing a bone aside, he fixed his eyes just above her head. "The name that was given me at birth was Small Fox. When I was in my seventeenth summer, Windhawk himself gave me the name Wolfrunner."

"My father told me that a brave had to win his name. I know my cousin Little Hawk has not yet won his name. What did you do to win your name, outrun a wolf?"

His eyes moved to her face. "Yes."

"What a strange man you are. Most men of my acquaintance love nothing better than to talk about themselves, but you don't, do you?"

"How many men have been in your life?" He hated himself for asking.

"None of importance."

Again he looked past her. "Say your name for me so I might know how to say it," he said softly.

"It is really very simple. Dan-ielle. Put it together

239

and it is Danielle."

". . . Danielle," he said with only the slightest hesitation. "Danielle."

"I was told by my father that my Uncle Windhawk once had difficulty saying Joanna's name."

"By many of the Blackfoot, your aunt is called Flaming Hair. She is well loved by my people."

"What about Sky Dancer?"

"She is a princess of the people, just as you are. She, too, is well loved."

To Danielle's surprise she found herself envying her cousin. She would like to have the love and respect of her mother's people. Where before she never wanted to hear about her mother, she now felt a need to know about the woman who had given her birth.

"Tell me what you know about my mother, Wolfrunner? I know very little about her."

He settled back against the grass, resting his head against his arms. "I remember Morning Song well. She was beautiful to look upon, and her manners were sweet. She loved your father, and had she lived, she would have loved you."

"I have always thought of my stepmother as my mother. It is difficult for me to think of . . . my real mother."

"That is because you do not want to think about the Indian part of yourself. You like the white man's ways and turn your back on the Blackfoot ways. You should never have come to our village." His dark eyes seemed to sparkle with anger, and Danielle, too, felt angered.

"It is not for you to say if I should have come. I didn't want to spend the summer with . . . my aunt and uncle. I wish now I had refused altogether."

240

Wolfrunner stared into the campfire. "It would be good for you to return to the white world when you get back to the village. You do not belong with the Blackfoot. You have only made trouble since you came."

Now Danielle was furious. How dare he blame her for being kidnapped. "You cannot think it was my fault that Scar Face took me away?" She jumped to her feet, angered at the man's audacity. "Nothing would suit me better than to go back where I belong. I wish I had never come to this country. You are mean and hateful and . . . and I despise you!"

His dark eyes seemed to snap. "What does this 'despise' mean?"

"It means I do not like you in the least. You are cruel and heartless."

A smile curved his lips. "Now you act like the white girl I first met. I wondered how long it would take for you to become your true self again. I care not what you think of me. You are as nothing to me!"

Danielle felt tears building behind her eyes. She would not cry in front of this man. She would show him that she was completely indifferent to him. "I cannot wait until I have seen the last of you. You are a . . ."

"Savage," he finished for her. "If I am a savage, it would be wise for you not to provoke me beyond endurance." He came to his feet and towered above her. "I will talk to you no more, white girl."

Danielle watched as he walked away, soon to be swallowed up by the shadows of the night. She gazed up at the rising moon and felt strangely saddened. Why did Wolfrunner have to be so impossible to get along with, she wondered. Why did she always seem to provoke him into anger?

Days passed since Wolfrunner had rescued Danielle from Scar Face. Now he seemed to regard her with little less than contempt. At night when they would make camp, he hardly ever spoke to her. Being of a prideful and stubborn nature, Danielle didn't again try to engage him in conversation.

Wolfrunner continued to see that she had food and water, but he rarely looked to her physical comfort. Danielle was learning how to survive in the wilderness. No longer was she frightened at night when he would go into the woods and leave her alone for long periods of time.

He had taught her how to clean and gut rabbits and other small game. He had shown her what berries were poisonous and which ones could be eaten.

They followed the river, often crossing at shallow points, when game was more plentiful on the other side. Each day Wolfrunner would backtrack to see if Scar Face was following them.

Danielle had begun to look forward to each new day. There was an excitement in the air as she trudged along behind Wolfrunner. She was learning many things from him. Sometimes, when he was unaware, she would watch him. He was almost beautiful, with his bronzed skin glistening in the sunlight. His dark eyes seemed to see so much more than normal human beings would ever notice. She had the feeling he could go the rest of his life living off the land. She came to admire and respect him and wished he respected her as well.

Deep inside Danielle was troubled. She wouldn't allow herself to think about the longings Wolfrunner stirred within her young body. He made her aware of the fact that she was a woman, and she was very aware that he was a man. She wondered if an Indian knew how to kiss? Did Wolfrunner ever think of her as a woman?

Sometimes when she lay beside him at night, and he appeared to be sleeping, she would watch him. A deep ache would surround her heart and her body would feel feverish.

There were times when Danielle was angry with him, and there were times he made her want to cry; those times she could handle. It was the times that he made her ache for his touch, that she fought against.

Chapter Eighteen

Many party and picnic invitations still continued to come to the house for Skyler. She was grateful, however, that her Aunt Alexandria and Uncle Tag no longer insisted that she attend any of the functions. The only person Skyler ever saw outside the family was Priscilla Wendham. Somehow Priscilla's lighthearted teasing often brought a smile to Skyler's lips and caused her to forget about her troubles for a time.

Apparently Morgan had taken Skyler at her word, to leave her alone. She hadn't seen him since the night in the garden. She knew it was for the best, but oh, she did wish she could see him just once more before she left for home.

Priscilla would often come to visit, and she and Skyler would ride over the estate, or just sit in the summerhouse, talking girl-talk and nonsense. Skyler was glad to hear that her friend was no longer infatuated with Bill Kirby. It seemed Priscilla was now interested in someone new. Priscilla was flighty and fickle, but then she was still young, Skyler thought.

One day she would lose her heart to a man.

It was a hot, humid day with no cooling breeze to ease the heat. Priscilla had been visiting, but she had now left for home. Skyler and Alexandria were in the morning room. It was the coolest spot in the house because of the many windows that opened out onto the garden. Since it was on the west side of the house, it was also shaded from the morning sun.

Alexandria was playing the spinet while Skyler sat on the bench beside her. It suddenly occurred to Skyler that she would miss her aunt very much when she returned home. It saddened her that she wouldn't be here when Alexandria's baby was born.

"I love babies, Aunt Alexandria, and do you not think there is something magical about children's laughter?"

"Yes, dear," Alexandria replied, thinking that Skyler would make a wonderful mother.

"I love to be with the children in my village. Sometimes my mother allows me to give them their reading lessons."

Alex smiled. "Is Joanna still trying to educate the whole world?"

Skyler nodded. "Yes. She believes that everyone should have an education. Did you know she even taught Farley to read and write?"

"Surely you jest?"

"No, I can assure you it is true."

Alexandria ran her fingers over the keys remembering the old trapper fondly. "Farley would do anything to please Joanna. That dear old man loves her more than anyone."

"I think he is a wonderful character. I always loved

to listen to his tales."

Skyler lapsed into silence and Alexandria knew she was troubled. Actually Skyler was thinking that summer had been a growing up time for her. She had learned many painful lessons, but she had also come to know and love her aunt and uncle. She knew that when she left she would never return to the white man's world. She was a stranger here and could never become one of them.

Just as Alexandria played the last note of "Irish Summer," the downstairs maid rapped on the door. "Begging your pardon, madam, but Mrs. Prescott and her daughter wish to see you."

Alexandria gave Skyler an inquiring glance. "I wonder what they could want? They only returned from France yesterday. I didn't expect them to call so soon."

· "Would that be Morgan's mother and sister?" Skyler asked. She had no wish to meet them.

"Yes, and before they come in I want to warn you that Nora Prescott is a very overpowering woman. She is one of my dearest friends, but she does speak frankly."

"Do you suppose they have come to see me?"

"I don't know. Why don't we just wait and find out. Holly, show them in, and then bring tea and cakes."

Skyler came to her feet as the two callers came rushing into the room. While they were greeting her aunt, Skyler had a chance to study Morgan's mother and sister. Nora Prescott was dressed in black and wore a matching bonnet with an ostrich feather as decoration. She appeared stately and assured and Skyler noticed that she had the same silver-gray eyes as

Morgan. Morgan's sister was small and pretty. She was dressed in a pale green gown, and her golden hair was pulled back in a matching snood.

Skyler was unprepared when the older woman rushed across the room to her. Taking her hand, Nora Prescott eyed her up and down. "I had to see you with my own eyes. I couldn't believe it when my son told me you were Danielle's look-alike. I can see he wasn't far wrong, except . . . you are prettier than your cousin, in an odd sort of way."

Alexandria laughed at Skyler's startled expression. "Nora, as you have already discerned, this is my niece Skyler Dancing. I warned her that you were outspoken."

Nora smiled. "Not so. I merely say what's on my mind. I'm too old to mince words. Besides, I don't give a fig for anyone who isn't truthful."

Morgan's sister stepped forward and took Skyler's hand. "I am Jenny Prescott, and I am hardly ever outspoken," she said, smiling brightly. "I think you and Danielle could easily pass for twins."

Skyler remembered her manners and made the correct replies. She had never met anyone who was as overwhelming as Mrs. Prescott, unless it was Morgan himself.

As they drank tea and ate the tiny tea cakes, Skyler listened to Nora Prescott and her daughter talk about their trip to Paris. She wondered what it would be like to visit faraway places. She thought of her brother who was traveling in Europe and hoped he wasn't feeling out of his depth.

Nora took a sip of tea and eyed Skyler closely. "So you are the one who has my son in a spin? I can see how

248

he could have lost his head over you, my dear. I am sure Morgan never met anyone with your kind of beauty before. You have a strange accent. I can't quite place it. Did you ever live in England, or perhaps Ireland?"

"No," Skyler answered. "But my mother comes from England, as does my Uncle Tag."

Nora was watching her closely. "I believe you may be the prettiest little thing I have yet seen. My son knows quality when he sees it. Yes indeed, Skyler Dancing, you have Morgan in a real spin."

Skyler felt her face flame. She felt tongue-tied, not knowing how to answer.

Jenny reached over and squeezed Skyler's hand. "Mama, you have embarrassed Miss Dancing. She isn't accustomed to your teasing."

"Oh, Tish. She doesn't appear to be the kind of girl who would be offended by straight talk. You aren't one of those flighty girls who has vapors and swoon, are you?"

Skyler caught Alexandria's eyes and saw the merriment dancing there. She was at a loss as to how to deal with this woman. "I have neither swooned in my life, Mrs. Prescott, nor did I set out to put your son in a spin."

"Well said, my dear. You've got spunk, and I like that in a young lady. Tell me all about yourself."

Skyler began to feel uncomfortable under the woman's silver gaze. "There isn't much to tell about myself, and my mother always said people do not want to be bored by listening to one's life story."

"You cannot argue with that logic, Mama. That's the same thing you have always told me." Jenny stood up and smiled. "Come, Skyler, let's walk down to the summerhouse before my mother asks you to share all your secrets."

Nora laughed jovially. "I'll let you off this time, but I have no intentions of giving up."

Skyler followed Jenny out to the garden, aware that Morgan's mother watched her closely. She was confused by Mrs. Prescott's attitude.

Jenny took Skyler's hand as they slowly walked down the winding path. "You really mustn't mind Mama. She was so excited when she learned that Morgan was interested in someone. She has been badgering him for years to take a bride. Morgan has had his pick of lovely ladies, but they always bored him. I can see why he wasn't bored with you."

"I will not be marrying your brother, Miss Prescott. Surely he must have told your mother this."

"Yes, but neither Morgan nor my mother gives up easily. I gathered from what Morgan said that you are going to return to your home."

"Yes, by the end of summer."

"It is so uncanny how much you resemble Danielle. When I first saw you I was surprised that Morgan fell for Danielle's look-alike, since he never paid the slightest attention to your cousin. But now I can see you are nothing like her. You are much quieter than Danielle."

"Did Morgan ask you to come here today?" Skyler wanted to know.

"Heavens, no. He wouldn't be at all pleased if he knew Mama had started grilling you." Jenny stopped and faced Skyler. "My brother loves you, Skyler. I had thought the woman would never come along that would settle him down. I can sense in him great pain and I was wondering if you would tell me why you turned him away?"

Skyler looked into bright, sensitive blue eyes and knew that Jenny was only concerned for her brother's happiness. "Your brother and I are simply not suited, Miss Prescott. I can tell you no more than that."

"Please call me Jenny, and please don't think I am prying. I just want to see my brother happy. Do you have a brother, Skyler? May I call you Skyler?"

"Yes, I have a brother and yes, I would like you to call me Skyler."

"Then you know how I feel. You would want your brother to be happy, wouldn't you?"

"Yes, of course. But my brother would never allow me to interfere in his life."

Jenny laughed. "Whoops, you can see I am more like my mother than I would like to admit. Will you forgive me for prying, Skyler?"

"Yes, of course. As you say, you love your brother."

By now they had reached the summerhouse, and both girls sat down on a cushion seat. Jenny arranged her gown and stared at Skyler. "You can tell me it's none of my affair, but do you love my brother? I somehow sense that you do."

Skyler smiled. "You said that you were not outspoken, but I find that you are."

Jenny smiled. "I guess it's a family trait."

"To answer your question, I do have some very deep feelings for your brother, but as I said, we are not suited to one another."

"I have always been a firm believer that love conquers all. If you love Morgan and he loves you, what is standing in your way?"

"I cannot explain, except to say that Morgan and I are from different worlds. I cannot live in his world, and he cannot live in mine."

"Let me tell you a story, and then you can judge for yourself if people from different worlds can ever find happiness. I know of a woman who was born into poverty in England. She was sent to America as an indentured servant to work off her father's debts. She toiled and labored in a wealthy man's house for a year. She and the son of the house fell madly and passionately in love. As you can imagine, the parents of the young man were violently against their son marrying beneath him. They opposed the marriage, but it took place all the same."

"What happened?" Skyler asked, getting caught up in the story.

"The two of them are deliriously happy. I have never heard them speak an unkind word to one another in all the years I have known them. Their love has warmed me for many years. You see . . . I was speaking about my and Morgan's mother and father. My family has always put love above all else. I hope you can now better understand why my mother wanted to meet you. You and Morgan couldn't have the gap between your worlds that my mother and father had. I can tell you are a well-brought-up young lady . . . unless you think Morgan isn't good enough for you."

"I could never in a million years make you understand about me, Jenny. You will just have to take my word that I am not right for your brother. My mother and father also reached far across two worlds to fulfill their love, but Morgan and I could never breach that gap."

"I don't understand."

"No, nor would your brother. I wish it could be different, but it cannot."

"Is this the way it will end?"

"I fear so. Some things just are not meant to be, Jenny. Morgan and I are not meant to be."

"Do you believe my brother loves you?"

"Strangely enough, I do."

"I think it's only fair to warn you that Morgan is persistent. He isn't a man to give up easily."

"He has given up on me, Jenny."

Morgan's sister laughed and shook her head. "Don't you believe it for a moment."

Jenny and her mother left a short time later. After they had gone, Skyler felt more confused than ever. Alexandria had gone upstairs to lie down, and the house was strangely quiet. Feeling restless Skyler went to the stable to saddle a horse so she could go for a ride to clear her head. She had many things to think about—many problems that didn't seem to have any solution.

It was almost sundown when Skyler returned to the stable. The ride had brought no joy to her heart, and no comfort for her loneliness. It had been torture talking to Mrs. Prescott and Jenny today. She knew neither of them would be anxious for her to marry Morgan if they knew about her Indian blood.

Chapter Nineteen

One day passed very much like all the others. Danielle didn't know what day it was, or for that matter what month. For a few days Wolfrunner had allowed a fire at night, but now they would make camp at night without benefit of a campfire. He had become cautious and watchful, and Danielle realized that he must think they were being followed by Scar Face once more.

They no longer followed the river, but moved among the tall grasses across the never-ending prairie. The winds were blowing strong and steady, bending the grass almost double. Danielle's mouth was parched and dry, and her skin felt as if it had been cooked by the sun.

As she trudged along, trying to keep step with Wolfrunner's powerful gait, her foot hit the edge of a large stone, and it threw her off balance. She stumbled and fell to her knees, crying out in pain as her leg twisted beneath her.

Wolfrunner glanced back and gave her a look of

scorn before he plodded on ahead, ignoring her pain.

She bit her lip in anguish and staggered to her feet. The pain was so intense that she could hardly bear it. Taking a deep breath, she moved forward. Each step she took felt like tiny needles prickled her ankle.

With stubborn determination, Danielle refused to falter. She would give Wolfrunner no cause to look down his nose at her. She would keep going if it killed her—and it probably would, she thought bitterly.

The morning passed, and still they continued. By now, Danielle's whole foot felt numb. She was long past pain and was moving on sheer willpower alone. She didn't think, as she placed one foot in front of the other—one foot in front of the other.

The sun beat down on her and the blistering hot wind stung her face. They didn't stop to rest, but plodded onward. If this was a new kind of torture Wolfrunner was dealing out to her, she would show him that he couldn't break her.

Keeping her eyes fixed on Wolfrunner's back, Danielle trudged onward. Hunger and thirst had no meaning—pain and weariness were as nothing. All that mattered was that she follow the man in front of her.

Many times she fell to her knees, but Wolfrunner never slowed his pace. She would get slowly to her feet and push onward.

Wolfrunner knew he was testing the girl beyond endurance, but somewhere deep inside he wanted to punish her. Why? he questioned. Did he punish her for the deep feelings she had invoked within him? Or was it because he wanted to make her regret the way she had treated him when they first met?

Looking back over his shoulder, he noticed she had

dropped farther behind. Realizing that if Scar Face were to come upon them now he would be unable to protect her, he stopped and allowed her to catch up.

This white girl had surprised him. He had deliberately been hard on her, and yet she hadn't complained. No Indian maiden could have endured what she had without faltering. She was stronger than he had thought, or perhaps it was her hatred for him that drove her onward.

When she drew even with him, she reached out her hand. He could see the pain in her eyes and grabbed her about the waist as she slowly sank to her knees.

Wolfrunner's heart was beating wildly as she threw back her curtain of ebony hair and gave him a pleading look. He noticed her lips were dry and cracked and her eyes were glazed with pain.

Leaning her back against the ground, he removed his waterskin and held it to her lips. He had wanted her to beg for mercy, but she hadn't. Even now her eyes seemed to defy him.

"We will rest here until the evening breeze cools the land," he said, sitting down cross-legged beside her.

Handing her a piece of dried meat, he watched her take a bite. Lying back, with the tall grass as a cushion, he closed his eyes. How strange it was, he thought. Even with his eyes closed he could still see the image of Danielle's face. The hardships they had endured had not detracted from her beauty. He wondered what her laughter would sound like. Was there a white man somewhere who waited for her return?

All at once, Wolfrunner's senses became alert. He could smell smoke! Jumping to his feet, he looked to the east and saw the grass fire that was burning out of

257

control. Smoke was billowing into the air! Deer and other smaller animals were stampeding in wild abandonment, trying to escape the fire.

The fire was spreading rapidly, destroying everything in its path! The orange and red flames were rolling in their direction! Wolfrunner's eyes moved quickly to the river which was at least five hundred paces away, wondering if they could reach it before the fire overtook them.

Jerking Danielle to her feet, he pushed her in front of him. She hadn't yet detected the fire, and she pulled away from him defiantly.

"No, I won't go another step. You said we could rest, and that's just what I'm going to do."

"Then you will die," he said, gesturing toward the raging grass fire.

Danielle felt wild unbridled terror as the cloud of smoke darkened the eastern sky. Taking a step forward, she fell to her knees. "I cannot make it. You will have to go on without me!" she cried.

Wolfrunner knew if he were going to save her he would have to act quickly. Rising his hand, he slapped her hard across the face with his open palm. "I always knew you were weak, white girl. You have not the will to survive. It will serve you right if you perish in the fire. I can then tell Windhawk and the Blackfoot people that you died a coward's death."

Danielle's head reeled from his blow. Tears of pain stung her eyes, but she ignored them. Again she would call on her inner strength to show this man she was not weak. With wings on her feet and pain forgotten, she ran in the direction of the far distant river. It was unlikely that they would make it to safety, but she wouldn't give up until Wolfrunner did.

Wolfrunner ran beside her, keeping his eyes on the advancing fire. He could see that they would never make it to the safety of the river at the pace they were going. Without even breaking his stride, he reached out and lifted Danielle into his arms.

His burden was light and had suddenly become more precious than his own life. He must save her because she was in his heart and mind. Looking down into Danielle's face, he felt his heart melt. Her lovely blue eyes seemed so trusting as they stared back at him.

His feet were swift and fleet as he raced the wind. He had not been given the name Wolfrunner for nothing.

The fire was gaining on them. Danielle felt the smoke sting her eyes and burn in her lungs. She realized she and Wolfrunner were faced with a painful death.

Suddenly she felt a calm wash over her. If she was to die, it seemed only right that she should die with this man. Looking up into his eyes, she somehow knew he was thinking the same thing. They had faced many hardships together. This might be their final test. But there were so many things that she wanted to tell him. Now they might never be said. She wanted to tell him how sorry she was for the cruel things she'd said to him. She wanted to tell him how her heart was filled with longings she didn't understand. No, there was no time. There might never be time.

All at once Wolfrunner became aware that a new danger threatened! The rumbling of many hooves drowned out the sound of the advancing fire. Wolfrunner glanced eastward and saw the huge herd of buffalo that had been stampeded by the fire, and they were heading right for him and Danielle!

There would be no time to make the river. They would soon be caught between the stampeding herd and the fire!

Making a quick decision Wolfrunner stopped and placed Danielle on her feet. Pushing her behind him, he faced the oncoming danger without flinching. He was faced with two ways of dying—to be crushed beneath the hooves of the buffalo—or to be burned to death by the fire. He would accept neither. As long as he breathed the air of life, he would fight to survive, for if he perished, Danielle would also die.

Danielle clutched at his shoulders, awed by his bravery. She knew he could have made it to safety if he had abandoned her. Why had he stayed with her?

Suddenly she knew that she loved this man. She didn't want to see him die because of her. "You must run!" she cried. "Save yourself, Wolfrunner!"

"No, I will not leave you," he shouted. "If death comes, it will find us both."

Wolfrunner knew that the end was near. With a glance at the sky, he prayed Danielle's death would be swift and she would not suffer. His heart cried out in protest. Had he saved her from Scar Face only to lose her now? Words of love had not been spoken, and she would never know that he gladly gave his life for her. She was as his own heart and filled his very life and soul. She was his love!

By now the dust caused by the buffalo herd swirled in the air, mingling with the smoke. The fear-maddened animals were so near that Danielle could see their small, beady eyes. She closed her eyes not wanting to watch Wolfrunner's death.

A wild cry rose from Wolfrunner's throat, and he

thrust his spear into the air and waved it about wildly. Knowing the buffalo were fear-crazed from the fire, he doubted they would stop for him, but still he had to make the effort.

The lead buffalo was bearing down on them, and Wolfrunner shouted louder. It seemed an eternity before the beast neared. To his surprise the animal turned, and he watched in amazement as the others followed suit!

Danielle opened her eyes in bewilderment. They were in the middle of the stampeding herd, and yet the animals were moving around them. They came so near, had Danielle wanted to she could have reached out and touched them.

Wolfrunner continued to shout and wave his spear in the air, and the buffalo continued to move aside. The air was filled with dust and smoke. The thundering sound from the buffalo hooves seemed to make the very earth tremble.

Wolfrunner could see the end of the herd now, and just behind them was the fire! Without pausing to consider, he grabbed Danielle in his arms and raced toward the river.

Danielle could feel the heat from the fire and realized they would never make the river. Clutching Wolfrunner about the neck, she silently urged him onward. No man could be so fleet, she thought. He was keeping pace with the buffalo!

The heat of the fire seemed to burn her face, the smoke burned her lungs, causing her to choke—she couldn't breathe or catch her breath.

How puny life was, she thought. How easily one could cross over the line between life and death.

Turning her face against Wolfrunner's broad chest, she felt darkness swirling about her. Gasping for breath, she reached a state of unconsciousness.

Farley entered Windhawk's lodge. His white head bent in sorrow, and he couldn't meet Joanna's eyes. He knew the sadness she was feeling and it tore at his heart. He'd loved her for many years. She and Tag had been the children he'd never had.

Looking into the dark eyes of Windhawk, he shook his head. "The warriors have just come back. They ain't found hide nor hair of Danielle."

"Has Wolfrunner returned?" Windhawk asked.

Farley scratched his grizzly beard. "No, there ain't been no word of him."

Windhawk bent down beside his wife and raised her face to him. "It is time for Farley to go to Tag and tell him his daughter is missing."

Joanna's eyes clouded over. "Could we not wait a while longer? Perhaps Wolfrunner has found her."

"No, Tag must be told as soon as possible," Windhawk said firmly. "You would want to know if Sky Dancer had come to harm," he said more gently.

Farley gave Joanna a sympathetic look. "I best be gone. It's been raining in the mountains, and I don't want to be caught in no flood. I'll bring Tag back with me."

Windhawk stood up and faced the old trapper. "Tell him not to lose heart. We will continue to search for Danielle. Tell him we are doing everything we can."

As the old trapper left the lodge, Windhawk gathered Joanna in his arms. He held her tightly, trying to bring her comfort. She knew without him telling her that there was very little hope that Danielle would be found alive after all this time. It was doubtful that they would ever find out what had really happened to her.

A short time later Farley rode away from the Blackfoot village that he now called home. His heart was heavy that he would have to be the one to bring the sad news to Tag that his daughter was missing. Deep inside he doubted the girl would ever be found alive.

As he reached the river, he glanced back. Joanna would get through this. She was strong and had weathered many hardships, and most likely she would weather a few more in the course of her life, still, Farley wished he could have brought her comfort.

Windhawk walked out of his lodge where two dozen warriors waited for him. Mounting his horse, he rode away, knowing he couldn't give up trying to find Danielle. The guilt he felt, that this should happen when she was under his protection, was nothing compared to the rage he felt toward whoever had taken her away. He would find out who had done this thing, and they would die a slow and agonizing death, he vowed.

Chapter Twenty

It had never been in Skyler's nature to allow anything to get her down for very long. She had been trained, as any young Blackfoot maiden, to hide her unhappiness from others. As the days of summer passed in rapid succession, she found it increasingly difficult to keep her heartbreak hidden from her aunt and uncle.

When Skyler was alone, she would often remember Morgan saying the only good Indian was a dead Indian. A part of her wanted to lash out at him for his cruel words, and another part of her wished she could make him understand about her father's people. How could he not love the Blackfoot children if he got to know them? How could he keep from respecting her father if he spent time in his company?

She hadn't seen Morgan in weeks, and she found herself wishing for the sight of his face. Priscilla had told Skyler that she never saw Morgan at any of the parties she attended. His mother and sister hadn't even come to call since that first visit. Alexandria had been told by Jenny Prescott that Morgan had asked his mother not to pester Skyler. He must have finally realized that their love was hopeless.

Morgan came down the wide, winding staircase and moved into the dining room. In spite of the fact it was early, he knew his mother would already have eaten breakfast and would be working in her garden.

As he took his seat at the head of the table, Letty, the cook, placed his breakfast before him. "It sure is good to have you home for a spell, Morgan. This house just hasn't been the same without a man in it."

Morgan unfolded the crisp white napkin and placed it in his lap. His father had been dead for ten years, leaving Morgan head of the family at the age of eighteen. Like his father before him, he had always wanted to be a doctor. The Prescott family owned several banks in Pennsylvania, but Morgan's uncle handled the business, leaving Morgan free to pursue a medical career. When the war had come along, he joined the Cavalry. Now he wasn't sure where his life would take him.

"I see you have my favorite strawberry jam, Letty. You will spoil me, and then I will be dissatisfied with army cooking."

"You could always give up your commission and stay home," his sister said, coming up to him and planting a kiss on his cheek.

"Good morning, Funny Face." Morgan winked at Jenny. "I am surprised to find you up so early. I thought you had decided it was fashionable to sleep late, since you got back from Europe and saw how the

266

Parisians set the fashion."

She tugged at a lock of his golden hair and made a face at him. "I don't like to sleep late. I tried it, but I just lay there in bed, watching the sun come up."

"I would imagine you were afraid you would miss something," Morgan said, smiling. "What do you do for excitement when you aren't bothering me?"

Jenny took the silver coffee server from Letty and poured her brother a cup of coffee. "There isn't anything exciting happening in Philadelphia, and you have become positively dull. I could sleep for a week without missing anything interesting from you or Philadelphia."

Morgan raised his coffee cup to his lips and studied Jenny over the rim. She was barely sixteen, but there was a promise of future loveliness. She was just past the awkward stage and was beginning to blossom. "What are your plans for today?" he wanted to know.

She smiled at him impishly. "Mama says we are going to a tca. Would you like to come along?"

"Spare me," he said, laughing at the funny face she made at him.

Her eyes looked into his. "Why don't you come? Skyler Dancing might be there. Wouldn't you like to see her?"

He ran his finger around the rim of his coffee cup. "Don't play with me, Jenny. I have no intention of satisfying your curiosity where Miss Dancing is concerned. Don't pry into things that don't concern you." Standing up, he tossed his napkin on the table and stalked out of the room.

Jenny stared after her brother. What was the matter with him lately? He didn't usually speak to her in such harsh tones. Lately he'd been biting everyone's head off. She realized he was upset because of Skyler Dancing and he was handling it the only way he could. She wished with all her heart that Morgan and Skyler would overcome their differences. Her mother was positive Morgan and Miss Dancing would eventually settle what was wrong between them, but Jenny wasn't so sure. Skyler had seemed very adamant that they would never be able to work out their problems, whatever they were.

The days of summer were quickly passing, and Skyler knew the time would soon come when she must think about going home. She was lonesome for her mother and father, but she also dreaded the time when she must leave. Once she left Philadelphia, she would never see Morgan again, because she would never return.

Skyler was riding in the cool of the afternoon. She was accustomed to riding across rivers and valleys with a freedom she didn't have here. She was beginning to feel confined behind the iron gates of the James estate. She was also not accustomed to riding sidesaddle, and wished she could rip the constrictions of civilization from her and fling them aside. She longed to feel free again.

As Skyler topped a small grassy hill, she saw a rider coming down the tree-lined road. Her heart soared as she saw the man was riding an Indian pony and was dressed in buckskin. She recognized the dear old Trapper, Farley!

Urging her mount down the hill, she rode toward

him, waving and calling his name. When she drew even with Farley, she bounded out of the saddle just as he did, and he lifted her off the ground to give her a tight hug.

"Farley, I am so happy to see you. Have you come to take me home?"

He didn't answer right away, and she glanced up to see the troubled expression on his face. "Has something happened to Mother or Father?" she asked hurriedly, feeling fear in the depth of her heart.

"I left your ma and pa in good health, but I have grave news. Come on up to the house, so I'll only have to tell it once."

Skyler nodded, and he picked her up and placed her on her horse. As they rode back to the house, she watched his face. "How is my grandmother?"

By now they had reached the front yard, and Farley stopped his horse and met her inquiring glance. "I ain't happy about being the one to tell you, but your grandmother walks in the spirit world."

A sob escaped Skyler's lips, and she reached out her hand to the old trapper. "I should have been with her at the end," she cried. "I cannot believe my sweet, gentle grandmother is gone. I will never forgive myself for not being beside her."

Farley dismounted and lifted Skyler from her horse. He held her closely as she cried out her misery. She was so deep in misery, she wasn't even aware when the groom led the horses away.

"You gotta get hold of yourself, Sky Dancer. Sun Woman wouldn't want you to cry for her."

"I cannot help myself, Farley. I loved her so much. It will never be the same without her."

"You best be strong, 'cause I got more bad news. Your aunt and uncle are going to need you to be strong for them."

"Farley, *no!* Has something happened to Danielle?"

"Is Tag and Alex at home?"

"Yes, they are in the morning room."

"Come on in the house, and I'll tell you all at the same time," he said, leading her up the steps.

Tag knew the moment he saw Farley that something was amiss. Alexandria placed her sewing aside and clasped her husband's hand. They could both see that Skyler had been crying, and they waited for the old man to speak.

Farley ambled over and sat down in a chair. He was thoughtful for a moment before he spoke. He decided it would be best to blurt it out and get it over with. "Windhawk sent me to fetch you. Danielle is missing."

"What do you mean Danielle is missing?" Tag's voice boomed out and he rose to his feet quickly. The color drained out of his face, and his eyes were probing Farley's, trying to read the truth.

"She was sitting with Sun Woman while the women were berry picking. When they got back to the village, it was as if she just disappeared."

Tag started pacing the floor, and Skyler went to Alexandria and gathered her into her arms to comfort her. She knew her aunt loved Danielle as she would her own daughter, and Skyler feared the news of her cousin's disappearance might cause Alexandria to lose the baby.

"How in the hell can someone just disappear?" Tag

270

demanded. "What has been done to find my daughter? Has there been an extensive search?"

"You know Windhawk has left no stone unturned. As we talk, warriors are out looking for Danielle."

"I have to go to the village immediately," Tag said, looking like a wild man. "I should never have made her spend the summer with her mother's people. I forced her to go when she didn't want to. It's all my fault."

"I don't rightly seed that it's anyone's fault. No one could have knowed this was gonna happen."

"I will leave first thing in the morning. You and Skyler must stay with Alexandria, Farley. I don't want her left alone right now."

"I'll stay, but Joanna wants Sky Dancer home. You will have to take her with you."

Tag turned to Alexandria, who was crying softly. Taking her in his arms, he gathered her close to his heart. "It will be all right. I'll find her, I promise you—I will find our daughter."

"Go quickly, Tag. I don't want you to lose any time getting to the Blackfoot village," Alexandria cried, laying her head against his shoulder.

"Come, I want you to go bed right away. The doctor said you weren't to get upset."

"I am fine. I don't want to lie down."

He helped her to her feet. "Nonetheless, Alexandria, you will do as I say," he said firmly. "I shall sit beside you while you rest."

Skyler watched them leave the room, sharing their fear for Danielle. When they were out of sight, she leaned her head back against the settee and allowed the tears to flow freely. "This is a dark day, Farley. I hope we all have the strength to get through it."

For the first time in his life, the old trapper had no ready remark. He just nodded his head in agreement. He had been with this family through happiness and sadness. He supposed he must be getting old, because this trouble had taken a lot out of him. "A black day indeed, Sky Dancer. This has just 'bout done your ma in, and your pa ain't had much rest either. I think he blames himself for what happened."

"I had better go and pack my belongings. I know Uncle Tag will want to leave first thing in the morning," Skyler said. She stopped in front of Farley and bent to kiss his cheek. "I am glad to see you, even if you are the bearer of ill tidings. I wish you were going home with us."

The old man watched her move out of the room, thinking she had changed, and it had nothing to do with the news he had dropped in her lap. It wasn't even the way she was dressed, all fancy like. He wondered what had happened to turn a happy carefree girl into a sad-eyed woman.

Skyler packed very little. Most of the gowns, bonnets, and shoes she was leaving behind. She would have no use for them in the Blackfoot village. She had been able to pack her meager belongings in one leather satchel. At the bottom of the satchel, she placed her doeskin gown, knowing she would change into it once they left civilization behind. When she was finished packing, she placed the satchel at the foot of the stairs to be loaded onto the carriage in the morning.

*   *   *

The house was unusually quiet and everyone had retired to their rooms. Skyler had already dressed for bed but felt a restlessness within her as if the walls of the house were closing in on her. Feeling the need to be under the stars, she slipped on her robe and went downstairs quietly and out into the garden, hoping she wouldn't wake anyone.

Tomorrow she would be leaving the white world behind, and Skyler knew she would also be leaving a large part of herself. Her heart was heavy for many reasons. She was worried about Danielle, she felt grief for her grandmother's passing, and she knew she would never see Morgan again.

When Skyler reached the summerhouse, she stood with her face pressed against a white supporting post and allowed her mind to wander. What would Morgan do when he learned she had gone? Would he put her out of his mind and find someone who would willingly give him the love he deserved? He was a fine man, and he would make some fortunate woman a good husband, she thought painfully. He was kind, sensitive, and so loving. The only fault she could find with him was his attitude toward her people. For some white women that would be nothing at all, but for Skyler it was everything.

She wished with all her heart that she could see him just once more. She wanted to tell him that she loved him . . . that she would always love him.

All of a sudden Skyler felt as if she were reliving her dream. Her heart was thundering within her body. Now she knew what the dreams had meant. The dreams had been a warning that she would have to give up the man she loved. Hearing footsteps behind her, she knew it was Morgan. Tonight she would see him for the last time. She had lived this scene before and knew what his first words to her would be . . .

"Do you wish upon a star, Skyler?" he asked.

Turning, she found Morgan standing just behind her. It seemed the most natural thing in the world that he had come to her on her last night in Philadelphia. "No, I was thinking about you," she freely admitted. "What are you doing here, Morgan?"

"I come here almost every night on the off chance that I might see you," he said, moving closer to her. "Tonight I was lucky."

"I am glad you have come. I didn't want to leave without telling you good-bye."

He gazed up at the night sky, while she watched him, trying to fill her heart and mind with his nearness.

"When are you leaving, Skyler?" he asked at last.

"In the morning."

"So soon. If I hadn't come tonight, you wouldn't have said good-bye to me, would you?"

"No."

"Tell me what madness is this to cut me from your life? I know you have deep feelings for me. Tell me about this thing that stands between us."

She closed her eyes. What she really wanted to do was be in his arms and pour out her heart to him, but her secret must never be told. It would only make him turn from her in contempt. If she just went away, without revealing her secret, perhaps he would remember her sometimes with love. Now she understood her dreams. They had been a warning to her. She could never reach out and take the love he offered.

"I can tell you no more, Morgan. This is the last time

I will ever see you. I am going home tomorrow, and I shall never come back to Philadelphia. Tonight is good-bye for us."

His hands gripped her shoulders and he pulled her back against him. "No, damn it, this isn't good-bye. Don't you know you are tearing my heart out? Don't you give a damn that I love you?"

Her eyes were tear-bright. "I would rather tear out my own heart than to cause you pain, Morgan. I do love you, but you will have to understand I must go away."

She could feel the shudder that shook him. "How can I let you go when I know you love me? I have never felt this strongly about a woman before. It seems to me that when two people are meant for each other, as you and I are, there should be nothing else to consider. What a proud woman you are. I think what I love about you most is your strength and courage. I do not admire that you can turn your back on love."

· Skyler rested her face against his chest, knowing this was the last time they would ever be together. "I am not strong, Morgan, and I would like to have your admiration above all others, but I have to do what is right."

"Is there another man in your life?"

"No."

"I can't believe that you are going away—leaving me with nothing to hold on to." He raised her face and rested his against it. "I want you, Skyler Dancing. I want you for my wife."

Skyler shook her head. "That can never be." She tried to close her eyes against the tears, but was unsuccessful. "I can never be your wife, Morgan, but I

275

will give you what should only be for my husband on my wedding night." She found herself saying the very words that she had spoken in her dream. For a moment she couldn't tell if she were dreaming or awake. Where did dreams start and reality set in, she wondered.

Morgan searched her face. "Are you saying what I think you are?"

"Yes. I will be with you tonight. This is all I can ever give you, Morgan."

Anger moved over his face. "How magnanimous of you, Skyler. You are leaving me, so you think to pacify me with a few crumbs. I don't want what you offer . . . now or ever."

She knew it was his hurt that was talking. "You do want me, Morgan. Your words may deny it, but your eyes never could. It will cost you nothing to take what I give you tonight."

"How many other men have you offered yourself to, Skyler? Am I the next in a long line of men to whom you have offered crumbs?"

She reached up and unfastened the neck of her robe. "I have never given myself to another, Morgan. I want to give myself to you so you will know how deeply I feel about you. I don't want you to remember me with anything but kindness and love."

"No! I will not take what you are so willing to give. If I can't have all of you, then I don't want anything at all. I could find plenty of women who are willing to give me what you offer so freely. Perhaps you were right, and I should just leave."

His mouth was moving, and he was talking, but he wasn't aware of what he was saying. His eyes were drawn to Skyler as she let her robe drop onto the floor

276

of the summerhouse. He stood mesmerized as she slipped out of her gown and stood before him naked. He took a step toward her, but stopped when she raised her arms to him.

The bright moonlight seemed to turn her body a golden color. Morgan felt his breathing close off, knowing he could no longer resist the lovely vision that stood before him with her arms outstretched.

"Skyler," he cried in a strangled voice. Suddenly she was in his arms, and his hands were running up and down her back. He sought and found her lips as his hunger for her deepened into a maddening whirlwind.

Skyler felt his hands sliding blissfully up and down her back and across her hips as he whispered her name over and over. She would give him all she had to give, for she couldn't bear to go away and leave him with nothing. There was no doubt in her mind that he loved her, and she doubted she would ever love another man as deeply as she loved Morgan. She would one day have to marry, but if she gave herself to Morgan tonight she wouldn't be cheating anyone but herself.

The dream was being fulfilled. Tomorrow she would go away never to see her love's face again.

Alexandria couldn't sleep, so she got out of bed and walked over to the window. She couldn't get Danielle out of her mind. The horrible part in all this was in not knowing if she was dead or alive. If she were alive, she would be a captive. It was tearing her apart to think how Danielle might be mistreated.

As her gaze wandered down to the garden toward the summerhouse, she saw someone moving out of the shadows. It was a bright night, and Alexandria had no trouble recognizing Skyler and Morgan. She didn't need to see clearly to know they were locked in an embrace. Alexandria remembered the time when she had freely given herself to Tag. She felt pity in her heart for Skyler and Morgan. Tonight was all they would ever have.

"Can't you sleep either?" Tag asked, getting out of bed and walking toward her.

"I think I can now, if you will hold me," she said, moving to his side so he wouldn't discover Skyler and Morgan.

Tag helped her back to bed and lay down beside her. She closed her eyes, wishing that Skyler and Morgan would realize that love was the most important thing in life. No one could tell them that—they would have to discover the meaning of love on their own. It didn't matter if they came from different backgrounds; all that mattered in the end was whether they loved each other enough to sacrifice some of their beliefs.

Alexandria thought of Danielle, and a sob broke her lips. Poor, sweet Danielle would never know love. Alexandria felt in her heart that she must be dead.

She felt Tag's hands move across her face, and he pulled her forward to rest against his shoulder. "Don't give up, Alexandria. I need you to believe that we will find our girl. If you believe it, then perhaps I can hope, too."

"I want to believe it, Tag, but Farley would never have come for you if he thought there was any hope."

Tag held her tightly, fearing she might lose his baby. Now when she needed him most, he was forced to leave her. "What kind of nonsense is that, my sweet love? I would be willing to bet that when I get to the village, Danielle will be there to greet me."

He closed his eyes, knowing he was only trying to pacify Alexandria. In his heart he feared Danielle had met a terrible fate. When she was gone, he would lose the last link he had with Morning Song.

In one of the guest bedrooms Farley swore under his breath because he couldn't get to sleep in the too soft bed. Tossing the wine-colored coverlet onto the floor, he climbed out of bed and lay down on it. Staring at the window he still couldn't sleep. There was much unhappiness within this family he loved, and there didn't seem to be a damned thing he could do about it.

Chapter Twenty-one

The prairie grasses no longer green were scarred with a thick black dust that covered the land. Smoke still rose into the air, mixing with the night shadows only to be lost in the ebony skies.

Wolfrunner bent over Danielle's unconscious body, examining her closely. Her face was streaked from the soot and ashes, but she didn't seem to be burned. He could see the steady rise and fall of her breasts, so he knew she was breathing.

Cupping his hands in the river, he proceeded to wash her face clean. When that was accompanied, his eyes traveled down to her ankle, and he saw it was swollen almost twice its normal size. She must have injured it when she fell earlier in the day, but she hadn't complained. He had pushed her mercilessly and she must have been in agony. Examining her ankle, his eyes wandered to her shoes. He saw the soles of her shoes had been worn through and the bottoms of her feet were raw and bleeding.

Gathering her into his arms, Wolfrunner held her

limp body against him. Great Father, he had thought her weak and unworthy, when she had possessed great courage. When the fire had raged out of control, and it looked like they would both be burned alive, had she not urged him to leave her and save himself? Never had he met a woman with such bravery and courage. His heart seemed to shatter, knowing he would never be worthy of her. In her eyes he was nothing but a savage—had she not said so herself?

Picking up her small hand, he held it to his face, rubbing his lips across the soft palm. Now, while she was unconscious, he could touch her and hold her in his arms. He could allow his love to wash over him without her being aware of it. He had been forced to hide his feelings from Danielle and himself. It had been difficult to pretend indifference and dislike when his heart had been crying out to touch her.

Lifting Danielle's head Wolfrunner cupped his hands in the water and held it to her lips. She stirred and her eyes fluttered open.

For a moment there was confusion written in her beautiful blue eyes. When she saw the look of concern on Wolfrunner's face, she smiled weakly.

"Are we not dead?" she whispered through parched lips. "Do I walk among your spirit world?"

Wolfrunner laid her back on the grass. "It would seem the Great One smiled on us today. We should be dead, but we somehow survived."

"It was because of you that we live," she said, sitting up. A grimace of pain flickered across her face and she reached down to her ankle. "How was it possible that the whole prairie caught on fire?"

Wolfrunner's eyes traveled across the river where earlier he had seen a lone Indian watching him, and he knew it had been his old enemy. "Scar Face set the fire. He must be very angry that we refused to die. He will try again."

Danielle's eyes searched the darkness. "Will he come tonight?" she asked fearfully.

"No, he is a coward and knows we will be watching for him. He will strike from behind when we least expect it, so we must always be on watch for him."

Danielle tried to stand, but pain shot through her ankle and Wolfrunner pushed her backward. "You will rest and I will tend you. Why did you not tell me you were in pain? I can see this is very bad."

"Would you have stopped for me had you known that I was injured?" she asked.

He plunged her feet into the cool river water and stood up. "I will find the soothing herb that will help you heal. It will be best if we remain here until you are well enough to travel. If you would have told me you were hurt today, we would not have to lose valuable time now." His voice was cold, and Danielle shivered at the anger on his face. She didn't know how to please him. If she had told him of her injury today, he would have accused her of complaining. Now, he claimed it was her fault they would lose time getting back to the village. Apparently anything she did would anger him.

Danielle watched Wolfrunner disappear, knowing he wouldn't be far away. He might have threatened to leave her in the past, but she now knew he never would have. He had protected her with his own life today. She had never known a man like him. She wished she knew the words to say to him to let him know how grateful she was. She had come to know him well enough to realize he wouldn't welcome her gratitude. What a proud man he was. Could no one break through that wall he erected about himself?

Danielle was experiencing a way of life that was as different from the way she had been brought up as day was different from night. Here in this lovely land of her Indian ancestors, she had lost her identity, but found herself. She had slowly been molded into a girl her friends would never recognize. Wolfrunner had helped her find the meaning of who she was. It didn't matter to her any longer that she would be considered a half-breed. To her surprise she found herself feeling that she belonged to this land. It was as if she had been searching for something and someone all her young life. The something was the land of her mother's people, the someone was Wolfrunner!

I love him, she thought. I love this man who has stood many times between me and death. She knew she could never tell him how she loved him—he would only scoff at her feelings. In the new person she had become, Danielle knew that she could be strong. She could face whatever the future held for her with pride and dignity.

How brave and noble Wolfrunner was. It would never have occurred to him to leave her today to save his own life. Again she found herself wanting to learn more about this man who had become her savior.

A short time later, Wolfrunner returned to her. He came so quietly out of the shadows that he startled Danielle. Sitting down beside her, he lifted her feet out of the river and gently dried them off. Danielle watched as he crushed some kind of leaves in the palms of his hands and then rubbed them on the bottoms of her feet. After that was done, he ripped a strip off her skirt and bound it tightly about her ankle.

"If you keep tearing my clothing, I will be wearing very little when we reach the village." Her smile told

284

him she was teasing, but he didn't seem amused.

"White women wear too many clothes. It is not good to cover the body when the sun is hot."

"Well," she said, looking down at the once expensive gown, that now came just above her knees. "You couldn't say I was overdressed."

He caught the humor in her voice, and inside he smiled, even though the face he turned to her held a grim expression. His eyes ran the length of her shapely leg, from foot to calf, and he quickly looked back to the binding on her foot.

When he was satisfied he had done all he could to make her comfortable, he bathed her face once more to remove the remaining smudges. "You must try to rest now. By tomorrow you will feel much better, I think."

When he would have risen, she placed her hand on his arm. "Stay with me," she whispered. "I don't want to be alone. Could we talk?"

Wolfrunner's dark eyes sought hers, and Danielle thought she detected a softness there. He said nothing as he stretched out on the grass beside her. Reaching out her hand, she found his and laced her fingers through it. He didn't pull away as she expected. Somehow they seemed bound together in that moment. They had faced death today; tonight they had been blessed with another chance at life.

Danielle sighed and closed her eyes, immediately falling asleep. She didn't know when Wolfrunner drew her into his arms, nor did she feel his lips brush against her cheek to rest at the side of her mouth.

Wolfrunner could feel his senses reeling. He felt as if he held the world in his arms. How easily he could have lost this wonderful gift today. Had the Great One placed her in his keeping for a reason? His hand wandered up to her silken hair. His heart felt as if it were overflowing. He wanted this woman—he needed her—she was the breath of life to him. His hand wandered down to her soft cheek. No, she wasn't for him. She was a princess of his people. Even though he was the son of a powerful war chief, Danielle was as far from him as the invisible line that separated his world from the white world. He could only have her for the short time that it took for him to get her safely back to the village. Then she would be lost to him forever.

Wolfrunner's body craved the closeness that was denied him. Sitting up, he moved down to the river and bathed his face in the cool water. He must not think of her. His only purpose was to keep her safe.

His eyes traveled across the river, knowing Scar Face was out there watching him. His trials were not yet over, nor would they be, until either he or Scar Face lay dead!

Danielle awoke with the sun shining on her face. Stretching her arms above her head, she smiled to herself. She had slept soundly all night and felt rested and refreshed. Rising slowly to her feet, she hobbled down to the river, cupped her hands, and took a cool drink.

Glancing about her, she looked for Wolfrunner, but apparently he was off scouting the area.

Turning her eyes toward the prairie, she gasped at what she saw. It was a wasted desert land now. Yesterday it had offered sanctuary and food to numerous kinds of wildlife. Today nothing could live on the ugly blackened land. Danielle shivered, knowing that if Wolfrunner hadn't saved them yesterday, their bones would soon be bleaching in the scorching sun.

Danielle looked down at her feet. Although they still bothered her, the herbs Wolfrunner had put on them had gone a long ways toward easing the pain.

Danielle's hearing had become attuned with the sounds about her. This time when Wolfrunner came up behind her, she heard his footsteps.

Placing the rabbit he had killed down on a rock, he smiled at her. "I have brought you a surprise, Danielle."

The biggest surprise for her was that he called her by name instead of "white girl." "What is it?" she asked, her eyes dancing with anticipation.

Pulling his hand from his back, Wolfrunner extended it out to her. Curled up in his palm was a tiny gray rabbit with a white cotton tail.

"Oh, the dear thing," she cried, taking the animal in her hand and raising it to her face. "Its fur is so soft. Where did you find him?"

"It is a she," he corrected. "I fear I unknowingly killed her mother. I try never to kill an animal if I know it has young to feed."

Danielle sat down on the grass and stroked the rabbit gently while talking to it softly. "I am going to call her Cottontail," she said, smiling up at Wolfrunner.

He raised a dark eyebrow. "Not a very original name."

"I don't care, I like her. May I really keep her?"

"That is what I intended. She is young enough not to be afraid of you."

"What will we feed her?"

"Grass, green leafy plants, and clover. You will have no trouble finding food for her."

She noticed for the first time that he was stacking

wood to build a fire. "Let me do that," she said, placing her newfound friend on the grass and bending down beside Wolfrunner.

"No," he said, picking Danielle up and sitting her beneath the shade of a tree. "Until you are recovered, I will take care of you."

She watched him turn away, wishing he would always take care of her. Danielle noticed the way his back rippled with muscles as he broke the firewood in half. Her eyes went to his strong hands, and she felt a physical ache for him to touch her.

Turning away, ashamed of her outrageous thinking, she picked up Cottontail and held her next to her heart. She couldn't touch Wolfrunner, but she could love and caress the living thing that he had given her.

Soon the aroma of cooking meat filled the morning air. Danielle watched Wolfrunner turn the wooden spit so the meat would brown evenly. She couldn't help but notice he was acting differently toward her today—he was being kind and considerate. How unlike him to bring her the baby rabbit.

Suddenly the irony of it all hit Danielle, and she started laughing. Wolfrunner turned to her with an inquiring glance.

"I was just thinking. Yesterday we were fighting to stay alive. Today we are acting as if nothing ever happened. Life is strange sometimes."

He said nothing, but turned back to remove the rabbit from the spit. Carrying it over to Danielle, he sat down and offered her a piece of meat.

"*No!*" she exclaimed, shaking her head from side to side. "I could never eat Cottontail's mother. It's like cannibalism."

He shook his head. "What is that word?"

"It means when a human eats the flesh of another human."

He chuckled just before he bit into the meat. "You have some strange ideas, Danielle. If you will not eat the meat, you must feast on roots and berries."

"That suits me fine. I'm not in the mood for meat."

Again he laughed. "It was not long ago that you declared you loved the meat of the rabbit."

"Well, I don't anymore. I will just have to eat something else from now on."

As his strong white teeth tore into the meat, he smiled at her. The two sides of you battle, Danielle. I wonder which is stronger. Which one will win in the end?

She turned away from him, thinking he could see too much. Curling up on the grass, she fell asleep with Cottontail cradled in her arms.

It was almost sundown and so peaceful beside the river, if Danielle didn't look to the south and see the ugly, charred prairie.

She sat with her back against a tree and Cottontail curled up in her lap. Wolfrunner had been gone all afternoon, and she heard him returning now.

As he dropped on the grass beside her, she couldn't help but notice his hair was wet. "Did you go for a swim?" she asked.

He smiled slightly. "I took a bath. Regardless of what you may have been told, not all Indians are filthy savages."

Shame washed over Danielle as the words she had once spoken to Wolfrunner came back to haunt her. "I never . . . I didn't . . ." she stammered, trying to think how to retract her cruel words. "I know my aunt

Joanna's lodge is spotless, as was my grandmother's."

All of a sudden their eyes met, and Danielle had the sensation she was drowning in the dark, mysterious glow in his eyes. He reached around her and plucked a blue wildflower and brushed her lips with the petals.

Danielle drew in her breath, astounded by the wildfire that seemed to churn through her veins. Cottontail was resting against Danielle's throat, and Wolfrunner reached up and softly stroked the rabbit. As his hand moved from the rabbit to Danielle's cheek, she felt as if an earthquake shook her body.

His dark gaze seemed to be drawing her to him. They moved toward each other, and she could feel his breath on her lips.

Her breathing seemed to stop—she waited for him to move the final distance so their lips would touch. As her heart pounded against her chest, she watched his eyes change. Where they had been velvet-soft before, they now sparked with anger.

Before she could reach out to Wolfrunner he was on his feet and moved away quickly. She was stunned by what had just happened between them.

Resting her face against the soft rabbit fur, she tried to regain her composure. This man kept pulling at her, and when she was ready to surrender, he pulled away. She didn't understand him at all.

Wolfrunner closed his eyes and allowed the night breeze to cool his face. He had almost lost control of himself a moment ago. He knew now that he was going to have to keep his distance from Danielle. He wanted her with every fiber of his being. Tonight he would fight the most bitter battle he had ever had to wage. He would fight his feelings for Danielle.

Chapter Twenty-two

Skyler moved out of the circle of Morgan's arms and glanced up at him shyly. "I have offered myself to you. Do you not want me?"

Her hair was streaming across her golden-colored breasts like a black velvet curtain. Her hips were well rounded, and her tiny waist could easily be spanned with a man's hands. Her legs weren't long, but they were perfectly shaped. Morgan didn't pause to wonder why her body was the same golden color all over. He stared at her in a half-dazed state, wanting her with every fiber of his being. His body trembled and he felt a need to touch her, to hold her against him forever.

"Damn you," Morgan growled, pulling her back into his arms. "You know I want you, but not this way. Why are you doing this to me . . . to us?"

Skyler could feel the strength of his arms as he pushed her aside. She could sense there was pain as well as anger in him. He took the cushions from the window seat and angrily tossed them to the floor of the summerhouse.

291

"If you want me to lie you down, I'll do it. I hope you know what you are letting yourself in for, Skyler. But I don't think you do," he said in a deep voice.

Her body trembled visibly as she watched him strip his shirt off and toss it aside. This wasn't what she wanted, she thought in a panic. She had wanted to give herself to Morgan with love, not with anger.

When he had cast the last of his clothing aside, he walked toward her slowly. Skyler stepped back a pace. His eyes were burning into her, and she could see that his jaw was set in anger. Her eyes went to the magnificence of his body. She started shaking all over as he drew nearer. Her eyes fastened on the golden mat of hair on his chest that ran further down his body than her eyes were willing to go.

Morgan reached out for her and slammed her against his naked body. His form was lean and hard and the feel of his hardness pressing against her caused Skyler to gasp.

"Damn you for making me love you, and damn you for making me want you," he growled in her ear.

"Morgan, please, I don't want it this way."

"How do you want it, Skyler?" he demanded to know. "I wish to hell I knew."

"I . . . wanted to give you this night to remember," she whispered through trembling lips.

He forced her head up so she would have to meet his gaze. "I don't need this to keep you in my mind and heart. Wherever I go and whatever I do, the thought of you will always be with me. How many ways do you want me to say I love you, Skyler? How many times must I prove that I want you for my wife?"

Tears blinded her, and she quickly brushed them

away with the back of her hand. "I love you more than my own life, Morgan. Am I not proving that to you tonight?"

His head dipped, and she met his kiss eagerly. His hot body was pressed against her soft curves, and she felt a new awakening from deep within. His tongue parted her lips savagely and his mouth plundered hers. She was vaguely aware that he was lowering her back against the cushions.

"This isn't what I envisioned for you and me, Skyler. I had thought to take you on our wedding bed," he whispered hotly in her ear. "Hell, who am I fooling? I'll take you any way I can have you."

"Tonight I will be as your wife, Morgan," she answered. "Take what I would have given you as my husband."

His lips moved down her throat and across her silken breasts. Skyler gasped for breath as his tongue circled the rosy peaks. A white-hot sensation rushed through her veins, and she felt as if an earthquake shook her body. She experienced the after-shock all the way to her toes.

"Sweet, sweet, Skyler," he murmured, and his hot breath sent shivers down her spine.

Morgan could feel his pulse beat madly as his hand drifted over her silken skin, down her smooth stomach, to rest against her thigh. He was inches away from paradise, and yet he couldn't bring himself to touch her forbidden womanhood. He knew she had never been with a man, and he questioned his right to take what she so readily offered.

Skyler could sense his reluctance, so she drew his face up to her lips. "Take the gift I offer you, Morgan.

It is all I have to give you."

He moaned as her lips sought his. He could no longer reason past the wild desire that kept pounding in his brain. Kissing her all the while, he spread her legs and positioned himself between them. One hand pulled her head closer to receive his burning kiss, while the other wandered slowly and sensuously down to the valley of her womanhood. His hand shook as it moved carefully into the velvety softness of her.

Skyler groaned as her body reacted to his soft touch. She felt something akin to pain yet beyond pain as his hand gently massaged her inner core.

Morgan found the barrier that proved she had never been with a man. Her breath was warm and sweet against his lips, and he felt his body tremble all over.

Yes, he would take what she offered him. Nothing could stop the tide of passion she had awakened within him. Never before had he had this deep craving for a woman. He tried not to think that this night was all they would ever share. He suddenly became obsessed with the need to show Skyler that it was meant that they should be together forever . . . not just for tonight.

Skyler felt Morgan move forward. When he slowly entered her body, she clamped her lips together tightly to keep from crying out at the beautiful feelings that encased her whole being. There was a slight stinging sensation as he pushed forward, but it didn't last long. She clutched at his shoulders when he moved slowly up and back in a slow, rhythmic motion.

The night seemed to have a thousand eyes as the stars twinkled down upon the two lovers. Each would give eternal love to the other, and so it had been since the beginning of time when the love is pure and the hearts intertwine. Skyler gave all she had, knowing this night was all she would ever have. Morgan took everything, hoping to bind Skyler to him for the rest of their lives.

Skyler sprinkled kisses across Morgan's shoulders. Loving the feel of his body united with hers, she wished this night would last forever. She had given to him, but he was giving back to her a hundredfold. His hands were gentle as they caressed her body, and his lips were sweet as they moved across her face to find her lips.

She knew that tomorrow, and a thousand tomorrows afterward, she would weep for what could not be. But now—at this moment, she had Morgan, body and soul.

"It is good between us, Skyler," he murmured against her ear. "You belong to me. Surely you can feel that."

His damp hair clung to the side of his head, and she ran her fingers through it. With an instinct that is born of woman, she moved her hips up, inviting him to drive deeper into her softness.

He groaned as his body reached dazzling heights. Never before had he felt this way with a woman. "You are me, and I am you," he whispered in a raspy voice. "I love you more than life, my dearest love. Say that you love me," he demanded, needing to hear the words spoken.

"Yes," she groaned as the tempo inside her body heightened by his softly spoken words. She had always wondered what love would be like between a woman and a man. Now she knew she would remember tonight for the rest of her life.

She gasped with pleasure when he thrust forward,

295

searing the insides of her with his stamp of ownership. Tears ran down her face at what she and Morgan could have had together. Tomorrow she would go away and they would never see each other again. How could she bear to leave him after tonight?

"I love you, Morgan," she whispered against his ear. "I love you with all my heart."

His eyes were soft, and clearly shone with an answering love. They stared into each other's eyes at the very moment when their bodies reached the final climax. As both their bodies shook with one tremor after another, they clasped each other to their hearts.

Skyler was never to know how long they lay in each other's arms, whispering words of eternal love, as they both pledged their love, one to the other. She wasn't brought back to reality until Morgan raised up on his elbow and looked into her misty violet eyes.

"Now you know that you were meant to be my wife, Skyler. I can't let you go after what has happened between us tonight. Say you will marry me." His voice was almost pleading as his eyes searched her face. "Say yes!" he urged almost frantically. "You know you want to, damn it!"

Skyler wedged her arm between them and sat up. "Do not ask this of me, Morgan. It will be hard enough to leave in the morning. Let us part with this beautiful thing between us. Do not spoil what we had."

Morgan stood up slowly and drew her up beside him. "What kind of a woman are you? Are you made of stone? Did you not say that you loved me?"

Tears were streaming down her face, but Morgan seemed unmoved by them as he gripped her arms and shook her. "Answer me, Skyler. What in the hell are you made of?"

"Please do not say anymore, Morgan. Let us both walk away without cruel words between us."

"What am I supposed to do—say thank you for a beautiful evening? Am I supposed to stand calmly by while you walk out of my life forever?"

"I will not ask anything of you, Morgan. You have my heart—I can give you nothing beyond that."

He grabbed a handful of ebony hair and jerked her head forward. "Why can't you tell me what is keeping us apart? If you really love me, at least give me that much. Whatever it is, we can work it out together."

"No, Morgan. What is wrong between us can never be worked out. I could not watch your love turn to contempt, as it surely would if I told you my secret."

Skyler moved away from him and picked up her gown and robe. While he watched, she slipped them on and then turned back to face him.

His eyes were wild as it began to sink in that she could not be swayed from her convictions. He searched his mind for some way to hold on to her. What could be so bad that she couldn't tell him?

"Don't you know you can trust me? Tell me about this thing that is eating away at you!" he cried, moving to her side and crushing her in his arms. "My God, don't do this to us. Don't you know you are killing my soul?"

By now Skyler was crying hysterically. She rested her face against the soft mat of hair on his chest, wishing he could hold her forever. He stroked her gently and spoke soothing words in her ear.

"Do not cry, little love. I shall move mountains if that will make you happy. I will sweep aside anything that stands between us, and I shall walk over anyone who tries to take you away from me."

Skyler closed her eyes, knowing the pain she was causing him. She raised her head and looked into his eyes. "Kiss me good-bye, Morgan," she cried softly. "My dearest, dearest love, kiss me one last time."

His face seemed to freeze. For a long moment he stared at her in disbelief. Suddenly he gave her a shove and turned away to pull on his clothing. Skyler watched through tear-blinded eyes as he pulled on his boots and tucked his shirt into his trousers.

When he turned back to her, his features were stormy. "It will be a hell of a lot better when you are gone from my life, Miss Skyler Dancing. I fared well enough before I met you—I can do so again."

Morgan moved across the summerhouse and turned to her one last time. Touching his fingers to his forehead in a salute, he then turned on his heels and moved down the path.

Skyler wanted to call after him, but she didn't dare. She could hear the sound of his boot steps fading into the distance. He was gone! She would never see him again!

Dropping to her knees, broken sobs came from somewhere deep in her throat. She never knew that crying could cause such pain. Agonizing sounds were filling the night air.

She had only borrowed Morgan's love for a short time—it had never really belonged to her. She had wanted him to remember her with kindness, but now when he thought of her it would be with contempt.

She cried until she was exhausted, then she stood up and made her way slowly back to the house. In a few hours it would be sun-up, and she and her uncle would be on their way back to her village. Perhaps her mother could help her understand why this had happened between her and Morgan. Yes, if anyone could understand, it would be her mother. Had she not had to face a similar choice when she married Skyler's father? But then her father had not had the contempt for her mother's race as Morgan had for Skyler's. Fate had been cruel to allow her to love a man who was not of her world. Morgan would never have accepted her if he'd known the truth. It was best that he never found out about her Indian blood.

It was barely daylight when the carriage bearing Skyler and her uncle moved out the iron gates of the James estate. Skyler had said a tearful good-bye to her Aunt Alexandria. It had been painful for Skyler to leave her aunt now that she needed her. She sat back, cloaked in her own misery. She was leaving heartbreak behind her in Philadelphia. Each mile the carriage traveled took her farther away from the man she loved.

Skyler knew when she reached her village she would be faced with other heartaches. She would have to come to grips with her grandmother's death and Danielle's disappearance. She prayed that by the time they reached her home, her cousin would have been found, unharmed.

Glancing at her uncle, Skyler saw he was sleeping. More than likely he hadn't slept all night and he must be very exhausted. She was traveling back to her world and to her old way of life. Skyler didn't know how she would ever be able to put Morgan out of her mind and just pick up her life where she'd left off. Wiping the tears away from her eyes, she stared out the window. The sound of the horses' hooves seemed to be echoing. You love him, you love him!

Morgan stood at his bedroom window, watching the sun come up. Skyler was leaving today. Where was she going? He knew nothing about her life, beyond the fact that she loved him—he knew that for a certainty.

He went over and over in his mind every word she'd ever spoken to him, trying to solve the mystery. Last night he'd held a woman in his arms and had poured out his love to her. Today that woman would walk out of his life forever, and he couldn't understand the reason for her going. What was this thing that stood between him and the woman he loved?

Skyler had thrown love away. Anger etched the stiff plane of Morgan's jaw. Waste had always made him angry.

Chapter Twenty-three

In three days' time, Danielle's ankle had healed enough so she and Wolfrunner could continue on their journey. Danielle was almost sorry to leave their haven. It was here that she had rested and regained her strength, and it was here that she found out that she was beginning to love this man.

Wolfrunner had cut strips of leather from the flap of his breechcloth and fashioned Danielle a crude pair of sandals.

He had bent down to strap the shoes about her ankle, when she laughed aloud. "I think it would be a good idea if we made it to the village before too long. The way we are using up our clothing, neither of us will have a stitch to our name when we get there."

Wolfrunner's dark eyes swept her face. He didn't smile, but she saw his mouth twitch, and his dark eyes were dancing. He scooped up the baby rabbit and handed it to Danielle. "Test your foot to see if you can walk," he told her while watching her face for any sign of pain.

Danielle tucked the edge of her skirt into the waistband and placed the baby rabbit in the makeshift pocket. It meant showing more of her legs, but she was past feeling modest by now. Testing her new shoes, she found them to be quite comfortable.

"I do not feel the pain any longer. Your cure worked miracles."

He nodded. "It is an old cure taught to me by an old medicine woman called She Who Heals. She once cured Joanna from snow blindness with this medicine."

He picked up his spear and started walking at a fast pace, and she fell into step with him. At first his strides were long, but he soon slowed them to match hers.

Once again they now followed the course of the river. To the south of them the land was blackened by the prairie fire. Danielle thought it would be years before the scars left on the land by the fire would heal.

Just ahead Danielle saw a huge mountain range. Some of the mountains were so high they still had snow on the taller peaks. She knew they must cross these mountains to find the Blackfoot village. She felt dread just looking at the seemingly impregnable wall, wondering how they would ever make it over the top.

The last few days Wolfrunner had become more silent than ever. He seldom spoke to Danielle, and she wondered if he would ever look at her as a woman. She tried in every way she could to please him, but still he seemed indifferent to her.

She found he was always alert to danger, and he could hear and see things that no normal person could. The threat of Scar Face still hung over them. Even though Danielle never saw any sign of Scar Face, she knew he would be following them. Wolfrunner often stopped and tested the wind. He would scan the horizon in every direction before they continued their journey.

They had to rely on small game for their survival. Wolfrunner knew Scar Face was aware of their every move, so he didn't bother to hide their tracks. Each night he would make a campfire to cook their food. There was no reason to hide from an enemy who knew where to find you. Danielle knew that he slept very little at night, since he didn't want Scar Face to come upon them unawares.

The weather had grown hotter, and the sun beat down on them with a punishing force. As they neared the mountains, the terrain became rocky, making it more difficult to walk. Danielle could feel every rock and stone through her thin-soled sandals. She took particular care not to injure her weak ankle, knowing Wolfrunner would not be pleased if they had to stop and allow her to heal again.

When at last they reached the mountains, there was the added burden of climbing very steep cliffs. But now it was much easier to hide from Scar Face, because Wolfrunner was very clever about covering up their tracks on the rocky face of the mountains. There was plenty of food to be found, and water was always abundant.

It was almost nightfall. Danielle stood on the high slope of a mountain and gazed out on the breathtaking countryside. This was a land of imperishable beauty. As she stood in the shadows of tall mountain peaks and deep canyons, she could see the reflections of numerous lakes and streams. Here nature had colored the land with every hue known to man. It was magnificent and spectacular. Somehow Danielle got the feeling that it hadn't changed since the beginning of time. This was the land of her past—did it also hold her future?

Gazing across a ravine, she saw Wolfrunner standing as still as a statue. He was looking at the same view, and Danielle wondered if he was having similar thoughts. How could he not feel pride in this land that belonged to his people. It was in his blood and a part of his heritage. It was as timeless and beautiful as the Blackfoot people who called it home. This love of the land came to her from out of nowhere, from some hidden recess in her mind. She thought it strange that she had never loved the land in Philadelphia.

Her eyes moved over the man who had come to mean so much to her. How magnificent he was with his dark hair blowing in the wind. The setting sun fell on his skin, turning it to a soft bronze color. He was as much a part of this land as the rocks and trees; he belonged here and she didn't.

Suddenly she wanted him to pull her into his world. Raising her arms, she held them out to him as if beseeching him to take her unto him. Her heart seemed to skip a beat when he raised his arms to her. Across the distance that divided them, Danielle could feel him pulling at her.

"I love you, Wolfrunner," she called out, but she knew he couldn't hear her, since her voice had been carried away with the wind.

She watched him lower his arms and disappear down the steep embankment. She knew she would always remember the moment when the two of them had stood apart and reached out to each other. Would the time ever come when they would reach across the gulf that separated them and their hands would touch? She doubted that he would ever think of her other than as Joanna's niece. Danielle knew Wolfrunner still didn't like her as a person, and she doubted that he ever would.

They had been traveling in the mountains for three days. Each day there seemed to be another mountain to climb. The barriers of rock and stone seemed to go on forever, and Danielle wondered if they would ever come to the valley of the Blood Blackfoot.

They had made camp beside a small stream with a magnificent view of a deep craggy canyon that seemed to cut its way into the mountains.

Wolfrunner had disappeared some time ago and Danielle was wondering where he was. They had food left over from the day before, so surely he hadn't gone hunting.

Gazing up at the sky, she noticed the dark clouds that were gathering on the horizon. She had never liked storms—for some reason they had always terrified her. She tried not to think of the impending storm. Dipping her hands in the cool mountain stream, she took a deep drink.

Suddenly, Danielle felt something brush up against her leg. Looking down in surprise, she saw a small furry animal curl up beside her. Her laughter rang out as she picked it up and held it in her arms. It was some kind of cat. Wouldn't it be wonderful if she could take the animal home with her as a companion to Cottontail?

she thought.

Danielle sat down and ruffled the animal's furry coat, which was soft and tawny with brownish spots. "You are just a kitten," she said, rubbing the animal beneath the chin and feeling delight in the way it cuddled up against her. The cat was making soft purring sounds, and Danielle laughed delightedly as it pawed at her finger playfully.

"How dear you are. I am going to keep you," she said, holding the kitten up to her face. Cottontail was curled up beside her while the newcomer lapped out its tongue and licked the tiny rabbit. "I can see that the two of you are going to be wonderful friends," she said, giving each of them an individual pat.

Danielle hadn't heard Wolfrunner come up beside her, and was startled when he yanked the kitten out of her arms. His eyes blazed dangerously and his jaw was set in anger. "You are a stupid white girl. Do you not know a cougar when you see one? The mother would tear you to pieces if she were to return," he said angrily.

"I didn't know," she said, lowering her eyes and feeling stupid indeed.

"I wonder that you are still alive. Do you know nothing about taking care of yourself?" His voice was deep with anger and his dark eyes were dilated.

She stood up and faced him. "If I am as stupid as you seem to think, why do you bother with me?"

"I wonder the same thing myself. Must I always keep you in my sight to keep you from harm?"

Her eyes flashed. "I did not ask you to look after me. I wish you would just go away. I don't want you here. You are hateful and mean. Nothing I do seems to please you."

306

He gave her a guarded look. "If I left you to yourself, you would not survive the first day."

"Who appointed you my guardian? I didn't ask you for anything. I don't want to be with you."

"Then leave. You are free to go. I am not holding you here!" Turning his back, he stalked away, carrying the cougar cub by the scruff of the neck.

Suddenly she feared what he would do to the cub. Racing after him, she caught hold of his arm. "You aren't going to harm this baby, are you? I am warning you, I won't allow it. Only an animal would mistreat another."

His dark eyes seemed to become storm centers. "I leave it to your white men to kill animals when it is not necessary. It is not the Indian way. The prairies and plains are dotted with the bleaching bones of slaughtered buffalo, which your people killed only for the hide. Go back to the stream and wait until I return." He turned away but she heard him mutter under his breath, and his words seemed to cut into her heart. "I grow weary of protecting you from yourself."

Danielle was blinded by tears. She wanted to strike out at Wolfrunner for causing her pain. If he thought she was such a burden, she would just remove herself. No man had ever dared treat her with such disrespect. She had no intention of staying with him any longer.

Watching him disappear up the face of the mountain toward a high ledge, she turned around and ran in the opposite direction. She ran and ran, until she dropped from fatigue. Sitting down on the ground, she pulled the baby rabbit out of its hiding place in the folds of her gown, holding it to her face. After she had rested, she got to her feet and ran some more.

Danielle was wise enough to move in the direction of the Blackfoot village. She didn't know how to get there, and she knew it was still several weeks' walk, but that didn't matter. The only thing she cared about was getting as far away from Wolfrunner as she could.

How could she ever have thought she had any tender feelings for that hateful man? All he wanted to do was boss and bully her while pointing out her short-comings. How could he expect her to know all the things that an Indian maiden grew up knowing about? What had been the harm in her playing with the adorable little kitten?

It was almost dark when the first drops of rain began to fall. Danielle saw the lightning streak across the sky and heard the thunder rumble down the mountain side.

She pressed her body tightly against a huge boulder and covered her ears. Fear deeper than when she had been abducted and more powerful than when she had been caught in the prairie fire, filled her being. A wild scream escaped her throat as a jagged streak of lightning split across the sky and struck a nearby bush, causing it to burst into flames.

It seemed as if the sky had opened up and rain fell to the earth in torrents. Danielle dropped to her knees, crying hysterically. She did have enough wits about her to try and shelter the baby rabbit from the rain. Finding where two rocks came together, she placed the ball of fur back as far as she could reach.

Danielle knew by now she was hopelessly lost. This time Wolfrunner could not save her, because he would never find her in this rainstorm. Her tracks would be washed away by the heavy rainfall.

She huddled against the boulder, clinging to it as if it

were her lifeline. Since she had been a small child, every time there had been a thunderstorm Danielle had been haunted by nightmares—nightmares more terrifying than any reality she had yet faced.

Just when she thought she couldn't stand it a moment longer, someone reached out to her and drew her into his arms. She threw her arms around Wolfrunner and pressed her body against him, trembling with terror.

"I was afraid you wouldn't find me," she sobbed.

He held her tightly, trying to still her shaking body. "I will always find you, little one," he whispered near her ear. "Do not fear the storm, I will protect you."

Danielle raised her face and looked at him as another streak of lightning flashed across the sky. For just a fraction of a second, his dark eyes reflected the lightning bolt. In that moment it seemed they were both suspended in time, drawn together not by the electricity of the storm, but by the electricity that came from within themselves.

For days they had been pulling against the force that tried to bring them together. Now, neither of them resisted.

Danielle's lips parted as Wolfrunner lowered his head. When his lips touched hers, she melted to his body.

Suddenly, the storm no longer mattered. It was pushed to the back of Danielle's mind to make room for a deeper and more meaningful emotion.

"I have wanted to touch you from the first time I saw you," he whispered in her ear. In a rush of feelings, almost as if a dam broke and pent-up emotions broke free in a flood of agony, he clasped her slight body to him. "Danielle!" He spoke her name as if it was ripped from his throat. "I cannot help myself for this weakness that burns within me."

Danielle felt her heart take wings. As he lowered her onto the ground, she held her arms up to him. "Hold me, Wolfrunner," she said softly. "Hold me very tightly."

"Danielle, I dare not," he said in a moment of sanity. "If I hold you now, it will not stop there. I desire you as a woman."

The rain was pelting her in the face but it didn't matter. She raised her arms to him once more. "Take me as a woman, Wolfrunner," she said, feeling a deep need for him to touch her.

He hesitated for but a moment before he scooped her up in his arms. She didn't know where he was taking her, and she didn't care. All that mattered was that she was in his arms and he wanted her.

Wolfrunner found a place where a bolder jutted out from the mountains, partially protecting them from the rain. He placed Danielle down and then knelt beside her. "If you do not want this thing, you must say so now. Later it may be too late, Danielle."

For her answer, she leaned forward and offered him her lips. She wasn't sure if the groan she heard came from her or from Wolfrunner. She only knew he was kissing her and making her feel all funny inside.

His hands were trembling as he gently pushed her clothing aside. There was a hard rocky surface below them, so he pulled her on top of his body so the rough stones wouldn't cut into her soft skin.

Danielle felt her head reeling as he lifted her up and placed her against his naked flesh. How glorious was the sensation of feeling his hard muscles fitting into her body as if they were meant to fit together.

"Danielle, Danielle," he whispered over and over. "Danielle!" he finally cried out in agony.

Wolfrunner knew he wasn't thinking clearly. All he knew was that he and Danielle might never make it back to the village. There was a chance that Scar Face would come out the winner in their contest of skill and strength. He would take what happiness he could tonight. The woman he loved was in his arms, and he knew she wanted him as much as he wanted her. Danielle's soft body had driven him to the brink of madness. Wolfrunner knew he had to have her.

"You are my heart," he whispered against her sweet lips. "I love you with my whole being." The words were spoken in Blackfoot—Danielle did not know that the man she loved had just bared his soul to her.

Chapter Twenty-four

So far the homeward journey had been a painful haze for Skyler. She and her Uncle Tag had little to say to one another. They were both worried about what they would find once they reached the Blackfoot village. In each of their minds dwelled the possibility that Danielle might already be dead.

Days passed and they pushed themselves past endurance. When they reached St. Louis, Tag bought horses and supplies and they pushed onward once more. They followed the Missouri River, sometimes by barge, other times on horseback, until at last they came to Fort Leavenworth.

As they rode up to the fort, a sentry passed them through the gates. Tag dismounted and helped Skyler from her horse. He remembered being here as a young boy. He and Joanna had briefly stayed with Colonel Jackson and his wife, Kate. He noticed that the fort had changed but little since then.

"We will need to stock up on supplies here, honey," he told Skyler. "If you are too tired to go on, we can rest a few days. I have been pushing you hard," he said with concern written on his face.

"I am not tired, Uncle Tag. I will be ready to leave when you are."

He smiled at her kindly. "This hasn't been easy on you, has it, Skyler?"

"It hasn't been easy on either of us, Uncle Tag. I know what you are going through. I just wish I could help you. I want to give you words of encouragement, but at the same time I don't want to raise false hopes. We both know the problems we are facing."

"We'll get through this, Skyler. We just have to take one day at a time." He tied their horses to the hitching post and motioned for her to follow him into the supply store where he purchased food and blankets.

They had decided to spend the night inside the fort and start out early the next morning. Tag took Skyler to her room and told her he would return later.

Skyler looked about the crude cabin with its wooden chairs and a bed with a lumpy mattress. It seemed curious that the farther they got from Philadelphia, the cruder the houses and buildings became. They were leaving the white man's civilization behind and moving on toward the great wilderness.

She opened her leather satchel and withdrew her beaded buckskin gown and moccasins. After today she would cease being Skyler Dancing. After today, she could be herself—there was no reason to pretend to be something she wasn't.

When Tag entered the room a short time later, he was startled to find his niece dressed in her Indian gown

314

and moccasins. He couldn't believe the change in her. Her hair was braided and encircled with a leather headband. Her knee-length moccasins disappeared beneath the fringe at the bottom of her gown. She was sitting on the bed dangling her feet just off the floor. She held her breath waiting for him to say something. For some reason she needed to be accepted as herself.

He smiled slowly. "I see no evidence of the elegant Miss Skyler Dancing. Is this some lovely young Indian princess I behold?"

"I am Sky Dancer, Uncle Tag. I will never again go by my white name. Please do not be hurt, but I want never to return to your world."

He drew her into his arms and patted her back affectionately, now knowing the harm that had been done to her. "I now believe it was wrong to try and take you and Danielle out of the lives to which you were accustomed. In your case we took a lovely wildflower and tried to strip it of its true beauty. Can you ever forgive us for that, Sky Dancer?"

"There is nothing to forgive. I just didn't fit into the white world," she said sadly, laying her head against his broad shoulder. "I am not even certain that I will fit back into the Indian world, Uncle Tag."

"You were deeply hurt by Morgan's attitude toward the Indians weren't you?"

Sky Dancer raised her head and looked at him. She loved this tall blond man who was almost as dear to her as her own father. She knew the torture he was going through, worrying over Danielle. She didn't want to cause him further pain, so she smiled.

"I will survive. All you need be concerned with is getting to my village as quickly as possible."

He looked deeply into the eyes that reminded him so much of Joanna's. "I don't know if I have told you this or not, but I am so proud of you. You are a credit to your mother and father."

Her arms went about his neck and he held her tightly. He'd never realized until now just how much she had been suffering. Sky Dancer was not given to complaining as Danielle had been. Rather she suffered in silence.

"Are you hungry?" he asked in a lighter vein.

"Starved," she admitted.

"Good, because I have brought us a feast, if you consider dining on army food feasting."

They dined on roasted corn, beans, and corncakes. After they had eaten, Tag stretched out on his bedroll, giving Sky Dancer the bed. They were both exhausted and soon fell asleep, thinking about the long journey that still lay ahead of them. There would be days and weeks of hard riding before they would ever know what Danielle's fate was.

The next morning as they rode out of the fort, Sky Dancer heard several of the soldiers calling after her. "Are you a squaw of a breed?" one man asked. "I'd like to be your chief," another called out suggestively. "Come warm my tipi any day, sweet thing," another hooted.

Tag watched Sky Dancer raise her head proudly, with her eyes looking straight ahead. Only he knew how she was hurting on the inside. He could have easily started trouble over the soldiers' remarks, but that would only have caused Sky Dancer more pain. It was better to let the matter drop, since the harm had

316

already been done. He was never prouder of her than when she glanced over at him and smiled.

"I am the daughter of Windhawk, Uncle Tag. No one can make me ashamed of that fact."

He gave her a warm glance, too choked up to speak. Indeed, he thought. She was a daughter worthy of the great chief of the Blood Blackfoot. A princess in her own right, an angel among the dirty swine at the fort.

Sky Dancer set her sights on the distant mountains. Soon, she thought . . . soon, she would be home! Perhaps the pain of the last weeks wouldn't be as acute when she was reunited with her mother and father.

Morgan sat in the Jameses' parlor, staring at Alexandria. He couldn't help but notice how her hand shook as she poured the tea and handed it to him, while trying to avoid his eyes. The doctor in him told him something was very definitely wrong here.

He had tried to stay away because that was the way Skyler had wanted it, but he couldn't get her out of his mind. He was here now demanding to know where he could find Skyler, and he was in no mood to be put off by unanswered questions. He noticed Alexandria's eyes kept darting to the door as if she were expecting someone.

"What's going on, Alexandria? I don't understand any of what has happened. All I want you to do is tell me where I can find Skyler—is that too much to ask?"

Her golden eyes met his and he saw sadness there. "I cannot help you in this, Morgan. You must not ask me any more questions."

"I can see you are upset. Is there anything I can do to

help? Would you like me to send for your doctor—or perhaps you would like me to give you something to help you rest?"

"No, I will be fine. I just cannot seem to talk to anyone right now."

Morgan stood up and started pacing the floor. "Do you have any idea what all this is doing to me, Alexandria? I feel like I'm battling a blank wall. You have got to tell me what is happening, or at least tell me where I can find Skyler. I don't care if she's at the end of the earth, I'll go after her. I have had two weeks to think this through, and I have come to the realization that all that matters is that I love Skyler and she loves me. Anything beyond that is unimportant."

At that point Farley, the grizzly old trapper, entered the room and looked Morgan over with a practiced eye. Nodding his head, he sat down beside Alexandria.

"Morgan, I would like you to meet a very dear family friend, Farley. Farley, this is a friend and neighbor, Dr. Morgan Prescott. He's also a colonel in the army," she said, glad for the interruption.

"Pleased to make your acquaintance," Farley replied. He'd overheard part of the conversation between Alexandria and Morgan Prescott, and was sizing the man up. His eyes went to Alexandria and he could see she was very upset.

"Don't you think you oughta be in bed, Alex?" Farley asked with concern.

"Yes, perhaps you are right," she said, standing up. "If you will excuse me, Morgan, I think I'll go and lie down. I'm sure you'll understand."

Morgan stood up and watched her rush out of the room, feeling frustrated. Everywhere he turned he seemed to meet with opposition.

Farley leaned back and popped a sweetcake into his mouth. "I seed you're in the Calvary," he observed.

"That's right, Mr. Farley. But not for much longer. I'm on leave until I receive my discharge papers," Morgan said, looking the old man over. The old trapper's manner of speech was coarse and he wore buckskins and scuffed boots. His beard and hair were as white as snow, and Morgan was puzzled as to how such an odd character could be a friend of the James family.

"Name's not Mr. Farley," the old trapper corrected. "It's just Farley, lessen you want to call me by my Indian name, Crazy Fox."

"How well do you know the James family, Farley?" Morgan asked, wondering if the old man might be able to help him find Skyler.

"I knowed them good as some and better than most," the old man said, eyeing Morgan shrewdly.

"How about the Dancing side of the family? Are you acquainted with them as well?"

Farley's eyes narrowed. "What iffen I am? I just heard Alex tell you she wouldn't help you find Sky . . . ler."

Morgan opened the top button of his uniform and sat down beside Farley. "If you heard me talking to Alexandria, you must also have heard me say that Skyler and I love each other. I want to find her, Farley. I know I can make her happy. Will you help me in this?"

"What makes you think you can make her happy?"

"Because she loves me. Something went wrong between us, and I don't know what it is. I am half out of

319

my mind, thinking I may never see her again."

Both men heard someone enter the room and turned toward the doorway. Alexandria paused as if she were having a hard time speaking. At last she looked into the eyes of the dear old trapper. "I have been thinking it over, Farley, and I believe you should tell Morgan about Skyler."

"Are you sure?" he asked. "Don't you want to think on it a spell longer?"

"No, my mind is made up. We must tell him everything," she said, sitting down on the edge of a satin-covered chair. "There has been too much unhappiness lately. It's time to tell the truth."

Farley stood up and placed a cushion at Alexandria's back. He poured her a fresh cup of tea and handed it to her, then drew up a footstool to sit beside her, as if he were her watchdog.

Morgan watched impatiently, wondering why they were acting so strangely. "For God's sake, will you tell me what's the big mystery," he ground out between clenched teeth.

"When do you have to report to Fort Laramie?" Alexandria asked.

"I resigned my commission a week ago. I won't be going to Fort Laramie—why?"

"How much do you love Skyler?" she asked point-blank. "Is your love strong enough to overcome prejudice?"

His eyes clouded over. "I don't really understand what you are asking me. I love her more than I ever thought to love anyone," he admitted. "Why do you think I'm here?"

"I wonder if you love her enough?" Alexandria asked

as she studied her hands that were clasped in her lap. "Do you love her enough to accept her no matter what you hear about her?"

"Nothing on earth could make me stop loving her. Did she tell you that I asked her to be my wife?"

Alexandria shook her head. "No, but then Skyler keeps much of her feelings to herself."

"Tell me where I can find her, Alexandria," Morgan said urgently. "I will go to her wherever she is."

"Do you recall the day you had just come from Washington?" she asked.

"Yes, of course. I was going to ask Skyler to marry me that day, but something happened. I remember very clearly that she became upset. What I don't know is why."

"I can tell you why, Morgan. She became upset when you were talking about the only good Indian being a dead Indian. You made the mistake that so many people make. You think just because someone doesn't act and think as you do that they are beneath you. You don't realize that the white race is stealing the Indian lands and when the Indian tries to protect what belongs to him, you say he is a savage."

Morgan was astonished by Alexandria's emotional outbreak. He looked at the old man and found his eyes cold as ice.

"What has all this to do with Skyler? I suppose you are telling me she doesn't like prejudice." He looked puzzled for a moment. "No. That couldn't be right. She wouldn't turn away from me just because I detest the Indians."

"Wouldn't she, Morgan?" Alexandria asked. "What if I told you her name isn't really Skyler Dancing . . .

321

but Sky Dancer! Would you understand then?"

Morgan closed his eyes, trying to digest what Alexandria was telling him. "My God," he said in an agonized voice. "Skyler is an Indian! No wonder I hurt her that day in the summerhouse. Why didn't someone tell me? I have been going over and over in my mind, trying to rationalize what happened. Now it all comes together."

"Now it ain't 'zactly true when you say Sky Dancer's an Indian," Farley spoke up. "Her pa's the chief of the Blood Blackfoot, but her ma's white. Sky Dancer is an Indian princess. She ain't never been near no one who looked down on her or her race before. In the Blackfoot tribe she is honored and revered."

Morgan stood up and walked over to the window. He had been a blind fool. Why hadn't he seen what was right before his eyes? He turned slowly back to Alexandria. "I don't understand any of this."

"It's all very simple, Morgan. Joanna is Tag's sister. She was once rescued by Windhawk, the chief of the Bloods. She fell in love with him and turned her back on the white world, and they were married. Sky Dancer is a child of that union."

He shook his head as if to clear it. "I can see how Skyler might . . . Dear God, I must have hurt her. She must have thought I would hate her if I found out about her father."

"That is exactly what she thought. She is proud of who she is, and most of all she is proud of the Blackfoot people. You hurt her more deeply than you can ever guess," Alexandria told him. "I wonder if you love her as much as you claim to? Knowing who she is, do you still want her?"

Alexandria watched as Morgan tried to digest all he had been told. She watched him wrestle with his conscience. "I have to go to her," he said at last. "Tell me where I can find her. I will make this up to her, you have my word."

"Not until you tell me how you feel about her," Alexandria said. "I don't want to see her hurt again."

"I will never hurt her, Alexandria. I want her for my wife more than ever now. I just hope she can find it in her heart to forgive me, blundering fool that I am."

"Can you accept who she is and what she is?"

"All I know is that she is the woman I love. I want her beside me for the rest of my life."

"Now, that might not be as easy as you be thinking it be," Farley spoke up. "You see, Windhawk may not want his daughter to marry a white man. While you ain't too fond of the Indians, they don't think too highly of you neither. Like I tole you, Sky Dancer is a princess, and Windhawk might think you're just a mite beneath her."

Morgan sank down on the settee and covered his eyes with his hands. "I only know I have to see her. Will you tell me how I can find her?"

"I will do better than that," Alexandria said. "Farley will take you to her."

"Now, I ain't too sure of that," Farley said. "Tag tole me to stay with you, Alex. 'Sides, Windhawk ain't gonna welcome this man into the village with open arms."

"Don't worry about me, Farley—I will be all right. Tag will be at the Blackfoot village to make sure no harm will come to Morgan. And you will take care of him on the way there. Do this for me, will you?"

"When can we leave?" Morgan asked eagerly.

"I ain't too sure 'bout this Alex," the old trapper said, shaking his head. "You knowed how Windhawk feels 'bout strangers."

Alexandria bent over and kissed the old man's cheek. "Do this for Sky Dancer, Farley."

Farley nodded reluctantly. "I'll do it, but Windhawk ain't gonna like it any too much."

"Can we leave in the morning?" Morgan wanted to know, pressing for an answer.

Farley nodded again. "I 'spect I'll have to take you or Alex won't let me have no peace. I don't knowed what Tag's gonna say, 'cause he tole me to look after Alex."

"Will you consent to having my sister stay with you, Alex?" Morgan asked. "I know Jenny would be delighted to look after you while Tag's away."

Alexandria stood up and offered Morgan her hand. "I'll consider it. I'm glad you love Sky Dancer, because she loves you a great deal. You are going to be in for a great experience. Farley knows the Indian Territory better than any white man alive. You will see things that will astound you. And you will meet a real legend. Sky Dancer's father, Windhawk, is like a god to his people."

Morgan raised Alexandria's hand to his lips. "Thank you—you won't regret this."

Alexandria's golden eyes gleamed brightly. "I had better not, Morgan. You had better know what you want before you stand before Windhawk, or God help you, because no one else will be able to."

Morgan didn't miss the hint of warning in her voice, but he would brave any danger to find the woman he

324

loved. He was even ready to face the legend, Windhawk, to ask for his daughter's hand.

Tag and Sky Dancer made good time. Her Indian training came to her aid, and she was easily able to keep up with her uncle. On and on they rode, from morning till night. They rode through rainstorms and dust-storms, with their eyes always turned toward the northwest.

They crossed the prairies following the deeply rutted trail that had been cut by wagon wheels.

Sometimes they would be so weary they would just throw their blankets on the ground and fall asleep. The urgency of the mission pushed them almost beyond endurance, but neither of them complained. They couldn't rest until they found out about Danielle.

Chapter Twenty-five

There was no earth and no sky. There was no today or tomorrow—there was only now. Wolfrunner's hands were gentle as they moved over Danielle's back, molding her to him so their thighs fit tightly together.

"So soft," he murmured against her ear. "I want to go on touching you until the end of time. I did not want this to happen to me."

"What?" she asked, wondering what he meant.

"I never knew a woman could make me feel so on fire. Do you know what you have done to me, Danielle?"

"No," she said, wanting to hear him tell her more. His strong hands were making a circular motion across her back then slipped slowly down to rest about her waist.

"You are as the earth mother, and I no more than the sands. You are the giver of life, and I am the seeker," he breathed against the soft column of her throat.

"I don't understand," she groaned as he moved his head and caressed her breasts with his lips.

"I want to fill you with my love. I want to show you what it can be like between a man and a woman." His voice came out in an agonized whisper.

"I have never been with a man before, Wolfrunner." Her breath came out in a gasp as he rolled her nipple around on his tongue. A slow fire had begun to smolder just below the surface, and Danielle was unprepared for the raw emotions that seemed to dance on her nerve ends. Her young body waited for his gentle, knowing instruction.

Another flash of lightning streaked across the sky, and she looked into his dark eyes that seemed to burn into hers. His hand moved down to her soft unexplored womanhood, and he began to gently massage her.

"I will go where no man has gone before, Danielle. Afterwards you will be changed from a girl to a woman. Do you want this?"

As his magic hands stroked and caressed her, she groaned softly. "I want to be a woman for you, Wolfrunner. Teach me how to please you."

His hot breath fanned her cheek, then his mouth settled on her lips. Danielle's hands tangled in his hair, and she yearned for something she didn't fully understand. There was a burning hunger in her—a void that needed filling. An ache that cried out to be soothed.

Wolfrunner lifted her hips and moved to her soft opening. "The first time there is pain, Danielle. I will not hurt you more than I can help. Hold on to me."

Danielle gripped Wolfrunner's shoulders, not knowing what was to come. His words seemed to echo in her head. She felt the warmth of his manhood move slightly into her body. There was slight pain as he slid slowly forward, but it was nothing compared to the hot, white, searing flame that sent the blood rushing through her body. When he was buried inside her, he gripped her waist and moved his hips forward—slowly, ever so slowly, he reached deeper inside her.

Wolfrunner could feel the barrier that proclaimed her maidenhood. Deep inside he knew he should stop before it was too late. Had he the right to take her innocence from her? His will and his resistance were as nothing as her soft lips opened beneath his insistent mouth.

The rain continued to fall heavily to earth, but neither of the lovers was aware of it. They were in a world that had been created just for the two of them. The electricity in the air came from their raw emotions that had been stripped bare.

Wolfrunner tasted the rain water on Danielle's lips, and it seemed to heighten his pleasure. His whole body seemed consumed by a fire that raged inside him. He had never been with a woman who made his blood run hot in his veins.

Danielle was riddled with new and pleasurable feelings. It was as if when Wolfrunner entered her body he had filled a void. She was his completely, and she knew she would never be the same after tonight. As he mastered her body, he also mastered her heart.

After the storm of feelings had moved over the two lovers, it left them strangely at peace. Wolfrunner held Danielle to him, feeling as if she belonged to him.

"After tonight I must never touch you again. You are too far above me, and it would be like reaching for the moon. I stole a little happiness tonight, but I cannot hold on to it, Danielle. You must soon go back to the white man's land. I will live in a world without you."

"I want to stay with you forever, Wolfrunner. Will you make me your wife? I know your father, Gray Fox, has two wives. I would never allow you to take another wife."

His eyes seemed to burn. If he had this woman for his wife, he would never want another. But he could never have Danielle. Now he had to convince her that they could never be together as husband and wife.

"It is true that my father has two wives. I will never have even one." He watched the pain in her beautiful eyes, and felt the intensity of it in his heart.

He rose to his feet, carrying her to a standing position. The storm had moved out of the mountains, leaving a bright moonlit night. Cupping her face in his hands, he stared into her blue eyes.

"From this day forward, you are the wife of my heart, but I cannot approach your father and ask for you. You must understand what it is to be a Blackfoot princess; you can marry only a chief worthy of you. Know in your heart that no other woman will ever touch me as deeply as you have. But I can never have you for my wife. Windhawk would never permit it, even if your father were to agree ."

Danielle's eyes sparkled with tears as he kissed the tip of her pert little nose. He was aware that he was the first man to ever love her, and that was the reason she thought she loved him. When they returned to the village Danielle would feel differently about him. She would remember that he was what she called a savage. Wolfrunner wanted to fight to hold on to her, but he knew he would have to let her go.

"Are you just saying this because you don't want

me?" It occurred to Danielle that Wolfrunner hadn't said anything about loving her. He talked of pleasure of the body, but he did not say he felt about her as she felt for him. She felt as if he were merely using the fact that she was a princess to be free of her. He had gotten what he wanted from her—now he wanted nothing more to do with her.

Wolfrunner's dark eyes settled on her face and she could see the pain written there. "I want you more than I have ever wanted anything in my life. I would die for you, but I cannot live for you. I didn't want to love you, but you drew me into your life. I thought you were spoiled and unfeeling, but I found out I was wrong. You are all that is good in the world, Danielle."

She became saddened and hurt, knowing he was pushing her out of his life. "I was both spoiled and unfeeling, Wolfrunner, but you helped me change. I have many things to learn. Will you not help me?"

"I have always walked alone. I have lived for twenty-seven summers, and before now never wanted to take a woman as wife. I will live the rest of my life alone, but I will keep the memory of this night to warm me through the years."

"If you love me, tell me. Can you not say the words? If you did love me, it wouldn't matter who I was or who you are. Look at Windhawk and Joanna. They are shining examples of two people reaching across different worlds to find happiness."

"Would you defy your family to be with me?"

"I would defy the whole world to be your wife."

Wolfrunner's heart seemed to melt as Danielle placed her small hand in his. "Keep me in your heart, Wolfrunner. Do not allow anyone to tear us apart."

He crushed her in his arms, fearing that even now forces were at work to separate them. They still had to make it back to the village. Then he would have to let her go. "If it were possible, I would live here in the mountains with you. Then no one could come between us, Danielle."

"I don't know what my father will say. Even though my mother was an Indian, I don't know what he would do if he knew we wanted to be husband and wife."

"I know, Danielle. He would say, 'Who is this warrior who reaches above himself to my daughter', and he would be right. You do not understand the Blackfoot. There are lines that cannot be crossed over. I am on one side of that line, and you are on the other."

"I had the impression that my Uncle Windhawk liked you very much. You always talk of how my aunt likes you. Why would they not wish us to be together?"

"Liking me has nothing to do with this, Danielle. With you it would be the same as with Sky Dancer. She will marry only a great chief. It is the way of my people."

"But if you love me—"

He silenced her by placing his finger over her lips. "There are some things that go beyond love, Danielle— honor is one of those things. I could never go against the teachings of my people. I will never go against my chief, Windhawk."

"Are you so sure that my uncle wouldn't welcome you as my husband? He will be grateful to you for saving me."

"Gratitude is one thing, Danielle, and granting the impossible is another. Do not make me say things that will only hurt you. Accept what I tell you as the truth."

Danielle raised her head and gave him a guarded look. It seemed that Wolfrunner didn't want her. Was he just making excuses to be rid of her? Her pride came to her rescue. She would no longer beg to be his wife.

"Yes, there is truth in what you say. I would never be happy living in an Indian village. What we had was amusing, nothing more."

He grabbed her arms and turned her to face him. "Do not make mock of me. I know you hide your true face because I have hurt you. You will one day know I was right."

With every word he spoke, he was rejecting her love. She would not let him see that she was dying on the inside. "How do you know I didn't show you a false face tonight? Perhaps the true me was the one you first met. I have many men in Philadelphia who would be only too willing to marry me. Why should I care what you think?" The words were spoken softly, and the lie Danielle spoke hurt her deeply.

Wolfrunner pushed her away. His dark eyes turned hard, and she actually watched him withdraw from her. "As you say, why should you care what I think. Come, it grows late and I need my sleep." He turned his back and walked off into the night, knowing she would follow.

Danielle retrieved the baby rabbit and held it to her face. She had humbled herself before Wolfrunner, only to have him reject her. She felt devoid of all feelings as she walked behind Wolfrunner. She knew she would begin to feel again tomorrow, but the pain was too deep to think about it tonight. She hoped he would never know how deeply his rejection had hurt her. Tears washed down her face, and she brushed them away angrily.

What she needed now was her father to tell her everything would be all right. Of course she could never tell her father about what had happened tonight. It was as if when she and Wolfrunner had loved each other, it had been in a dreamworld created by the fierce storm. When the storm had moved away it had swept everything—feelings, emotions—away with it.

When Wolfrunner reached the point where they would sleep for the night, he lay down and turned his back to Danielle. Bracing her back against the cliff wall, she allowed her hand to drift down to her stomach. She felt so different inside. She couldn't blame Wolfrunner for taking her innocence, because she had brazenly offered it to him. What she had also given him was the gift of her love, but he gave her nothing in return. He didn't want her.

Little Cottontail curled up in her lap, and she placed her hand on the rabbit's soft fur. A cloud drifted over the moon, and Danielle watched it shadow the land. Oh, yes, she had changed, but it had been a very painful experience for her. Nothing would ever hurt quite as much as having the man she loved turn away from her. After this night, she knew she could face whatever came her way. Now, more than ever, Danielle wanted to go home to Philadelphia. Perhaps then she would forget how she had humbled and humiliated herself before an Indian who didn't even want her.

After the night Wolfrunner made love to Danielle and then rejected her, she changed toward him. Now she, too, was silent and brooding. The tension between the two of them was heavy and uncomfortable.

Inside, Danielle burned with uncertainty and anger. She had given herself wholeheartedly to Wolfrunner, only to have him throw her love back in her face. She was angry with herself that she had been such a fool. She had been willing to give up her life in Philadelphia, her family and friends, to remain with him. Now, all she wanted to do was go back to Philadelphia and never see Wolfrunner again.

Danielle was still bothered by the thought that Scar Face was following them. Since they had been in the mountains, they had seen nothing of him. She hoped he hadn't trailed them into the mountains, but deep inside she had the feeling that he was watching them.

The day was unbelievably hot. Above them on the highest peaks, the snow was melting, causing streams of water to flow swiftly down the mountainside and making their progress even slower and more difficult. In the places where the streams were too wide, they would have to climb down the mountain until they found a narrow point to cross.

Danielle stood by one of the gorges which had been cut into the side of the mountain by the water. The water cascaded down the mountain in a breathtaking waterfall. It was wide and swift, and she was wondering how they would ever get across.

She held her breath as Wolfrunner positioned his spear on the ground and used it to smoothly vault across, landing safely on the other side.

"I will throw you the spear and you must cross as I did," he called out to her.

"No," she said, backing up and looking at the swift current which cascaded down the mountainside in a sheer drop-off. "I cannot do it."

His dark eyes narrowed. "You must. Do not fear, I will catch you. You have not been a coward in the past—why should you be one now?"

Danielle tensed as he tossed the spear across to her. It landed near her feet, and she reluctantly bent to pick it up. She knew if she should slip, her body would be carried over the cliff wall.

Wolfrunner could see her indecision. "You must do it now, Danielle. Just remember to swing your legs out so you will land clear of the stream."

She gripped the spear tightly, knowing if it had supported Wolfrunner's weight, it would surely support her. Her eyes wandered to the sheer drop-off, and Danielle realized if she lost her footing, she would go over the side and plunge down below to her death.

"Come to me," Wolfrunner ordered. "The longer you wait, the harder it will be."

Danielle took a deep breath and quickly placed the smooth end of the spear on the ground. Without allowing herself time to think, she swung her body forward.

As soon as her feet left the ground, she felt the spear slip and knew she hadn't cleared the stream! Frantically reaching out, she tried to grasp Wolfrunner's hand but failed. She landed in the water, and the swirling force carried her toward the edge of the mountain!

Danielle could hear Wolfrunner's voice calling out to her as the edge of the cliff yawned in front of her. Before she could cry out, she was washed over the side and seemed to be suspended in the air for what seemed an eternity.

Danielle knew that if she didn't save herself, she would be carried to her death in the deep crevice below. Reaching out her hand, she grabbed hold of a bush that grew out of the side of the mountain. Gripping it tightly, she held on with all her strength. The force of the water seemed to tear at her—she could feel her hands slipping. With a strength she didn't know she possessed, she held on and swung her legs around so they touched on the ledge that jutted out above the crevice. When she felt the tip of her feet touch solid rock, she pushed herself forward and dropped down to the ledge.

Danielle's whole body felt bruised and battered, but she was alive! Hearing Wolfrunner call out to her, she lifted her head and saw him peering down at her.

"Are you hurt?" he cried out.

She stood up slowly and gazed up at him. She was still too shaken to speak.

"Do not move. I will come down to you," he called out. He needn't have worried; at the moment she was too scared to move. Glancing over the ledge, she knew she had narrowly escaped death. Fear made her body tremble. Had she gone over the side, she would have been dashed on the rocks below.

Suddenly she remembered the baby rabbit, Cottontail. Earlier she had placed her in the fold of her skirt. Now she was gone! Dropping to her knees, she looked over the side of the ledge. She cried out in pain as she saw the tiny furry body that had been dashed on the rocks below. Tears blinded her as she buried her face in her hands. She had loved the rabbit because Wolfrunner had given it to her. But for the grace of God, she, too, would now be lying on the rocks below.

She rose to her feet and stared at Wolfrunner. His dark eyes were clearly visible, and she read the same fear in his eyes. Why should he care if she had met her death? Had she died, he would be rid of her. In that instant she realized that he had only saved her in the first place to impress Windhawk. He didn't really care about her.

She was about to voice that thought when she saw movement above Wolfrunner. It was Scar Face! He had his battle axe poised, ready to strike the unsuspecting Wolfrunner!

Her voice seemed ripped from her throat. "Wolfrunner, behind you!" she screamed.

She watched helplessly as Wolfrunner turned over on his back and assessed the danger immediately. He quickly grabbed the hand that held the battle axe. For a long moment the two men struggled at the edge of the cliff in a life-and-death struggle. Danielle could do no more than hold her breath and look on helplessly. After a time the two men were on their feet and had moved out of Danielle's view.

Without pausing to think, Danielle started the long and difficult climb to the top. Fear for the man she loved wiped out any thoughts of danger to herself. She used roots, rocks, and anything she could to gain a hand-hold. She was unaware that her hands were cut and bleeding from the sharp stones. Several times her foot slipped on the upward climb, but that didn't deter her. All she could think of was that Scar Face might kill Wolfrunner, and she had to try and help him.

As she made her way to the top of the cliff, she felt

burning anger toward Scar Face. He was a savage—an animal who preyed on others to satisfy his lust for revenge. She prayed she could reach the top before he harmed Wolfrunner.

Pulling herself up to the top, she watched the struggle that was going on between the two men. They were locked in a struggle of strength, and she knew it wouldn't end until one of them was dead. Neither man seemed aware of her as they each battled for supremacy over the other.

Wolfrunner seemed to have the superior strength, but Scar Face had the weapon. A scream escaped her lips as the Piegan warrior swung wide, catching Wolfrunner across the shoulder. Blood flowed freely down Wolfrunner's arm, and he fell to his knees. Scar Face took advantage of Wolfrunner's momentary weakness and hit him with the butt of his battle axe, sending him sprawling backward. Scar Face then leaped on top of Wolfrunner and raised his axe to strike the final blow!

Danielle knew she must do something quickly or Wolfrunner would die! In her panic, her foot struck a hard object and she looked down to find Wolfrunner's spear lying on the ground. Picking it up, she aimed it at Scar Face's back, hoping her aim would be true. She knew she wouldn't get a second chance, so the first one had to count.

Throwing all her weight into the thrust, she watched and prayed as the spear sailed through the air. She had not been trained to fight as a Blackfoot maiden might have been, so she had very little faith in her ability to hit the mark she had aimed for.

Her heart was drumming in her ears as she watched

the spear enter Scar Face's back. He seemed to freeze at the moment of impact. Then he turned slowly to gaze at Danielle with a puzzled expression on his face. Staggering to his feet, Scar Face stumbled toward Danielle with his battle axe now aimed at her.

Danielle's eyes were wide with fear as he slowly advanced on her. There was nowhere to run. Behind her was the swift stream that had carried her over the edge of the cliff earlier, and Scar Face blocked her front exit. Helplessly she waited for him to draw near. His weapon was poised in the air, but he never launched the missile. Falling to his knees, he muttered something in the Blackfoot language. His eyes glazed over and blood flowed from his mouth. Tears of relief stung Danielle's eyes as Scar Face pitched forward, his body twitched, and lay still.

Gathering up all her courage, Danielle walked toward him slowly. It was all she could do to force herself to touch the man who was her enemy. She jerked the axe from his hand and stepped back. There was little doubt in Danielle's mind that Scar Face was dead, for his blank eyes stared at the sun without seeing it.

Today she had committed murder, but she wasn't sorry. She would kill a hundred men like Scar Face if it was to save Wolfrunner's life.

Turning her gaze to Wolfrunner, she ran quickly to him. Going down on her knees, she took his hand in hers. His eyes were glazed with pain and blood was freely flowing from his shoulder. She didn't know how badly he was wounded, but at least he still lived.

"I . . . owe you my life . . ." he whispered. "Can . . . not seem to move."

"We are even now," she answered. "From this moment forward, neither of us owes the other anything."

Wolfrunner tried to rise, but he was too weak and fell backward into unconsciousness. She leaned forward to examine his wound. She knew she would have to do something to stop the flow of blood or he might bleed to death. His head wound didn't appear to be serious, but she didn't know about the other wounds.

Danielle tore a strip from her skirt and plunged it into the stream. She could do nothing beyond cleansing and bandaging the wound. She prayed that would be enough.

Danielle raised him up and rested his head in her lap to make him more comfortable. How strange it seemed for him to be so still. He had always been so full of life. Her hand rested against his cheek. She loved this man beyond anything she could imagine. Today she had killed so he might live. Surely God wouldn't take Wolfrunner away from her now. She didn't know how long she sat there holding his head in her lap, but the evening shadows were creeping across the mountain when she finally decided she had to do something.

Gently lying Wolfrunner's head down, Danielle stood up. Her legs felt stiff and cramped from sitting so long in one position. Knowing she had to move him away from the edge of the cliff, she took Wolfrunner's arms, pulling and tugging with all her strength. Danielle made slow progress, but at last the deed was accomplished and he was safely against the face of the mountain.

As night began to fall, Danielle could hear the eerie sound of howling wolves in the distance. Gripping the axe tightly, she hoped her courage wouldn't be tested further. It had turned colder—a chilling wind blew down the mountainside. Lying down beside Wolfrunner, she curled up against his body, trying to keep him warm.

"You cannot die," she cried. "I will not allow you to. A brave warrior should not die at the hands of a coward."

All through the night, Wolfrunner didn't stir. Danielle held him, loving him with her whole heart. Deep inside she knew that a man with his strength and courage couldn't die so easily. She would hold on to him, and by sheer will keep the flame of life burning within him.

When morning came, Danielle had fallen asleep from exhaustion. She wasn't aware when Wolfrunner sat up and looked around. His eyes rested on Scar Face who lay facedown with the spear sticking out of his back. His dark eyes then moved to the lovely face of the woman he loved. Danielle had saved his life! He didn't know how she had accomplished it, but then, did not the blood of chiefs run in her veins?

His hand gently brushed a tress of hair from her face. Surely she had been meant to be his woman. Why had the Great One placed her out of reach for him? He would never be allowed to step over the line to take an Indian princess as his bride. Wolfrunner knew he would have to be content to live on memories of the many days and nights he had spent with Danielle.

Chapter Twenty-six

Sky Dancer turned her face to the sun and felt its warming rays. The very air she breathed was reviving her spirit and filling her with a renewed sense of belonging. She and her Uncle Tag had been traveling in Blackfoot country for two days—she was almost home. But would it still be home to her?

Her eyes drank in the beauty of the green grasses, the mountains , and the rivers. She was coming home to be reborn. This was where she drew her strength. This was where she would finally heal her mind and spirit.

Tag moved his mount closer to Sky Dancer's and she noticed his hand was resting on his rifle. Her keen hearing picked the sounds of riders, and she watched as a dozen warriors topped the hill in front of them.

In a split second, Sky Dancer knew they were warriors from her own tribe. Her heart lightened, and she nudged her horse forward to join them. Riding up the hill with the wind on her face, she felt joy ripple through her heart.

When she drew even with the leader, she drew up her

mount. Smiling brightly, Sky Dancer looked up at Gray Fox, her father's best friend. "Has there been any word of Danielle?" she asked hurriedly, wishing with all her heart that her cousin had been found unharmed.

Gray Fox looked at Tag with sorrow in his eyes. "We have found no trace of your daughter, Night Falcon. Your sister, Flaming Hair, sent me to ride with you to the village. Windhawk would have come, but he is out searching for your daughter."

It had been many months since Tag had been called by his Blackfoot name, and it seemed strange to him. "It is good to see you, old friend," he said, speaking in the Blackfoot language. How far to the village?"

"We will be there tomorrow," Gray Fox told him.

"Let us go forward with haste," Tag said, spurring his horse forward with an urgency, knowing the others would follow his lead.

That night they made camp in the pine forest. They were in the heart of Blackfoot country, so there was no need to fear an enemy would come upon them in the night. This was Windhawk's land, and rarely did the Blackfoot's enemies cross into his territory.

Tag was talking to a group of warriors, and Sky Dancer walked away from camp. Her eyes drank in the beauty of the forest. She quietly watched the abundant animal life that thrived in the woods. Across a small meadow, she watched a doe and its fawn drinking from a stream. There were no town noises here to distract one from the serenity—there was only peace and beauty. The other world, the white man's world, was a lifetime away.

344

"It lightens my heart to look upon your face once more, Sky Dancer," Gray Fox said, coming out of the shadows. "It was not the same with you away."

She smiled at her father's war chief. Gray Fox and Windhawk had grown to manhood together. He had always been a part of her life, and she had missed him.

"I am home to stay, Gray Fox." She moved her hands to indicate the countryside. "This is where I belong."

"All will be glad that you have returned. Your mother needs you right now."

Sky Dancer watched the softness that came into Gray Fox's eyes when he spoke of her mother. She had always suspected that the war chief secretly loved her mother. "This is a sad homecoming. My heart is heavy that my grandmother no longer walks the earth, and I am so frightened at what might have happened to Danielle."

"Everything has stopped at the village. The warriors no longer hunt the buffalo because Windhawk wanted all available warriors to search for your cousin. I do not think it is a good sign that we have, not yet, found any trace of her."

"What do you think could have happened to her, Gray Fox?" Sky Dancer questioned.

Gray Fox raised his hands in a hopeless gesture. "It is hard to say. You know Windhawk has many enemies. The man who took your cousin must have planned carefully, perhaps for years. We have come to think whoever took her thought that they had taken you."

Sky Dancer's eyes widened in horror. "Poor Danielle. I am grieved that she should be mistaken for me. She has soft manners and is not accustomed to the

Indian ways. I wish . . . I wish she could be found quickly. I will not allow myself to think that Danielle is . . . dead."

Gray Fox watched the lovely face of his princess. Deep in his heart he couldn't help but be grateful that Sky Dancer was not the one who had disappeared. Joanna was grieving now, but if she had lost Sky Dancer, her heart would break. In Gray Fox's heart, anything that hurt Joanna also ripped him apart on the inside. He had loved her in silence for many summers. No one knew that he felt great love for the wife of his best friend, his chief. Gray Fox would carry that secret with him until he died.

He reached out and took Sky Dancer's arm. "Come, you must get some sleep. The hour grows late, and tomorrow we shall ride hard all day. I made a promise to your mother that I would look after you."

Sky Dancer nodded. Tomorrow she would be home but everything was different now—she was different. She could hardly wait to be with her mother and father. They didn't have to know she would never come all the way home. Sky Dancer would never tell them that she'd left a part of herself behind with Morgan Prescott.

The next afternoon it was a grim party that crossed the Milk River and rode into the Blackfoot village.

When the people saw Sky Dancer and Tag, they rushed forward to greet them. Happy faces smiled at their returning princess. Many hands reached out to touch her with affection. There were many who sadly welcomed Tag home, knowing his mission was not a happy one. He had once been a part of this tribe and was still held in high regard.

Sky Dancer's eyes were fixed on the big lodge in the center of the village where her mother and father waited. This was not to be the happy homecoming Sky Dancer had hoped for. There was too much sadness that hung heavily in the air.

As Sky Dancer drew even with her parents, her father reached up and pulled her into his arms. He said nothing as he held her tightly to him, but Sky Dancer knew that he was happy she was home. Joanna rushed to her brother and was enfolded in his embrace. The tribe members, knowing of the sadness that would be in the chief's lodge this day, went to their own tipis, not wanting to intrude on their sorrow.

As Joanna drew her daughter into her arms, her eyes were wet with tears. "I have missed you sorely, my daughter. It is good that you are home."

Sky Dancer gazed at her beautiful mother with an aching heart. There were so many things that she needed to share with her mother, but now was not the time. "I never want to leave again, my mother," she said, feeling that she had come home at last .

As the four of them entered the lodge, a silence settled over the village. There would be no ceremonies of welcome for the returning princess tonight. There would be only sadness in the chief's lodge.

Windhawk and Tag had ridden out with several warriors. They had decided to go to the Piegan Blackfoot village, which was three days away. Windhawk would now enlist the brother tribe in the search for Danielle.

Night had fallen—Sky Dancer and her mother were talking quietly while Joanna told her daughter about the death of Sun Woman. They both cried softly for the loss of the woman they had loved so dearly.

As they drank the tea Alexandria had sent to Joanna, Sky Dancer talked of her life in Philadelphia. "There is happy news in all this sorrow, my mother. My uncle and aunt are expecting a baby."

Joanna smiled. "I know. Tag told me." Joanna searched the face of her daughter. There was something different about her, a deep kind of sadness, and she knew it had nothing to do with Sun Woman's death or Danielle's disappearance.

"You are troubled, my daughter. Would you like to talk about what is bothering you?"

Violet-colored eyes met violet-colored eyes. "I wasn't going to tell you about what happened to me in Philadelphia, Mother. I thought it would not be right to talk of my troubles when there is so much sadness here."

Joanna pulled her daughter to her. "I will always want to hear what is bothering you, no matter what. Can you talk about it now?"

Sky Dancer again met her mother's gaze. "I have met a man called Morgan Prescott. He is a doctor and an officer in the United States Cavalry."

Joanna pushed a tumbled tress of ebony hair out of her daughter's face. "Are you telling me that you have

348

some deep feelings for this man?"

Sky Dancer's eyes filled with tears. "Yes, I love him. I never thought it was possible to love anyone the way I do Morgan. You never told me that love could hurt so much, my mother." Sky Dancer had kept her feelings bottled up for so long that they now came out in a rush.

Joanna held her daughter while Sky Dancer told her about herself and Morgan Prescott. Her heart felt heavy that her lovely sweet Sky Dancer should have met with ugliness and prejudice. "Cry all you want to," she said soothingly, rocking her daughter back and forth as if she were a baby.

Joanna had come to the same conclusion that her brother had earlier. It had been a mistake to separate the two girls from their worlds. She had no words of comfort to give Sky Dancer. All she could do was hold her and feel her pain in the depths of her own heart.

When they reached St. Louis, Morgan followed Farley's direction and exchanged his blue uniform for a buckskin shirt and trousers. The Old Trapper had wisely pointed out that in his uniform he would be a sitting target for every Indian in the territory.

As they made their way across the seemingly neverending prairies toward the great wilderness area, Morgan began to experience a way of life that he never dreamed existed. He began to enjoy Farley's wit and humor and to realize that there was a highly intelligent man behind the bushy hair and colorful manner of speech.

They rode hard and made good time. Often they would be in the saddle before sunup and ride until long after dark. Farley knew the country so well they would sometimes ride on with only the moonlight to guide them.

A few days after they left Fort Leavenworth, Morgan set his sights on the tall mountains in the distance. His heart grew lighter each day, knowing he was getting closer to the woman he loved. He didn't know what he would say to Sky Dancer when he saw her, but he hoped he could convince her to be his wife. First, he would have to prove to her that he was sorry for his rash statements about the Indians—that would be the hard part. She might never forgive him.

They were camped by a small stream and Farley handed Morgan a cup of his thick coffee. Over the weeks Morgan had become accustomed to the strong brew with the coffee grounds floating in it, and even welcomed it now.

"How many more days until we get to Blackfoot Country, Farley?"

The old man leaned back against his saddle and smiled. "You ask me that near every day."

"Do I? I wasn't aware of it."

"We'll sleep in Blackfoot Country tomorrow night," the old man said, pulling his wide-brimmed hat down over his eyes. "I'm gonna get some shut-eye. You might want to douse that fire and keep your eyes peeled. This here's Arapaho land, and they ain't none too friendly to white folk."

"Farley, I have been doing a lot of thinking lately, and I am puzzled by something. How can it be that Danielle and Skyler look so much alike."

The old man sat up and eyed the young man. "'Cause Tag was married to a Blackfoot princess, Morning Song, when he was younger, and Danielle was their daughter."

"I didn't know. What happened to Danielle's mother?"

"She were killed by white men. She were also Windhawk's only sister."

"What is Skyler's mother like? I have seen her portrait hanging in the James's house. She was very lovely."

The old man sighed wearily, knowing he wouldn't get much sleep tonight, since Morgan was in a talking mood. "In the first place Sky Dancer don't want to be called Skyler no more. And I don't know how to tell you 'bout Joanna. She ain't like no one you've ever seed afore. I think I'll just wait and let you judge her fer yourself."

"I am trying to figure out why a well-brought-up young lady like Tag's sister would turn her back on her way of life and live as an Indian."

"You are making the mistake so many folk make. You think the way you live is the only, and best, way. That just ain't so. There is a strong peacefulness and brotherhood among the Blackfoot. They take care of one another. When you meet Windhawk, you'll be meeting more than a man. You'll be meeting up with a legend. He is . . . Windhawk!"

"I keep trying to envision the kind of life Sky Dancer has led. It was apparent to me that she was very well educated. Her manners are above reproach, her speech impeccable. I realized when I first saw her that she was different from all other young ladies I had ever met."

"Sky Dancer owes her manners and her education to her ma. Joanna always insisted that she know about both the Indian and the white world. I knowed she wasn't too happy in the white world. You may just have to face the fact that she won't go with you. I think I should warn you that there is unhappiness in the Blackfoot village. Danielle has disappeared."

"Danielle is staying with the Blackfoot?" Morgan said in amazement. It was hard for him to visualize the spoiled girl he'd always known living among the Indians.

"We don't knowed where she is. That's why her pa and Sky Dancer had to return to the village. Now douse that fire and let me get some sleep," Farley said, rolling over to his back to indicate their conversation was at an end.

Morgan threw dirt on the campfire, and then settled down to ponder the old man's words. Somehow, someway, he had to convince Skyler of his love for her.

As he listened to the stream washing over the rocks, he felt an urgency within himself. All he wanted to do was take Skyler in his arms and tell her how sorry he was for hurting her. Would she ever be happy living in his world? he wondered. Could he convince her that they would overcome any obstacle that stood in their path?

He picked up his rifle to make sure it was loaded, then leaned his back against a tree. What a strange twist his life had taken. He had been forced to rethink much of what he had been taught. He was ashamed that he had condemned a whole race of people just because they were different from himself.

Glancing up at the moon, he watched a cloud move

over it, shutting out the light and casting the countryside in shadows. Each day brought him closer to the woman he loved—each night he felt the differences that separated them.

He tried to visualize Skyler as an Indian, but he couldn't. She had fit so well into the life in Philadelphia. She had been so convincing in her role that he had never suspected she was any part Indian. It was even hard for him to think of her as Sky Dancer, since Skyler Dancing was the woman he'd fallen in love with.

His heart ached at the unhappinesse he had caused her. He would make it up to her somehow. Please, God, he prayed, let me convince her that she belongs with me.

Sky Dancer walked down by the Milk River feeling lost and misplaced. She didn't feel at home here anymore, and she hadn't belonged in Philadelphia. Where did she belong? The river was cast in silvery light and she turned her face up to the moon. The same moon shone down on the Indian world and the white man's land. Sky Dancer had now walked in both worlds, and felt like she belonged to neither.

Chapter Twenty-seven

Danielle had spent a miserable night and as she awoke, she looked about her in a sleep-drugged state. The first thing her eyes fell on, when she could focus them properly, was Scar Face's dead body. She shivered when she saw the spear sticking out of his back.

Turning her head, she met Wolfrunner's dark gaze. "You saved my life, Danielle," he said softly.

"It was nothing. I merely paid a debt," she told him, feeling as if she were going to be sick. She wished the grim reminder of her daring deed wasn't lying so near with his eyes open in death.

Sitting up, she tucked a strand of ebony hair behind her ear. "Are you well enough to move on, Wolfrunner? I don't want to stay here." She couldn't resist another glance at Scar Face's body, or the shiver that followed.

"I have tried to get up, but find I am too weak. If you will allow me to lean on you, we will move away from this place," Wolfrunner said weakly, feeling shame because he had allowed Scar Face to get the better of him.

Danielle helped him to stand. With him leaning heavily on her, they made it around the side of the mountains. Danielle watched Wolfrunner's face, knowing he was pushing himself beyond endurance. Beads of perspiration popped out on his forehead, and he staggered backward.

When Danielle felt they were a far enough distance away from the dead Scar Face, she helped Wolfrunner lean up against the rocky face of the mountain. With his face a mask of pain, Wolfrunner slowly sank down to a sitting position. Leaning back, he closed his eyes.

Danielle knew he was too weak to go on. She retraced her steps to the stream. Ignoring Scar Face's body, she ripped another strip from her skirt and wet it in the icy water. By now, her skirt was midway up her thigh She tried not to think about her half-clad condition—there were more important things to worry about.

Returning to Wolfrunner, she washed his face and tried to make him as comfortable as possible. She would tend his wounds, as best she could, but beyond that there was very little she could do for him. They didn't have anything to say to each other. Too much had happened between them—their feelings were still too raw.

Danielle had to make several trips to the mountain stream. On one occasion she realized she would have to retrieve the spear from Scar Face's back. Approaching the body slowly, she tried not to look at him. Grasping the spear in both hands, she gave a tug, but it wouldn't budge. Drawing a deep breath, she tightened her grip and braced her foot against Scar Face's back. With a strong yank the spear finally came loose. Danielle felt herself getting sick and clasped her hand over her mouth. She would never, as long as she lived, forget how it had felt when the spear had entered Scar Face's body. Nor the sound of its sharp point grinding against bone when she pulled it out.

In two days' time, Wolfrunner had recovered sufficiently from his wounds so they could continue their journey. They traveled slowly for the first day, allowing him to regain his strength.

It was a week after Danielle had killed Scar Face. Although there was no longer any need to fear pursuit, Wolfrunner pushed them harder than ever. It was almost as if he was obsessed with the need to get her back to the Blackfoot village as quickly as possible.

Wolfrunner looked behind him and saw that Danielle had dropped to her knees. Leaning his spear against a tree, he walked back to her and helped her to her feet. Her hair was matted and tangled and her face was streaked with dirt, but he could see the pride that shone in her sky-blue eyes. Seeing she was in a near state of exhaustion, he picked her up in his arms. When she weakly tried to struggle out of his grasp, he silenced her with a dark glance.

"I will carry you now," he said in a commanding voice. "You have been brave long enough."

Her eyes drifted shut, and she managed to open them with great effort. "So tired," she whispered. "I cannot . . . go on."

Wolfrunner held her close to his heart, knowing he

had pushed her past human endurance. She had not complained, and he now knew her well enough to realize her proud spirit wouldn't allow her to ask for help.

Setting his eyes on the mountains ahead of him, he walked in that direction. His burden was light, but his heart was heavy. Soon they would reach his village, and then he would have to turn his precious burden over to Windhawk. She would no longer have to depend on him for her survival. Soon she would be going back to her people, and he would never see her again.

Danielle had fallen asleep. Her head fell back against his shoulder, and he laid his face against hers. He loved her with every breath he took. His whole being was filled with her. He was considered a great warrior, and yet he had found a weakness within himself—Danielle was that weakness. He knew he could no more chase her from his heart than he could will the sun not to shine.

He carried her until the sun began to set, hardly noticing her weight. When he stood on the banks of the Milk River, at the foot of the last mountain that formed a barrier between them and the village, he decided to stop and make camp.

Wolfrunner was hot and weary, and he knew that Danielle must feel the same. Gathering her close to him, he waded into the river and allowed the cool water to wash over them.

Danielle's eyes fluttered open as he set her on her feet then proceeded to wash her all over. No words were spoken as he lifted her up and carried her up the bank.

Setting her on the soft grass, he knelt and ran his

fingers through her mass of black hair, trying to remove the worst of the tangles.

All this Danielle suffered in silence. She was so exhausted, it was all a filmy haze to her. She wished Wolfrunner would just leave her alone and let her sleep.

Laying Danielle back on the grass, he moved away from her and began gathering wood to build a fire. She hadn't stirred, so he lay down beside her and pulled her to rest in his arms. He would hold her tonight, for all too soon she would be taken from him.

Danielle awoke during the night, feeling something warm on her cheek. Opening her eyes, she found she was lying against Wolfrunner's shoulder and his head was resting against her face.

In that moment his eyes opened, and she was staring into deep, soft ebony pools. His hand moved up to touch her cheek, and she felt warm all over from the gentle gesture. His mouth was so near hers, she had but to move the slightest bit and they would touch. Suddenly his lips brushed against hers and she shivered with delight.

Against his will, Wolfrunner reached up and pushed Danielle's gown off the shoulders, baring her breasts. Dipping his head down, his mouth settled on one of the ripe mounds and he felt it swell as his tongue circled the tip.

Danielle threw back her head and allowed him the freedom to explore her body. She was a trembling mass as his hands pushed her tattered gown down her hips.

Before, when he had made love to Danielle, she hadn't known what to expect. Now her body knew that it could find new heights of joy when it became united with Wolfrunner's.

Forgotten were the harsh words he had spoken to her. All she could think about was the warm tingling sensation he was stirring within her body.

Somewhere in the distance, the call of a wolf penetrated the valley and echoed across the night sky. Wolfrunner was swept away by feelings deeper than lust and warmer than desire. Danielle's lips were sweeter than the nectar of the honey bees, and her skin was softer than the petal of a wildflower.

"Danielle, Danielle," he muttered in a thick voice. "I had not meant this to happen again."

Danielle thrilled at the sound of his voice. He might not like her, but at the moment he wanted her. She reached up and captured his head, bringing his lips down to hers. She could tell he was mentally trying to resist her. It was apparent that she had some power over him, and that thought warmed her with unspeakable pleasure.

Parting her lips, she offered them to him. He groaned as his mouth settled on hers. He had no will to fight the pull of this Blackfoot princess who was forbidden to him. She was in his blood and he couldn't get her out.

Wolfrunner's heart raced frantically as his hands moved down to explore her body. Danielle's mind was a swirling tide. Like a leaf that was riding the wind, she had no control over her emotions. Seeing his eyes darken with passion as they roamed the length of her now naked body, Danielle stifled a groan. With a violent tug, he stripped off his breechcloth and clasped her tightly against his hot flesh.

Wolfrunner became aware of the smallness of her

body. She was delicate, fragile, and small-boned. There was a need in him to protect her from any hurt—even if it should come from himself.

With an agonizing force of will, he pulled away from her. He had taken her once; he must not do it again. Suppose he should plant his seed in her—what would that do to her life?

Danielle could feel him pulling away from her. She knew he wanted her. Why was he fighting against this feeling between them? Realizing she had the power to move him, she reached out and touched his hard chest, then allowed her hand to drift up to his mouth. He moved back and she followed him, covering his body with hers.

A savage groan escaped his lips as she moved her silken body against him. Grabbing her by the shoulders, he rolled her over and positioned her hips so she could receive his thrusting manhood. He had meant only to take her quickly to release the fever that raged in his loins, but when he entered the velvet softness of her, it shook his whole world.

Wolfrunner moved forward and back slowly, trying to prolong the beauty of the mating. The earth touched the sky and the soft wind joined with the mountains. There was beauty all about him, and Wolfrunner felt a strange wetness in his eyes. There was no shame in him because of the tears—he cried from the beauty of his love for this woman who had taken his heart. His hands moved gently across her breasts and he sought her mouth. He could feel Danielle quiver, and knew she was experiencing the same deep emotions he was.

Danielle could feel Wolfrunner pulsating hotly inside her, and she threw back her head and clamped her lips tightly together to keep from crying out. She writhed beneath him, not knowing what to do to find relief. His hands moved to her hips and he gently guided her forward to meet his thrusts.

"It is good, beloved," he whispered thickly in her ear. Danielle only half heard his softly spoken words. She knew without being told that she had met the one man who filled her, body and soul.

With a strangled cry, Wolfrunner clasped her tightly to him, as wave after wave of fiery passion rocked both their bodies. Their bodies were intertwined—it seemed that neither could get enough of the other. They touched and caressed until the passion built and they coupled once more.

This time they made love with an urgency. It was as if both realized they might never have another time together. Danielle's head was reeling and she held on to his shoulders as he built up the pace faster and faster. This time when their bodies exploded in a white hot flash, each lay trembling from the aftershock.

After Danielle's heart rate had slowed and her breathing became even, she turned to Wolfrunner and found him staring at her. His gaze was probing, searching, as if he were trying to find something.

Suddenly he rolled over and sat up, pulling on his breechcloth. "I did not mean this to happen," he said in a cold voice which wounded her as well as himself. "It was wrong. I should never have touched you again." He avoided Danielle's eyes, knowing he dared not look at her. He had to clamp his jaw tightly together to keep from crying out that he loved her.

Danielle reached out her hand to him, but he merely turned over and pretended to fall asleep.

Tears ran down her cheeks and onto the grass she lay upon. Where moments ago, Wolfrunner had given of himself, he now turned a cold face to her. She was wounded to the quick, not understanding how he could be so cruel after what they had shared.

Closing her eyes, she decided to harden her heart against him. Never would he have the power to hurt her again. From tonight on, she would never again turn to him with love. She would show him she could be as cold and heartless as he was.

Chapter Twenty-eight

Farley, with his keen eyes, had spotted a large war party of Assiniboin warriors about an hour behind him and Morgan. Knowing they would soon pick up their trail, he and Morgan had been forced to travel in the mountains so they couldn't be easily tracked. It would mean taking a longer route to get to the Blackfoot village, but the way he saw it, they had little choice.

Morgan reined in his mount and gazed down the mountain. He couldn't see any sign of Indians but he knew if Farley said they were there—they were there.

"I take it that the Assiniboin are enemies of yours and the Blackfoot, Farley," Morgan said, watching as the old trapper dismounted and tightened his horse's cinch.

"Yep. Them Assiniboin would like nothing better than to have my scalp hanging from one of their spears. It's a treasure they seek second only to Windhawk's scalp."

The old man remounted and then let out a long spew of tobacco juice. "We best be moving on. I don't want them devils to pick up on our whereabouts."

As it neared dusk, Farley and Morgan made camp at the foot of the mountains. There would be no campfire tonight because the Assiniboin were camped just down the valley from them. Farley knew the Assiniboin were aware of their presence in the mountains. He knew they would send out scouts to try and locate him and Morgan, but he was a wily old fox and it wouldn't be the first time he had thrown an enemy off the track.

The old trapper chewed on a piece of jerky, wishing he could have a cup of coffee to wash it down with. He watched Morgan who was reclined against his saddle. As he studied the man who claimed to love Sky Dancer, he found much to admire in him. Farley knew Morgan wasn't the kind of person who could live with the Blackfoot. This man was a doctor, and his talents and skills were needed elsewhere. He didn't know how it would work out between Morgan and Sky Dancer, but he knew the young doctor loved Joanna and Windhawk's daughter—but was love enough to overcome their differences?

Morgan heard a twig snap just behind him and turned his eyes in that direction, while placing his finger on the trigger of his repeater.

"That ain't nothing but a deer nosing about," Farley said, taking another bite of jerky. "You act skittish; you ain't fretting 'bout them Assiniboin, are you?"

"I can't say I like the notion of them being so near. Especially since you said they would like to have your scalp, Farley."

"I just can't figure what they're doing in Blackfoot territory. They are either awfully brave, or mighty, mighty stupid. Windhawk don't look kindly on anyone invading his land—specially them Assiniboin. Was you thinking 'bout how your scalp would look hanging from one of their battle axes?" The old man chuckled. "They would be mighty partial to yellow hair like yourn."

Morgan smiled. "They would have to kill me first, and I expect you to see that doesn't happen."

Both men lapsed into silence. Farley unlaced his boots and eyed Morgan. "What you looking so thoughtful 'bout?" Farley asked, feeling in one of his talkative moods.

"I was thinking about what I'm going to say to Skyler when I see her."

"Sky Dancer," Farley corrected. "You best start thinking about her as Sky Dancer."

"How far to the Blackfoot village, Farley?"

The old man grinned widely. "I done tole you this morning, it ain't more than a two day ride, iffen them Assiniboin don't give us no trouble. 'Course iffen they was to chase us, I reckon we could make the village in one day."

"I grow impatient, Farley. I need to know if she loves me enough to leave her people."

"Are you planning on taking her back to Phila-delphia with you?"

"Yes. I realize it would be asking a lot for her to leave her home and return to Philadelphia with me. Do you think she would do it, Farley? Do you think she will be happy that I resigned my commission?"

"That's two questions, and I can't answer nether of em. I don't 'spect you are gonna have an easy time of it when you see her. I need to warn you that you'll not be able to go near her, lest Windhawk or her ma says it's all right."

Farley thought of Sky Dancer. She was almost as dear to him as Joanna was, and he loved Joanna more than anyone. He couldn't help but think Sky Dancer belonged with this man. He only hoped Windhawk would see it that way.

"You best get some sleep, Morgan. I'll take the first watch. We have to keep an eye peeled for them Assiniboin. I'll wake you 'bout midnight and you can take the watch."

Morgan turned over on his back and played a game, counting the stars. He didn't want to think too deeply, or he might never get to sleep. Sky Dancer was with him night and day. He couldn't get her out of his mind, and he didn't want to get her out of his heart.

Wolfrunner awoke before sunrise. He knew they were no more than four days' walk from the village. He hoped they would soon come across one of the Blackfoot hunting parties, because he didn't know how much farther Danielle could go before she collapsed.

For a long moment, he stared down at her. Last night, when they had made love, would be burned in his memory for all time. He knew when he was an old man, he would still remember the night when he had held the world in his arms.

Bending down, he shook her gently by the shoulders. Her eyes fluttered open. For a fleeting moment he saw them soften before they turned cold as ice.

"We must move on," he said, helping her to stand. When she cried out in pain, he looked down at her feet. Picking up one of her feet, he saw they were cut and bleeding again. Evidently the hard pace they were traveling had broken the wounds open again. Scooping her up in his arms, he carried her to the river and plunged her feet into the cool water. He avoided her eyes as he washed the dried blood from the bottom of her feet.

"We will go slowly, and if it becomes too painful to walk, you must tell me," he said with a softening in his eyes.

Danielle stood up and turned her back on him, knowing he would never hear a word of complaint from her. If it killed her, she wouldn't allow him to see how badly her feet hurt. Nor would she allow him to see how bruised and battered her heart was.

"You lead, I will follow," she said stubbornly.

Wolfrunner handed her a slice of meat. "You must eat or you will not be able to walk at all."

She took the offered food and ate it hurriedly. As far as she was concerned they couldn't reach the village too soon to suit her.

As they started out, she was aware that Wolfrunner had deliberately slowed his pace, and she knew it was because of her feet. She knew if she asked it of him, he would stop and allow her to rest, but she would never beg him for mercy.

The morning passed quickly. They moved out of the mountains to follow the winding path of the Milk River that would lead them home.

Danielle was following along behind Wolfrunner, wishing she dared ask him to stop so she could rest. She watched him whirl around and look back toward her. Leaping through the air, he caught her about the waist and threw her to the ground. Scrambling to her knees, it was on the tip of her tongue to scold him for being so rough and knocking her down—but the look in his dark eyes stopped her.

Wolfrunner had become alert as if he sensed danger. His eyes scanned the countryside, and he jumped in front of Danielle as if to shield her with his body. Danielle was startled when he grabbed her by the arm and pushed her behind a huge boulder. Shoving her forward, he thrust her face down on the ground.

"Stay down," he commanded. "No matter what you hear, do not show yourself."

Danielle watched him unsheath his knife, and he shoved it into her hand. Picking up his spear, he quickly turned away and moved behind the trunk of a tree.

In the next moment all the demons of hell seemed to be unleashed! Savage cries split through the stillness, and out of nowhere came a dozen or more painted Indians. Danielle gathered from Wolfrunner's reaction that they were not Blackfoot.

She watched in horror as Wolfrunner leaped from behind the tree and started running away from the river. She realized at once that he was trying to draw the Indians away from her hiding place. He was sacrificing himself for her!

Disregarding his warning, she stood up and screamed just as an arrow whizzed through the air and entered Wolfrunner's body. She watched in horror as he crumpled and landed hard against the ground.

In a frantic haze, she ran toward him, praying she would reach him before it was too late. If he was to die, then she wanted to die with him. Danielle paid little heed to the mounted men that were bearing down on her. All that she could think about was reaching Wolfrunner!

She stumbled and fell, only to jump up and race forward. When she reached Wolfrunner, she dropped to her knees. His chest was covered with blood, and his eyes were glazed with pain. He tried to raise his hand and touch her but he was too weak.

Clasping his hand in hers, she laid her face against his. "Don't die," she cried. "Do not leave me!"

"Run . . . go," he whispered weakly. His eyes were sad, and they seemed to speak of things that had been, and others that could never be. He tried to rise but couldn't, and slumped backward. His eyes seemed to glaze over and his hand slipped from her grasp. Danielle's hand tightened on the knife he had given her earlier. No longer was she the polite young lady from Philadelphia. She was an Indian maiden and she would revenge the life of the man she loved!

By now the Indians had reached her. One of them jumped from his horse and grabbed her, pushing her to the ground. Danielle jumped to her feet, and slashed out at him with the knife, but he easily wrestled it out of her hand. The Indian grabbed her around the waist, and was about to remount his horse when a shot rang out and his grip loosened. He seemed to crumple and fell to the ground, taking Danielle with him.

Danielle fearfully tried to wriggle out from under the Indian, whose weight had pinned her beneath him. She saw that he'd been shot through the head! Other shots rang out in rapid succession and the remaining Indians rode away in a cloud of dust.

Danielle gave no thought to who her rescuers could be. She only knew she had to get to Wolfrunner.

Crawling over to him, she dusted the grains of sand from his face with a trembling hand. The arrow was still embedded in his chest but she didn't dare remove it. His eyes were closed and she didn't know if he was unconscious or dead. Leaning forward, she placed her ear against his chest and could hear the faintest heartbeat.

Raising her face to the sky, she prayed in a broken voice. "Dear God, don't take this brave man. Please allow Wolfrunner to live!"

Looking down at Wolfrunner's face, she noticed his pallor was ashen. She could barely see the rise and fall of his chest. He had made the supreme sacrifice by protecting her today. She feared this time he would pay with his life.

Grasping his limp hand in hers, she held it to her lips. "I love you, Wolfrunner!" she cried. "Don't die!"

Farley heard the Assiniboin's war cries. He halted his horse, ready to take cover when he spotted Danielle, and Wolfrunner on the ground with the enemy all about them. He knew if he didn't do something quickly it would be too late.

"Well, hell and damnation—that's Danielle!" he yelled out to Morgan. "We gotta save her!"

Both men took careful aim. Morgan had the Indian in his sight who was trying to place Danielle on his horse. He squeezed the trigger, and watched the man crumple.

Farley fired twice in succession, and two more Indians fell. Pointing their mounts in the direction of Danielle, they rode swiftly, firing all the while. Several more Indians fell, and the others rode away in a cloud of dust.

Morgan jumped from his horse, and pulled Danielle to her feet. An amazed look washed over her face when she saw him. Before she could ask Morgan why he was there everything turned upside down, and she collapsed in his arms!

Farley decided they would make camp by the river until Morgan could tend to Wolfrunner and Danielle. Morgan knew it wouldn't be wise to move the wounded Indian in his condition.

Farley stood guard with his rifle aimed and ready in case the Assiniboin decided to return. Danielle was watching Morgan cleanse the skin around the arrow that was still embedded in Wolfrunner's chest. She felt dizzy and faint when he broke off the shaft and tossed it aside.

Danielle held Wolfrunner's hand, and gritted her teeth when Morgan began probing the wound. She was thankful that Wolfrunner was unconscious when Morgan finally removed the arrowhead.

"Save him, Morgan please save him," Danielle cried.

Morgan gave Danielle a strange look before he dropped the bloody arrowhead into her hand. "A souvenir to show your friends back in Philadelphia," he said lightly.

"Will Wolfrunner make it, Morgan?" she asked hopefully.

"It's too soon to tell, Danielle. The arrowhead went deep. He's lost a lot of blood."

"You have to help him, Morgan," she said, grasping his shirtfront. "Do everything you can!"

"I always do the best I can, Danielle," he said, pouring disinfectant over the wound.

Danielle watched as Morgan removed a roll of bandages from his bag and bound Wolfrunner's wound.

"I have done everything I can for him, Danielle," Morgan said, rising. "Now let's have a look at you."

"I'm not hurt," she told him. "I will just sit beside Wolfrunner in case he awakens."

"He isn't going to regain consciousness for a long time, Danielle," Morgan said. "I see some pretty nasty cuts on your feet. I want to clean and apply medication to them."

She shook her head and clamped her jaw stubbornly. "No, I said."

His brow knitted in a frown. This wasn't the Danielle he had known. She had changed not only in appearance, but in character as well. "I am the doctor here, and I will tend your wounds, Danielle," he said firmly.

She had little choice when he scooped her up in his arms and carried her down to the river. She was silent and sullen as he cleaned and applied medicine to her cuts.

After he had bound her feet in white bandages, he sat back and took a long look at her. Smiling slowly he carried her back to the wounded Indian and plopped her down beside him.

"Since you seem so concerned about him, you can watch over him, Danielle, while I clean my instruments."

She placed her hand on his arm. "I don't know what you are doing here, Morgan, but I thank God that you came when you did."

Morgan smiled, and pushed a tumbled strand of hair from her face. Danielle's resemblance to Sky Dancer was almost uncanny. But she stirred no passion in his heart as Sky Dancer had. At the moment he just felt pity for her. He was glad that he and Farley had found her alive.

"After you have rested and had something to eat, we will talk. I'm sure we both have a great deal to tell each other, Danielle."

When Danielle had drifted off to sleep, Morgan stood beside Farley and they both scanned the countryside.

"Do you think the war party will return, Farley?"

"Nope. We gave them a licking today and they ain't likely to come back asking for more. Still, I'll keep an eye peeled."

Morgan's eyes moved over the wounded Wolfrunner. "Do you think he's the one that abducted Danielle?"

"Nope, not Wolfrunner. He'd be the one who rescued her from whoever took her in the first place. Do you think he'll make it?"

"I just don't know, Farley. It seems Danielle is very fond of him." His eyes moved over Danielle and he noticed she was sleeping fretfully. "It looks like they have both been through a lot."

"It 'pears so. I don't understand Danielle caring

nothing 'bout no Indian. She don't like the fact that her ma was a Blackfoot."

Morgan watched the stars twinkle in the ebony skies. He could hardly curb his impatience to see Sky Dancer. Soon, he would be able to gaze upon her lovely face. He hoped she would be glad to see him.

Chapter Twenty-nine

Sky Dancer sat on the bank of the Milk River glancing every so often toward the village. They hadn't heard anything from her father or Uncle Tag. She hoped that they would have found some clue to Danielle's disappearance. But if they had, wouldn't they have sent word by now?

She watched several children playing in the river remembering a time when she, too, had been carefree like those children. She realized she hadn't yet come all the way home. A part of her still remained in Philadelphia.

Sky Dancer knew she would never be the same carefree young maiden she'd been before she had gone to Philadelphia. She realized that her parents had shielded her from hurt in the past, but they could no longer stand in harm's way for her. She now had to face life on her own terms, and come to grips with it, no matter how painful an experience it was.

Gathering up the reins of her horse, she bounded onto its back. She would ride out alone so she could think. Waving to the children who cried out her name, she nudged her horse forward at a fast pace. With the wind in her face, and the sun lending its golden rays to the summer skies, she felt a new kind of unhappiness. She no longer belonged to this world. She was caught halfway between two worlds.

Joanna was sitting under the shade of a wide cottonwood tree. She was surrounded by several young children who were eagerly hanging on to every word she said. It had become her habit to teach them to read and write English one day a week. She found she looked forward to these times as much as the children did.

Suddenly the stillness of the village was interrupted by two riders crossing the river. Joanna laid her slate aside, and dismissed the children. Walking quickly toward her lodge, she hoped the newcomers would have some word of Danielle. If they did, they would come to the chief's lodge first.

Morgan balanced the unconscious Wolfrunner across his lap while Farley carried Danielle behind him. Morgan felt a prickle of uneasiness when he rode up the bank, and was suddenly surrounded by fierce-looking Indians. Their dark eyes seemed to burn into him, but no man approached him. He followed Farley's lead, and rode to the center of the village.

As they stopped before the huge lodge, Morgan watched the flap being pushed aside, and the most beautiful woman Morgan had ever seen came out. Her hair was red-gold, her eyes were the same violet-blue as Sky Dancer's, and her face seemed to be like a figure out of a beautiful painting. He knew without being told that this lovely creature must be Joanna, Sky Dancer's mother.

Joanna couldn't believe her eyes when she saw her niece Danielle slumped over, with her head on Farley's shoulder.

"Farley, thank God you found Danielle!" she cried. "Is she unconscious? Has she been hurt?"

"Nope, she's just plumb tuckered out. I'll just carry her into your lodge," he said, agilely dismounting and lifting Danielle into his arms.

Joanna placed her hand on Danielle's face to assure herself that she was really all right. When she felt the warm even breath against her hand, she was overcome with relief.

When Farley carried Danielle into the lodge, Joanna turned for the first time to the white man. Her eyes went to Morgan and her lovely face creased into a frown. Stepping forward she glanced down at the wounded warrior.

"Oh, no," she gasped. "Wolfrunner!" Turning to one of the men, she spoke rapidly to him in the tongue of the Blackfoot. Moments later a woman came rushing out of one of the tipis. White Dove, seeing her wounded son, began to wail and cry.

Joanna asked one of the warriors to help the white man carry the unconscious Wolfrunner to Gray Fox's tipi. When they had laid him on the buffalo robe, Joanna dropped to her knees and began to examine him carefully. Seeing the bandage that was wrapped about his chest, she looked up at the white man inquiringly.

"Don't remove the bandage," Morgan said, dropping down beside Joanna. "I am Dr. Morgan Prescott and I just put fresh bandages on the wound this morning."

Joanna's eyes met soft silver eyes. She knew this was the man Sky Dancer had told her about. She didn't know why he was here, but she could guess. There were many questions that formed in her mind, but they would keep until later.

"How is Wolfrunner, Doctor?" she said, voicing her concern for the warrior she had loved almost like a son.

"I'm not sure. He's lost a great deal of blood, but the wound is clean, and that's always a good sign."

Joanna spoke to White Dove, telling her what Morgan had said. She then turned back to Morgan. "How is my niece, Danielle?"

"As Farley told you, she is suffering from no more than exhaustion. Other than scratches and bruises, she is doing just fine."

"Come with me, Doctor, I would like you to have another look at Danielle. There is no telling what conditions she has had to suffer through."

As they walked out of the tipi, Morgan couldn't keep his eyes from straying to Sky Dancer's lovely mother. He didn't know if she knew who he was, or why he had come. Even though she was a white woman, she wore the doeskin gown and moccasins as if she had been born to them.

"I am curious, Doctor. How did you and Farley find Danielle when the whole Blackfoot nation has searched for her in vain?"

"It was a strange quirk of fate . . ." He paused, not knowing what name to call her.

She smiled slightly and he drew in his breath at her

loveliness. "You may call me Joanna," she offered, seeing his dilemma.

"Joanna, Farley and I were on our way here when we ran into a party of Assiniboin warriors. They had wounded Wolfrunner, and were trying to carry Danielle away with them."

Joanna took a deep breath. "It was very fortunate that you came along when you did. You have my gratitude, Doctor. As a matter of fact you will have the gratitude of the whole Blackfoot tribe."

Morgan looked into the violet colored eyes that were so like Sky Dancer's. "I don't want your gratitude, Joanna. I want your daughter."

There was no surprise on Joanna's face at his announcement. Seeing the sincere light in Morgan's eyes, she knew that he loved her daughter. She was not ready to deal with Sky Dancer going away with this man, but hadn't she always known it might happen?

"My daughter isn't mine to give, Morgan Prescott. I am sure Farley has told you that she can only be given by her father."

"Where is she? May I see her? I have come a long way to find her."

They had reached the lodge, and Joanna turned to Morgan. "It will not be permitted that you see her alone. But you will be allowed to see her in the company of others. She is not in the village at the moment, but I expect her any time now." She reached out and laid her hand on his arm. "Don't hurt Sky Dancer. If you cannot accept what she is, ride away right now, and she will never be told that you were here."

"It is because I accept who she is that I am here,

381

Joanna. My problem now is whether Sky Dancer will accept who I am."

For a long moment the two of them looked into each other's eyes. "I cannot imagine that will be a problem, Doctor. The problem you will have to face will be with my husband, Windhawk."

Farley chose that moment to come ambling out of the lodge grinning at Joanna. "Danielle will be stirring soon, and I 'spect she'll be hungry too."

Joanna slid her arm about Farley's waist, and kissed his cheek. "It seems as if you are always showing up at the right time, my dear friend. Countless times you have turned defeat into victory for me and mine."

Farley's eyes danced merrily as he warmed under Joanna's praise. Morgan was seeing a different side of the old trapper. It was apparent that he adored the redheaded goddess.

"I couldn't a done it without Morgan," Farley said, watching Joanna's eyes. "He were right beside me when I was chasing them Assiniboin."

Joanna's eyes twinkled as she looked at Morgan. "I have already offered the good doctor my gratitude, Farley, but he didn't want it."

"You don't say—now is that a fact," Farley said, scratching his head.

"That's right, Farley. He said he wanted my daughter instead," Joanna said, moving quickly into the lodge, leaving Morgan with a startled expression on his face.

Farley turned to Morgan, shaking his head. "You damned fool. Do you want to get yourself killed? You'd better watch what you say or it might get back to Windhawk. You best not be forgetting that Sky

Dancer is a princess of the Blackfoot tribe, and these Indians don't take kindly to an outsider staking his claim on her."

Morgan was still staring at the lodge flap where Joanna had just disappeared. It was beyond his imagination how someone with her obvious breeding and beauty would bury herself in a Blackfoot village. He was anxious to meet the man who had won her heart and fathered Sky Dancer.

"Come on," Farley said, walking away. "You can bunk in my tipi, but I warn you that I ain't much of a cook. I make a hell of a good cup of coffee though."

Morgan couldn't help but laugh at the strange character whom he had come to respect over the weeks since they had left Philadelphia. "Oh, no, Farley, let us hope your cooking is better than your coffee."

Suddenly Morgan felt lighthearted. The long journey was at an end, now he was anxious to face Sky Dancer.

It was an hour later when Morgan came out of Farley's tipi. He gazed about the village as the Indians went about their normal day-to-day chores. He looked at the children with a doctor's eye. They seemed to be well fed and happy. A group of them were gathered about an old white-haired Indian man, and seemed to be listening to him attentively. He wished he could understand the Blackfoot language, because whatever the old man was saying made the children laugh delightedly. Apparently the Indians revered their elderly, which was more than could be said for the white race. Remembering what he had said about

Indians that day in the summerhouse made him feel deeply ashamed as he looked at the dark-eyed children.

The women went busily about preparing their evening meal, and wonderful aromas drifted through the air. This village was so totally different from anything Morgan had been led to believe about the Indians. He had watched them cry over the wounded Wolfrunner, and he now saw them laugh. There was a peacefulness here, and it seemed to settle on him like a tonic.

If it weren't for the ache in his heart to see Sky Dancer, he knew he would feel totally at ease.

Suddenly there was a thundering of hooves, and the children looked up from their playing. Morgan tensed as he watched a young Indian maiden ride her big black stallion into the village. The children ran along beside her, and she smiled down at them.

Sky Dancer was riding astride, and agilely slid off her mount. Picking one of the smaller children up in her arms, she walked toward the chief's lodge with the other children tagging along beside her.

Morgan heard her speak to them in the language of the Blackfoot. One little boy held up his hurt finger, and Sky Dancer kissed the hurt away.

Morgan's eyes roamed hungrily over Sky Dancer. She appeared so different in her fringed buckskins, knee-length moccasins, and beaded headband.

Morgan was at a loss as to how to approach Sky Dancer. Suppose she were to look at him with contempt? She had just reached her lodge when the mother of Wolfrunner called out to her. Morgan watched as the Indian woman spoke to her, and he assumed she was telling Sky Dancer about Danielle and Wolfrunner.

Sky Dancer glanced over to Farley's tipi and drew in her breath at the blond-headed man who was dressed in buckskins. Surely that couldn't be Morgan! No, Morgan wouldn't be here!

Morgan took a step toward her, and she felt her heart leap with joy! There could be no mistake—it was Morgan!

Without pausing to think, she ran toward him. Her feet seemed to fly as he reached out his arms to her. He caught her about the waist, and lifted her into the air!

As her tears wet his face, Morgan murmured her name, over and over. It was too public for a kiss, but Sky Dancer gloried in his warm embrace.

"You came, Morgan!" she cried. "I cannot believe you are really here."

He set her on her feet, and smiled deeply into her eyes. "I came to take you home with me, Sky . . . Dancer. Did you think my love so puny that I wouldn't follow you?"

She brushed the tears away with one hand while he clutched the other. "I wasn't sure. I didn't think you would want me when you found out who I was. When did you come? How did you find me?"

"There was nowhere you could go that I wouldn't find you, my little Indian princess." His eyes spoke of his love for her, and she wished he could take her in his arms.

Sky Dancer saw his eyes move over her, taking in her appearance. "You find me . . . different?" she asked hesitantly, fearing he wouldn't like the way she was dressed.

"You are no different now than you were when I fell

in love with you." He gazed at the soft buckskin that molded her soft curves. Taking both her hands in his, he worshipped her with his eyes. "Well, perhaps you are a little different, but I like what I see, my little Indian princess."

She smiled up at him. "You look a bit different yourself, Morgan."

Farley came out of the tipi and sized up the situation in a flash. He hurriedly stepped between Sky Dancer and Morgan, breaking their hands apart. "Have you both gone clean out of your mind? Sky Dancer, you know better than to let Morgan touch you with the whole village looking on. You best go to your ma at once."

Sky Dancer nodded, suddenly brought back to reality. "Farley is right, Morgan," she said, stepping back a few paces. "I must leave you now."

"When will I see you?" he wanted to know, taking a step toward her.

"I do not know. Perhaps Farley can bring you to my father's lodge later." Turning away, she moved gracefully toward her lodge. Just before she disappeared inside, she turned back, and waved at Morgan.

"You are a fool, Morgan. This ain't Philadelphia, you know. Iffen you want to keep your scalp, you better play by the Blackfoot rules. You ain't allowed to touch Sky Dancer lessen her pa says you can."

"Morgan's eyes narrowed. "I can be patient, Farley, because I know he will have to give her to me sooner or later. I will not give her up."

"You don't know Windhawk if you think that you have any say in the matter. He don't have to do nothing he don't want to. Damn it, don't you knowed he's the

386

same as a king here in this village. Would you go walking up to the king of England, and demand his daughter?"

Morgan merely nodded. "No man, be he king, or chief of the Blackfoot, can keep me away from Sky Dancer. I didn't come all this way to lose her."

"You won't be so damned sure of yourself when you meet Windhawk!" Farley told him.

Chapter Thirty

Danielle was dreaming she was being chased by savage Indians. Their faces were painted with hideous colors, and she couldn't get away from them. She watched as one of them shot an arrow, which struck Wolfrunner. She clawed and struggled to get to him, but they were holding her back.

She turned her head from side to side, moaning. Suddenly she felt a cool hand on her forehead, and she opened her eyes. For a moment she thought she was looking into a mirror, for her own image was looking back at her.

"I am dreaming," she whispered through parched lips. "It was a nightmare."

"You are safe now, Danielle," a soft, sweet voice said. "You have nothing to fear. Morgan and Farley brought you safely back to us."

"Sky Dancer? Is it you?" Danielle said in confusion. "I don't understand."

"Yes, it is me. You must rest because you have been through a great ordeal. My mother said you were to

389

stay in bed until she says you can get up."

"I don't understand. Where am I?" Danielle asked, looking about her.

"You are in my father's lodge."

All at once the whole ordeal came back to Danielle in a flash. She tried to sit up, but was too weak. "Wolfrunner, I have to find him!" she cried. "They killed him! Someone has to help me find him."

Sky Dancer touched Danielle's forehead and discovered she was feverish. That must be why she was talking irrationally. "No, Danielle, Wolfrunner is not dead. He is recovering in his father's tipi."

A tear rolled down Danielle's cheek, and she clasped Sky Dancer's hand. "You wouldn't say it if it weren't true, would you, Sky Dancer? Is he really going to be all right? Do not lie to me. I can take the truth. If he is dead, I want to know it."

"I can assure you Wolfrunner is resting comfortably. He is most certainly not dead. Dr. Morgan Prescott is here, and he assures us that Wolfrunner will soon mend. Please try to rest now."

Danielle looked confused. "What would Morgan be doing here? I don't understand. Yes . . . I remember . . . he and Farley rescued me from the Indians."

"You don't have to think of anything but getting well. Are you hungry?"

"Yes . . . I think so."

Sky Dancer picked up a bowl, and lifted a spoon to Danielle's mouth. "You will love my mother's stew. I will feed you myself."

Danielle had many questions to ask, but she was content to satisfy her hunger at the moment. Nothing mattered but that Wolfrunner was going to recover.

Sky Dancer held a waterskin, allowing Danielle to drink deeply. Danielle noticed her feet were bandaged, and looked at her cousin inquiringly.

"Morgan tended you," Sky Dancer said, answering her cousin's unasked question.

"Tell me how I got here? What is Morgan Prescott doing here? Did my father send him?"

"Lay back, and I will explain some things to you. Wolfrunner has already told us about your adventure. It seems that the warriors who abducted you thought they had taken me." She smiled. "That is an easy mistake for one to make."

"Yes, he died without ever knowing he had made a mistake. If it hadn't been for Wolfrunner I don't know what would have happened to me."

"There is no need to dwell on the unpleasant. I have a surprise I think you will like. Your father is here. Farley rode all the way to Philadelphia to tell us of your disappearance."

"Where is my father? When can I see him?" Danielle asked, needing to see him, to assure herself he was really in the village.

"He and my father returned earlier. Uncle Tag sat beside you for a long time and then he and my father left to visit Wolfrunner."

Danielle reached out for Sky Dancer's hand. "I have come to know a great deal about your life. I wanted to be more like you, Sky Dancer. When I came here I was a spoiled little girl, but I have changed."

Sky Dancer pushed the damp hair out of Danielle's face. "I have walked in your world, and I found many wondrous things, not the least of which was love."

Danielle frowned thoughtfully. "You love Morgan

Prescott, don't you?"

"Yes. I love him and he loves me."

Danielle laughed delightedly. "You have managed to walk off with the prize catch of Philadelphia. I began to think Morgan would never find a woman to his taste."

"I do not know if my father will allow me to marry Morgan," Sky Dancer said sadly. "I fear he will not."

"What will you do if my uncle won't let you and Morgan marry?"

"I will obey my father."

"You are far more fortunate than I, Sky Dancer. I, too, have found love, but the man I love does not love me. I think I shall never know true happiness."

Sky Dancer clasped her cousin's hand. "How could anyone not love you?"

"Wolfrunner thinks of me as nothing more than an irritant. He will be only too happy to be rid of me."

"Wolfrunner," Sky Dancer said in amazement. "He is a noble warrior."

Tears spilled down Danielle's cheeks, and Sky Dancer gathered her close. "I am lost, Sky Dancer. How can I go on without his love?"

"Do you know for a certainty that he does not share your feelings?"

"Yes, he has told me very clearly that he doesn't want me. I cannot really blame him. You know what I was like when I first came here."

"If he does not love you then there is nothing you can do. You must be brave, and never look back. There is every chance that my father will send Morgan away. I fear we may both be in for a heartache."

Danielle glanced into her look-alike's eyes. "I am glad I have come to know you. In all that has hap-

392

pened, I always felt close to you. When I felt I couldn't go on, I would try to think what you would do, and it helped me to be strong."

"My mother says that we both nursed at her breast after your mother was killed. She always told me that gave you and I a special bond."

Danielle smiled. "And so it does. My one regret is that we shall soon be separated. I will go back to Philadelphia, and you may have to stay here."

"I fear that is just what will happen."

"At least you have the comfort of knowing that Morgan loves you a great deal. Why else would he have come so far to see you, Sky Dancer?"

"Yes, I do have that."

"Have you had a chance to talk to Morgan?"

"Just for a moment."

"Wouldn't it be possible for the two of you to have some time alone?"

"No, it would never be allowed."

"Let us hold on to each other as long as we can," Danielle said. "I feel so close to you."

"And I you, Danielle, for when I was in Philadelphia, I walked in your shoes."

It was long past nightfall when the Indian came to Farley's tipi. He told the old trapper that Windhawk wanted to see him and Morgan at once. As the two men walked slowly toward the big lodge, Farley eyed the young doctor.

"You have been summoned by the great man himself. I 'spect he'll be wanting to thank you for saving Danielle's life. Tonight isn't the time to bring up how

393

you feel 'bout Sky Dancer," Farley warned.

As they entered the lodge, there were several men sitting around the fire. Tag was one of them, and the other four were Indians. There were no women present, and Morgan suspected they might be behind the curtained off area, thus dashing any hopes he might have had for seeing Sky Dancer.

As they approached the men, Morgan's eyes went to the one Indian who seemed to stand out among the others. He could only be Windhawk. It wasn't that he was dressed any differently from the three other Indians—it was more that he was a commanding personality. He held his head proudly, and his dark eyes were alert with intelligence.

Tag motioned that Morgan and Farley should join them around the council fire. Morgan took a seat next to one of the Indians, and all the while he was studying Windhawk. The dark eyes seemed to see inside him, and he felt as if Windhawk could read his every thought. He could see now how Joanna had been drawn to this man, for Morgan had met no other like him.

"You are Dr. Morgan Prescott," Windhawk stated in near-perfect English.

"Yes, and you would be Windhawk," Morgan answered.

Windhawk inclined his head. "Tag you already know—this is Dark Warrior, Hunting Bear, and Gray Fox. Gray Fox has something to say to you and Farley. He will speak in English so you will be able to understand him."

The Indian named Gray Fox stood. "I want to thank you both for saving my son Wolfrunner's life. Once before I gave my thanks when Joanna saved my son's life. It is no less precious to me now than it was when he was a baby. I offer each of you the choice of my best horses."

"I do not want your horses, Gray Fox. We did nothing that . . ."

"What he means," Farley spoke up, jabbing an elbow into Morgan's side to silence him before he insulted the war chief, "is that me and Morgan would be honored to accept one of your horses, Gray Fox."

The Indian, Gray Fox, nodded and took his seat. Tag was the next to speak. This was a different Tag than Morgan was accustomed to. He was dressed as an Indian and his golden hair was encircled with a leather headband.

"You both know that my gratitude goes past anything material, yet I would also like to offer you the prized beaver skins that were left to me by Sun Woman," he said solemnly.

By now Morgan was totally confused. "Why was Tag acting so strangely? He acted like this was some solemn ceremony, when a handshake would have sufficed.

Again Farley poked him in the ribs. "We are happy to accept your gifts," the old man said. "Although we were proud to save the life of Danielle and Wolf-runner."

"Tag, I don't want your thanks," Morgan spoke up. "I did nothing that you wouldn't have done in like circumstances. Why are you saying this to me?"

Tag motioned for Morgan to hold his tongue, but Windhawk spoke up. "I give you leave to speak, Doctor Morgan Prescott. For saving the life of my dead sister's daughter you can ask what you will of me, and if it is in my power, I will grant it to you."

Morgan remembered Farley warning him not to mention Sky Dancer at this time. "I want nothing but to talk to you on a matter that concerns us both, at a later time, Windhawk. Will that be agreeable to you?"

Windhawk nodded his head. "I will let you know when the appointed time comes." Then Windhawk did something that startled Morgan. His face eased into a smile, and he looked at Farley. "You were once a burden I had to bear, old man, because Joanna loved you. In later years, you have become my valued friend, and not so much of a burden."

Farley's laughter crackled out. Evidently the ceremony was over, and they could relax. "There was a time when you woulda killed me sure enough iffen Joanna hadn't stopped you. I still get nightmares remembering it."

"You are a wily devil, Farley," Tag spoke up. "One would have to get up very early in the morning to get the better of you. You have been my friend since I was but a boy. Since I have grown to manhood, that friendship has deepened."

Suddenly the lodge flap was thrown wide, and Joanna entered. Morgan watched Windhawk's face as his eyes followed his wife. He could see the adoration sparkling in the dark depths, and the warm glance that passed between the two of them. It was possible to cross over the forbidden line and love someone outside one's race. Windhawk and Joanna were living proof of that. Morgan just hoped Windhawk would feel that way when he asked for Sky Dancer's hand.

"Am I intruding?" Joanna asked.

Windhawk's mouth eased into a smile. He said no words but then he didn't have to. The look he gave her said she could never intrude in his life.

"Doctor Prescott, White Dove asked if you would mind looking in on Wolfrunner before you turned in for the night," Joanna said, looking directly at him. "I told her I was sure you would want to check his wound."

"Yes," he said, rising. "I was going to do so anyway. If you will excuse me," he said, standing up.

"Farley will take you to Wolfrunner," she said, moving to her husband's side.

Morgan cleaned and dressed Wolfrunner's wounds. "You are healing nicely," he said, looking into dark, brooding eyes that seemed void of any feeling.

"I will be up soon. I will not lie on my mat like a woman," Wolfrunner said in a harsh voice.

"Even the strongest of us need time to heal. You have been gravely wounded. I wouldn't be in such a hurry to get up if I were you."

"You are not me," Wolfrunner said coldly. "No white man could know how an Indian feels."

Morgan closed his black bag, and stood up. "I will stop by to see you again tomorrow."

Wolfrunner looked up at Morgan. "I have not thanked you for saving my life. While my life is no great thing, I am grateful that you saved Danielle."

Morgan was getting weary of everyone thanking him. Apparently the Blackfoot people were generous with their praise. "I did nothing. If you want to show your thanks, then follow my orders."

"There is something you can do for me, Doctor," Wolfrunner said in a soft voice, as if he didn't want to be overheard by his mother, who was seated nearby.

"If I can."

"I would like it if you would say that I can have no visitors. Sometimes when someone is very ill, the medicine woman of my tribe says this."

"Your visitors should be restricted, but I do not think—"

Wolfrunner held up his hand. "I do not want Danielle to see me. You must say that she is not to come."

Morgan looked puzzled for a moment. "I will pass the word," he said. With a nod of his head, he left the tipi and stepped out into the night.

Morgan thought of the strange conversation he had just had with Wolfrunner. His patient was still weak, but he suspected with the stamina the Indians displayed it wouldn't be long until he was up and about.

As Morgan walked toward Farley's tipi, several Indian braves smiled and nodded at him. Evidently he and Farley had been made into some kind of heroes because they had rescued Danielle and Wolfrunner.

He was so deep in thought, he didn't hear the soft moccasin footsteps that approached him from behind. When Sky Dancer touched his shoulder he turned around to face her. Her eyes met his, and he was reminded of the night they had made love in the summerhouse in Philadelphia. By the light blush to her cheeks, Morgan suspected Sky Dancer was also remembering.

The sweet scent of the nearby pine forest hung

heavily in the air, and the night birds' song danced on the warm breeze. Morgan was aware that this was where Sky Dancer belonged. She was nature's child, and was more a part of the land than he would ever be. This was her land—did he have the right to ask her to leave it? He wanted to reach out and take her in his arms. For the first time he began to realize that he might really lose her to this land that was a part of her heritage. Here she was a princess, with him she would have to face prejudice and hatreds. She would have to mask who she was, and deny her own heritage.

"My mother has given me permission to walk with you, if we stay on this side of the river, and if Farley comes with us," she said, looking up at him with bright, shining eyes.

Morgan felt as if he had been delivered a blow to the stomach, so badly did he ache to hold her.

The old trapper chose that moment to poke his head out the tipi. "Did I hear my name being mentioned?" he asked, with a quirk of his bushy eyebrows.

"Will you walk with Morgan and I, Farley?"

"Iffen it's all right with your ma and pa," he agreed. "I ain't looking to rile Windhawk."

"My mother gave her permission."

"Well let's be off and about it then, I got little time to go lallygagging about."

Sky Dancer only smiled. She knew Farley would do anything for her. "Let us walk toward the woods," she said, leading the way. Morgan watched her clasp her hands behind her back, evidently she was not allowed to touch him.

Farley could see that Morgan and Sky Dancer were watching each other with intense longing. Shaking his head and muttering under his breath, he wondered how this would turn out. He couldn't imagine Windhawk allowing his daughter to marry Morgan Prescott and move off to Philadelphia.

"How is Wolfrunner?" Sky Dancer inquired.

"What's he to you?" Morgan asked, feeling a prickle of jealousy.

"A friend."

"He's recovering very nicely. It wouldn't surprise me in the least if he were to be up and about in a few days. Is he always so short-tempered and angry? I got the feeling he wasn't too fond of me."

"What do you mean?" Sky Dancer asked in a puzzled voice. Wolfrunner had never been one to express anger to a stranger; especially one who had saved his life.

"I don't know. It was as if he were brooding about something. Of course I don't know him very well—perhaps it's his nature to be sullen and quiet."

"No, Wolfrunner is not like that. I have a feeling that he has a lot on his mind. Danielle would like to see him, but she was told that he is not to have any visitors. Was it you who gave the order that he was not to see anyone?"

"No. Wolfrunner himself doesn't want to see Danielle. I thought it strange when he asked me not to allow her in his tipi."

"Oh."

By now they had reached the edge of the woods. Farley was trailing along behind whittling on a piece of wood, acting as if he wasn't paying the slightest attention to them, but Sky Dancer knew the old trapper was always aware of everything that was going on around him.

The village was barely visible through the trees as Sky Dancer stopped beneath a tall pine tree. Farley seated himself on a stump some distance away and turned his back. Morgan stood beside Sky Dancer, gazing down into her eyes and watching as her lovely face eased into a frown.

"When will you be leaving, Morgan?" she finally allowed herself to ask.

"What makes you think I will be leaving?" He answered her question with a question.

"I had thought you would be reporting to Fort Laramie before too long."

"No," he said, watching her face. "I am no longer in the Cavalry. I have decided to retire to public life."

"I see."

"Do you?"

"No, not really—it just seemed the correct answer," she said, plucking at the fringe on her doeskin gown.

Morgan smiled to himself. She looked so adorable he could hardly keep his hands off her. "We have discussed everything but the weather and what I really want to talk about, Sky . . . Dancer."

Her long silken lashes brushed her cheek as she gazed down at her moccasins. "I . . . do not know what we can say to each other, Morgan."

Suddenly Morgan reached out and crushed Sky Dancer in his arms, knowing that was where she belonged. "You little fool—did you think so little of me that you decided I would turn away from you because you are half Indian? When I think what you put me through because of your damned stubborn pride I could just shake you."

"I am not ashamed of who I am, Morgan," she told him, raising her head proudly, meeting his gaze. "I would have told you about being Indian except that you seemed to have contempt for my people."

"Did you really think I would reject you when I learned the truth."

"I wasn't sure. In many ways I was a coward. I didn't want to see you look at me with contempt."

He laughed deeply. "You sweet adorable little fool. What we have between us goes beyond bloodlines and family ties. If you will marry me, I would shout to the world that my wife is an Indian."

Sky Dancer felt her heart swell to overflowing. "You still want me for your wife?"

He gave her a smile that melted her heart. "Why do you think I am here? I want you in every way a man can possess the woman he loves. Will you marry me, Skyler?"

Her eyes seemed to cloud over. "I am not Skyler. She was a girl who did not exist."

"I would love you no matter what your name happens to be, Sky Dancer. Now, will you marry me or not?"

She shook her head sadly. "You will have to ask my father, and I do not think he will allow me to be your wife."

Morgan felt a prickle of uneasiness. He had the same doubts himself. He knew he might face powerful objection from the chief of the Blood Blackfoot. "Would you go away with me if your father refused my offer?"

"No. I love and honor my father. He is not only my father but my chief. I could never go against what he says. His word is law with the Blackfoot."

"What is the customary way for a man to ask an Indian chief for his daughter's hand?"

Sky Dancer couldn't help but smile. "If you were an Indian, you would bring my father many horses. I am a princess, so my bride's cost will be high."

"Where will I find horses in your land?" he asked, returning her smile.

Suddenly Sky Dancer became serious. "I think perhaps in your case, my father will overlook the bride's cost. But I do not think he will overlook the fact that you are a white man. You will find him in the lodge if you wish to talk to him. But I believe it would be better if you wait until he asks you to come to him."

Their eyes met, and they both remembered the night they had been so close. Farley cleared his throat, and stood up knowing he must remind them of his presence.

"I 'spect we best mosey on back to the village. I wouldn't want anyone to come looking for us."

Morgan watched Sky Dancer walk away, knowing she might never belong to him.

Danielle was asleep in the curtained off area at the back of the lodge. Sky Dancer was with Farley and Dr. Prescott, so Joanna and Windhawk were alone.

Windhawk watched his wife as she mended one of his buckskin shirts. The light from the torches fell on her face. She frowned, as if concentrating on her needlework.

"Put that aside and talk to me, Joanna. I know you well enough to sense that you are troubled about

403

something, and I believe I know what it is."

Her eyes sought his, knowing she had never been able to hide anything from him. "There are so many things on my mind, that I don't know where to start, my husband. Much of what I would tell you may make you angry."

"I am not blind, Joanna. Many things have not gone unnoticed by me. Will you tell me why Morgan Prescott has come among us, or must I guess?"

Joanna drew in a deep breath, and laid her mending aside. "Doctor Prescott came for Sky Dancer. I believe they love one another."

The expression on Windhawk's face didn't change, but his dark eyes seemed to glisten with anger. "I will never consent to my daughter marrying a white man. I will send him from the village in the morning." His words were softly spoken, but they were laced with anger.

"I am white, Windhawk. Are you saying it was all right for you to marry me, but it would be wrong for Sky Dancer to marry where she loves."

"Why do you say this to me? Would you have this man take our daughter away so we would never see her again?"

Joanna reached forward and rested her hand on Windhawk's. "It will tear my heart out to let her go but I would have her marry where her heart lies."

Windhawk shoved her hand away, and stood up. "No! I will not listen to you in this, Joanna. Sky Dancer would not be accepted by the white world. She does not understand how it feels to be made to feel inferior. Even though Sky Dancer has said nothing about it, I know she was hurt by something that happened to her

404

in Philadelphia."

Joanna slowly stood, knowing her husband was agonizing over allowing Sky Dancer to leave. He was a proud man, and she knew he would make his own decision, and nothing she or anyone else said would sway him.

"Think on this, Windhawk. Perhaps it is time to let her go. She may have to face bigoted people, and they may hurt her. But I have a feeling Morgan Prescott will take very good care of her."

"There is nothing to think about. Sky Dancer will stay here," he said, turning away and disappearing out the lodge opening.

Joanna moved to the back of the lodge where Danielle lay. Going down on her knees, she touched her hand to her niece's forehead. Finding it cool, she sighed with relief. Four lives were in a tangle and Joanna didn't know what to do about it.

Chapter Thirty-one

Wolfrunner stood up slowly. The pain in his chest felt like a red-hot poker, and his head was spinning dizzily. Grasping the lodge pole tightly, he rested his weight against it, allowing himself time to catch his breath.

"You should not be up, my son," White Dove said, looking at him with concern. "The white man of medicine said you should stay on the mat for awhile longer. You must not do anything that will harm you."

"I will not lay down like some youth who has not won his feathers, my mother. I am a warrior."

"Even warriors must rest when their body needs to heal," she persisted. "You must go back to the mat. The white doctor told me rest was important."

Wolfrunner's eyes went to the tipi opening. He could see that the sun was shining brightly, and he felt a strange restlessness stir inside him. While he had languished upon his mat, his thoughts had been mostly of Danielle. The pain in his chest did not compare with the pain in his heart. Soon she would be leaving, and he would never see her again. His mother had told him that she was fully recovered from her ordeal, and he realized her father would soon be taking her back to the white world.

As a sick feeling washed over him, Wolfrunner made his way back to the buffalo robe, hating the weakness that made him as helpless as a newborn baby.

Lying down, Wolfrunner thought it might be best that he was confined to his tipi because he wouldn't have to face Danielle. It would be far better if she just went away without him seeing her again. Perhaps in time he would put her out of his mind as well as his heart.

Danielle rode beside her father knowing this was her last day in the village. As they halted their mounts, they both gazed down at the lush green valley below them. How magnificent this land was, with its tall mountains, pine forest, rivers, and streams.

Danielle felt her heart wing its way across the lush, green valley. This was the land of her mother's people, and this was now the land of her heart. She hadn't realized until this moment what it would cost her to ride away, never see this land again. This was also the land of the man she loved. Wolfrunner didn't love her, he didn't even like her, but still she couldn't stop loving him.

"I will always feel as if I am leaving a part of myself behind when I leave this land," Tag said as he watched a herd of antelope grazing beside a stream.

"I too feel this way, Father. I wish I could remain here forever."

Her father looked startled. "Can this be the same girl, who only a few months ago swore she wouldn't live like an Indian savage?"

She met his eyes squarely. "I have changed in many ways, Papa. It's hard to explain, but I feel the pull of this land. I don't want to go back to Philadelphia. Could I not stay here a while longer?"

Tag saw the mist in Danielle's eyes, and felt as if he were losing a part of her. "You haven't told me this before. When did this all come about? I know you have been through a rough time, honey. You'll feel differently when we get back home."

Danielle didn't want to think about going home. If only Wolfrunner loved her, she would be content to stay here forever. "I didn't tell you because I didn't think you would understand. I love . . . Wolfrunner."

"You are right, I don't understand. I know you too well and you would never be happy living here. They don't have balls and parties here in the Blackfoot village. The latest fashion in gowns will be one you make with your own hands. Do you think you could be happy working with your hands until they are no longer white and soft?"

She drew in her breath. "I deserved that, Father. I know in the past I have been very selfish. I have changed—I'm surprised you haven't noticed."

"Well, miss, you can just put the notion of staying here out of your mind. I will never allow you to stay here. It would break your mother's heart!"

"My mother's heart would be glad if she knew her daughter embraced her people. My mother is dead— you remember her, don't you, Father? Her name was Morning Song."

Tag looked perplexed. "I was speaking of Alexandria, and you know it. I hadn't told you this before, but she is going to have a baby. She needs you at home."

A tear ran down Danielle's cheek. "She will have me, Father. I said I loved Wolfrunner, I didn't say he loved me. The truth of the matter is that he doesn't have a very high regard for me at all."

Tag's eyes narrowed against the glare of the afternoon sun. "It's all for the best, Danielle. I will buy you a whole new wardrobe when we get back to Philadelphia. In the spring we will all take a trip to England, and you will forget all about your bad experience this summer. After a time this will all seem like no more than a bad dream."

Danielle smiled at her father sadly, knowing he would never understand what she was feeling. She would go with him to Philadelphia, but her heart would remain here in this lovely Blackfoot country.

When Sky Dancer entered the tipi she saw that Wolfrunner was lying on his mat with his eyes closed. White Dove had asked her to come and talk to him. It seemed his mother was concerned, because Wolfrunner didn't want to eat. All he did was lay on his mat and stare into space.

Wolfrunner's eyes opened, and he turned to face her. For one brief moment, she saw his eyes sparkle with a soft warmth—then it was as if a mask moved over his face, and he looked away.

Sky Dancer dropped down on her knees beside him. "I have brought you some of my mother's honey cakes—I know you always liked them, Wolfrunner," she said, reaching out and touching his arm.

Slowly he turned back to her. For a long moment he looked into her face, then at last he spoke. "Your eyes are different from Danielle's."

She smiled. "Yes, I am told that. At first when I came in, you thought I was Danielle, did you not?"

His eyes drifted down to slits. "Yes, but I recognized my mistake immediately. You and Danielle look very much alike. People who do not know the two of you cannot see the differences."

"But you can, Wolfrunner. You know that Danielle and I are not the same."

"Yes, I know."

Sky Dancer stood up, and placed the honey cakes beside White Dove's cooking utensils. "You love my cousin, Danielle," she said matter-of-factly. "I have known you all my life, so I can see this in your eyes."

"Love is not the great thing that people would have us believe it to be. I can go the rest of my life without loving."

"What if Danielle loved you in return?"

Wolfrunner's eyes blazed, and his mouth eased into a straight line. "If you came to see me because we are old friends, I will talk to you. But if you have come to talk about your cousin, I will not."

"I do not know why you are acting this way. I have always been your friend. You are changed, Wolfrunner. Have a care, or you will lose all your friends."

Wolfrunner closed his eyes and turned his face to the wall. She knew he was shutting her out as his mother told her he had shut everyone out. She knew him well enough to see that he was deeply disturbed about something. It had never been in his nature to be cold to his friends. She had never known him to brood about anything. He had always been the fun-loving warrior, always laughing and teasing.

"If you love Danielle, why do you not tell her? You might find that she loves you also."

"Leave me in peace, Sky Dancer. I do not want to talk to you anymore." He didn't turn back to her, and she could feel that he wanted her to leave. Shaking her head sadly, she quietly left him.

Windhawk studied the face of Dr. Morgan Prescott through half-closed lashes. He knew why the white man had come to him. He had pondered long and hard about what Joanna had told him. His heart was heavy knowing he must give his daughter to this man who would take her far away.

Morgan shifted uneasily under the dark gaze of the chief. "You told me I could ask what I would of you, and I could have it—I have come to you to ask for your daughter's hand in marriage, Windhawk. I want you to know if you give Sky Dancer to me I will take the greatest care of her. My life will be spent making her happy."

Windhawk was quiet for a long time, and when he spoke his words were soft. "I think that you must love my daughter since you came so far to find her. Can you say to me that Sky Dancer will never be hurt, or be made to feel ashamed of who she is?"

"You know I cannot make this promise to you. There will be those who will know she is different. But I will say to you that for anyone to hurt Sky Dancer they would first have to go through me. You must know how I feel about her since you yourself married a white woman. I am proud of who Skyler is, and you need not worry about her if you give her to me."

"Her name is Sky Dancer, not Skyler," Windhawk said with feeling.

"I know this. I was told that your wife was called Joanna until she was given the Indian name of Flaming Hair. The name is not important, it is the love that counts. I have seen the love in your eyes when you look at your wife. Pity me because I feel that same deep love for your daughter, and yet I know she will never marry me without your blessing."

Windhawk was quiet for a long time. Finally he reached out his hand to Morgan. "I will give my daughter to you, Morgan Prescott, because I know her happiness lies with you. I will charge you to love and care for her."

Morgan felt his heart lighten with joy. He gripped Windhawk's hand with a firm handshake. He hadn't expected Windhawk to give in so easily. He had prepared many arguments in his defense, but he hadn't needed to use them. This chief *was* the great man everyone claimed him to be. Morgan knew Windhawk could easily have decided against him, and if he had Sky Dancer would never have married him.

"I am more than grateful that you trust me to care for your daughter. I can tell you now, if you had said no, I was prepared to live as a Blackfoot for as long as it took to win your consent."

Windhawk smiled. "You would have made a good Blackfoot. I have seen your courage."

"I never needed my courage as much as today when I entered this lodge."

Windhawk's eyes seemed to darken. "You were afraid, and yet still you came."

"Yes."

"Go to the river now and wait until I send my daughter to you."

"Can I see Sky Dancer now?" Morgan asked.

The two men stood head to head. "No, it is not for you to talk to her just now. I will tell her of the decision I have made."

Sky Dancer was grooming her horse, Degobar, when her father, Windhawk, came up beside her. She had known that Morgan had gone to speak with her father, and her eyes now sought his questioningly.

"This mare was a gift from me on your sixteenth summer," Windhawk said, patting the horse's sleek neck.

"Yes, she was one of your finest. I have always been so proud to ride her."

Windhawk felt a tightening in his chest. He had to pause before he could speak. "Will you be taking Degobar to Philadelphia with you?"

Sky Dancer thought she had misunderstood her father. She felt her heart pounding against her chest, and placed her hands there to still the tremor. "What are you saying?" she asked softly.

He reached out, and drew her into his arms. "It is a hard thing for a father to let his only daughter go. Especially when she has brought such joy into his heart. I could not do so now, if I loved you less."

"Oh, Father," she cried, placing her head against his shoulder. "My heart is both happy and sad. I love Morgan, and I want to be with him, yet it tears at my heart to leave you and Mother."

Windhawk's arms tightened about her. He would miss her because, like her mother, she had brought sunshine into his heart. "Go to Morgan with a happy heart, my daughter. Give him strong sons . . . and a daughter with laughing blue eyes like yourself. Give him the joy your mother gives to me."

Sky Dancer raised her head and brushed the tears away. "I will come back often to visit, Father. I will always remember where I came from."

He studied her face carefully. "Always remember who you are. Never lower your eyes, but hold your head up and say to yourself that you are part of two proud races. Teach your children to look into a man's heart, to find his worth."

She pressed her cheek against his. "I will teach my children what you and Mother have taught me. I will always keep you both in my heart."

"Go now, my daughter. Morgan awaits you down by the river."

Joanna was standing in the shadow of her lodge, watching when Sky Dancer kissed her father's cheek, then ran away to find the man she loved. Joanna turned away quickly not wanting Windhawk to find her crying. She knew how hard it had been for him to let Sky Dancer go. He had always been such a strong man—but he never ceased to amaze her with his love and understanding. She knew how anguished he must be at the moment—indeed, she herself felt heartbreak at the thought of her daughter's leaving.

Morgan propped his booted foot on a log, watching several healthy brown-skinned children swimming in the river. He couldn't help but think how it must have been for the Indian before the white man landed on their shores. They had neither worried about famine nor the white man's diseases then.

Looking across the river, he allowed his eyes to wander to the great wilderness beyond. One day this would all be under the white man's domination. Already Washington had claimed this as their territory. What would happen to the Blackfoot when the white world came crashing in on them?

The sound of the children's laughter filled his ears, and he remembered the time he had foolishly stated that the only good Indian was a dead Indian. He hadn't realized that day that he had condemned Sky Dancer, and her people, to obscurity in his mind. He couldn't help thinking how sanctimonious men were in their ignorance.

Hearing soft moccasined footsteps, Morgan glanced up to observe his love's laughing blue eyes, sparkling at him. Sky Dancer was standing on an incline just above him, and he drew in his breath at her loveliness. The summer breeze was blowing her long ebony hair, and his heart swelled with the warm feeling that she would soon belong to him.

Holding out his arms, she laughingly jumped into them. "So it would seem your father is willing to rid himself of your tiresome person," he said in a teasing light. "Had I known he was so anxious to give you over to me, I might have asked a high price to accomodate him."

Sky Dancer wrapped her arms about his neck feeling as if her heart would burst with joy. "I give my heart and hand to you willingly, Morgan Prescott. I believe I shall make an admirable doctor's wife."

His expression became serious as he studied her beautiful face. "I shall love and cherish the gift of your love, for the rest of our lives. God only knows, it was hard enough to make you love me."

Touching his face softly she shook her head. "Not so, Morgan. You had my heart almost from the beginning when you mistook me for my cousin."

"Is there some kind of ceremony that we need go through before I can take you home with me? I find I am very impatient to have you to myself."

"I would very much like it if you would go through the Blackfoot marriage ceremony," she admitted.

"Consider it done. When we get to Philadelphia you will stay with your Uncle Tag until such time as I can arrange a marriage for us."

Disappointment showed in Sky Dancer's eyes. "Can we not be man and wife after the Blackfoot marriage?"

"No, my dearest love. I want to tie you to me, all legal and proper. I want no slur cast on your name. After all, you are a princess from a very old and proud people."

He placed her on her feet. "Go along now. I need to be alone. When he turned away, she could hardly catch the words Morgan muttered under his breath. "Lord only knows, it will be difficult enough to keep my hands off you, after today."

Sky Dancer smiled to herself, and moved back toward her village. She wanted to find her mother so they could spend some time together. There would be so little time before she and Morgan would be leaving. Her heart was so filled with joy, she wished Danielle could also find happiness.

Chapter Thirty=two

The night was warm, and a full moon lit the sky, making it appear almost as if it were daylight. The drums were beating out a haunting tempo, and people were chanting the age-old song of the marriage ceremony.

Sky Dancer, dressed in her white doeskin gown, stood beside her father and mother feeling as if her heart would burst with happiness. Her eyes were on Morgan who walked slowly toward them. When he drew near, he reached out and clasped Windhawk's hand.

"I bring unworthy gifts to show my respect for your house, and my love for your daughter," Morgan stated solemnly.

Windhawk nodded, and Morgan continued.

"I give to you one hundred horses for the bride price. Is this acceptable to you?"

A gasp rose from the crowd, for it was a high price the white doctor paid for the princess, Sky Dancer. Morgan and Farley had spent three days buying horses from the Piegan Blackfoot, because Morgan knew it was important to Windhawk that his daughter not be shamed. Seeing the pride in the chief's eyes, he knew he had done the right thing.

Danielle watched her cousin take the hand of the man she loved and felt her heart break. She was happy that Sky Dancer was marrying Morgan because he would take her to Philadelphia, and they would be able to see each other often. But she was sad that she would never have Wolfrunner, the man she loved.

Unable to watch any longer, Danielle silently slipped into her uncle's lodge, where she lost herself in tears of misery and heartbreak.

Sky Dancer felt Morgan's hand close about hers. There were tears of happiness in her eyes as she looked first at her mother, and then to her father. Willing her emotions under control, she allowed Morgan to lead her to the tipi which had been prepared for them.

Once inside, Morgan pulled her into his arms. For a moment neither of them moved—they just held each other, feeling overwhelming joy.

"You are almost mine, Sky Dancer. One more ceremony and you will fully belong to me."

She raised her face, and rested it against his. "I belong to you now, Morgan. I believe I have belonged to you from the very first."

He smiled down at her. "Oh, yes. You caught me in your tender web the first time I met you. I was confused by my feelings for you. You looked like Danielle, and yet I had never had any desire for her. I wondered what it was about you that kept me continuously on my mind. Now, I realize it was love, pure and simple." He laughed, and his eyes twinkled. "Or . . . perhaps it was love, not so pure and not so simple. I wanted to possess your body as much as I wanted your love."

"You have already had both," she whispered, pulling his head down so she could reach his lips.

Morgan's arms tightened about her as he deepened the kiss. Both of them were aware that they belonged together, as the wind belongs to the everlasting sea and this land belonged to the Blackfoot people.

Lifting her into his arms, he carried her to the buffalo robe, and they both sank down into its softness. "I hadn't intended this to happen until we were married in Philadelphia," he whispered as his hands slowly slipped her gown over her head. "I am not very strong when it comes to denying myself your body, Sky Dancer."

Holding her arms up to him she seemed to beckon him to the softness of her body. With a groan, Morgan gathered her tightly to him as a tremor of desire shook his tall frame.

They had all night to love and explore each other's bodies. Morgan had many things to teach her, and he would take his time tonight.

When he pulled her beneath him, her silken legs opened to the pressure of his knees. Caught up with a burning fire of urgency, his mouth moved to her breasts, taunting and teasing the rosebud tips.

Sky Dancer's hands moved to Morgan's hips, and she urgently guided him down to her. With the wild tempo of the drums still echoing through the night air, he thrust forward, penetrating her softness. They seemed to fit together perfectly.

"I will give all to you with a happy heart, my husband," she whispered in a voice that seemed to rip through his senses.

This was love, he thought. This was why he had been unable to get Sky Dancer out of his mind. She was a part of him, the other half that would make him a whole.

With the tempo of the drums, he set his rhythm. As the drum beat built up, so did his rhythmic motions. There was a wildness about their lovemaking—it was primitive and sensuous. Sky Dancer was caught up in the beauty of Morgan's lovemaking. Their hot skin became moist from perspiration, almost like an inferno.

Resting his face against her soft breasts, Morgan penetrated deeper into her moist body. Their desire for each other rose higher and higher. The drums beat faster and faster. Sky Dancer could feel the ache building up inside her as his manhood stroked her inside.

In a moment of beauty, their bodies reached the ultimate joy of surrender. The drums had slowed, and the last haunting beat faded into the night air. Morgan felt his body relax, satisfied as it had never been before.

Raising his head, Morgan's mouth found Sky Dancer's. His kiss was soft and sweet, and her lips trembled from the deep love she had for this man who was her husband.

As Sky Dancer held Morgan to her breast, she thought the world had never known a man such as he. He with the sparkling silver eyes. He had a wonderful sense of humor, and he was so loving. She knew her days would be filled with happiness and her nights with wild passion.

His finger trailed down her breasts, pausing to circle

each satiny peak, then to continue down to her stomach, causing her to shiver with delight. "You are all I shall ever want," he whispered hotly in her ear.

Once more her legs opened to him and he took what she so freely gave.

When they lay exhausted in each other's arms, Morgan looked deeply into her eyes. "We leave in two days. I think I had better find a parson in the first town we come to."

"If that is what you wish, but nothing could tie me more tightly to you than the ceremony we had tonight. I am your wife in every way that counts."

"Will you never regret marrying me, Sky Dancer?" he asked in a burst of uncertainty.

"No, my husband. I shall miss many things—there will be times when I will ache for the ones I love, but I shall be with you, my husband. I know when I go from here, I must leave Sky Dancer behind forever. I must again become Skyler Dancing."

He smiled as he traced a pattern across her face. "Correction, you will be Skyler Prescott," he said with amusement dancing in his silver eyes. However, I believe I shall miss the lovely Indian maiden who gave herself to me tonight."

"I am both Skyler and Sky Dancer, Morgan. I was brought up by my mother, who instilled the white man's ways and customs in me. I was born into the Indian world and the two parts of me walk side by side in harmony. I am proud of both my bloodlines."

Morgan chuckled, and drew her tighter into his arms. "And so you should be, for they make you into the person I fell in love with. When we have children, you will one day tell them how their father once followed you to the ends of the earth to make you his bride."

"Oh, Morgan, how I will love giving you a child. I would love to have a little boy with silver eyes."

He buried his face in her sweet-smelling hair. "I would like a daughter, with violet-blue eyes."

They lapsed into silence as each felt a completeness. After a moment, Sky Dancer spoke. "Morgan, will we live with your mother and sister?" she asked.

"My mother is going to love you, but no. I have a house that was left to me by my grandmother. It is at this very moment being prepared for you and me. I'm afraid it's very large, so we will have to have many children to fill up so much space."

She smiled up into his face. "Like Mr. and Mrs. Pinwinkle?"

His laughter warmed Sky Dancer's heart. "Indeed, like Mr. and Mrs. Pinwinkle.

Sky Dancer snuggled tightly against Morgan's hard body. "You said that the house was being prepared for you and me—were you so positive that I would return to Philadelphia with you?"

"No. I was only sure that if you didn't, I would drag you away with me," he said, laughing deeply.

Sky Dancer's heart softened in the warm glow of Morgan's love. She liked the idea of having Morgan's children. She wanted a little boy with the laughing silver eyes.

As they made love once more, they were both drawn into the wonder of their feelings for each other. There would be times in the future when their love would be tested, but they would always walk hand in hand. What they had was precious, and it would last a lifetime.

As her whole being was caught up in a swirling storm of passion, she couldn't help but feel pity for Danielle. She wished with all her heart that her cousin would find everlasting love as she had.

The village was quiet, with the exception of an occasional barking dog. Wolfrunner stood in the shadows, watching the chief's lodge with dark haunting eyes. Would Danielle be sleeping, or would she be remembering the times she had lain in his arms and had given herself to him? He was tortured by this love that he felt for her. He had been told by his mother that Danielle would be leaving in two days. The thought of never seeing her again ripped at his heart.

Wolfrunner wished they had never found their way back to the village. Danielle had belonged to him when she had to depend on him for her survival.

He tried to tell himself that she was selfish and shallow, but deep down he knew that wasn't true. She was generous and loving—he envied the white man, who would one day make her his wife. Wild jealousy built up inside him at the thought of another man touching the woman he loved.

Wolfrunner reminded himself that Danielle had never said she loved him. There had been the time she had begged him to keep her with him, but that was only because she was dependent on him for her survival. He knew how she loathed and despised the Indian. Had she not told him that he was a savage?

He hadn't seen her since they had been brought back to the village, with the exception of one brief glance tonight, when Sky Dancer had married the white doctor.

His heart burned with anguish, and his dark eyes closed for the briefest moment. He wished he could tear this love from his heart, and cast it to the wind.

Hearing soft footsteps he turned to see Joanna just behind him. "I thought all were asleep in the chief's lodge tonight," he said to her.

"No, not I. Red Woman just delivered a son, and I was with her."

"It grows late, and you should be asleep, Joanna."

"You should be also, Wolfrunner. What are you doing out here all alone?"

"Just thinking."

Joanna followed his eyes to her lodge, and she caught the anguish in his gaze. She knew he had been thinking of Danielle. She knew that Danielle and Wolfrunner were trying to hide their love from each other, and from everyone else. Since Joanna had such a great love, she wanted to see everyone as happy as she was.

"Why do you not tell Danielle that you love her, Wolfrunner? It could be that you will find she returns your feelings."

His eyes sought her hopefully. "Did Danielle say this to you?"

"No, but unless one asks, they will not find the answers."

He looked away from her, and fixed his eyes on the nearby Milk River. "One does not need to ask when they already know the answers, Joanna. Danielle is not for me."

"Do you say this only because she is a Blackfoot princess?"

Again he met her eyes. "I do not have a hundred horses to give her father as the white doctor did."

Joanna placed her hand on his arm. "Some things go beyond price, Wolfrunner. I am surprised you have not found this out for yourself."

Without another word, Joanna stepped around him, and walked toward her lodge. She did not see the misery in Wolfrunner's dark eyes, but she felt his pain in the very depths of her own heart. Wolfrunner had always been special to Joanna, as were all the children of this village.

Wolfrunner mounted his horse and rode away from the village. He would not see Danielle before she left, but he would give her a gift that would clearly tell her how he felt. If she scoffed at his meager gift, he would never know it.

Danielle felt the heat of the night. She was dreaming that soft dark eyes were looking at her lovingly. In her dream, Wolfrunner's hands ran over her body, pulling her against him. Her heart soared on silver wings as he whispered words of love in her ear. She happily took his hand, and raised it to her lips.

Suddenly she came fully awake. Sitting up, she realized she had only been dreaming. Pressing the palms of her hands against her eyes, she lay back down. Wolfrunner had never said that he loved her—nor would he ever.

Turning to her side, she closed her eyes. Dreams were so fleeting, and they always ended when one awoke to reality.

Chapter Thirty-three

Tearful goodbyes were said in the privacy of the chief's lodge. Sky Dancer hugged her father tightly, knowing she wouldn't see him again for a long time. Windhawk's eyes were shining as he handed Sky Dancer over to her mother.

Joanna pushed a tumbled ebony tress from her daughter's face. "Be happy, my dearest one. I will not worry about you because I know Morgan will take care of you."

Morgan gripped Windhawk's hand in friendship. "I will bring Sky Dancer back for a visit in the spring."

Windhawk nodded. "It is good. She will need to see her people now and then."

Joanna linked her arm through Morgan's and kissed his cheek. "I believe my daughter will be happy with you, Morgan. I see in you a good man."

He smiled into laughing violet-colored eyes. He could feel himself being drawn into the family's deep love for one another. "I will try to live up to your faith in me," he said with sincerity.

Danielle was drawn into her Uncle Windhawk's arms, "I feel in you a deep sadness, little one," he said so no one but Danielle could hear. "I wish that I could give you what you most desire."

She looked up into his eyes. "Do you know what that is, my uncle?"

"Yes, I know what you desire. Sometimes you have to find your own way, Danielle. There is no guarantee in this life that we will always be happy—not in the white world, not in the Indian world."

"Yes, I have come to believe that. I have also come to love my mother's people."

He smiled. "I knew that you would."

Joanna hugged her niece tightly in her arms. "Come back to us soon, Danielle."

"I think I shall never come back, Aunt Joanna."

Her aunt only smiled. "Do not be too sure. One cannot always see what the future holds."

Lastly, Tag pulled his sister into his arms and hugged her tightly to him. "I will miss you, Joanna, but then I always do."

"You will come next spring and bring Alexandria and the baby with you."

"We shall see," he said. "It will depend on how Alexandria is feeling."

"Tell her for me that I miss her," Joanna said.

The time for good-byes was over. As Sky Dancer stepped out of her father's lodge she allowed her eyes to roam over the dear faces of the people she loved. She felt a sadness at leaving them. She was leaving her way of life behind and going into a world that she didn't fully comprehend. There would be many times when Sky Dancer would long for the peace and tranquility of her Blackfoot home, but she would go to her new home with a happy heart.

Danielle saw that everyone in the village had turned out to say their last farewells—everyone except Wolfrunner. She knew he was healed from his wounds, but he had not tried to see her. Even if he didn't love her, they had been through a great deal together. The least he could have done would have been to come to see her off.

Danielle felt someone tugging at her gown. Looking down, she saw a dark-eyed little girl. The child extended her cupped hands out to her and Danielle's heart stopped beating. There, nestling in the palm of the little girl's hand, was a baby cottontail.

Tears wet Danielle's lashes as she lifted the soft animal to her face, breathing in its soft scent. Glancing down, she saw the child had disappeared. Frantically Danielle looked about, trying to locate Wolfrunner, but she couldn't find him. Wolfrunner had given her this gift, and she wondered what it meant. Could it mean that he loved her? No, if he loved her, would he not have come himself?

Danielle wished she had the courage to walk into his tipi and demand that he talk to her. Shaking her head, she gently placed the tiny ball of fur in her pocket and mounted her horse.

Turning her mount, Danielle fell in beside her father. She would like to think that this gift represented Wolfrunner's love for her, but she was afraid to allow herself to hope. If only he had come to see her off. She had too much pride to beg Wolfrunner for anything.

As they rode across the Milk River, Danielle turned and looked back, hoping against hope that she would see Wolfrunner. Even if he'd been there, she wouldn't have been able to recognize him in the sea of faces that were slowly fading in the distance.

Danielle would not cry. If Wolfrunner didn't want her, she would just put him out of her mind. Oh, but the deep ache inside her hurt so badly. She felt as if she were leaving the very essence of her being behind.

Wolfrunner stood in the shadows of a pine tree and watched Danielle ride out of his life forever. Closing his eyes, it felt as if the sensation of her was still with him. As he watched her disappear across the river, he was suddenly jolted by reality. He would never see her again!

He felt a burning urgency deep within. The woman he loved would soon ride out of sight and out of his life forever.

Running swiftly to where he had tied his horse, he bounded onto its back. Kicking his mount in the flanks, he knew he would have to race the wind to catch up with Danielle. He would not approach her, but watch her from the nearby hills. He would allow his eyes to behold her until she was lost from sight.

When Wolfrunner topped the hill, he saw the dust cloud and knew they were just ahead of him. Putting the whip to his horse's flanks, he raced across the hill and down into the valley. A strong need in him was pushing him onward. If he could just have one more glance at Danielle's face, it would stay with him for the rest of his life.

Sky Dancer was the first to see Wolfrunner. Her keen sense of hearing picked up the sound of his unshod horse's hooves before anyone else detected them. Turning her head, she recognized Wolfrunner's horse and her heart soared with happiness. Apparently he was trying to stay out of sight. He wasn't trying to pull even with them, but just to keep them in view. Surely he must love Danielle—why else would he be following them?

Dropping back to ride beside her cousin Danielle, Sky Dancer caught her eye. "If Wolfrunner were to come after you, would you go with him?" she asked point-blank.

"Your jest is in poor taste, Sky Dancer. Why do you torture me with things that can never be?"

"Answer me," Sky Dancer demanded, knowing her cousin must make up her mind quickly.

"You know I would go anywhere with Wolfrunner. I love him."

"Then turn your eyes to the hills on the right," Sky Dancer said. "I think he comes for you although he hasn't the courage to approach too near."

Danielle turned in her saddle and allowed her eyes to scan the hills. At first she didn't see him since he was hidden behind the cover of a thicket. Her heart was pounding against her chest as she watched him ride into view. He wore only a breechcloth, his dark hair was flying in the wind. He rode with such precision that from this distance it appeared that horse and man were one and the same.

Was it possible that he had come for her, she wondered wildly? If he wanted her, why did he not come closer?

They were now approaching a wide stream and slowed their pace. Danielle glanced back to find that

433

Wolfrunner was nowhere in sight. She felt her heart sink, feeling as if her stomach held a heavy stone. He was gone!

Frantically she halted her mount and allowed her eyes to scan the horizon. Tears of grief stung her eyes, and she felt as if her heart had been ripped open. Why had he come if he didn't intend to take her back with him? How cruel he was to hurt her so deeply. Was he not satisfied with hurting words he had spoken to her? Had he not gotten his satisfaction from rejecting her as unworthy?

At that moment, Wolfrunner reappeared on the top of a hill about twenty horse leagues away. He was closer now, and Danielle could see the sad expression on his face. His eyes seemed to be pleading with her. It was as if they were a magnet, drawing her to him.

Wolfrunner's horse reared up on its hind legs, and he quickly brought the animal under control with the force of his strong legs. He felt his heart racing across the distance that divided him from Danielle, and he willed her to come to him. He needed her as surely as he needed the air that filled his lungs. He had no pride where she was concerned. She was his whole world, and if she should go, there would forever be a deep, dark void.

Tag caught Danielle's reins, fearing she might try to go to Wolfrunner. Everyone had halted their horses and were watching the silent struggle that was taking place between father and daughter.

Danielle glanced up at the man she loved and then back to her father. She knew in an instant that if she went back to Philadelphia she would never know one day of happiness. There was no question in her mind now that Wolfrunner loved her. Everyone could see what he was feeling by looking into his expressive face.

A pain ripped through Danielle's heart as Wolfrunner slowly reached his arms to her. It was as if silently pleading with her to come to him.

"No!" Tag cried, realizing he could lose his daughter. "You can't do this, Danielle. I forbid it!"

Sky Dancer placed her hand on her uncle's, drawing his attention. "It's time to let go. Would you keep her with you at the expense of her happiness? My mother and father made the supreme sacrifice; will you not do the same?"

Tag slowly released his hold on his daughter's hand. He said nothing as Danielle leaned forward and hurriedly kissed his cheek. She turned to Sky Dancer and looked toward the heavens in a gesture of pure happiness.

Without a word, Danielle turned her mount and raced up the hill toward the man she loved. There was no regret in her heart for what she was leaving behind. All she could think about was that she would soon be in Wolfrunner's arms and he loved her!

Wolfrunner couldn't believe his eyes as Danielle rode swiftly toward him. He had reached out to her, thinking she would probably turn away from his love. He watched her approach with tears sliding down his cheeks.

When Danielle reached Wolfrunner's side, he saw the tears glistening in her eyes. With his heart soaring to the skies, a strangled cry issued from his throat. Reaching out, he lifted her from her horse and held her tightly against him. Danielle must love him—why else would she turn away from the white world?

Danielle was crying so hard she had to hide her face against Wolfrunner's broad chest. She was ashamed of the weakness within her.

Wolfrunner raised her face and gave her a soft look that said so much more than words could ever reveal. She could read love and adoration in his dark gaze. Reaching across her, he gathered up the reins of her mount and spun his horse around. Not once did either of them look back at the riders who watched beside the river—not until they topped a hill. Then Wolfrunner halted his mount and raised his hand in a silent salute to Danielle's family.

Sky Dancer caught the eye of her uncle and saw the misery there. "She will be happy, my uncle. My mother and father will be there to counsel her wisely."

Tag took a deep breath and nudged his horse forward. Somehow a peace descended on him. It seemed only right that Danielle should return to her mother's people. He felt as if Morning Song's spirit would always look after her. It was as if he had only borrowed Danielle for a short period of her life. She was a Blackfoot princess and belonged to the earth and its people.

Morgan rode up beside his wife and gave her a warm smile. Sky Dancer couldn't help but ponder what a strange world it was. She would walk in the world of her cousin, and Danielle would walk in her world. Their lives had crossed but briefly, but she knew in her heart there would always be a special bond that tied them together.

Each girl had found her love in the most unexpected place. Now each would walk in happiness.

*　　　*　　　*

No words had been spoken as Wolfrunner carried Danielle upon his mount. She lay against his shoulder and he rested his chin against her sweet-smelling hair, lost in the wonder of her loving him. How was it possible that she wanted to be his woman?

Seeing a secluded place beside the stream, he rode in that direction. There was a burning need in him to possess her, thus binding her to him with love's bonds.

Danielle looked up shyly and met his dark eyes. A small tremor shook her at the naked love she saw reflected there. His mask had been stripped away and all that he was feeling was reflected in those magnificent eyes.

By now they had reached the stream, and he dismounted with her in his arms. He didn't place her on the ground, but stood holding her against his heart.

Danielle wriggled out of his arms, laughing. "Would you crush the little pet that you gave to me this morning?"

Reaching into her pocket, she withdrew the baby rabbit and placed it gently onto the ground. Turning back to Wolfrunner, she allowed him to lift her into his arms.

Danielle could feel the naked strength of his back and shoulders beneath her fingers, and a weakness washed over her.

"Have you no regrets?" he asked in a voice of uncertainty.

"Yes," she told him, lacing her hands in his midnight-colored hair. "I regret that it took you so long to know you loved me."

He could hardly speak through the catch in his throat. "I knew from the first that I was to love you. I fought against it, but it did little good. I realized today that I would never live without you beside me."

"You love me," she said, pondering the sound of those words as if they were more precious than gold.

"You fill my heart and leave no room for any other thought. I will live to make you happy," he said, placing her on her feet and holding her tightly against his body.

"I will work to make you a home, but you will have to be patient with me. I realize I have much to learn."

Raising his face to the sky, Wolfrunner felt as if he had been reborn. How does a man react when he has just been handed the most precious possessions a woman could give him? He felt almost humble, and certainly unworthy of this lovely Blackfoot princess.

"Will you then be my woman? Will you walk beside me in the summer rain, and lay with me in the winter snow?"

"Yes, my love. I will stay with you as long as God will allow it," she cried, offering him her lips.

They sealed their love with a burning kiss. Later they would go home to the Blackfoot village, but for now they wanted only to be alone in their newfound happiness.

As the warm breeze kissed the leaves on the tree and the lazy stream cut its way across the valley, they made love, thus binding themselves tightly one to the other.

Danielle knew there would be times when she would falter, for one doesn't change overnight, but she knew Wolfrunner's love would mold her and make her into the woman he wanted her to be.

Soft words of love were spoken, and hearts were pledged for eternity. There was music on the wind and laughter in their hearts. As they discovered new things about each other, they were drawn into an everlasting love.

As night began to fall they returned to the village. The people of the tribe didn't seem at all surprised to see Wolfrunner return with the Blackfoot princess. They had known for a long time what Danielle and Wolfrunner now openly admitted.

It was with a happy heart that the Blood Blackfoot welcomed Morning Song's daughter back home.

Joanna felt Windhawk's arm on her shoulder, and turned to smile up at him. "I knew Wolfrunner would never allow Danielle to leave, Windhawk."

The tall chief of the Blood Blackfoot looked down at his wife. "From the way they are looking at each other, I think they had better be joined in marriage soon."

Joanna reached for Windhawk's hand, and together they entered the lodge. "Make it today, my husband."

As Windhawk enfolded Joanna in his arms, he thought of all the happy years he'd spent with this flaming-haired woman beside him. He looked forward to many more.

Epilogue

Now that the Civil War was over, the people of the United States turned their eyes westward. There were rumors that they were coming in droves to the lands that belonged to the Indian.

They wanted to till the soil and plant their crops. They sought the precious silver and gold metal that came from the sacred mountains. Soon . . . soon they would push the Indian back, and force him to fight for what belonged to him.

Windhawk looked down in the valley below him and watched as his people moved slowly toward the north. There was a great cloud of dust which was stirred up by the many horses. Deep in his heart there was an ache that they must forever leave this land of their birth. But had he not made his mother a promise that if the white man came, he would move his Blood Blackfoot to the Canadas?

Perhaps it was best, he thought. It would rip Joanna's heart out if he had to war against the people of her past.

441

As his eyes roamed over the winding Milk River and across the Sweet Grass Hills, Windhawk knew he looked upon them for the last time. The beauty of this land would remain in his heart. He felt as if he were in tune with the past. His fathers and their fathers seemed to cry out at the injustice of it all. Could a man keep his honor when he turned his back on his ancient home? he argued. Was it not better to leave a place where his people might die from the white man's bullets? he reasoned.

He saw Joanna riding up the hill to join him. He knew she was part of the reason he was leaving. He did not want to turn his war weapons on her people.

Her red-gold hair was flying in the wind, and her cheeks were kissed by the warmth of the sun. His heart seemed to swell within his body as he caught the look in her beautiful eyes. This was his woman, he would do anything to keep her from hurt and sorrow.

Joanna said no words as she drew up beside Windhawk. Both knew what the other was feeling so there was no need for words. Each sat for a long time watching the Blood Blackfoot ride away from the land of their grandfathers.

Reaching out, Windhawk caught Joanna's hand in a firm grip. He knew he could live anywhere with his woman beside him.

Silently they rode down the hill to join their people. The Bloods would start a new life. They would cast off the old life and embrace the new. For Joanna and Windhawk there would be no looking back with regret. They must look to the future and concentrate on the survival of their people.

They were not leaving their homes, rather they were

riding toward a new beginning.

YOU ARE GONE O NOBLE BLACKFOOT
WARRIOR
TO DISAPPEAR FROM EARTH AND SKY.
BUT YOUR MEMORY LIVES IN THE HEARTS
OF MEN,
FOR LEGENDS . . . DO NOT DIE. . . .

Author's Note

With *Savage Summer* I conclude my four-book saga on the Blackfoot Indians. While writing these books, I became aware of a way of life that has disappeared forever. With a heavy heart I cannot help but regret that we, our children, and our children's children will never know the peaceful world of a wise and noble people. We will only be allowed to visit them when we find them in the pages of a book.

SWEET MEDICINE'S PROPHECY
by Karen A. Bale

#1: SUNDANCER'S PASSION   (1778, $3.95)

Stalking Horse was the strongest and most desirable of the tribe, and Sun Dancer surrounded him with her spell-binding radiance. But the innocence of their love gave way to passion — and passion, to betrayal. Would their relationship ever survive the ultimate sin?

#2: LITTLE FLOWER'S DESIRE   (1779, $3.95)

Taken captive by savage Crows, Little Flower fell in love with the enemy, handsome brave Young Eagle. Though their hearts spoke what they could not say, they could only dream of what could never be. . . .

#4: SAVAGE FURY   (1768, $3.95)

Aeneva's rage knew no bounds when her handsome mate Trent commanded her to tend their tepee as he rode into danger. But under cover of night, she stole away to be with Trent and share whatever perils fate dealt them.

#5: SUN DANCER'S LEGACY   (1878, $3.95)

Aeneva's and Trenton's adopted daughter Anna becomes the light of their lives. As she grows into womanhood, she falls in love with blond Steven Randall. Together they discover the secrets of their passion, the bitterness of betrayal — and fight to fulfill the prophecy that is Anna's birthright.